W9-BNP-276

INCIDENT AT ASHTON

INCIDENT AT ASHTON

a novel

JAY MILNER

with a new foreword by

John Tisdale

TCU Press

Fort Worth, Texas

Library of Congress Cataloging-in-Publication Data

Milner, Jay Dunston, 1923-2011, author.

Incident at Ashton : a novel / by Jay Milner; with a new foreword by John Tisdale.

pages cm

First published in 1961 by Appleton-Century-Crofts, New York.

"The characters, the town, the county and the incidents described herein are fictitious. The attitudes and atmosphere are not.-Jay Milner."

Summary: "Philip Arrow Jr. returns to his deep South town of Ashton after six years in New York to take over the editorship of his father's newspaper the *Dispatch*. Far from 'liberating' him, New York has had an inverted influence on his feelings about his hometown and its main concern -- segregation. He was forced to leave Ashton once before because of what was considered his extreme liberal position, but dismayed by what he calls New York's 'hothouse' liberalism, he is now determined to align himself with the main body of sentiment in his town, going slow. But the death of an African American male who was about to test the voting registration laws causes Arrow to take a more discernable stand."-- Kirkus Review.

ISBN 978-0-87565-652-6 (alk. paper)

1. Newspaper editors--Southern States--Fiction. 2. Social justice--Southern States--Fiction. 3. Race discrimination--Southern States--Fiction. 4. Southern States--Race relations--Fiction. I. Title.

PS3563.I4295I53 2016

813'.6--dc23

0150

36363

Cover photo by Betty Press
Bridge from where Emmet Till's body was dumped in the back waters of the Tallahatchie River. Glendora, Mississippi, 2014.

Designed by Vicki Whistler

TCU Press
TCU Box 298300
Fort Worth, Texas 76129
817.257.7822
www.prs.tcu.edu
To order books: 1.800.826.8911

KENNEDY

*This book is dedicated
to those Southern newspapermen
who are truly dedicated to the profession;
and to Donna, Pettis Boyd, and Carter.*

FOREWORD

Depending on the weather or the traffic, the drive from our home in Southeast Texas to visit relatives in Mississippi took between four and one-half hours to five hours. We visited often. It was our version of vacation. Normally, these visits involved awaking before five in the morning on a Saturday and returning shortly after noon on a Sunday.

As my father steered our green Chrysler Newport across the midsection of Louisiana, we always searched the horizon for the top of the Natchez-Vidalia Bridge, a 1940 Works Progress Administration structure that signaled our arrival at the Mississippi River. For my parents, it meant they were back home.

The final stretch of these quick trips to Mississippi routed us through the town of Fayette on Highway 61 (the famous Blues Highway). The first town of any size located north-northeast of Natchez was Fayette, where I was introduced to the civil rights movement.

Medgar Evers served as the first field secretary for the NAACP in Mississippi. A World War II veteran who served in Europe, Evers had experienced a Europe that treated him more nearly as an equal than anything he'd experienced growing up in the United States. He returned home and felt the continuing sting of racism when he and his older brother, Charles, tried to register to vote after the war. That experience, coupled with the encouragement from the NAACP and its legal team headed by Thurgood Marshall, persuaded Medgar to apply to the University of Mississippi School of Law. The university denied admission, citing irregularities and missed deadlines in his application. The Supreme Court had recently (and unanimously) struck down the "separate but equal" part of the *Plessy* decision in the *Brown* decision. Still, most everyone, including the NAACP, knew that the university would deny admission to Medgar Evers. The application was tactical. The thinking was that you have to start somewhere. A short time later, the NAACP asked Medgar to open its first field office in Mississippi.

In his work as field secretary, Medgar Evers investigated the murders of Mack Charles Parker, Emmett Till, and many more "missing persons." He regularly received requests from family members wondering what happened to the aunt or uncle who tried to register to vote on Monday or was last seen at the courthouse but not seen since. Evers also organized meetings, primarily in churches that tended to serve as the safe harbor for activists in an environment of unsympathetic or hostile law enforcement and an even less tolerant populace. He also handed out flyers and organized protests.

In June 1963, Byron De La Beckwith pointed a rifle from behind a bush and murdered Medgar Evers with a single shot to the back. All of this I would discover much later in life. . . .

I do not remember my age at the time of my awareness of Medgar Evers or of the civil rights movement in general, but at some point I noticed something unusual in Fayette.

I remember just a single traffic light and a twenty-mile-per-hour speed limit that forced you to observe the benign qualities of the small town.

On that main street, several businesses had signs with the name "Medgar Evers" attached to facades and over the glass doors. I remember asking my dad, "Who is Medgar Evers?" I honestly cannot recall whether he answered or just ignored me. And just as quickly as I made the observation and asked the question, I turned my attention elsewhere—to a comic book, the roadside or the trees, or the speed at which our Newport barreled eastward toward my relatives' homes.

And, thus, my early recognition and introduction to the *Second*

American Revolution, the subtitle of Anthony Lewis's early-1960s firsthand account of the civil rights movement. (I would not think about Medgar Evers for another twenty years, when I sought a dissertation topic.)

Fayette was the home of Charles Evers, Medgar's older brother, who also happened to be the first African American mayor in post-Reconstruction Mississippi. I met and interviewed Charles for my dissertation. Medgar had died before I turned five years old.

The 1950s and 1960s in Mississippi and other states in the South proved to be dangerous places where civil rights workers sought to navigate a culture dedicated to preserving white political and economic dominance.

This dominance also involved the news media. In Jackson, Mississippi, the Hederman-owned newspapers enthusiastically supported, both in coverage and on its opinion pages, the maintenance of white rule and African American subjugation.

Newspaper editorials in the South tended to cite states' rights when federal court decisions threatened the separate worlds of whites and African Americans. Most newspapers and media outlets either ignored or buried the stories in the back of Section A or at the end of the radio broadcast. In fact, the majority of newspapers and television stations in the South ignored the movement for as long as possible. In 1947, the *New York Times* sent Johnny Popham to Chattanooga, Tennessee, to set up its first bureau in the South. Soon other national media followed. The Emmett Till murder trial in 1955 and the subsequent national media coverage it generated moved the story of the civil rights movement onto the front pages of newspapers across the country.

Jay Milner covered the Till trial for the *Greenville Delta Democrat-Times*, where he served as managing editor for Hodding Carter II's newspaper before moving to New York City to work at the *Herald Tribune.*

Milner is Phil Arrow.

Milner's *Incident at Ashton* closely mirrors the Emmett Till murder. It should, because the Till trial occurred just a few counties east-northeast of where Milner worked at the *Delta Democrat-Times.*

It is at the intersection of the civil rights struggles and media coverage that *Incident at Ashton* best illustrates the difficulty in covering civil rights issues, specifically for those news organizations in the South. If you covered the news as honestly and fairly as possible, the risk of losing advertisers and subscribers increased exponentially, especially where the orthodoxy of segregationist culture went unquestioned by a significant majority of the population.

To Kill a Mockingbird captured this racial tension in book form when published in 1960. Milner published *Incident at Ashton* the next year.

It is part civil rights history and equal parts journalism history set in the volatile South of the 1950s. The novel chronicles newspaper editor Phil Arrow's return to his hometown of Ashton after working in New York City for six years. He has returned to be editor of his father's newspaper. It is also a story about journalism ethics and the difficult balance between reporting what has occurred and what advertisers and subscribers want to read. It's a story of orthodoxy and change. How much changed during this period of US history? It depends on one's perspective. The willingness to change, however, was not always a shared value.

Any journalist in the South who challenged the culture of segregation faced the threat of violence. It's not difficult to find journalists who challenged orthodoxy and suffered dangerous consequences.

The consequences varied. The threats varied. It could be a neighbor not returning a greeting. It could be a brick through a window or the grocery store owner threatening to cancel Thursday's full-page advertisement. It could be a typed but unsigned letter with no return address threatening to cancel a subscription or to hurt your family, or it could be losing a seat on the board of trustees at the First Baptist Church or a seat on the board of the First National Bank. The threats varied, but they came. Moderation on the editorial page came with a cost.

The "war stories" of reporters, editors, and publishers being threatened is best chronicled in *The Race Beat*, the Pulitzer Prize-winning history of covering civil rights by Gene Roberts and Hank Klibanoff. Civil rights workers and supporters suffered. It was the second revolution.

In Mississippi, Milner's employer, Hodding Carter II, was the target of a state House of Representatives resolution, passed by a vote of eighty-nine to nineteen, calling Carter a liar because of an article he wrote for *Look* magazine that was critical of the state of Mississippi.

Other editors and publishers experienced the wrath of a culture with deep resentment toward change, especially when that change was perceived to come from outside the South's recognized borders. Occasionally, however, the change was generated by some of the state's bravest editors and publishers.

Besides Carter, others suffered for adopting and expressing moderate views.

Ira B. Harkey Jr., who owned the *Pascagoula Chronicle*, found few others interested in his insistence on using "Mrs." in writing about African American women and also dropping the word *Negro* as a label to distinguish white from black. He eventually won a Pulitzer Prize in 1963 for editorial writing but soon left town, worn down by years of threats.

Other editors and publishers in Mississippi came under attack. Hazel Brannon Smith's *Lexington Advertiser* came under intense pressure because whites suspected she printed the NAACP newspaper. She won the Pulitzer Prize for editorial writing in 1964. The Citizens Council boycotted her newspaper. She received death threats.

J. Oliver Emmerich, the publisher of the McComb newspaper, suffered from boycotts and threats. So, too, did P. D. East with his weekly newspaper in Petal. These were the few who stood up to racial orthodoxy. It was not easy.

In Milner's novel, Phil Arrow's return to Ashton was not easy, either. It was complicated.

His hometown friends remembered him—and not in a good way. He's remembered as an agitator, a favorite sobriquet bequeathed by southerners on anyone who opposed segregation. Before Arrow left for New York City, he used the newspaper as a platform to have the names of African American veterans of World War II recognized the same as white veterans. He left town shortly afterward.

He angered his fictional father. He angered friends and relatives, but he returned, and the story that follows is an accurate reflection of the cost of moderation.

The question of whether to republish a novel can be dependent on whether the message or central tenet continues to resonate and, thus, whether there exists an audience for that message. It's the most basic of Business 101 questions for any publisher. Why should this book be republished? How does it merit, more than fifty years later, another printing?

Although we are now well into the twenty-first century, the topic of race continues to dominate national headlines. *Incident at Ashton*, a historical novel that parallels the murder of Emmett Till several years earlier, is as important today as it was in 1961, when first published by a reporter who actually covered a trial that further exacerbated a racial divide that we continue to study.

Stories like Jay Milner's *Incident at Ashton* should be retold and republished until we finally start to understand the lessons he begs us to learn.

John R. Tisdale
Associate Professor,
Department of Journalism
Texas Christian University

INCIDENT AT ASHTON

*The characters, the town, the county and
the incidents described herein are fictitious.
The attitudes and atmosphere are not.*
　　　　　　　　　　　　—JAY MILNER

1.

THE SLENDER MAN in the gray suit looked out at the squatty, flat-topped buildings, none higher than the third-story window where he stood.

Funny how he had forgotten about the shifting earth and the flat, squatty buildings. When they put up the new city police building nine years ago, seventy-nine creosoted pilings, each eighty feet long, were driven into the ground to keep the foundation from sliding and cracking the walls. Tall buildings won't sit still on ground like that. The hotel, which he could not see from his window, was eight stories tall and, although it was built after the war, splitting like an overripe watermelon. Until now he had never thought of how the shifting earth shaped his town's appearance.

"Will someone *please* take a picture for me? Right now?"

Only Laura could make a simple request come out as the last desperate cry of a drowning woman. He smiled and turned from the window. It was Laura, all right. She led two eager-eyed matrons off the elevator.

"Take it easy, Laura," said the big, balding man sitting at the easel-shaped desk near the center of the long, cluttered room. "We're right on deadline. You can wait ten minutes." He spoke without looking up from the stack of green paper.

"Don't shout at me, Ranch Harden," Laura pouted. "All I did was make a simple request. Where's Tommy? He can do it."

"Tommy's at the police station—where he's supposed to be this time of day—and I didn't shout. Why can't you point a camera and pull the trigger? My two-year-old daughter can take pictures with a Speedgraphic."

"That old thing's too heavy for me and you know it." If you didn't know Laura you would think she was near tears. If you knew her, you knew this was her "poor, defenseless, Southern belle" act and it would be followed—if necessary—by more aggressive maneuvers, sometimes including ashtray tossing and surprisingly expert cursing.

"I'll take the picture, Laura," the slender man said, grinning as he stepped away from the window. "That is, if I haven't forgotten how to point a camera and pull the trigger."

"Philip Junior! You darling! I didn't see you there. Come here and let me hug your neck." She ran to him and put her arms around his neck and kissed him on each cheek.

Her skin felt thin and lifeless as tissue paper against his. She carried the musty odor of expensive old furniture in storage. He remembered the musty odor. She had carried it when he was a boy and she was his father's "glamorous young society editor." In those days she tried to cover it with wonderful perfume and he had a crush on her. Now she was a skinny spinster with tissue-paper skin. She no longer used perfume.

She pulled away from him. "Now—please take the picture for me. These ladies—you remember Bertie Mae and Pearl—have to hurry on out to the Country Club. They're late now."

Phil walked past Bertie Mae and Pearl. They nodded and smiled and said they were happy to see him home again. He nodded and smiled and said he was happy to be home. He opened the long doors of the steel cabinet. Two four-by-five Speedgraphic cameras, bellows extended, were on the middle shelf. He took one out, set the lens and shutter speed, and walked back to where Bertie Mae and Pearl waited. Laura told them where and how to stand and when he pointed the camera they stiffened. They blinked and giggled when the flash went off and said it always blinded them like that. Then they said hurried goodbyes and went back into the elevator.

"Thanks, darling," Laura said and looked at the big man at the desk and added, "It's nice to have a real Southern gentleman around this place again." She took the film clip from him and walked a few steps toward her desk, then stopped and came back to Phil and put her arms around him again. She kissed him on the mouth this time and there were tears in her pale eyes.

The telephone on the easel-shaped desk jangled and Ranch shouted into the intercom box, "Hold it a minute down there. I'm on the phone."

Laura dabbed at her eyes with Kleenex and went to her desk.

"Yes, Mrs. Auld," Ranch said pleasantly as he frowned at the phone. "No, ma'am. I don't think we will be able to use the picture on the front page. Yes, ma'am. I know it was a district meeting. All right, Mrs. Auld, you call Mr. Philip Arrow, Senior. (He looked up at Phil and winked.) Whatever he says I'll do."

"Dear Mrs. Auld." Phil smiled. "I thought she was dead."

The strident voice from the composing room rushed out of the intercom box. "Ranch! you off the phone yet? This god-damned streamer headline is too long."

"Relax." Ranch leaned forward and put his mouth an inch from the rusty box. "Take out the 'the.' That's simple enough."

"Don't talk like I ought to know what to do," the voice from the floor below answered. "I don't get paid to write this crap. I just put it in type."

Phil walked back to the window, leaving Ranch with the last-minute problems which must be solved from that easel-shaped desk to get the *Dispatch* out on time each day.

He had forgotten the feel of this room.

The three wire service machines lined against the wall opposite the window where he stood clattered out news from London and Memphis and New Orleans and Paris. It was piped into the room from all those places at sixty words a minute. If Ranch read it all—and he must at least scan it all—he read the equivalent of a good-sized novel every day. Laura pecked at her typewriter in the corner she had occupied six days a week for twenty-two years. Ranch scowled at the words on the paper and jabbed at them with his pencil. The dirt-stained floor was pocked from the thousands of cigarettes stomped into it. Eight desks were scattered about, placed according to each reporter's desire to face a wall or face Ranch. And those beer labels were still on the ceiling over the desk where Ranch sat. Phil's father put them there on V-J Day.

His dad was a ripsnorter in those days. He was so proud of the beer-label feat that he ordered they never be painted over. Phil had not been able to persuade him to tell how he put them up there. The ceiling was about twenty feet high and Laura, the only one of the old bunch around then, swore there had not been a ladder in the room. All his father would say about it was "When I get high, son, I get high."

He looked out the window again. He had forgotten too how old the buildings were—or appeared to be. But, he told himself, from this window he could see only the ugliness of the flat, gray, asphalt roofs. They were old, yes, but they weren't so ugly when seen from the street. If Southerners would only use more paint . . .

"Some town, eh? Guess it looks pretty small now."

Phil turned and faced a white-haired man. A man almost his exact height and with evidence of the same sharp facial features. Once people said they looked like brothers, he and the white-haired man who seemed to have been standing there behind him for some time before he spoke.

"Hi, Dad," Phil said. "I didn't hear you come up. Naw, Ashton looks good to me. I missed it."

"Fine," his father said. "It's good to have you back. You didn't have to come down here today though. Take it easy a few days. I'll last awhile."

"I haven't turned a hand. . . . I take that back. I took a picture for Laura. But I intend to sneak out soon, before she puts me to work again."

"Sure. Take it easy a few days. No hurry about anything. The *Dispatch* will survive us both." He turned away then and walked slowly toward the elevator.

"Hi, Mr. Arrow," Ranch said.

"Oh, hello, Ranch. Good-looking front page today."

The paper isn't out yet, Phil thought, as he watched his father go into the elevator.

Ranch answered the ringing telephone. "Phil, it's for you."

Phil walked to the desk and took the phone. "Yes?"

"Phil, this is Janie," a pliant feminine voice said. "I know it's terrible to ask the guest of honor to help fix for the party but would you run an errand for me?"

"Sure, Janie, what is it?" Odd how the cadence of a Southern drawl is so exaggerated on a telephone. He wondered if he had lost his Southern accent and cadence.

"Jerry won't be back from Jackson until late and we need more liquor for that bunch. Would you be a dear and go to the bootlegger's and get a case of bourbon and half a case of gin for me? I can't get away and you know I can't send Andrew. I'd not only lose my liquor, I'd probably lose a good yard man. And I must have Andrew tonight. He can mix wonderful martinis and he looks exactly like one of those Virginia footmen when he wears his white coat."

"Be glad to, Janie. What about Scotch? Got plenty? Why don't I contribute half a case of Scotch? You and Jerry are going to a lot of trouble throwing this shindig for me."

"Don't flatter yourself, goofy," Janie laughed. "We've planned a turkey hash party for weeks. Your homecoming just gave us a good excuse to set the date. I suppose you better get some Scotch though. There'll be that couple from Pennsylvania and my cousin from Kansas City. I guess all Yankees drink Scotch, don't they? You never drank Scotch before you went up there, did you?"

"Before I went up there I was exactly like I am now. I'd drink anything."

"Silly. You talk so big and tough. But I remember when you

passed out on a pint of sherry on graduation night. I've got to run, honey. See you tonight. Thanks for being a dear. Tell Mannie to charge it to us."

"Okay, Janie, 'bye." Phil cradled the phone and smiled. What was it that distinguished Southern women, even in a telephone conversation, from all other females in the world? In addition to their Southern drawl that is. They seem always ready to play mother to the mischievous child in a man. And that, of course, brings forth the child in him, with all the accompanying frustrations. New York women, on the other hand, are a bit too eager to accept for themselves the standards of a man's world. Too eager for his taste, that is.

An apprentice from the pressroom brought in copies of the first edition. Ranch took them and handed the top one to Phil and began studying another one.

Phil scanned the front page:

117 Receive Diplomas
Ashton High's Biggest
Senior Class Graduates

This 30-point Bodoni bold headline was two columns wide in the upper left-hand corner. At the end of the story, below the fold, was a one-column 18-point headline:

Negro High School
Graduates Fifty-one

The day's main story, dropping from a 72-point headline in the far right column, was by Tommy Dunham. Dunham was one of the two young reporters Phil had not yet met. His story was a roundup of the opinions of some local public officials and civic leaders on the school bond issue election scheduled for July 22. Most of those interviewed said they favored the bond issue, although their enthusiasm seemed forced the way Dunham had written the story. The mayor said taxes were too high already, but that the bond issue should be approved by the voters because of "the tensions of the times." The mayor went on to say, according to Dunham's article, that "we must stay two jumps ahead of those who would destroy our Way of Life. Most of the money from this proposed bond issue is designated for the construction of Negro classrooms. If we approve this bond issue it will show the professional South haters of the North that we do take care of our Negroes." The tone of the story was accurate; Phil knew the people interviewed well enough to know that. It looked as if Ranch was still hiring "bright, young Southern liberals."

"Good job Dunham did," he said.

"He's a good boy," Ranch nodded. "He worked on this half the night. He knew you would be here today. I told him this morning it was good and he asked if I thought you would like it."

"Oh?" Phil hoped Ranch and his crew did not expect things to be as they were six years ago.

"I better shove," he said. "I've got an errand to run for Janie before the party. You going to be there, Ranch?"

"Nah. The Windham parties are strictly for the elite and the intellectual. I'm neither."

"They say they always have a few old characters at these turkey hash parties. I thought you might have been invited in that category."

Ranch grinned and turned his attention back to the news copy he was editing for the inside pages of tomorrow's *Dispatch.*

"See you at the party," Laura said.

"Which category are you in?" Phil asked, and dodged the copy pencil Laura threw as he boarded the elevator.

Outside, it was cool for a June day. The sky was more gray than blue and utterly infinite, the way Ashton skies are on cloudless days. Phil looked at his watch. Almost five o'clock. The party was to begin at eight. He had time for a short nap before he dressed and went after the booze for Janie.

He drove three blocks south on Main Street and turned left to take the Hooker Street short cut. When he saw Shine Tatum's store he decided to stop and buy a dill pickle as he had done so many times when he was a schoolboy. No one had pickles as good as those Shine kept in that old churn. He bet Shine didn't change the vinegar once a year. The pickles at the bottom were best.

The store looked the same. The false front appeared to be constructed of soft drink signs. Phil parked behind a 1951 Ford pickup truck. When he opened the tinkling screen door he saw Shine bent over a stack of credit books on the high, narrow counter.

"Gimme a pickle and an R.C.," he said.

Shine looked up quickly. A broad smile followed the near-startled expression on his face. "Mister Phil, I'll be doggoned."

"How are you, Shine?"

"Good as new almost. My, don't you look fine in that New York suit."

"Narrowest lapels in Ashton County."

"I heard you was coming home. Lord, it's good to see you."

Shine had walked around the open end of the long counter and was shaking Phil's hand enthusiastically. "I'll bet you know what I came after," Phil said.

"I bet I do too."

"Still have them?"

"Sure do. Don't sell as many as I used to when your bunch came around nearbout every day. But I still keep them." Shine went behind the counter and reached deep into the mold-colored churn and pulled up a large cucumber that was soft with juice. "How's this one?"

"My mouth's watering already."

"You want an R.C. too?"

"No, thanks." Phil bit the dripping end of the pickle. "Wow! I'd forgotten how good these were. How many times have you changed that vinegar since I left?"

"Not many," Shine smiled. "I mostly put in a little more dill and vinegar now and then. It's like gumbo. The older it gets the better it is."

"Is it true you found a mouse in the churn once and didn't change the vinegar because you had a new batch of cucumbers in there?"

"You know better than that." Shine laughed. "I poured every one of them pickles out the back. You're joshing me, Mister Phil."

They laughed and Phil ate the pickle. Then he pulled the handkerchief from the breast pocket of his coat and blotted his mouth and fingers.

"Way you do that," Shine said, "it's like you was sitting at a banquet table with the governor. You know, neat, and gentleman-like? Wish my Cooter could see you do it, just once."

Phil felt his face flush. The compliment, strange in itself and stranger because of Shine's simple sincerity, embarrassed him; almost angered him.

"I've got to run," he said, stuffing a hand into his pants pocket for change to pay for the pickle. He saw disappointment on the old Negro's face and he added, "I'll drop around again soon . . . when there's more time to talk."

Shine pushed his hand away. "You can't pay me for that pickle, Mister Phil," he said. "It's your homecoming present."

"Thanks."

They walked to the door in step.

"There're some things I would like to talk to you about," Shine said. "I'll come over to the paper if you want me to."

"Sure. Any time. Better check by phone before you come the next day or so though. I'm kind of resting now and may not be around the paper much for a while."

"I'll give you time to rest before I come."

"Good to see you again, Shine. And thanks again for the pickle." Phil stepped outside, released the screen door, and heard it tinkle shut behind him.

The store faced east and when he stepped onto the sidewalk Phil saw that the shadow cast by the old building now reached the middle of Hooker Street. The lots were still vacant on each side of the long, low, unpainted store building. A block and a half south, however, buildings were jammed wall to wall on both sides of the street and dirty neon signs hung over the sidewalks. They would be blinking dimly over crowded sidewalks in a few hours. This was "the Block." Ask an Ashton Negro where he was going or where he had been on Saturday night and, if he was over fifteen and wasn't sick or living with an aunt or mother who had got religion too recently, he would say, "On the Block," meaning he had walked the four blocks of the Negro "Main Street" of Ashton and socialized under the dim neon lights. You seldom saw a white man, never a white woman, on the Block after dark.

As a boy, Phil remembered, he was afraid to ride his bicycle along this street at night.

2.

PHIL HUMMED "That Old Black Magic" as he steered his father's sedan into the narrow driveway between the rows of pecan trees. The old Crutchfield home, which Jerry bought seven years ago as an anniversary gift for Janie, loomed ahead of him. Janie grew up in the rambling frame house with the quartet of pillars in formation across its wide front. Phil remembered telling Janie and Jerry the house was a caricature of the Southern Way of Life. "It's majestic and complex and somehow it plucks the romantic instincts in every man. But it's ugly and crumbling and termite infested and economically impractical, if not impossible." He talked that way a lot before he went to New York.

Jerry said he bought the house because it was important to Janie that her children grow up in it.

Phil eased the sedan past the hedge that had replaced the grotesque iron fence and parked behind Janie's station wagon. He got out and stood by the car and looked across the two acres of green which flowed down the slight incline to the neat hedge. Maybe living in this house would give a country schoolteacher's son the added confidence Jerry now seemed to have. Being a state senator at thirty-six helped too. Phil felt again the excitement he felt the night before as he and Jerry talked. That was when he realized for the first time that in his absence his generation had taken long strides toward positions of leadership. The years he lived in New York were key years in that progress.

The party was one of those known as "Janie and Jerry's turkey hash get-togethers." Phil had attended one or two like it. But while he was away they had achieved a status that was nearly institutional. Jerry and Janie would entertain Ashton's various homogeneous social cliques individually at formal dinners and informal cook-outs, depending on the weather and the nature of the clique. ("When a guy's in politics," Jerry said last night, "he's got to do a lot of that sort of thing.") Then they would have one of the turkey hash parties, inviting carefully selected representatives from each of the cliques and a few newcomers, out-of-towners—if any "acceptable" ones were available—and a local "character" or two for conversation pieces.

Thirty minutes after Phil arrived there were twenty-eight people in the large playroom off the formal living room. Phil counted them. He sat in the brown leather chair at the right of the fireplace and sipped his second Scotch and water. When he finished the drink he stood up and walked into a group directly across the room. He had been examining the back side of a woman in a red knit dress and wanted to see what she looked like in front. He was in that kind of mood tonight.

"Personally, I'm not bothered by all the talk about intermarriage," the woman in the knit dress said as Phil walked up. "Simply because my son goes to school with nigras doesn't mean he would marry one. What I would worry about would be his sex life."

"There's a modern mother for you," the man on her right said, and the two other men laughed. "My mother never worried about my sex life."

"Oh, shush, Marvin," the woman said. "What I mean is his sex development."

Her face was less stimulating than her backside, but her breasts were worth any red-blooded male's attention. Phil wondered why women with boyishly slender hips always had large breasts.

"My mother never paid any attention to that either," the man said. He was Dr. Marvin Holbrook, a general practitioner with the reputation of a "ladies' man."

"What I mean is an adolescent boy is at the experimental age," the woman said. "He's too shy to try anything with his nice girl friends and too scared to go into the nigra quarters and buy his sex. But if he sits next to a nigra girl in school all day he might work up the nerve to ask her. And you know as well as I do that nigras aren't as discreet as we are about sex and . . ."

"Now, would you deny your son the opportunity of experimenting the easy way?" Holbrook said. "You wouldn't do that, would you, Grace?" He grinned and looked down the loose front of her dress.

"It isn't that," Grace said, unconsciously raising a hand to her breast. "Nigras aren't as discreet as we are. Aren't as careful. You're a doctor, you should know the venereal disease rate is high among them. I don't want my son to come home with V.D."

Phil remembered her now. Her husband was the Standard Oil distributor. Gossip had it he was impotent. I should have let well enough alone, Phil thought. Knowing what he did about her, he could no longer enjoy watching her self-conscious hips.

"You have a point there, Grace," Holbrook said.

"Wouldn't you say so, Phil? Or would you?"

Phil did not want to become involved in their conversation. Was Holbrook being sarcastic? "Not being a parent disqualifies me," he said. "Look, folks, I'm heading for the bar. Anybody want a refill?"

"No, thanks," Grace said. "This is my third and I better slow down. I don't know *what* I might do if I have many more."

She smiled at Holbrook and Phil could see they had something going. Or were pretending to, for the thrill it gives cautious people. He moved away, nodding and murmuring how nice it was to see them again.

He walked to the bar and while Andrew mixed the Scotch and water he found his cigarette package and took one out and lighted it. He wasn't pleased. He felt alone. An outsider. He didn't know half the people here. This party was in his honor, according to Jerry, and he couldn't find anyone he wanted to talk with. What were all these people discussing? Grace and Holbrook were talking about sex and warming up their motors. What about that group over there? The one including the short woman in the plaid skirt and green blouse and the two tall men, what were they talking about?

"Thanks," he said to Andrew as he took the glass. He walked back to the leather chair and sat down. He wished Jerry would hurry. Hell, what had he expected? He'd been away six years. These people's lives had gone on without him. If he could hold his infernal impatience in check he would become a part of this community again.

"Technically you're a good newspaperman," his father had said that day. "Emotionally you're a spoiled kid. You don't like what you see and you want to wave the *Dispatch* like a magic wand and change this town and this state overnight. You saw some things in France and wherever the hell else you went during the war and now you think all Southerners are stupid jerks. Running a newspaper is no job for a spoiled kid."

He had been out of the Army two years when he assumed the responsibilities of managing editor of his father's newspaper. He had made some mistakes, he knew, but he put out an exciting newspaper that had attracted some attention. His father seemed willing to let him learn from his mistakes until Copeland killed that Negro prisoner.

"I'm not saying you are wrong to be upset about what Sheriff Copeland did," his father had said. "I'm saying only that you were set to handle it wrong. You can't do anything with a newspaper if you lose your audience. I won't stand by and allow you to do that to the *Dispatch.* I'm still head man around here, you know."

"Hi, you bunch of drunks," Jerry shouted, entering the room with a big hand raised in an all-inclusive greeting. "What's the big argument tonight?"

Phil looked up and away from his thoughts.

"Hi, Jerry!" came simultaneously from the various groups as Jerry's entrance momentarily halted all conversations, giving some a chance to slip away to another huddle and some the opportunity of grabbing the offensive and expressing views they had been cataloguing all day in preparation for the party.

"Soberest turkeys I ever saw," Jerry said. He was tall and blond and handsome in a trustworthy way and he moved easily from one group to the next, shaking hands, slapping backs, making appropriate remarks.

Phil admired his friend's entrance. It was showy, and could have been obnoxious if the enthusiasm were faked.

But, Phil observed, everyone in the room was smiling warmly at Jerry, just as he was. Jerry had always been gregarious and had developed that part of his personality expertly since the days when Phil wrote the speeches that got him elected president of Ashton High's senior class.

"Hi, Phil," Jerry said when he reached the chair by the fireplace. "Come over here with me." He pulled Phil to his feet and guided him to the bar at the east end of the room. "Friends," he said, raising one hand to signal for silence and placing the other hand on Phil's shoulder. "I'm a little late but I want to announce officially that everyone is obligated to be extra nice to this galoot tonight. Janie and I were looking around for an excuse to toss this brawl and he furnished it by coming home. . . . And so, my dear friends, we are gathered here tonight to honor the return of Philip Arrow, Junior—known as Flip in the glorious days when he wore the colors of dear ole Ashton High." The last was said in the tones of an old-time political orator. Then Jerry added, "Or maybe I should say, we are here to relaunch Phil Arrow into the gay social whirl of Ashton County. And, as you all know, to launch anything properly you must use alcohol."

Abruptly, he turned a whisky glass, which appeared to be filled, upside down over Phil's head. Phil jumped aside instinctively. But nothing came from the glass. It was one of those trick glasses, with its inside painted a whisky color. "Don't think I'd waste good liquor, do you," Jerry laughed, "even on you?" He turned to the crowd. "Okay, folks, back to the serious drinking. I'm way behind." Then he whispered to Phil, "Stick around after the last body's dragged out. I want to talk a minute."

Janie came, properly stiff-backed despite the several drinks she had had, and kissed Phil on the cheek. Laura walked to him, a bit unsteadily, hugged him tightly and kissed him on the mouth. A few others filed by and shook his hand. Others waved and shouted greetings. It was as if he had walked into the room with Jerry instead of almost an hour before. Then the party settled back into its previous pattern, and he was alone again.

He watched her—trying to do so as subtly as possible—for maybe thirty minutes before he found the opportunity (or got up the nerve) to walk over where she stood and force their meeting. He hadn't felt shy about walking into the group to see the other side of the woman, Grace, with the self-conscious hips. But this was a different kind of woman. In the first place nothing about her manner revealed any self-consciousness. She seemed too absorbed in what others were saying—and maybe her own thoughts about what they were saying, because sometimes he thought he saw a secret smile attempt to show itself on her face—to be conscious of her own physical self. He kept trying to see whether she wore a wedding ring because, although there was something faintly familiar about her, he was certain she wasn't an Ashton girl and, therefore, might well be married. Few, very few, women moved to Ashton seeking careers or husbands, with the exception of schoolteachers, and schoolteachers ordinarily stayed clear of, or weren't invited to, drinking parties. Ashton parents expected, demanded really, that teachers be better moral examples to their children than they were themselves.

She was standing beside Ches Blinken when Phil decided to stop wondering who she was and find out. He and Ches had been fairly close friends in high school, although Ches was a year or two younger, so he had a perfectly legitimate excuse for walking into their conversation. Ches was sitting on the piano bench, picking at his banjo, which he always brought to parties. She seemed to be teaching him the tune of a song that Phil did not recognize by the banjo string sounds resulting from Ches's red-faced concentration.

"Hi, Ches," he said, succeeding in his conscious effort to avoid looking at her. "Don't tell me there's a song you haven't learned yet."

"Oh, hi, Philip," the chubby, red-haired man said. "Good to have you home again. I was going to come over soon as the mob cleared away and welcome you officially. Then Ann here got me all involved with this darn song. . . . Oh, you know Ann here? Ann Davis, Philip Arrow."

Phil allowed himself to look at her. "How do you do, Miss Davis, I . . ."

"Yes," she interrupted quietly, "Mr. Arrow and I have met."

"Oh?" Phil said, ". . . Yes." He didn't believe it possible, however, that they *had* met and he had forgotten. The teasing mischief in her remarkably green eyes made him uncomfortable, the way they studied his own face and eyes openly.

"I figgered you must have," Ches said. "Say, Phil, you ever hear this song?" He plunked a few notes from the strings of his banjo.

"Gee, I don't believe I have, Ches." Phil heard himself put sincerity into the words—sincerity the question neither deserved nor asked for. He heard himself playing the part of the fairly bright, very well-mannered and conscientious son of the owner of the town's newspaper; heir to the town's courier of information about tomorrow's weather, next week's social and cultural events, next spring's weddings, yesterday's football scores, deaths and births, and editorials in praise of the Rotary Club for its progressive and unselfish attitude toward such projects as taking up a special collection to buy playground equipment for a small vacant lot donated by one of its members as a park in the Negro quarters. Yes, by just standing there looking at him she made his careful plans seem sophomoric, embarrassingly ordinary. And, for a moment, he resented her—because he knew he was right. He had to be right—and he wasn't a sophomore. He would, in three months, be thirty-five years old; the age when a man should—*must*—have his direction set.

"Ann says it's real big in New York and I figgered you'd probably heard it," Ches said, bent over his banjo again, picking the same few notes repeatedly.

"Well . . . I didn't . . . maybe I didn't go around with the right people." Phil looked at her now. "Are you from New York?"

"I've lived there the past two years or so." She smiled, not mischievously this time, but friendly and warm. "Don't worry about the song. You lived in New York long enough to know there are no such animals up there as the 'right people.' Just depends on which people you happen to enjoy."

"I was a copy writer for an advertising agency," he said, realizing it came out as an apology and resenting that too. It was a long time since he had met a girl who made him feel like a child, an adolescent—disturbed and incompetent and excited, all at the same time.

"Everybody's got to make a buck," she said, still friendly and without the snicker in her eyes, so some of his discomfort began to ebb.

"Can I get you a refill?" He nodded at her empty glass.

"Thank you." She handed the glass to him and, for the first time, he was looking directly into the green depth of her eyes at the same time that she was looking into his and the other adolescent-like disturbances, except excitement, disappeared. The excitement grew with almost breath-taking quickness to replace the other sensations in those spots in which emotional stimulation, good or bad, reveals itself anatomically—the pit of his stomach, the palms of his hands, the back of his neck, his loin region.

He took her glass and turned away. Dammit, he thought, if coming home is going to cause me to revert to childhood, maybe it was a mistake. Then he remembered he had not asked her what she was drinking. He turned back, grinning.

"Scotch and just a little water," she said.

When they had settled, with their drinks, in an unoccupied corner, sitting cross-legged on two floor cushions facing the party crowd, her uninhibited acceptance of him as her conversational partner for at least a major part of the evening restored him rapidly to adulthood. He asked her about the song and she said it really wasn't "big" in New York, only a catchy tune with lyrics spoofing "the mess the world is in." She and some friends heard it at an Off-Broadway revue and learned the melody and words for party singing. She was teaching it to Ches as an excuse to remove herself from a conversation she had got involved in with a woman named Grace and a man introduced to her only as Dr. Holbrook.

Phil laughed. "Yeah," he said, "I almost got caught in that trap too." He spotted Grace's self-conscious rear again, but it no longer interested him, despite its increased nervousness.

Ann gazed into the crowd, giving him a chance to concentrate on her. Ordinarily redheads didn't appeal to him. Her hair wasn't exactly red, however. More auburn. Light auburn. Sort of copper colored, with sun-bleached highlights. The subtle puff around her eyes put an Oriental cast to the mold of her face. Her hair, visibly soft, was cut short, so it framed her puckish, but not "cute," face closely. He always had preferred a generous mouth on a woman. Women with small mouths seemed consistently tense somehow. Unlike so many New York women he had known, she wore no make-up, except lipstick, and no earrings. He liked that too. He always felt that heavily made-up and bejeweled women were hiding from themselves.

"Where'd you live in New York?" he asked finally.

She turned her attention from the party going on in front of them—although he sensed that she was thinking about something else and only appeared to study the people here. "On West End Avenue," she said, "near Eighty-sixth."

"I went to parties over there a couple of times," he said. "Real arty groups. I was the only Madison Avenue specimen there. I got the feeling I was invited for scientific purposes. You know, so they could all see one in the flesh?"

"There are phonies on both sides of Central Park. No one's yet found a way to segregate phonies. Be dull if they did, I suppose. Segregation of any kind tends to cause sterility of one kind or another. . . . Or does that kind of talk get you lynched in this territory?"

"I haven't lynched anyone in years." He grinned. "Been out of the territory lately."

"I know. . . . It was a silly remark, especially to you. Just the kind of thing one of my hothouse liberal friends on West End Avenue would say."

"You said, 'especially' me. And awhile ago you said we had met before. You seem to know something about me but darned if I can believe we could have met because I can't remember you and I think I definitely would have if we'd met."

"I'm sorry. I was teasing. It's the way I compensate for nervousness as well as boredom. You couldn't be expected to remember. I'm Janie's cousin from Kansas City. I met you at a Country Club dance, years ago when I was visiting here one summer. I was seventeen. The braces had been off my teeth such a short time I could still feel them and . . . well, I got a mad crush on you. When I found out you were married I sulked for days."

He still didn't remember, but it wasn't important now. "I'm not married any longer," he said.

"I know."

He took a deep breath. It was almost a sigh. "Well, how long you going to be around this time?"

"Until mother gets settled. She's moving back here. Father died a year ago and she decided to move in with Aunt Amy. You know how the Crutchfields stick together."

She didn't ask him about his divorce and he was grateful for not being forced to recite his memorized explanation. He would tell her about it later, if he was lucky enough for her to be interested later. They talked about books and plays (he was repeatedly amazed at how easily he could express himself to her) and their favorite places in New York and how remarkably similar their separately discovered favorites were. Then, long before he was ready to stop talking to her, Mary Lee Blinken interrupted to tell Ann it was time to "pour my husband into the car and take him home." Ann had come to the party with Ches and Mary Lee. Phil looked around and discovered only a few of the hardier drinkers remained. He was about to ask Ann if he could take her home when he remembered that Jerry wanted to talk with him "after the last body's dragged out." He walked to the car with the Blinkens and Ann, helping support the shaky but very happy Ches. Then he went into the library where Jerry was waiting for him.

It was past two o'clock and Phil had drunk a lot of Scotch and was sleepy now that Ann was gone. He lit a cigarette and flopped into a wide leather chair near the fireplace (the old Crutchfield house had a fireplace in almost every room). Jerry stood by the window, puffing at his pipe, looking out into the night.

"What's the big secret, Jer?" Phil asked. "I'm sort of bushed. Not used to this fast Ashton life, I guess."

Jerry took a match from his coat pocket, struck it on the fireplace stone, and put the flame to his pipe.

"Remember how we used to talk about what we were going to do and be when we grew up?" he asked.

Phil nodded.

"You were going to win the Pulitzer Prize and I . . ."

"You were going to be governor," Phil said.

"That's right." Jerry puffed on his pipe then took it from his mouth and knocked it out in the fireplace.

Phil looked around him at the antique plushness of the library. "This looks like a governor's study," he said; then after a brief pause added, "and you look like you belong here. I don't mean that any way but as a compliment. You've come a long way, Jer. You'll be governor one day. I'd bet my last dime on it."

"I'm going to run for governor, Phil—next time around," Jerry said. "That's next year."

"I'll be damned!" Phil sat up straight. "That soon? Do you have a chance to win or is this a feeler race? Why didn't you tell me last night?"

"I didn't tell you last night because I have a *damn* good chance of winning. I've been working on my organization for three years and it looks good. But I didn't know you were coming home."

"I don't understand."

"Those talks we had in high school and later were important to me. You probably didn't realize it but you had a terrific influence on me. Hell, you were class and I was a poor country schoolteacher's kid."

"Thanks, but I still don't understand why you didn't tell me last night."

"I remember *everything* we planned, Phil. You were going to be my campaign manager when I ran for governor."

Phil frowned. "I was, wasn't I? But hell . . ."

"No, when I heard you were coming back—that was only last week, you know—I thought, Okay, now we can do it just as we planned it. Then I realized that was impossible. That's why I didn't tell you last night. I had to think about it a little more. I thought about it all the way to the capital and back today. I think better when I'm driving."

"Hell, you didn't have to worry about that."

"I think I did. I already have a guy lined up as campaign manager, but I could have changed that. But I couldn't change the fact that you have been out of the South six years. And that you aren't exactly the most popular person in the state, to put it mildly. You understand, don't you?"

"Sure. Hell, I'd forgotten about it anyhow. Seems I've forgotten a lot of our plans. I sure as hell haven't won a Pulitzer yet."

Jerry laughed. He was relaxed again. "There's plenty of time for that. I haven't been elected governor yet either."

"But *you've* been working on it," Phil said. "Look, it's late and I'm tired. You are too. We'll talk about this later. So, I won't be your campaign manager. I can help you in other ways. The important thing is to get you elected."

They shook hands and Phil went home. He went to sleep quickly and dreamed of 75-foot-long pickles driven easily into the earth to support the new Time-Life Building in New York and of Grace's self-conscious rear and of him and Ann laughing and eating pickles on the Staten Island ferry.

3.

A RABBIT APPEARED in the path cut in the night by the headlights. It sprang out of the darkness and hung there in the light. The man's fingers tightened on the steering wheel and his legs tensed to stomp the brake pedal if it became necessary. Then the rabbit was on the hard surface of the highway running ahead of the car, unable to see beyond the light on either side, so staying in the geometric pattern of the beam.

Little rabbit, the man thought, you ought to be blind, then you wouldn't be afraid to run into the safety of the darkness. He swerved the car left and then right, trying to cast the light off to one side and then the other so the rabbit would run into one of the flat fields. But his speed was so great he was forced each time to swerve back before the rabbit escaped. The rabbit disappeared then as suddenly as it had appeared. The man's skin tightened as he waited to hear the soft thump the small body would make against the steel. He knew how the thump would feel in his feet and legs because he had once run over a dog. Finally he decided the rabbit had simply pooped out and fallen on the pavement and the car had rolled over it, not touching it, leaving it crouched there trembling but unharmed. "If rabbits think," the man said aloud because he had been driving alone a long time, "that one must be thinking how foolish all that running was."

He wondered if it was a jack rabbit. He'd heard or read somewhere that a few jack rabbits were in the delta country, although he could not remember ever seeing or hearing of one when he was growing up here. It is said that jack rabbits can run—how fast?—seventy-five miles an hour? As scared as this one was running it's not improbable it had, for that brief time, equaled the car's registered eighty mph.

The dog in the back seat stirred and whined and the man moved his foot off the accelerator and let the car's weight slow itself before he pressed the brake pedal.

When the dog had relieved itself and was scratching in the grass the man decided that because he no longer knew this country he'd better do the same, here beside the road. Then he thought how good a cup of coffee would taste and how it might steam some of the cobwebs from his tired mind. Then he thought of food. Then he thought a bottle of beer might taste better than coffee.

He and the dog got back into the car and soon they were rushing past vast stretches of young cotton he knew was peeking out of the earth in the fields that extended in unbroken flatness to the tree-fringed horizon on his right and to the low hills that rose in the fog on his left.

His foot moved off the accelerator again and the big car reduced its speed gradually until the power-line poles moved toward him and floated past instead of flipping by in a flickering blur. The lights of a village, scattered across the highway and the flatlands on both sides of it, approached directly ahead.

He glanced at the clock on the dashboard and saw it was 10:30 and thought that an eating place should be open in a town of this size. Maybe a truck stop if nothing else.

Then he was electrically aware of the color of the hands gripping the cold, white steering wheel.

He silenced his thoughts until a feather of anger brushed over his body and he found himself thinking of the rabbit running up there in the beam of his headlights. He shrugged off the anger and remembered his hunger and that in the area there were restaurants divided in half by the display and dish shelves and the utensil cabinet. In these places the whites sat at a counter on one side of the wall of shelves and Negroes were served at the counter on the other side. He remembered such a place in Ashton when he was in his teens. The drawer holding the knives, forks and spoons slid all the way through the segregating partition and the waitress pulled the spoon for his coffee out on the Negro side then walked around and pulled the same drawer out on the white side and got a spoon for the white man's coffee. But, somehow, pulling them out of the drawer on separate sides of the shelves like that made it acceptable under the rules of the System.

The trouble is, he thought, you can't tell whether a restaurant is one of that kind until you get inside. Even if he saw several restaurants open here he did not have time to make the rounds, peeking cautiously inside until he found one with the characteristic ceiling-high divider of shelves. He saw a dimly lighted drive-in restaurant approaching on his right. A dirty white plank building squatted in the center of a graveled parking area. Neon tubing fringed the top of the building with a sputtering green glow. He jerked the steering wheel with his right hand and the tires crunched onto the gravel.

The woman, or girl, or girl-woman (how does it go, he thought, "the fairest creature that walks God's terrestrial ball") stood leaning against the dirty white of the building, which in turn appeared to lean against, or toward, her. His headlights splashed on her.

He switched the lights off and her image dimmed to a shadowy, more attractive version of the squinting, half-sneering girl-woman in the spotlight.

He wondered if she could see him and he became tense wondering and felt his temper rouse because he became tense.

She leaned there for a while, long enough to take two long deep sucks on the cigarette.

Damned if it don't look like a jig in that Chrysler Imperial, she thought. What's a jig doing stopping here? What's a jig doing in a brand-new Imperial, for that matter? She decided to just stand there and maybe he would go away. Then she thought he might be a chauffeur with his boss man drunk on the back seat or waiting at home or in the motel for the jig to bring him some food or a couple of beers to put him to sleep. She looked inside and saw Pete talking to the kid from the Teachers College. Well, I guess I have to go out there and see what the jig wants, she decided; if he tries to rape me, Pete and the kid will hear me holler. What will I say to him? A jig never stopped here before.

She dropped the cigarette and stepped on it and walked toward the Imperial. When she stood beside his window, which he had opened by pressing a button, she said nothing until the dog in the back seat moved toward her and made that half-whine, half-bark sound friendly dogs make at strangers.

He saw now she was younger than he would have guessed during the brief time his headlights were on her. She was twenty or less. Her hair, under the dim exposure from the three poled lights some distance away and from the green neon trim around the top of the boxy building, was a burnt blond and shoulder length. He could not see the texture of her skin (her skin looks green in this light) but he could see the defensive sneer, conveyed by her half-lidded eyes and a slight curl of her upper lip.

(He remembered now. "There is nothing so fair on God's terrestrial ball as a well-bred Southern white woman and her blond, blue-eyed daughter." That's the way Mississippi Circuit Judge Tom Brady wrote it in his book, *Black Monday.*)

"That dog yourn?" she said, her voice farmyard coarse but with less authority now than she would have liked. It was the only thing she could think to say. She damned sure wasn't going to say, "What can I do for you?"

"Yes,'" he said, "ma'am." (You're green, he thought, not white. And he wasn't as nervous as he had been. He was glad his tan Palm Beach suit could not be mistaken for a chauffeur's uniform.)

She took a cigarette from her breast pocket. "Never seen one like him before," she said. "What kinda dog is he?"

"He's a Weimaraner."

"A Vi-mah what?" She giggled.

"Weimaraner. German dog."

"You don't say." She was impressed. "A German dog, huh? Well, I'll be dad burned. Say does he understand us—English, I mean?"

"Oh, yes. He was born in America. He's a show dog."

"Well, now you know I thought he lookt like more'n jist a common houn' dog. Even though you know he does look something like a houn' at that. But with . . . well . . . with more class somehow. His fur looks like velvet." (She reached to touch the dog, but withdrew her hand when the man leaned forward to give her room.)

"By damn, he looks green under this light. Like a green velvet dog," she said. "What television shows has he been on? I see Lassie all the time."

"He's not that kind of show dog. He . . . I enter him in contests. He's won lots of prizes . . . for the way he stands and the way he's built." He tried to simplify it for her.

"Oh, I see," she said. "You said *you* enter him? Is he yours? Your dog, I mean?"

"Yes."

The light from the neon tubing sputtered over the head of the kid from Teachers College as he walked unsteadily out the door and got into his hopped-up, forty-something model Ford coupe and roared away.

"Yeah, that's some dog, all right," the waitress said. "He really looks like he's covered with green velvet, don't he? It's this green light."

"Yes. Well, the reason I stopped here is that I've been driving a long time and he's hungry. My dog is, I mean. Could I get him something to eat?"

She frowned at his words. Then she said hesitantly, "Yeah, I guess that'd be okay. Whadda you want? I mean what do you want for your dog?"

His hands sweated inside the tight grip they had on the white steering wheel. He inhaled.

"A hamburger, I suppose," he said, letting the breath out softly with the words, "and a bottle of beer."

"Beer?" She took a half step away from the car and glanced at the building. She could still see Pete in there. He was reading a newspaper now.

"Yes. He's a German dog. Remember?"

"Oh . . . sure." She wrote the order on a pad that looked green too.

She went inside the building to give Pete the order instead of shouting it to him through the shelved hole in the wall. While Pete fried the meat she went to the toilet.

While she secured the tray to the door of the car she concentrated on the task until it was done and then went back to her post at the leaning wall. As he reached for the hamburger she shoved away from the wall with the foot that was cocked up behind her, went inside and sat at the counter with her back to him as he ate the hamburger and drank the beer. When he had finished he blinked his lights and she came out again.

She laid the ticket on the tray. He took it and held it up and twisted in the seat to see the amount written there and reached in his pocket and drew out some change and counted out the fifty-one cents and another twenty cents and placed the coins on the tray.

"It's only fifty-one, not seventy-one," she said curtly and picked up the fifty-one cents and stood looking over the top of the car until he shrugged and picked up the two dimes. Then she picked up the tray, balancing it on the palm of her left hand, and turned to go.

"My dog thanks you," he said. She looked back at him and nodded, her face still expressionless, her eyebrows pulling together slightly.

He turned the key and the motor growled under the long black hood, then ran silently again. He punched the black button marked with the white "R." The gears under his feet meshed and the car moved backwards until he touched the wide rubber brake pedal and pushed the button marked "D." As he and the car surged forward, the headlights bounced over the figure of the carhop, standing in the shadows of the crackerbox building, cigarette smoke filtering through her nose; standing there watching the long car flow away, her eyebrows pulling a little closer together now in what might have been the beginning of a frown.

His rear tires kicked gravel behind him noisily. The Imperial grabbed the highway and he could see the white center line far ahead on the flat road.

He wondered how scared this Shine Tatum was at this very minute. He must be as scared at least as that rabbit had been, running up there in the headlights ahead of those three hundred horses charging at it, silently, from the rear. This Shine Tatum, whoever he is, was being smarter than the rabbit. He was sucking up his guts and heading out into that dark on the side—out where you couldn't see while you were running in the beam, but where dignity was available to those who had the ability to earn it; only ability; that's all it took, out there. A rabbit has no business on a paved highway. He loses his rabbit dignity there. Most everybody and everything but cars and trucks lose their own peculiar dignity on a paved highway. Just as he—Duval P. Stoneham, LL.D.—momentarily lost his dignity, his hard-earned dignity, at the drive-in faced only by an ignorant carhop; but an ignorant carhop whose green skin would turn white when the neon sign was turned off. He tried to evaluate his actions back there. Had he played the game with the white waitress because he was afraid not to play it? Or worse, had he, after all these years, automatically fallen in step with the System because he lived under its rules during his early, "formative" years? He wanted to believe what he had done was a joke on the white girl, the man inside who cooked the hamburger, and the System. But he wasn't certain.

What made Shine Tatum decide to test the darkness, he wondered, after all those years of running in the beam? According to the data in the briefcase at his side, Shine Tatum was sixty-four years old. Been running so long maybe he couldn't stop suddenly and crouch and hope the car would roll over him without smashing him. How long does the desire to be free burn in a man? Would it still be burning inside Duval Stoneham if he had not taken that bus ride north that day? If he hadn't gone north at fourteen would he have had the courage, now, to do what Shine Tatum was going to do?

———————

The light from a car ran around the walls of the room and the noise of the tires and motor made the boy stiffen in his sleep. The book slid off his chest and hit the floor and the boy sat up, rubbing his eyes sleepily. A moment later he heard the front door open and his Uncle Shine greet a newcomer. He struck a match and looked at the clock on the table by his bed. Almost one. He got out of bed, tiptoed to the door and pushed it open just enough so he could see the men, five of them, seated around the table with the green oilcloth cover on it. Yellow light from the kerosene lamp in the center of the table glistened on their black faces. The boy knew all of them but one, the man who had come in the car a moment ago. Dr. Ramos, who gave him his polio shots, sat with his back to the boy's bedroom. Brother Walthall, the preacher, sat across the table facing Dr. Ramos. Mr. Jackson, the undertaker, dressed even finer than Brother Walthall, sat over beside the preacher. The new man sat at the end of the table nearest the bedroom. He wore a silky tan suit that was almost the same color as his skin. He was the grandest Negro the boy had ever seen. He sat straighter, looked bolder and more relaxed than the others. The boy watched him. There was something about him; something you couldn't describe right off. Then the boy knew what it was: he acted like a white man. There was that something about the way he moved his hands and held his head.

The boy's Uncle Shine, older than the others and seemingly detached from their talk, was at the other end of the table, leaning back in his chair. His arms were folded on his chest and his eyes were closed. The boy had seen him sit that way many times in the two years he had lived with him since his mother—Uncle Shine called her "baby sister"—died. He knew this was the way his uncle sat when he was thinking hard about something. He appeared to be asleep but he wasn't. He sat that way when the boy came home from school those first few weeks he came here to live. Just sitting there, leaning back with his arms folded and his eyes closed until the boy came in. Then he'd rub his eyes and say, "Well, Cooter, how was school today?" and Cooter would say, "Okay, I guess," and Uncle Shine would say something like "Looks like we got some studying to do tonight from all the books you carrying." And he would try to help Cooter with his studies until he would get mad, not at Cooter but at himself because it was easy to see, even though he was a grown man, that he didn't know much about schoolwork. Finally, one night he slapped his hands down on the table and said, "Doggone it, Cooter, I just can't do it any more. I'm doing you more hurt than good. Truth is, I never went to school past the third grade myself. The school on the place where my folks sharecropped didn't go no further'n four or five grades, I guess. Our school, that is. And I couldn't see then the sense in wasting my time going two or three more years when I was big enough to pick and chop and work off-season too. Neither did Maw. So, please forgive me, Cooter, but let's don't play this game no more. If you want to know about farming or folks just ask me. But if you want to know something about them books, you'll have to ask your teachers. I can read the stories. Learnt to do that good enough by reading my Bible. But that 'rithmetic is too much for me." He chuckled. "Maybe that's why I always came out on the short end when I was settling up in my sharecroppin' days. Fact, maybe that's why the white folks don't care about colored folks going to school. Least I don't have to worry about settlin' up no more now that I got my own place here."

Uncle Shine sure was proud of his old buckshot farm. Prouder of it than he was of the store down on the block because he only rented the store and he owned the farm. It was all paid for. Cooter guessed the farm would be his someday. Uncle Shine said so often enough.

The men were talking so low Cooter could hear only occasional words. They kept mentioning "a lawsuit." Then Cooter heard the stranger, who talked louder than the others, say, "Gentlemen, I want you to know that when Mr. Tatum goes down to that courthouse and files that suit I will be right there with him and will stick with him all the way. All we need at this time from you is your moral support and your prayers. Later, perhaps, there will come a time for you to speak out. But for the time being I believe it will be wisest if you went about your business as usual. Let the fire be directed at us for a while."

Then the voices got low again. Finally, the men seemed to have finished their talk, and they stood to go, thanking Uncle Shine for his hospitality as they walked slowly toward the door, shaking his hand and patting him on the back and taking longer to leave than men usually do. Then Cooter heard the two cars start and move away from the cabin and he pushed the door open and stepped into the room.

"Oh, hello, Cooter," Shine said. "I thought you was asleep long ago."

"I was but I woke up when that new man came," Cooter said. "Uncle Shine, who was he?"

"He's a Mr. Stoneham from New York City."

"I knew he wasn't from Ashton."

"Yeah, he got a different look about him, don't he."

"Yes, sir."

"You better get on back to bed."

"Yes, sir. Uncle Shine, what kind of lawsuit were they talking about?"

Shine stood at the door staring out into the warm night where his visitors had gone. He closed the door and turned to the boy.

"Maybe this is as good a time to tell you about it as any," he said. "Did you see who was here, Cooter? There was a preacher, a under-taker, a doctor, and a farmer, me. There was supposed to be a teacher too, but Mr. Pierce said he took sick at the last minute. Anyhow, all of them but me has college degrees. College degrees and can't a single one of them go down and vote for who's gonna be mayor of this town. Can't a single one of them walk in a white man's office without his hat in his hand. They all gotta live in a certain section of town. None of them will ever have that look that Mr. Stoneham has."

"Why don't they go to New York City?"

"People can run away only so long. Anyhow, it wouldn't be much better for most of them up there. I worked in Dee-troit one year. Folks, even up there, don't have much respect for people who are running away. No, if you can't be somebody where you were borned and raised, then it's mighty hard to be somebody somewhere else."

"You gonna get the court judge to make the white folks let Mr. Jackson and them be somebodies right here in Ashton?"

Shine smiled sadly. "That's about it, I guess. . . . No, I don't suppose nothing we can do now will be much help to the ones of us that are our age." He reached out and put a hand on the curly head of the boy who, as far as he knew, was his only living blood relation. "But what we do might let you be a somebody. Your teachers say you're a smart boy. More than ordinary smart. If that's so, you got a right to be a somebody—and be it right here where you was borned and raised and where your folks have lived ever since this land was settled. Did you know your great-grandfather was a chief in Africa? Well, he was. I don't know what kind of chief, but some kind. I remember Granny telling about him. She said the white folks who owned her brought him to her one day. She was scared to death might-near, but he wasn't mean like some of them and she and him lived together till she got pregnant with Mamma. Then they came after him. He didn't want to go and he fought like a painter, Granny said. Took two white men and three buck slaves to take him off. She never saw him again. When Mamma was borned, she said, the captain was mad as a wet hen 'cause he wanted that chief's child to be a boy. But Mamma was so pretty the captain's wife took right to her and moved her into the big house when she wasn't more'n five or six and taught her how to wait on fancy tables. She never even had to work in the fields until the slaves was freed and she married Papa. . . . I never told you about all that before, did I?"

"No, sir."

"Well, I should have. Some of these white folks around here always bragging so much about their kin."

The old man smiled. Then his face was serious again.

"But that ain't the most important, Cooter. What's most important is what *you* are. That's why we're filing that lawsuit. That's why. I want you to have a chance to live right here where you and all your folks was borned and raised and stand up as straight as Mr. Stoneham does. You may not understand it all now, but someday you will. Nobody can generate much respect for you or me or nobody who can't go down on election day and speak his piece."

4.

"WHAT'RE YOU MUMBLING ABOUT, you old warhorse?" Phil said.

It wasn't seven o'clock yet and there was no one but Ranch in the newsroom. Phil had walked instead of taking the elevator and had eased up behind Ranch and stood there grinning at the big man who had served so loyally and efficiently for so many years as city editor, feature writer, sports columnist, photographer, reporter, public relations man, and done a little janitorial work on the side when necessary. Phil thought of the many bright young reporters who had worked here over the years, learning the fundamentals and ethics of journalism from Ranch and his father and going on, after a year or two, to bigger, better-paying jobs on city papers or wire services throughout the country and the world while Ranch stayed on, the stabilizing force around which the small, ever-changing but somehow always adequate news staff functioned. He remembered the time the big, bald man he now watched had insisted that a particularly good reporter get the salary raise he should have got himself so the reporter would stay on with the *Dispatch* instead of taking a job offered him by the New Orleans *Picayune.* The reporter had left a few months later for a job on the Memphis *Commercial Appeal.*

"Mornin', Phil," Ranch said when Phil spoke. "Aw, I just got the regular Monday morning reds. Baby kept me awake all night and I got here this morning and the god-damned AP machine was out of ribbon and we missed the last fifteen or twenty minutes."

"Good thing we got the UPI machine in last year."

"Sure is. This has happened before." Ranch picked up a stack of green paper he had torn from the machine and stepped over to his desk and laid the paper on it. "We cleaned out your desk." He nodded toward the corner where Phil had worked six years ago.

The twin AP machines and the UPI machine clattered in Phil's ears. Someone in the composing room shouted through the intercom and Ranch shouted back into the rusty box on his desk. The two young reporters came in together, tossed their sport coats on the table by the elevator, nodded respectfully when Ranch introduced them to Phil, and began opening the envelopes filled with memos from Ranch to guide them through their day's work. Nick Sparacino, the sports editor, came in and stopped to shake hands with Phil.

"Good to have you back," Nick said. "It hasn't been much fun around here lately."

"How was the baseball game Friday?" Phil asked, remembering that when he was in on Friday afternoon Ranch had told him Sparacino was covering a game.

"Pretty good," Nick said. "Greenwood beat us nine to six, but we got a couple of good boys who are just sophomores. Oughta have a good team next year."

"Glad to hear it," Phil said. He saw out of the corner of his eye that the two young reporters were watching him now instead of reading the memos.

"Here's some pictures I took at the game," Nick said, turning to Ranch. "Which ones you like?"

Ranch and the sports editor went into a huddle over the pictures and the reporters turned their attention back to the memos. Phil sat down and looked at his typewriter. He felt strangely out of place. He wanted to write something wise or dramatic for today's paper. He felt that these people in the newsroom with him now expected him to write something wise or dramatic. But what could he write about?

"Think I'll make the rounds at the courthouse and city hall this week sometime," he said. "I need to catch up on things before I can be of much help around here. I'm out of touch with local issues."

Ranch looked up at him. "That reminds me. I need to talk with you soon as possible about something. I'll have this early copy down in a few minutes if you have some time then."

Phil looked back at the silent typewriter. "Sure, I've got plenty of time this morning," he said.

"Hey, Ranch," the voice from the intercom shouted, "we need a three-inch editorial to fill out the column. And hurry up, will ya, we're behind schedule with this page now. It should have been locked up five minutes ago."

"Think you can write a three-inch editorial in the next five minutes?" Ranch asked Phil.

Phil laughed. "I'd forgotten about that too. You have to be wise to a stopwatch in this damn place. What the hell can I think of and write in five minutes?"

"Four and a half minutes now," Ranch said.

Phil saluted and put his fingers on the typewriter keys. Write something, he told them.

He wrote about the city sanitation department's trash cans in the downtown area. They needed painting, he wrote. "These cans are part of an Ashton visitor's first impression of our city. They are, in their present condition, a disgrace."

Oh, well, he thought, I have to start with something.

He hoped the two young reporters weren't too disappointed when they read the editorial that afternoon.

When the stack of paper on Ranch's desk had gone downstairs or in the wastebasket Ranch walked to Phil's desk.

"Got time for a cup of coffee now?" he asked.

"Sure," Phil said and they rode down on the elevator and walked across Main Street to the grill.

"What's the big secret?" Phil said when they were settled in a booth near the rear of the dimly lighted café. "I know it's something big or you'd have asked me about it in the newsroom."

"Well, since we don't have much time I'll get right to the point," Ranch said. "There's a strong rumor going around in the Negro quarters that a test case is going to be filed here soon . . . real soon."

"Schools?!"

"No, voting."

"Oh? . . . That should be interesting."

"Interesting is right. Since you left, Phil, the Citizens Council has gotten pretty damn high and mighty around here."

"They been givin' the paper trouble?"

Ranch looked down at the checkered tablecloth. "Naw. We . . . well, we haven't been giving them any trouble, so they leave us alone. We're at a sort of arm's-length truce, you might say."

"Oh?"

"Yeah. Your dad had a long talk with some of them. Old Man Auld over at the bank and some of them. He told me to kind of lay off as long as they didn't bother us. That was right after you left. It's been pretty quiet ever since."

"I see."

"Does that still hold? I mean now that you're back?"

"For the time being, yes."

A frown of disappointment passed across Ranch's ruddy face.

"Don't go getting your damper down," Phil said. "We aren't going to play press agent for them like most papers in this state do. We're just going to take another approach. I did a lot of thinking in New York. I was up there a long time without an audience for my sermons. I don't want to lose my audience down here. And that's exactly what would happen if we went off half-cocked. These are good people. Damn good people. If we meet them halfway they'll listen to reason."

"Yeah," Ranch said, "they love their niggers."

"I know. I know. But the point is if they're ever going to change that attitude they're going to have to change it themselves. From inside themselves. It has grown there for a long damn time. And we can't cut it out with a few front page editorials calling them bastards."

"You mean we're going to worm our way into their confidence

and tell them politely that they're race-baiting bastards?" Ranch said.

"Not exactly," Phil said. Ranch's sarcasm irritated him.

"We're going to put out a good newspaper that tells the truth and let the truth do the job.

"What is the truth, Phil?"

"That's not for you to decide," Phil said. "Your job is to put the news in the paper the way it happens. I'll write the editorials."

Ranch stood up as the waiter arrived to take their orders. "I've got to get back," he said. "The coffee is lousy here anyhow."

Phil gazed at his hands on the table in front of him.

"Do we print that rumor about the voting test case?" Ranch asked.

"We don't print rumors," Phil said. "When it happens, if it happens, we'll print exactly what happened."

When the presses began to roll with the final edition that afternoon and Phil had got a copy and glanced at the front page, which was the only change from the first edition, he decided to drive around and look his town over. He maneuvered his father's black sedan through the late afternoon traffic which was multiplying now as if by mitosis as the time approached for the business places to close their doors for the day. He drove toward the courthouse, south on Main Street. In the rear-view mirror he saw the river bridge loom silver in the sun behind him. After he looked the town over, he would drive along the river road. No, he had a better idea. He was to pick Ann up in an hour. He would wait until then and they would drive along the river together. Or, better still, they would have a picnic on one of the sand bars some afternoon this week. He had seen Ann as much as possible since the party. They played nine holes of golf together Saturday afternoon after the party, then sat in the lounge at the Country Club and got loaded together that evening. They never seemed to run out of things to say to each other. The next day, Sunday, they went swimming at the Country Club pool and spent most of the afternoon sitting on the bank, dangling their feet in the water, talking. But they had not yet talked about themselves. He had never been with a woman who could talk so sensibly about any subject. If Ann was not informed on a subject, she listened. That alone put her head and shoulders above most women.

He was approaching the courthouse and he smiled at the large glazed-tile billboard directly ahead of him. It was put there to honor Ashton's World War II dead. There were no names on the red, white, and blue surface and he regarded its sterile ugliness as a personal reminder of the fruitlessness of his pre-New York, "young Turk" days as his father's managing editor. Fresh from the war himself, he had chosen for his baptismal crusade the task of convincing local patriots that names of Negroes killed in the war should go on the billboard alongside the names of white men who had given their lives for their country and democracy. At first there was no expressed opposition to the idea.

"I guess it's all right, Phil," Chester Blinken, Sr., chairman of the Chamber of Commerce committee in charge of the project, had said. "Won't hurt nothing that I can see. We can put the niggers' names on one side and our boys names on the other."

That had been satisfactory with Phil. He knew a crusader must sometimes compromise, and this was a minor concession. The important thing was to get the names up there. "German and Jap sharpshooters," he wrote in a front-page editorial backing his stand, "certainly did not check the color of the skin under those American uniforms before triggering the bullets that tore into the flesh and let the uniformly red blood gush."

But somewhere along the way somebody had spoken out against it. Phil always suspected it was Hampton Auld, president of the Farmers' Bank and Trust Company. Old Hamp was one of those "ag-inners." Phil and Jerry used to laugh and say he studied the *Dispatch* carefully every night only to find local projects he could be against the next day.

Anyhow, whoever ignited it, opposition to putting the names of the Negroes on the billboard blazed. In the end the nameless monstrosity facing him now was erected. Now folks were calling it an eyesore and there was talk of tearing it down.

He made the U-turn instead of driving around the square and headed north again toward the bridge. At the post office he waved at Old Man Auld, who was standing alone on the steps peering cautiously at an envelope as if he weren't sure he would or should open it. Auld didn't see him or pretended he didn't.

"The old son of a bitch stills looks like a skinny Neanderthal man in a Brooks Brothers suit," Phil chuckled.

He recognized three of Ashton's leading lawyers hurrying out of the Buscher Building toward the parking lot half a block away behind the Rex movie house. Rushing to the Yacht Club, Phil thought, each to buy a half pint of bourbon and drink that rapidly—with water—then buy another half pint each and attempt to get that down before their wives telephoned that meaningful third time. It had been a long time since he'd thought about the local men's unique custom of buying liquor in half pints. The bums in New York bought whatever they had money to buy in small quantities. And rednecks in the hill section honky-tonks carried half pints or pints on their Saturday night rounds. But in Ashton even men whose daughters were debutantes preferred half pints unless they were going to a Country Club dance where the bottle, a fifth, sat on the table. He remembered going on a picnic on a plantation once and his host, when his half pint was dry, took Phil to the car and opened the trunk and took another half pint from a case of them. Phil had always enjoyed the Yacht Club, which was a spruced-up Negro tenant house built on stilts at the river's edge, and he considered going there now for a couple of drinks and some conversation before he went home to dress for his date with Ann. He decided against it, however, and continued his ride, crossing the bridge into the town's oldest residential section.

Few families whose ancestors had built these huge homes still lived in them. More modern houses were easier to manage and this was no longer considered a "good part of town." But the beauty of River Street, with its row of giant trees dividing the traffic lanes, had not yet been covered completely by what sociologists call "creeping blight," which does not actually creep but is pushed in by money-hungry real estate brokers or by the descendants of the builders of the homes themselves. Paint was peeling off most of the gabled, two- and three-story frame houses and few of the once grand and manicured garden yards were cared for any more. But the nineteenth-century dignity of the homes had not yet been completely hidden by the carpenters who divided them into as many apartments as possible. The trees were still there and did wonders to camouflage the man-made blight.

As he drove slowly in the friendly shade of the trees—pecans, oaks, cottonwoods—he felt a surge of happiness because he was home again; and home to stay this time. He wasn't sorry he had gone to New York. If he had not gone there to work and live in that frantic center of almost everything he might never have lost the nagging restlessness that asked him if he had the ability to "make it" there. Now he knew he could "make it" there—maybe not in a sensational way, he wasn't the type, but he had been a mild success and knew he could have done even better if his heart had been in it. He liked to think of New York as a glamorous woman he had admired, with not a little awe, for a long time and finally persuaded to go to bed with him. She hadn't fallen in love with him, nor he with her. But the awe was gone because the mystery was gone. He had had his fling and now he was back with his "family." Ashton had its faults, but just as its virtues were smaller than New York's virtues, so were its faults— if not smaller at least faults he understood because he shared many of them with the people he had grown up with and among.

A man wants to have something important figured out by the time he is thirty-five. Not everything, but something important to him. Ashton and its people were important to him and he believed he understood them now. Living in New York had helped him reach this understanding. And helped him appreciate it. He had never learned how to anticipate the reaction of a New Yorker, man or woman, in a given situation. Initially this had intrigued him but as the months and years went by the uncertainty of it built a constant, gnawing discomfort inside him. He was told that New Yorkers react logically, with a minimum of emotion, while Southerners don't *react,* even in normal business transactions; they *act* according to a ritual. Maybe that's bad to a New Yorker, but if you were born and reared in the atmosphere of that ritual you know instinctively what to expect and, therefore, how to proceed. That had been his trouble when he came home after the war. He had shoved the knowledge of the ritual aside in favor of the belief that the shortest distance between two points is along a straight line. This simply is not true in Ashton and now he knew it and could promote his pet community projects within the framework of the ritual. He had become too impatient while away at war. At war you learn to think only of getting through each day— alive under some circumstances and with a minimum of boredom under others. This day-by-day scheming to escape death or boredom builds within you an almost frantic distaste for ritual and routine, a distaste which takes time to overcome when suddenly you are a civilian adult who should, must think past today, and even tomorrow.

He absorbed the familiar landmarks with a sensual pleasure and inhaled the familiar air. The air down here, heavy and humid as it is, has character, he thought, even the ugly, unpainted shacks in the Negro quarters. I prefer it here. This is home. All my memories are here, at least most of my pleasant ones—those filled with the wonderful background music of youth. And by God I'm going to be an accepted part of all of it again.

He had circled back and was again approaching the courthouse. This time he turned right at the glazed memorial billboard and drove slowly around the ancient building which rose three stories high from the center of the lawn that was already green (it was soothing just to see so much green again) and above the giant oaks. Unlike their counterparts in the public square and parks of New York, Southerners who spend leisure hours on the benches of the courthouse squares don't make speeches. They sit quiet and whittle and chew tobacco or suck snuff and talk in low tones to whomever they are sitting near. There are no stand-up speeches and arguments except at election time, and these are by the traveling vote seekers and their aides. Knowing this, Phil was curious about the crowd at the northwest corner, under the largest oak on the square—the one with the gnarled and twisted trunk encompassed by benches. He drove nearer and stopped the car. Immediately he wished he had not noticed the crowd and driven over to see what attracted it.

A white man, his back to Phil, barked military orders. A large, heavily muscled Negro paced back and forth, carrying out—or trying to carry out—his orders. Phil recognized the Negro. He was the one called Crazy Tom, an imbecile who probably should have been placed in a mental institution years ago, but who was "kept around and fed," Phil's father had once said, "to prove to some of these people that Negroes are inferior."

Crazy Tom had lived off what he could beg until about 1951 when Shine Tatum gave him a job in his store. He still lived in a lean-to on the river a mile north of town. As a puppy learns to retrieve a stick tossed by the man who feeds it, Crazy Tom had learned that it pleased white men when he performed and that afterwards they were likely to give him dimes or a drink of whisky.

"Hut, two, three, four," the white man in the red leather hunting cap shouted and Crazy Tom marched back and forth, limping and shaking his knees, making deep-throated animal noises. Anything to make the big man laugh louder.

"Okay, nigger," the white man in the hunting cap said, "let's go on a weekend pass. What are you going to do when you meet up with one of them Yankee gals?"

Tom moved his hips and threw back his head and screamed. The men around him laughed and Tom went through the motion again and screamed again.

"Now dance like your granddaddy did in the jungle," the man in the leather cap said, and Tom began a low, guttural chant, bent forward at the waist and danced around an imaginary campfire as he had seen Indians do in Western movies. The men slapped their thighs and nudged each other and laughed and winked at each other.

"That Mike Heaney is a card, ain't he," a man in faded blue overalls and a khaki shirt standing near Phil's car said to the man at his side.

"He sure is."

The man in the red leather hunting cap turned and stood facing Phil. Phil remembered him. Mike Heaney. Mike had been painfully shy and fat in high school. Lived in West Ashton somewhere near the river. He wasn't fat now and certainly not shy.

"Well, if it isn't *Mr.* Phil Arrow," Mike Heaney said.

"How are you, Mike?" Phil said, reaching to turn the key and start the car's motor.

"Enjoying the show, *Mr.* Arrow?" Mike said, grinning and glancing at the men around him.

An angry nausea stirred in Phil's bowels and his face burned. "Yeah, some show," he said and he drove away.

5.

PHILIP ARROW, SR., sat on the side of his bed and cursed whatever it was that made it impossible for the old to sleep late. If he could sleep late, the day would be shorter. He limped barefooted to the door, made certain it was locked, shuffled back to his rumpled bed and got the silver flask from the bedside table's bottom drawer. He started to pour the Scotch into the glass that waited there on the tabletop but stopped when he saw chalky beads hanging in clusters halfway down on the inside of the glass. The Alka-Seltzer he drank before he went to bed a few hours before had left its mark. He shuffled into the bathroom with the glass, rinsed it, returned and poured what he estimated was two jiggers. He drank that and sat on the bed with his eyes closed until he felt the warmth course through his aching body.

I'm not an alcoholic yet, he thought. I don't want liquor, at least my body doesn't cry for it. I drink it this morning because I can't sleep past eight o'clock no matter how late I stay up the night before. The liquor shortens the day.

He felt no better but he knew the next drink would begin to reach him. Then, as he did every morning, he thought of the newsroom at the *Dispatch.* At eight o'clock it was more alive than at any other time during the day. He should be there—a part of its aliveness—as he had been for twenty-five years. As he had been until he lied to his son and set him adrift by telling him that all he had taught him was false. If the boy hadn't set out for Copeland's hide at just that time. If he could have sent him away on some wild goose chase until he had time to adjust to the kick in the face the town had given him. When you spend your life building a run-down biweekly into an honest-to-God daily newspaper with a reputation for integrity and guts you are really spending your life building a one-horse, history-burdened town into an energetic little city. He had done that. He—Philip Arrow—had done that. How many thousands of inches of copy had he run on page one promoting Chamber of Commerce projects? How many committees had he been chairman of? How many trips to the East had he made at his own expense begging for industry? How many terms had he served as president of the god-damned Chamber of Commerce—four? Sure, he had built a profitable business for himself, but no other business, except a bank, has as much to do with the growth and energy of a community as does a newspaper. Show me a dead newspaper and I'll show you a dead town around it.

But what did he get for his ulcers and bad liver and spent energy? Hate. That was his reward—hate. He woke up one morning and discovered he was the most hated man in town. He had, through the columns of the *Dispatch,* goaded these people into prosperity over the decades and they hated him for it. Sure, he was wrong to have been so rough on Phil Junior. But what was a man to do?

He poured another drink, swallowed it and went into the bathroom to shave. He wouldn't go to the paper this morning. Let Phil jump right in and learn for himself what it was like. Then maybe, if he lived long enough, he would hear his son say, "Now I know why, Dad."

It was Monday, and at noon, after riding down to the Yacht Club and drinking a few beers and watching Colonel Pierce and Roger Blake play gin rummy, he sat stiffly in the straight-backed chair and watched his fellow Rotary Club members. He watched their faces reshaped with laughter and their mouths move as they spoke or chewed the bland hotel food. He shook his head to dislodge the vision of each Rotarian spitting poisoned darts at his tablemates. He wondered if the compulsion to murder friends and loved ones was peculiar to

Americans. Probably not. The low hum of the voices now roared in his head. Then he was able to hear not only many of the actual words of those around him but the real meaning behind those words: *"Hey Joe, how's your daughter?"* (*"I thought it was my duty on this day as your friend to spoil your meal by reminding you of your alcoholic, nymphomaniac daughter."*) *"Hey, John, that son of yours looks more like you every day."* (*"I say that because everybody knows he was sired by that Air Force captain who lived next door to you while the air base was open here."*)

Then as on television their conversation faded out of and back into focus and he saw them at home with the women to whom they had been joined until death parted them—physical death, that is; dead souls don't count:

"Darling," each mate said to the other, *"people treated me badly today so I am going to stab you again and again throughout the evening with this barbed instrument."* And he could see them do as they said they would do, throughout the evening.

He saw the plantation owners walk from their homes where their wives were and go to tenant shacks to bludgeon a Negro psyche or two before supper.

"You no'count black bastard, lay'n up here in the sack all day when there's work to be done. Who's sick? Somebody gonna be sick if that tractor ain't fixed tomorrow."

And he saw the black eyes glaze as all emotion vacated them until the tirade passed, so there would be no anger to prod the black-skinned man to talk back to the white men, who for all practical purposes owned the black-skinned man because despite the fact that the black man had worked for the white man all his life he somehow owed him more money than he could ever hope to repay. "The way to keep a nigger in line is to keep him in debt to you." The Negro didn't plan revenge and wouldn't talk it away later. He simply would not think about it. He would live the best he could between visits from the white man who owned him and not think about the fact that it was the twentieth century and Mr. Abraham Lincoln was dead and gone. Not think and not feel, that was the way.

"... I dint do nothin' but I done done so many bad things I's due to be whipped anyways ...."

"... When you singin' you forgit, you see, and the time just pass on 'way; but if you just get your mind 'voted on one something, it look like it will be hard for you to make a day, see ... so to keep his mind from being 'voted on just one something, why, a nigger he just sing ...."

Philip Arrow, Sr., wished he could sing away the days. He couldn't. But he could drink them away. It was almost the same. He rose abruptly and walked out of the room.

Outside, he took the flask from the glove compartment of the car and drank. But the flywheel in his head had already started whirling and the liquor only made it whirl faster. If he hadn't gone to the god-damned Rotary Club he could have kept it still.

"Look at me, Mommy! Look at me, Daddy!" the child cries ... expectantly at first, then puts on his mask of nonchalance to cover the hurt, because neither Mommy nor Daddy looks.

"Help me, help me," sob a husband and a wife, standing back to back, each pleading away from the other until their voices die out and they slump in two separate lumps.

"Lord, I woke up this morning, man, I feelin' bad. Wah, baby, I was feelin' bad."

"When you singin' you forgit, you see."

It's much better to forget, Phil Arrow, Sr., thought, than to spend your life trying to rehabilitate the god-damned human race through the columns of a fifteen thousand circulation newspaper and see people pick up the paper day after day and hear them say, "Now what did he have to go and print that for?"

———————————

When Phil got home that night, after taking Ann to her Aunt Amy's, the telephone was ringing. It was Chief Hedgepath calling to say that a patrol car had found his father out on Bayou Lane asleep behind the wheel of his Ford sedan. He hadn't been there long, the chief said, because, to be real frank, he hadn't slept long enough to sober up. He said Phil had better come on down to the station and get him and by the time he'd finished saying it Phil had hung up the receiver and was running down the stairs, putting his jacket on as he ran.

Thirty minutes later, as he undressed his father in the big bedroom, the silver-haired old man tried bravely to hold his tall gaunt frame erect. He docilely obeyed each order Phil whispered to him, as if he were the child and the son were the father, a little bewildered at being alone with the baby for the first time. "Lift your left foot up, Dad."

"Uh-huh."

"A little higher. That's it. Now the right one. Easy does it. We'll get those damn pants off yet. There . . ."

"Son . . ."

"Never mind now. You just lie down and get some sleep. We'll talk tomorrow."

"Son . . . be hard. Be hard!"

"Sure, Dad. Sure. Now lie back easy and I'll pull up the cover. There's a chill out tonight."

"Son, be hard. Be hard. You gotta be hard or they'll split you wide open and your guts will spill out all over your dignity."

"Sure, Dad. We'll talk about it tomorrow."

"Just go at it to make money. You can't rehabilitate the entire damned human race with that little old fifteen thousand circulation paper, son. Can't be done. Try to be their conscience and first thing you know you'll hear them say, 'Now what did he go and do that for?' And you'll know what I mean then. . . . What did he go and spend his whole life serving on committees, advertising civic things, fighting for the good guys and against the bad guys for and not even really doing that . . . just wanting to and not doing it . . . and passing everything worth stopping for. Not even putting the worst things in the paper—cause you'll lose your audience, Ranch—know what I mean? You'll lose your audience."

"Just lie back now, Dad. We'll talk about it later."

As he closed his father's bedroom door gently, leaving the lights on, Phil murmured to himself, "We damn sure will talk about it tomorrow." But he knew when he said it they would not. Not tomorrow.

He wiped tears from his cheeks with the back of a hand and, head down, walked to his room where he smoked four cigarettes before he got into bed. After he smoked the cigarettes and was in bed, his body relaxed because he had long ago trained it to relax under any circumstances. But he could not stop the painful unpackaging that had begun in his mind. It was like tearing at old scar tissue but he could not stop the tearing. Seeing his father so drunk started the tearing and it continued until his mother's voice burst forth: "You are filthy. You are filthy, Philip Arrow." Then he saw her. The telegram in her hand. The yellow, crumpled paper. "Here is her message. Take it and answer her. Tell her you will meet her. Tell her, because I don't care now. You are already filthy from her. A woman like that wouldn't send a message like this if you weren't." And he saw his hero's face. And he saw a small boy standing at the top of the stairs looking down on his mother and his hero. His small bare feet numb. His arms strangely light as if they wanted to float away from his body. "Don't ever come to me again." His mother dropped the yellow paper and it fell at his hero's feet. "You may stay in this house for my son's sake. But don't ever come to me again. Speak to me only when necessary. Don't ever try to rub your sin on me." The boy tiptoed down the stairs to the violated spot when they had gone. He picked up the yellow paper and read: "Will be in Memphis Tuesday. Call me. Peabody Hotel. K.S." In the months that followed he saw his mother's face become rigid from the absence of emotion. Her face relaxed again only in death. Her own father, looking to be from another world in his black Presbyterian suit, paused at her casket, his long, veined hand resting on the boy's shoulder, said, "That was one of the finest little girls God ever put on this earth, Philip. She was too good for most mortals."

All this spilled over into Phil's consciousness for the first time in many years. In the years after the night he had stood on the stairs he reconstructed his father's image in heroic proportions (because he had to), using his love and dedication to journalism and the *Dispatch*. Men of great passion for a profession or art, the teenage Phil reasoned, often need more than one woman can give. History books are full of the proof of this. But to remain intact his hero had to maintain his passion for his profession. When he went to New York Phil believed his hero had lost even this. Then he had, he thought, begun to understand.

But before he could sleep Phil had carefully to wrap up the memory of what the boy at the top of the stairs had seen that night. As he wrapped it up he cursed his Bible Belt upbringing and whatever it was that made him want to vomit when he saw an old man drunk.

6.

WHEN A MAN and a woman are falling in love but haven't yet spoken of it, for fear it may not be as eternal as it feels, it's as if a vibrant mist surrounds them when they are together and they neither can nor wish to see beyond it. They communicate each mood with incredible quickness and share it with delight that is, simultaneously, painful and religious.

That's how it was for Phil and Ann from the time they met at the Windham's party. It was less than a week after the party when they went to the river sand bar with a picnic basket, but it seemed—as each said many, many times—they had grown up together. ("Why do people always say that?" Ann asked once. "I don't know anyone I grew up with that I have so much fun with.") Phil had not kissed her although he had sensed, several times, that she wanted him to kiss her. Each time something—he didn't know what—held him back.

That day at the river he parked where the two-rutted road ended and hurried around the car to open the door for her. They raced to the sand bar, kicked off their shoes and stood with the yellow sand crawling over their feet, wiggling their toes like children, laughing like children. Then they were silent as they watched the debris that moved past in the river's brown current. Phil threw a piece of drift-wood into the current. It was snared by an eddy and circled with increasing speed until it was sucked down. This made them laugh and they began chasing each other up and down the sand bar. Finally, breathing heavily from the exercise, Ann ran over to the blanket they had spread, lay on her back, closed her eyes tightly and stretched her arms over her head.

Phil stood over her, wondering how he could have thought, as he did at the party, that her body was less noticeable in a crowd than Grace's. She just didn't throw it around in a crowd the way Grace did, but stretched out as it was now it could stun a man. He dropped to the blanket, propping his head on his left hand, and studied her face. A man shouldn't be afraid to love a woman with such a face, he thought, regardless of how badly he had been hurt before.

She lay silent and motionless for a while; then she turned onto her stomach and drew pictures in the sand. Suddenly she looked at him and asked, "Why did you come back to Ashton, Phil?"

"What do you mean?"

"I mean, why did you come back here—from New York?"

"This is my home. The *Dispatch* . . ."

"I know. But I'd always heard you were one of those freaks—a real Southern liberal. I think a liberal might find living here intolerable, especially if he ran a newspaper. Maybe I'm wrong. *You* tell *me.*"

"That word 'liberal' has gotten so fouled up with issues, specific issues I mean, it doesn't mean anything any more." He hoped she wouldn't insist on staying on this subject.

"Well, what *do* you consider yourself? A moderate?"

"Hell, no. That doesn't mean anything either—unless it means you're trying to stay out of trouble. Or please everybody." The mysterious mist of their near-love was lifting fast. He felt anger stirring inside him, although he knew it was foolish to be angered by her questions. It's not her questions, he thought, it's because she is turning us into two people—any two people—talking politics, or philosophy, or whatever to hell she's building up to. And a moment ago we were almost lovers.

"Isn't that what you plan to do? It sure sounded like it to me when you were telling me the other evening about, quote, 'becoming a part of this community again,' unquote."

He sat up and took a cigarette from the package that lay between them and offered one to her. She shook her head. He lighted his cigarette and inhaled the first puff.

"Okay, Ann. You asked for it. I'm going to take a chance and be corny with you."

"Why do you say 'take a chance'?"

"Because, dammit, it's impossible to explain—to most people. If you're talking to a Northerner either he has to admit he doesn't know what the hell you're getting at or he's so arrogant he tries to fit everything you say into his own ideas about how it is. To explain, I've got to say I love the South—and how can anyone really understand that? Unless maybe he has an alcoholic mother, or some other crazy emotional relationship to compare it to."

The way she looked at him made him even more uncomfortable than what he had said. But he had to go on now. He couldn't stop even if she were willing. Maybe it is just as well we talk this out now, he thought, if there's ever to be anything *real* between us she has to know, and understand. Maybe if he tried to put it all into words—for her—he would even understand it himself. He waited to continue because she seemed to be running his words, or maybe her next question, over and over in her mind.

Finally she said, "I always liked Kansas City—at least the neighborhood where we lived. But I have never wanted to go back there to live. I certainly don't feel I owe it anything. Somehow I sense that you believe you owe the South something—if nothing else, mental anguish for it. Why?"

"But you didn't grow up continuously conscious you were a Midwesterner. Down here you're born knowing—or believing—somebody, somewhere, is trying to take your home away from you. . . . There's a problem in genetics for somebody—I never was told by either of my parents that the South was in danger of being invaded, but I felt it. As far back as I can remember I felt it. It seeps into you from out of the earth maybe. Like hookworms. The earth Union soldiers walked over. . . . Did you know this town was burned to the ground during that stupid war?"

"Mother has told me that story a thousand times, I guess," Ann said thoughtfully; then added, "But you admit it was a stupid war. And I *hope* you believe the right side won it. How could those old ancestral scars bother you?"

"Sure, I believe the right side won—now I do. But it's an atmosphere a kid breathes when he's growing up down here. The war is seldom, if ever, mentioned outside the classroom, but somehow the fear, or distrust, of outsiders gets in him. Maybe it's because you remember stories your grandmother told you about Union troops riding up to her house; how they buried the family silver . . . I don't know. Maybe it's just that at a certain age you have to be violently loyal to something and have a special, common identity with your buddies. You sing 'Dixie' at the top of your voice and it's a song of defiance. That terrible adolescent defiance against everything that restricts you. You don't think about reasons when you're a kid. You just *feel*. Then, when you become an adult, in years, it's tough to shake the habit."

He watched the clouds and puffed on the cigarette. Then he said, "Well . . . let me put it this way. Say, a kid's father is a drunk and sleeps with every two-bit wench in town. And everybody knows it but the kid, of course. He doesn't know it, or think about it, because his father is, to him, a happy, warm, loving person—that's in addition to being his father, which means a lot to a kid—so he loves him very much. Then one day he grows up and discovers that his father is a drunk and a . . . a rounder. What happens? After the first big slap of disappointment, he loves the old scoundrel even more than before, that's what."

"So you went off to war and came back and discovered your 'fatherland' was in an alcoholic-like daze—not dashing and romantic—and you went off to New York to sulk; then came back loving it more than ever. Is that it?" Ann's eyes were moist.

"I guess that's about it," he said. "In fact, you explain it much better than I do."

"What is it, Phil?" she asked, sitting up abruptly.

"Nothing. Why?"

"Your face. For a second it looked as if someone had slapped you." She laughed self-consciously. "Or you got a stomach cramp, or something."

"I was just remembering," he said, "the first time I went to a Citizens Council rally. They prayed to God to help their cause, of course, and that's bad enough. But I think what hurt me most was hearing them sing 'Dixie'—my song. I had never really paid attention to the words. The song just stirred me up. You know, made me determined to 'win the game for dear ole Ashton High' and things like that. Then, all of a sudden, here they were singing it with the same fervor we sang it in high school, but singing it to get all riled up to go out and fight against the Negro's right to be a human being. I heard the words that night—'I wish I was in the land of cotton. Old times there are not forgotten' . . . .I knew then it fit their cause better than mine. I've hated the damn song ever since."

He had told her only part of the truth. He had remembered that first Citizens Council rally when the pain showed on his face. But at the same time—the way thoughts can pile up in your mind—he was thinking too of his father and the "charming, loving drunk" he used to explain, or try to explain, his feeling toward the South and Ashton. Did he love him more now? He was thinking too of the little boy at the top of the stairs and the two people the boy saw—the woman shouting and the man, head down, silent, not denying anything. Did he love him more now, after putting him to bed as he had a few nights ago? Or did he only pity him now? It might be better for a son to hate his father, he thought, than pity him.

He frowned. "Let's talk about something else . . . about you, for instance."

"What'll we say about me?"

"There's not much about you I know, I regret to say. . . . But I intend to find out plenty." He wanted this to sound casual, maybe even a little suggestive. No, he'd settle for casual. Every time he tried to make a risqué remark around a woman it came out just plain vulgar. He didn't have the knack some guys had. Some guys could tell a dirty joke to a Baptist preacher's wife and she'd laugh and not be offended. If he propositioned a whore, with his money showing, she'd probably slap his face.

"You have more secret thoughts than any man I ever knew," Ann said. She lay on her stomach again. "Ask me something. I'll tell you anything you want to know about me. Don't just sit there wondering."

"I was just wondering why you—why some man hadn't already taken you out of circulation—married you."

She watched her finger make furrows in the sand. "I want a man who can love me as unselfishly as my father loved my mother and a man I can love as unselfishly as Mother loved him. I just haven't found him yet. I've thought so a couple of times . . . but it always turned out, no." She drew two more furrows, side by side, in the sand, then she looked up at Phil. "Now tell me about your wife."

"You sure sneak up on a man," he said, feeling the old resentment creep back in him. "What do you want to know about her?"

"Just tell me about her. I wanted to hear you talk about the South. Now I want to hear you talk about her."

"I warn you, it's pretty dull stuff." The familiar inner tension, which he once tried to laugh off—in his thoughts, not aloud, ever— as his "cuckold complex," returned for the first time in two or three years. It had been at least that long since he allowed himself to talk about her.

"Such things are never dull," Ann said. "Painful maybe, but never dull."

"Okay." He inhaled deeply. "Well, we went to Vanderbilt together. You know, dated pretty steady and all. Then when Pearl Harbor was bombed I signed up. The Navy let me finish that semester because it was my last one and we got real serious during those months. Me going off to war soon. You know how it was . . . or you've heard . . . lot of people were getting tangled up the same way."

Ann's smile was warm and understanding and suddenly he wanted to tell her about Kathy, all about her.

"Well, we got real serious. I felt pretty heroic and she was . . . is . . . a darned attractive girl. Anyhow, one night we wound up in a motel together. I asked her to marry me. Practically forced her to say yes before we went to bed. That's something else about being brought up in the South—before the war anyhow, I understand it's changed since—that Northerners don't understand. I had fooled around some before that, but not with what we called nice girls." He hesitated.

"So you thought because you went to bed with a nice girl you had to marry her?" Ann said. But she said it kindly, not mockingly as he feared she might react.

"Yes. Oh, I liked her. Maybe even loved her, some. But . . . well, anyway, we got married the next day. The semester was about over then and I went to a special naval school near Philadelphia. She got an apartment in Philly and I came in on weekends." The rest he told hurriedly, to get it over with as quickly as possible. "One night . . . it was a Wednesday . . . I popped in unexpectedly and found this other guy there. A Marine. And it wasn't just a friendly visit. They were both in bathrobes . . . sitting on the sofa, smoking cigarettes and drinking brandy. . . . So, that was that. I didn't even get to blame it on being overseas so I could feel heroic about getting a 'Dear John' letter. She just couldn't wait until weekends . . . or something."

He swallowed the lump in his throat and lit a cigarette. Neither of them spoke for a while, then he said, "When are you going back to New York?"

"I had planned to go this weekend. Mother and Aunt Amy are pretty well settled now. But . . . I think I'll wait. I like it here better than I thought I would."

He tossed his cigarette away and kissed her. It seemed exactly the right moment to kiss her.

"Ann," he said against her mouth, "I feel like a kid in love for the first time."

"Me too," she whispered.

His hand moved down from her shoulder, over her hips. When

he felt the smooth warmth of the bareness of her leg he moved his body against hers.

"I've got to get close to you," he said, "I need to."

"Not here, Phil, please . . . let's go somewhere."

He picked her up and carried her to the car. She laughed and kissed him and pulled away and ran back to the sand bar to get the unopened picnic basket, their shoes and the blanket. He followed her, a hint of the uncertainty he was beginning to feel showing on his face, and helped her carry the things to the car. They kissed again before he started the car and again after the motor was running and he stopped before they turned onto the highway and kissed her again. He needed the reassurance.

Automatically he turned north on the highway, toward Ashton. Then he realized he had no idea where they might go. His father would be at home, or likely to come in at any time. He could not take her to a motel in Ashton. They could not close the door before the news would be all over town.

"Where can we go?" he asked, feeling stupidly unsophisticated. He should know where to go. And take her there immediately, before she changed her mind.

"I don't care." She closed her eyes and snuggled against him. "I just want to be indoors."

She's so damned sure of herself, he thought. How many men have had her? There's no "where to go" problem in New York. She must think I'm pretty damned adolescent.

"What are you thinking about?" Ann asked. She did not open her eyes.

"What the hell do you think I'm thinking about at a time like this?" he said roughly.

She opened her eyes and looked up at his face. "Well, if you're not the grouchiest lover I ever saw."

"How many lovers have you seen, Ann?"

"What kind of question is that?"

He felt her grip loosen on his arm.

"A stupid kind of question," he said. "Forget it."

"How can I forget it?"

"Then don't."

It was getting dark. He reached to turn on the lights and when he put his arm back she did not renew her hold on it. They reached the graveled road that led from the highway to the Country Club and he turned.

"Let's have a drink first," he said.

"Let's have a drink anyway." She took her comb from her purse and ran it through her hair several times before he parked near the entrance to the Country Club bar.

The bar was empty except for the Negro bartender and his helper. It was too late for the men who dropped by for a quick drink before going home and too early for those who would arrive in an hour or so to make an evening of it. Phil led her to a table in the corner near the jukebox.

"Two Scotch and waters," Phil told the smiling Negro waiter. "No, make mine a double."

"Make mine a double too," Ann said.

The waiter nodded and walked away.

"Wanta hear some music?" Phil asked, nodding toward the jukebox.

"Sure."

"What do you like?"

"It doesn't matter."

He went to the rainbow-colored machine and fished two quarters from his pocket and put them in the slot. He paid no attention to the number of buttons he punched or the selections they would cause the machine to play. He stared at the jerky moves the pieces inside the glass made as the first record was picked up and transferred to the turntable.

What a damned fool, he thought. You want her more than you ever wanted a woman—even the one you married—and because you are back home in Ashton you are botching it. In New York you didn't chase them away with your stupidity until you had stayed with them a night or two. No, that is not the way it was. You kept your doubts to yourself with those women because it didn't matter whether you were the first or the fiftieth man who'd slept with them. Only your own sin mattered to you then. Is it because you are in Ashton that her sin matters?

He went back to the table. "Ann, forgive me for being a child," he said. "I . . . I've just had . . . I don't know. . ."

She reached across the table and put her hand on his.

"I don't know either, darling," she said. "But I want to know. I somehow believe it's worth finding out. Let's forget it for now. Okay?"

He smiled. "Let's get out of here."

"Where are we going?"

"Leave that to me." He hoped he didn't sound as boyish as he felt.

"No, darling," she said. "Sit back down a minute. Let me tell you something. Something important to both of us, I believe."

He sat down slowly.

"I don't know how to begin," she said. "Which is a stupid way to begin. But, well, I can't go with you anywhere tonight. Not now. And please don't get that hurt look. I won't let sex be something bounced between us like a ball. Something we make up with after a quarrel. I want to go with you. I would even if I hadn't had a crush on you when I was in high school. I would have gone anywhere with you from the river. But it's different now."

"But, Ann . . ."

"No, darling. I'm very sorry. More than I like to admit. But, no. I'll sit here with you and get drunk with you. I'll neck with you later. But I won't go to bed with you tonight. And I don't want you to expect me to. Not tonight."

Phil raised a hand to signal the waiter.

"Bring us two more doubles," he said.

7.

PHIL OVERSLEPT the next morning. It was one-thirty when he took Ann home from the Country Club. The bar closes there at one. He spent thirty minutes after their last drinks trying to convince her everything between them was as it had been when he picked her up at the sand bar and carried her to the car. She said she knew it was the same, but, now that she knew how it really was between them back at the sand bar, the answer was still, "Not '*no*'—but '*not yet.*'" He thought she was so cute saying it—both were a little drunk by then—that he laughed. Then she laughed and he took her home and drove home himself, feeling remarkably happy for a guy who'd just been turned down. But it was three before he put out his last cigarette and went to sleep.

When he woke up and saw how late it was he telephoned Ranch and told him he'd go straight to the courthouse from home, so he wouldn't be at the paper until afternoon. This was the day he planned to get reacquainted with the politics and people at the courthouse and city hall; to pick up again the lines of information about his community a small-town newspaperman must have. Most of the people who read his paper were personal friends, or handshaking acquaintances, of the public officials he would be praising and criticizing, so he must know them personally too.

While he shaved and dressed he tried to think about the people he would see at the county courthouse, his first stop. But Ann kept popping into his mind.

She had taught him a lesson. At least she had begun his education in something you might call the Proper Relationship of Lovers, Married or Unmarried. It was a subject he always had been backward in. If they had gone to the motel, what they shared could have been little more than common disappointment, under the circumstances. And that's a fragile bond. He was in the wrong mood to go before he got tight, and after he got tight he probably would have been even more disappointing to her than he would have before. He marveled at the way she somehow had the wisdom to know all this last night, even after matching him drink for drink for several hours.

Now he wanted to begin her education in How to Live with Southerners. She would be a willing student. She had shown him by asking why he loved the South, then by understanding his answer, despite the vagueness of it. But, even though she seemed to understand his feeling about Ashton, he was convinced she still thought of it as a village of bigoted idiots. She had to be shown the basic goodness of these people, if she stayed here with him.

It was the first time he had allowed himself to think that she might stay with him. The thought pleased him.

Before leaving the house he peeked into his father's room. Mr. Arrow was asleep and Phil frowned as he watched a moment and heard his father mumble some unintelligible protest.

He went first to the weekly meeting of the county board of supervisors. Four farmers, a storekeeper and a lawyer sat at a long mahogany table in a small room with seven extra, cane-bottomed chairs lined against the wall near the door. The extra chairs were for the "interested public," a group from which Phil was the only member present. The storekeeper was chairman and sat at the head of the table. The lawyer sat at the other end. He was not an elected member of the board, but the others let him make the decisions. "The lawyer knows about those things," the chairman would say when a question was posed. Phil was sitting only a few feet from the table, but he was unable to hear enough of what was said to know if anything besides bill paying was being discussed. He watched the circle of expressionless, sunburned faces and listened to them mumble over the stack of the county's monthly bills until his head began to nod and his forehead perspire. Then he stood and stretched—no one at the table looked at him—and walked out and into the adjoining office, a long room with the high walls lined with ledger-filled bookcases. It was the chancery clerk's office and he asked Luther Renfro, who had been chancery clerk eighteen years, if the board had anything important coming up at today's meeting. Luther said no, not that he knew about, but then he didn't know, of course, what each board member had on his mind. Phil said of course and asked what roads and bridges were under construction in the county now. Luther said the biggest county road project now was a concrete bridge over Loose Nigger Creek, a few miles north of town. The old wooden span, he said, burned six months ago. Phil thanked him and walked out and along the narrow, brown corridor to the office of the superintendent of county schools. Harland Singletree, the county school superintendent as far back as Phil could remember, had died three years ago and he found Mrs. Singletree behind her late husband's old desk near the only window in the small office. When her husband died she was appointed to serve until a special election could be held; then she was elected on her own. She shook Phil's hand roughly and told him to "have a seat." He smiled, thinking how perfectly the old news writers' cliches for describing police on a manhunt fit her. She was "grim-faced, tight-lipped and hard-eyed," even "tall and gaunt." She smiled (She has her own little joke maybe, he thought) and he wondered how she had managed to win an election with a smile like that.

"I'm happy to see you, Mr. Arrow," she said and he could see that she didn't trust him. Maybe it was because she remembered some of his editorials criticizing the county schools when her husband was superintendent or maybe, like most public officials in the South, she instinctively distrusted newspapermen.

"Nice to see you again, Mrs. Singletree," he said.

"I heard you were back in town. You've been up north, haven't you? Up in New York City, I hear."

"Yes'm."

"Well, it must be awfully good to be home again," she said. "I guess young folks have to try their wings now and again. But they always find out the grass is greenest right in their own back yards, I always say."

"I'll bet you do." Phil said it before he could stop himself.

"Yes. Now what was it you wanted to see me about?" she said. "I always say the press is welcome in this office as long as I am superintendent of schools. This goes for the voters too. We try to run this office on an efficient and reasonable basis for the benefit of the most people. We have nothing to hide."

"No'm. I was just kind of nosing around this morning trying to get acquainted again. If I'm going to run the *Dispatch* I need to know as much about the public's business as possible. I had nothing special in mind."

"Oh, you going to be running the *Dispatch* again?" she said, looking at him over the tops of her glasses.

"Yes'm."

"I see. Well, let us see what we can do for you. This map here"—she stood and pulled down a large map of the county from one of the wall rolls behind her desk—"shows the location of all our county-operated school plants. You'll notice, if you were up on it before you left town, that we have a number of new plants now. We've done some consolidating. The state made us, you know. I never thought it was a good idea. Many of our fine little communities will just dry up now that their schools are gone. A lot of learning has been done in the one-room schools in this state in the past and a lot more could have been done if they'd just left them alone. Anyway, here are our schools."

She pointed to pins with tiny, flesh-colored knobheads. There were five of them outside Ashton, which was a school district not under the jurisdiction of the county board.

"And here are the nigra schools," she said, pointing to three pins with black knobheads. "And here is where a new nigra school is now under construction. That'll make three brand-new ones they'll have, which, I might add, is more'n our children have. But you know how things are now."

"Yes'm."

"You ought to do a story for one of those magazines like *Life* or *Look* about these new nigra schools. They're always writing about the bad things down here. Why don't you do that? Or don't you think they'd take it?"

"I don't know," he said. "I've never written a magazine article. I'm just a newspaperman."

"What I mean is, I heard they won't use stories that are favorable to the South. You know how they are."

"I imagine if someone did a well-written, logical, interesting article on anything they would use it."

"Well, then, why don't you write one about the money we're spending right here in Ashton County on schools for the nigras? It would be a service to the community. Isn't that what a newspaper is for?"

"I'll think about it. I could do one or have one of our reporters do one for the *Dispatch*."

"Oh," she said, obviously disappointed.

Her disappointment that the story would appear in the *Dispatch* instead of a magazine angered Phil. The *Dispatch* has served these people like a public official for a quarter of a century, he thought, yet they seem to have little more than contempt for it.

"Well," he said, "guess I better rush on. There are several other places I want to stop by before I go to the city council meeting."

"Glad you came by here," Mrs. Singletree said, rising to her full, masculine height and stepping toward the door. "Any time you want information don't hesitate to call me. Think over the magazine story idea. I believe the good people of the United States would like to read the truth for a change."

"Yes'm," he said and walked into the corridor.

As he waited for an old man to drink from the water fountain marked "For Whites Only," he thought how fantastic it was that some of these people—Mrs. Singletree included, obviously—believed they could, if given the opportunity, convert the rest of the country to their way of thinking on segregation of the races. The thought was amusing until he remembered the North had its system of segregation too, more subtle but just as devastating, in its own way, to the morale of the segregated. There are, of course, important differences in the two systems. New York newspapers, for one thing, defend the rights of minority groups energetically. Perhaps they do it to build their subway-rider circulation, but the point is they do it. Phil supposed he could name no more than five Southern newspapers whose publishers allowed their reporters and editors absolute freedom in reporting and commenting on incidents of racial conflict. Another, more important, difference is that in New York anyone who can qualify can vote. City and state governments must pay attention to a man who can vote, regardless of his color. In the South few towns are large enough to support more than one newspaper and fewer can support competitive newspapers; so publishers cater to advertisers rather than subscribers. If someone invented a method of printing newspapers that would cut the cost in half, small-town editors could concentrate again on putting out good newspapers, guided by only their professional consciences, not by bookkeepers' figures. And if Southern Negroes could vote, uninhibitedly, they wouldn't have to worry for long about their other basic rights. They could demand them and, once they got basic rights, the wonderful fringe benefits which white people take so casually for granted would come to them quickly. He wondered if the tip Ranch had got about a Negro planning to file a voter test case in Ashton was more than a rumor. He shouldn't have snapped at Ranch for asking what the *Dispatch*'s editorial policy would be if this test case actually were filed. But, dammit, he'd been home only a week and he needed more time to get his ideas organized.

He stopped at a closed door with "Office of the Ashton County Sheriff and Tax Collector" painted in black letters on its upper panel.

The sudden concern about the kind of reception he would get in that office took his mind away from the long-range thinking he had been doing. This was something he had to face now.

Slim Copeland, who had not been slim in many years, was seated behind his desk cleaning a pearl-handled pistol. He was sheriff six years ago and had beaten a Negro prisoner so badly the prisoner died a week after the beating. Phil had written two front-page editorials asking for a grand jury investigation and was set to get really tough about the case when his father stepped in and stopped him. He didn't know how much of this Copeland knew. The first two editorials were cautious enough. Maybe he didn't know about the one that never got into print. There had never been an investigation by a grand jury. The thought of this caused Phil's face to flush now as he watched Copeland sitting there cleaning that pistol. He wondered if it was the same pistol he had whipped the old Negro drunk with.

"Well, if it ain't Phil Junior," Copeland said. "How's the boy?"

"Fine. Just fine. How are you?"

"Couldn't be much better. Have a seat, boy. What can I do for you?"

"Nothing special," Phil said. "I'm just making the rounds trying to catch up on things. Any good trials set for the next term of circuit court?"

"Naw, nothing special. Five nigger cuttin's and a couple of white trash shootin's that took place out at the tonks on the highway. We got guilty pleas from all the niggers and one of the white men. The other white feller'll plead guilty fore court time, I predict. He ain't from around here. Was bumming through from Texas and got in a scrap out at the Travelers' Inn. Pulled a snub-nosed thirty-eight on a kid and shot him. Had a head lock on him, they say, and shot the top of his head clean off. It was the middle Russell boy he shot. You oughta know him. His older brother went to school 'bout the same time you did."

"Yeah, I think I remember the Russells."

"Too bad we ain't got a nigger killing for you to cover now that you're back," Copeland said, his face expressionless so that Phil could not tell whether he was bringing up their old conflict or making a distasteful joke.

"I'd as soon not get mixed up in anything like that now."

"Me neither." Copeland fondled the pistol with both hands as his eyes searched Phil's face. "I never did understand why you was so all-fired upset about that old nigger. Shit man, niggers are killed nearly ever' day in some jail or other and nobody runs around trying to stir up trouble about it. If a law officer don't show 'em who's boss once in a while they'd take over. You can't go around forgetting, son, that they's more of them in this county than there is of us."

"Well, I've got to get over to the city hall and listen to the council for a while," Phil said. "Good to have seen you."

"Yeah." Copeland pushed his 250-pound, five-foot-eight-inch frame up from the cushioned chair. "Come back to see me any time. If I'm not here just ast for my brother, Hoke. He's my chief deputy."

Outside the sun was high and a clean-smelling breeze met Phil as he stepped onto the wide porch that stretched across the front of the courthouse. He inhaled the fresh, country air deeply. It may not be as easy to work with these people as I had imagined, he thought.

———————

City council meetings were held in the mayor's office in the city hall, which was four blocks north of the county courthouse on Main Street. It was almost eleven when Phil got there and the meeting had been under way for some time. Mayor Reginald Dobbs nodded when he entered. He was the only council member facing the door. The others were seated on either side of the long table jammed against the mayor's desk to form a "T" with the desk crossing the "T." Mayor Dobbs was talking.

". . . now that's the way I see it. As long as Miz Ash lives in that house that street won't be cut through there. Not while I'm mayor, anyhow."

Phil was relieved. He was beginning to think there were no issues in Ashton that did not concern, in some way, the Negroes. This was an old issue that the paper could, and had in the past, have fun with. The town was divided over it, but nobody, except the few at the core of it, took it seriously enough to lose any sleep over it. The mayor was one who probably lost sleep about it.

Mrs. Gardner Ash, 3rd, last of the Ashton County Ashes, although she was a Dobbs before she married Gardner Ash, 3rd fifty years ago, lived in a crumbling ante bellum monstrosity on Lee Street, a block behind the city hall. This meant a block from the center of the downtown business district. The town was built around the house, you might say, since the house was there first. When Phil was a child the old house was surrounded by carefully manicured grounds as large as five city blocks and guarded by a high iron fence. It was a showplace, much like a park in the middle of town, except no one could go inside the fence without an invitation and few were invited. As the town grew, the Ash fortune dwindled. The only Ash children for several generations were girls who grew up to be neurotic women and a boy or two who grew up to be "sissies" or who were "strange" and took their inheritances on reaching legal age and went to live in Paris or Rome and were never heard from again. Gardner Ash 3rd was one of the "sissies." He just about finished off the Ash fortune and died drunk. Mrs. Ash buried him in style and retreated into the old house. The town was, in general, happy there were no more Ash men around to embarrass them. It was better to be able to point out the house to visitors and say, "That's where the Ash family lives" and then say you were kin to the Ash family in some indirect way. It was good to be kin to either the Ashes or the Crutchfields or the Dobbses or the Halberts if you had social ambitions. If you could find one of them on your family tree somewhere your daughter, for instance, could be a debutante without any trouble. Otherwise you might have to dig up some Virginia relations with a name folks knew. If you had enough money, neither was necessary, of course, but not many socially ambitious people around here had that much money.

Anyway, the Ash house was the topic before the city council today. After Mr. Ash's death Mrs. Ash was forced, every few years, to sell a few lots off the estate. Finally she sold the last parcel to the city for the new post-office site. That was about twenty-five years ago. When she let that go (Mrs. Ash was always able to make people believe she was doing the city a favor when she sold a lot although if she hadn't sold it she probably would have starved to death in a month) she made Mayor Dobbs, who was then city attorney, promise that the street in front of her house would never be opened. If it were opened, she said, a lot of noisy cars and trucks would be whizzing by keeping her awake at night and kicking up dust all over the place. She seemed to forget that streets nowadays were paved. Dobbs promised to keep the street closed and, although the post-war business boom fed the Ashton business district until it needed every possible traffic outlet, Lee Street stopped abruptly at the corner of the Ash property; azalea bushes, which bloomed beautifully in the spring, seemed to grow right out of the pavement. The street continued again on the other side of the single row of azaleas, but since it went nowhere but to the Ash house, the only vehicles that came down the street from the crowded Main Street a block away were driven by strangers who didn't know about the flowery roadblock. Periodically some council member or civic group petitioned to have the street opened, pleading the cause of progress. But Mayor Dobbs, now serving his fourth term, always vetoed it.

"There wouldn't be an Ashton," he was saying, "if it weren't for the Ash family. I will not have a part in breaking the city's solemn promise to Aunt Pearl." (Mrs. Ash 3rd was Mayor Dobbs' mother's third cousin, but he always called her Aunt Pearl.)

So that was that. The council moved on to other business. There were bills to approve, subdivision plats to approve, a recommendation from the zoning board that a lot on the corner of Spruce and Forrest streets be rezoned for commercial use so a gasoline station could be erected there. A request from Southern Airlines that the waiting room at the city airport be air-conditioned was put aside for consideration later, and four petitions for street-paving projects were referred to the city engineer.

Phil's lack of sleep the night before and the routine of the council's business lulled him to sleep. When his head fell forward, waking him with a start, he heard Les Hogarth, the councilman who owned a hardware store, say, "Let's talk about this swimming pool for the niggers matter."

"It's not a legitimate matter for discussion," Councilman Alvin Presley said. "It's never been put before the council in the form of a motion. Do you want to make the motion and have it put on the book that you did?"

"I want to talk about it first," Hogarth said, "and see how you fellows feel about it. I say if we beat the niggers to the punch and build them a pool they won't be filing one of them suits like they did in Atlanta."

"Well, I say we oughta just sit still," Mayor Dobbs said, pulling on his second chin. "I know niggers. Been around them all my life. I was raised on a plantation, you know. And I know if you got a nigger working and you ask him if he wants water, why, he'll say no. But if you keep on asking him, sooner or later that nigger'll decide he's the thirstiest nigger alive. It's the same with this. Best thing to do is just go along and keep quiet. Then they won't get thirsty."

"You mean they haven't even said they wanted a swimming pool and we're settin' here talking about building them one!" Presley said. "That's the craziest thing I ever heard of."

"Well, we haven't asked them to vote either," Hogarth said, "but from what I hear there's gonna be a try at that—and pretty soon too."

"Awww, that's just another one of those rumors," Mayor Dobbs said. "I know these niggers and none of them ain't going to try nothing as foolish as that."

"They say they're going to appoint a nigger to the Supreme Court and let him rule on all the integration cases," Councilman Spriggs, a bald, nervous man who was manager of the cotton compress, said.

"I wouldn't be at all surprised," Hogarth said. "That's what I mean. What can they say if they have a pool that's just as good as ours?"

"Hell, Les, they overruled that separate but equal argument years ago," said City Attorney Percival, who until then had been sitting quietly in the corner near the big window.

"Senator Wakefield tells me there's a good chance of getting the ruling on that reversed," Hogarth said. "He says people all over the country are getting damned sick and tired of the way the Supreme Court's trying to run the country. Someday the good white people up in New York and Washington are going to realize that integrating the races is the cause of all their troubles and then they'll put that separate but equal doctrine back in effect. I say we ought to be prepared for it."

Six years ago Phil would have been taking notes furiously. He would have taken down the exact words of each councilman and put those words, grammatical mistakes and all, into his news story. He took no notes now. What should a Southern newspaperman do when he hears public officials talk in such an unbelievably fantastic manner? He wasn't sure now. He did know that these were serious-minded men, who loved their families and their community. They served on the council for a hundred dollars a month, a mere token salary. They were churchgoing men. They taught their children the Ten Commandments. They worked hard to give their children more than they had had. They contributed generously to the Community Chest. They probably tithed. Was it his duty as a newspaperman to hold them up to ridicule?

As if they heard his thoughts, Councilman Hogarth and Mayor Dobbs turned suddenly to face Phil.

"Now, Philip, you understand this is just a friendly little discussion," Hogarth said, taking his unlighted cigar out of his mouth for the first time since Phil arrived. "We haven't taken any official action one way or the other on it. It hasn't even been brought up as a motion for consideration. I think it would be best if you didn't mention it in the *Dispatch.* It'd just stir up a lot of trouble."

I'm glad you know what would be best, Phil thought. It must be nice to have definite opinions on such matters.

Councilman Presley whispered to Hogarth, "Dammit, Les, see

what you've done. How could you forget that son of a bitch was here?"

"We ain't had to worry about newspaper reporters in so long I just forgot," Hogarth whispered back.

Phil stood and stepped to the end of the long table. He faced the mayor. The council members lined the table to his right and left.

"Gentlemen," he said, after clearing his throat, "I don't know exactly how to say this. It's very difficult to admit you might have been wrong once in doing something you felt so strongly about at the time. But, well, just let me say this. I'm not going to embarrass you. I want to work with you—the council. I came back to Ashton to be a contributing citizen. I know you feel you do what is best for Ashton. I want you to believe that whatever I write in the *Dispatch* is written with the same conviction."

"Yeah, but what about this . . . this nigra swimming pool matter?" Presley said. "You not gonna write nothing about that, are you?"

Phil inhaled deeply and let the air out slowly before he said, "No, gentlemen, I suppose not, under the circumstances. I want to prove to you that I am not an irresponsible yellow journalist. I too believe that to print this today probably would cause some trouble that might otherwise have been postponed."

"You mean you're not going to write about all this . . . all that was said here today?" Presley said. "Is that it, Arrow?"

"Yes," Phil said. "That's it."

"Well, let me shake your hand, son," Presley said, standing and reaching across the table. "That's the spirit we like around here and you'll find that out."

What do you mean I'll find out what the people of Ashton like? Phil thought. I was born here and grew up here. This is my town too. I'm not a stranger.

"I've been meaning to come by the *Dispatch* and see you," Mayor Dobbs said, smiling. "Wanted to welcome you back. But you know how it is. I get tied up with the people's business and have to put off pleasures sometimes."

"Yes, sir," Phil said. "I know."

All the councilmen were standing now, shaking his hand and telling him it was good to have him back. When he had shaken everybody's hand, including the city attorney's and the police chief's—who had slept through most of the meeting—Phil said he had to get back to work and left.

"I knew that boy was a winner," he heard Presley say as he closed the door. "Anybody who could play football like that rascal could in high school is bound to be an all-right guy. We haven't had a team like that since him and Jerry Windham graduated. You remember the time . . ."

In the hallway Phil drank from the water fountain marked "For Whites Only" and walked outside to his car and drove to the *Dispatch,* three blocks away.

He nodded as he walked past Ranch's desk. He sat staring at his typewriter several minutes; then he began writing:

The population of Ashton has increased in the past ten years from less than 20,000 to almost 40,000. Growth such as that does not just happen. It does not come about accidentally, unless oil is hit and oil has not been discovered in Ashton. That kind of growth, and the economic growth that goes with it, is the direct result of the dedication of the men and women of the community who give generously of their time and talents for the betterment of the community as a whole.

These dedicated men and women are your city councilmen, your supervisors, civic club officers, your church leaders, your PTA leaders, the women who hold positions of responsibility in your garden clubs, and many others. But these community leaders could do nothing if it were not for the cooperation they receive from those of us who are not privileged to serve in positions of leadership. In other words, when a town grows into a city, every citizen of that city can look about him and say proudly that he had a part in bringing about that growth. Let us look about us and see some of the evidence of growth and prosperity that is the result of the citizens of Ashton taking their duties as citizens seriously. A wing has been added to our courthouse; Main Street has been widened; a beautiful and functional four-lane highway now cuts through the eastern edge of Ashton, stimulating commercial growth there and in the downtown area; most of the motels now have swimming pools, bringing more tourists here; impressive new school buildings have replaced some of the decaying, old structures in which you and I attended classes; four new industries have located here in the past ten years, putting new payrolls into the economic mainstream of our community . . .

He wrote on until four pages were filled. He knew it read as if it had been written by a high school civics student. But he knew also that it would cause favorable comment all over town and that was what the *Dispatch* needed now.

When he finished and reread it he realized painfully not only that was it classically naive but it was written exclusively to and about only one half Ashton's population. He could, he thought, title it most accurately with the messages on the water fountain at city hall: "For Whites Only."

He clipped the four pages together and laid them on Ranch's desk.

"Run this on page one tomorrow in ten-point type," he snapped as he stepped into the elevator.

When he pulled away from the curb and drove south past the post office Phil did not know where he was going. When he reached the courthouse he decided to go talk to Jerry. He needed to talk to Jerry. He could ask him if he had heard anything about the rumor of the voting test case. Jerry would know if there was anything to it. It was his business to know. It was Ranch's business to know too. Maybe he did know. He hadn't had much of a chance to tell what he knew that day in the café.

It was almost three o'clock when he parked behind Jerry's red convertible and walked onto the long, pillared porch and rang the doorbell. There was no response, so he opened the door and stuck his head in and hollered, "Jerry."

"That you, Phil?" Jerry's voice came from the back of the house. "Come on in the kitchen."

Phil walked through the long, narrow hallway that split the house in two almost equal parts. The house was a grand, two-story version of a sharecropper's shotgun or dogtrot house, he thought. A wall covered with large purple flowers rose on his left. The mahogany banisters on his right began at the library door, which was closed, and angled up steeply to a big portrait of a dead Crutchfield he did not recognize, then turned to meet the second floor. There were no sounds coming down from upstairs. On his left the wide doorway to the beige-carpeted living room was open and on beyond the living room he could see into the playroom where the turkey hash party had gathered.

He was conscious of a dark, musty odor. The odor that moves into a house when there are no people living in it. He wondered how long the young Windham family would have to cook and complain and laugh and sweat and cry inside these old walls before the odor of their aliveness chased out the odor of those years the house had been dead.

At the end of the hall he turned right and entered an old-fashioned kitchen, as big as a studio apartment in New York. Jerry was sitting at a heavy, round, oak table scanning the pages of the Memphis *Commercial Appeal*. The Negro cook was bending over, peeking into the oven, holding the door handle with a hand protected by her apron.

"Don't you read the *Dispatch?*" Phil said.

"Caught in the act." Jerry grinned. "Sit down. I'm running down tonight for a Senate committee meeting and Precious is fixing me a good home-cooked meal. I've got to be there two or three days and Precious wants to fill me up before I leave. She can't stand to think of me eating restaurant food that long."

"Where's Janie?"

"At one of her damn club meetings. Had lunch yet? I know you can take some of Precious' cooking, even if you have."

"Hi you, Mista Phil," the cook said, standing a few steps from him now.

"I'll be damned," Phil said. "I didn't recognize you, Precious." She worked for his father when he was in high school, their first "sleep-in" cook after his mother died.

"I didn't think you did." Precious laughed.

"You look too young to be my Precious," Phil said. "I'll be older than you before long."

"Go long with you, Mista Phil," the old Negro said. "I'm so old I can't hardly get up when I get down and you know it."

"But she can still cook like an angel," Jerry said.

"That's one thing about me," Precious admitted. "I can cook. And I better get to it if I'm going to get you off when you said. Nice to see you, Mista Phil."

Having paid her polite respects, she returned to her work.

"What's up?" Jerry asked.

"Nothing special," Phil said. "It's just been a rough day already. Thought I'd come out and relax before I faced the rest of it."

"Anything wrong?"

"No. At least not anything you can put your finger on."

"Well, I always say if you can't put your finger on it it's not worth bothering about."

"You mean 'in' it, you horny bastard," Phil laughed.

"Son, I haven't stopped long enough to put my finger in anything first since I was a teenage football hero."

"If you boys don't quit talking ugly I'm going to walk right out of here and leave you hungry," Precious said from across the room.

"If you'd stop eavesdropping you wouldn't be embarrassed." Jerry laughed, then turned back to Phil. "What is it, buddy? You look worried."

"I don't know. I came home with good intentions. I was going to put the race issue where it belongs, I said, second to the welfare of Ashton as a whole. But, dammit, these people won't let me. Everywhere I turn they're talking about it."

"Maybe you're like the guy who went to the psychiatrist because he always had his mind on sex," Jerry said seriously. "The doc drew a picture of a bush and said, 'What does this suggest to you?' The guy said, 'A man and woman are behind that bush screwing.' The doc said, 'Mister, you need help,' and the guy says, 'What about you, doc? You drew the dirty picture.' Maybe you're seeing a nigger in everything these people say."

Phil rubbed a palm over his short-cropped hair, then on down over his face.

"Maybe so," he said. "Maybe so. But all old Mrs. Singletree could talk about was the, quote, nigra problem. And then Copeland jumped me about putting it in the paper six years ago when he killed that Negro. And the city council was arguing about whether or not to build a swimming pool for the Negroes. Then, to top it all off, Ranch is mad because I won't get excited about a rumor he's heard that a Negro vote test case is going to be filed here. And, dammit, worse than that, when I take Ann out I have to try to explain to her why I don't put on my armor and go out hunting for Ku-Kluxers."

"You have to remember, Phil, you had a reputation when you left here," Jerry said. "You're going to have to prove to these people you're not a wild-eyed liberal anymore."

"You talk like you thought I was a wild-eyed liberal, as you call it, yourself."

"You gotta admit you did some . . . well . . . unnecessary things six years ago."

"Like what?"

"There wasn't any reason for you to get in a stew about that billboard. If you really wanted to help the nigras you should have concentrated on the important things. Not crap like that. It only made things worse."

"What is important to a Negro, Jerry?"

"It should be getting good schools and improving himself. He ought to worry about that before he thinks about trying to get the name of some dead nigra soldiers on the same billboard with some dead white soldiers."

"How can he be expected to improve himself—or even want to—when he knows that if he goes out and gets killed fighting for his country even his monument will be separate but equal?"

"You were right in principle. I'll admit that," Jerry said. "You remember I voted with you at the Chamber meeting. I only said you went at it wrong. You've got to go slow on things like that, especially now that the pressure's on. People around here have gotten damn sensitive since the Supreme Court decision. You could lose ground instead of gaining it. I shouldn't have to tell you that."

"I know. I know. I'm trying to go slow. But these damn people keep pushing it in my face."

"The trouble is you're all keyed up. We need to go off by ourselves some weekend. Fishing or fox hunting."

"Sounds good. I haven't been fishing in years."

"Remember when me and you and Sneed went up to Sardis that weekend. Man, that was a long time ago, but I'll never forget it. We had just graduated from high school and we told those State girls we were seniors at Vanderbilt."

Phil laughed. "Yeah, that's the weekend you decided to, to go to State instead of to Vanderbilt with me. I still think the State coach sent those girls out there and that you were taken, not them."

"Who cares? What a way to be taken! You know, the little old gal I laid that night is president of the Junior League in the capital now. She's agreed to organize the women voters of the county for me." He grinned. "For the governor's race, I mean—imagine! Makes a man feel old."

"That's life," Phil said. "One night you're getting screwed at Sardis and next thing you know you're president of the Junior League organizing women for the guy that screwed you."

"Or running for governor," Jerry said. "You know if I hadn't got that piece from Martha Jean that night I might *not* be running for governor now. I'd have gone off to school with you and wouldn't have so many old classmates scattered around the state to work in my campaign. I know I wouldn't have worked with Governor Sullivan's campaign that summer or with Wolfe or Henry later. That's experience you can't buy, Phil. Goes to show what a piece of ass will do for you sometimes."

"I told you about that kind of talk," Precious said, but she was putting the plates before them, already filled with field peas, slices of onion and tomato, and fried chicken. She put a plate of hot cornbread in the center of the table and went back to the cabinet for the pitcher of buttermilk.

"Boy!" Phil said. "I haven't eaten food like this in years!" The two men concentrated on eating until Phil said, "You heard anything about the test case?"

"Nothing but rumors," Jerry said, "and I don't believe them. Every year before school starts there's a rumor that some nigra's going to try to register his kid at the white high school. Nothing ever comes of it."

"How many Negroes vote in this state now?" Phil asked.

"About twenty thousand are registered."

"There were that many six years ago. I thought I read where some Negro leaders were holding classes to help their people learn to pass the registration tests."

"There's been some of that and a few more are registered in the capital and on the coast maybe. But in other places things have tightened up. The Citizens Council has gotten pretty big since you left. Some counties have just wiped all names of nigras off the voter books. It's nothing to get excited about, Phil. These nigras don't worry about voting. Hell, they wouldn't come out and vote if you begged them. They're not ready yet, these things take time, like I told you."

Phil turned to Precious, who was standing at the kitchen sink eating from a plate she had filled for herself.

"How about it, Precious?" he said. "Would you vote if you had a chance?" He immediately wished he hadn't said it. It was cruel, putting poor Precious on the spot.

"Mista Phil," Precious said, her dark eyes cool and expressionless, her hands nervous under her apron. "I hears some of 'em talking about such down on the Block. But I tell 'em to leave me out of it. I'm older'n your daddy and I don't want to worry my mind with trouble with the white folks now."

"See what I mean," Jerry said.

"No, sir," Precious went on, "I been actin' like I act too long to change now. I always worked for good white folks for the most part and I ain't gonna complain about them now. It's too late for me. I don't have no trouble with the traditions they talks about, so I don't try to bust none. If it please you for me to say 'sir' to you when I'm old enough to be your grandmomma, it don't bother me none. If it please you to call me 'girl,' then it's all right with Precious."

She paused and her hands clenched. Phil saw the knot form under the apron.

"But don't mistake me. I got a grandbaby . . . Margaret . . . what's nineteen and me and her momma saved enough to send her over to college in Baton Rouge. She's smart and she's pretty. And she ain't gonna be put in the rut her momma and grandmomma's in. Don't call her 'girl,' Mista Phil. Don't nobody call her 'girl.' When she gets outta that college in Baton Rouge she gonna vote if she wants to. Don't you think she got a right to if she got a college education?"

The old Negro turned away. "I got some dustin' to do out in the living room," she mumbled. "I ain't got time to fool around with you ugly-talking boys. Call me when you gets finished and I'll wash up after you."

8.

THE COUNTY SPREADS ACROSS the break in the geography of the northwest part of the state and half of it is flat alluvial plain and half of it is red clay hills. If you have a farm in the flat, rich, delta half you are a "planter." If you have farm land in the hills you are a "dirt farmer" or "redneck" or "peckerwood," depending on how much land you have. The town of Ashton lies at the foot of the hills, technically in the delta. But the hills are more thickly populated than the plains, so Ashton merchants cater as much, or more, to redneck tastes and incomes as to the tastes and incomes of the planter trade. Planters' wives and daughters like to go to Memphis or New Orleans, or even New York, to shop anyhow.

When he felt he must escape physically, as he did today, Philip Arrow, Sr., ordinarily drove into the flat country. Most of the time he drove northwest, speeding past the neat row patterns and abandoned tenant shacks in the fields. Sometimes he would park on a side road and watch a crop-duster plane dip and dive at the fields and drop its sprays of insecticide. Sometimes he drove all the way into Mississippi to talk awhile with Hodding Carter and wish some of Ashton's civic leaders were as broad-minded about controversy as at least a few of his readers had learned to be over the decades that Carter's newspaper had dealt news and opinion straight from the shoulder. Carter had trouble, all right. But most of it came from outside Greenville. When the state legislature brought in that professional witness that time and he said Carter was a member of "several Communist front organizations" there were influential men and women in Greenville who had the courage to step forward and defend Carter. "Carter may be a son of a bitch," one of his old political enemies had said, "but he's no Communist." Yes, Greenville was unusual. The legacy of Alexander Percy maybe. But it was an island.

When he passed the Country Club two men, putting on the eighth green, waved at him and he waved back. Hell, he thought, think I'll drive into the hills today. It's too late to drive to Greenville now. He made a U-turn and drove back past the Country Club without looking at the golfers, who had finished putting and were striding down the fairway.

He glanced at the dashboard clock. It was 4:47 if the damn thing was working. He wanted a drink but knew he would have to turn back into delta country to buy liquor. Maybe the store at Crutchfield Crossing sold beer. He saw the unpainted cabin in the clearing approaching on his left and knew Crutchfield Crossing was just over the next hill. A barefoot white child of five or six was playing with a bony, brown dog in the dusty yard. The child wore only white cotton underpants. The cabin sat on log sections approximately three feet high, putting the cabin off the ground as if on stilts. The child's play was listless, as was the dog's response. The child paused to watch the car pass. The dog didn't look as if he even wanted to chase. The child's blank stare stayed in Arrow's mind until he topped the hill and saw Old Man Perthman's feudal bailiwick in the small valley below him. This hill country half of Ashton County is another world, he thought. No wonder those who live in it resent those who live on the delta. They have to scratch out meager existence in this red clay while their delta neighbors worry, not about whether everything they plant will grow but whether the weevils will take it. Irrigation removed the fear of drought from the delta planter's mind. He still had to worry about too much rain. But this summer was beginning like a dry one, which meant good crops in the delta and more worry for the hill farmer. Maybe that's why they pray more in the hills.

A tiny roadside sign let you know the name of the community by the river bend ahead was "Crutchfield Crossing." But a giant neon sign atop the Perthman General Store said simply, "PERTHMAN," causing most strangers to believe Perthman was the name of the tiny town and not just the name of the man who owned the general store. The store was surprisingly modern, a brick building behind a smooth concrete driveway which swooped from the highway past the bright blue gasoline pumps. It was a long building with three front entrances. One of the wide doors entered the grocery department, another the farm implement department, and the third the clothing department. Old man Perthman opened a new department when each of his three sons graduated from State. The sons married and moved into the three modern, air-conditioned brick homes you saw coming into town, as they got their diplomas certifying their four years in college studying bookkeeping, accounting and the other courses a State University student must study to get a degree in business administration. The Perthman Consolidated School stretched along the highway across from the store. All three Perthman boys had been president of the student body there. Behind the school were scattered fifty or so homes, most of them white frame structures with tree-shaded yards. Old Man Perthman was now "retired" and the boys split up his public duties. The oldest son, Reuben, was mayor. The next oldest, Gavin, was Beat Five Supervisor. Richard, the youngest, was president of the school board. The Old Man had held all three titles for sixteen years. Now, with his sons carrying the official titles, he still dictated major policy to all three groups without having to go to the trouble of attending the routine meetings.

The Perthmans are very important cogs in the machinery of the System, Arrow thought. The Aulds of the state control the Perthmans and the Perthmans control the rednecks. The world, to a Perthman, was his county district. He depended on the men he had learned to trust—the men his father had trusted before him—to tell him about the goings on in the outside world. The Aulds told him what went on in the rest of the county and the state. Senator Wakefield told him what went on in Washington. If a newspaper or magazine persisted in trying to tell him something different, he stopped reading that newspaper or that magazine.

Arrow parked by the first gasoline pump. He told the young Negro who ran out of the store to check the oil and fill the tank with gas. He walked into the grocery department. Four men were playing checkers at a table by the big picture window. He dismissed the quick urge to walk over to them and ask, "What do you gents think of the Algerian situation?"

"Howdy," one of the men said. He was tall and there was little flesh on his bones. The sleeves of his khaki shirt were too short and the bones of his wrists were knobby. He was about sixty and stoop-shouldered the way some men are after years of following a plow.

"Hello," Arrow said. "You gents have a drink with me?"

"Don't mind if we do," the stoop-shouldered man said, pushing away from the table and walking to the drink box.

Arrow looked into the red box, then reached in and pushed aside the Cokes and fruit-flavored drinks. "Do they sell beer here?" he asked.

"Yeah," the stoop-shouldered man said. "It's in that box at the back of the store."

"Thanks."

The stoop-shouldered man opened the four Cokes he had taken from the red box and carried them to his checker-playing friends at the table.

"It's a pretty day," Arrow said, back from the beer box, sipping from the can.

"Need rain bad," the stoop-shouldered man said. Arrow wanted to say that rain at this time would be bad for delta cotton, but he realized in time that he was thinking of the irrigated crops on the plains and not the parched hill patches.

"My name's Arrow," he said, pushing his hand at the stoop-shouldered man as he said it. "Philip Arrow."

"Yeah, I know you," the man said. "Course you probably don't know me. I'm Pat Grubbs, the Reverend Pat Grubbs."

"Oh, sure."

"I got that church up the road. The store next to it too."

"Sure. Sure. I place you now."

"You ain't never been up there, have you?"

"I've hunted all over this county."

"That so?"

"Yes. I came here almost thirty years ago. Been living around here ever since." Arrow warned himself to calm down. "There was a baby lost out your way one winter. I stayed out there all night until they found her. Your wife fixed me a cup of coffee, in fact."

"That was the Richter child. He's a boy. That was back in thirty-seven."

"Yes. I used to cover most stories myself in those days. That was before my son got old enough to be my reporter. Then the town grew and we hired some reporters. Always think those were the good days, though, when I was out seeing things happen myself. Nothing like seeing things yourself."

"Never could figure out why you newspaper folks wanted to hang around other folks when they're in trouble. Funny way to earn your bread."

The three men at the table—two in khaki and one in pale-blue overalls—nodded and sipped the Cokes. Arrow looked across the shoulder-high partition between the grocery department and the clothing department. Two young women were talking with one of the Perthman boys, who held a bolt of broadcloth. The Negro youth came in. "Dint need no oil," he said. "Put in six gallons of gas. Anything else, sir?"

"No, I guess not. You can put me about four cans of beer in a sack though."

"Yes, sir."

The four men nodded at each other silently, with no change in their expressionless faces.

Arrow took the beer, paid the Negro for it and the gas and the Cokes the four men had drunk.

"Won't you have a Coke too?" he asked the Negro.

"No, sir. I just had one a few minutes ago."

"Well . . . guess I'll get on down the road." He looked over at the checkers table. "You gents be careful now, you hear."

The four nodded at him. He wanted to laugh because he had told them to "be careful." He hurried out and got in the car and turned back in the direction he had come. There was a liquor store not far from the highway a few miles from here, back in the delta half of the county. When he passed the stilted cabin the child and the dog seemed not to have moved.

He pressed hard on the accelerator and the sedan lurched forward. He vowed never to venture this far into the hills again without a bottle.

It was dusk dark, that half hour of a delta day when everything seems to suspend its motion. Arrow felt he was violating the dusk by chasing time along the highway. At dusk it is neither daytime nor night. It's too near supper time to take a short nap and too long until supper will be on the table to start washing up. It is too long until the boys gather at the Yacht Club to start drinking again and too early to go to bed. The night will be too long anyhow. There's something about that suspended half hour that stirs even an ordinary man on an ordinary day. He had seen them walk out into their yards and look up into the leafy branches of the trees which had grown too large for a town lot. They walked among their trees and wondered if it would rain.

No, he shouldn't be out here on this highway now, going sixty-four miles an hour. But where should he be?

9.

PHIL LEFT Jerry's house and drove to the Werner Park section (referred to once in a news story by Ranch as "semiexclusive Werner Park"). While he talked with Jerry the sky had clouded and now, as dusk neared, a few drops of rain splashed on the windshield. He turned left at Azalea Drive and stopped in front of the neat, square, frame house where Ann's Aunt Amy and mother lived now. He walked from the car, between the twin magnolia trees, to the front porch, rapidly because it was raining harder now. Ann answered the doorbell and was surprised to see him. He was an hour early for their date.

"Hope you don't mind," he said. "I've had a pretty rough day and didn't feel like going home just yet. I thought we might drive out and see John Allen and his wife. I haven't been out there since I got home and I think you'll enjoy them."

"Come in out of the rain," she said, and he did. "What happened?"

"Nothing you can explain really. People just kept harping on the Negro issue one way or another. I came back here to run a newspaper, not to argue sociology all day, every day."

"I see," Ann said. "Let me get my raincoat. I *have* wanted to meet the Allens."

She waved him a kiss as she went through the doorway by the tall mirror with the baroque gold frame. Phil looked around. It was the first time he had been in the living room of Amy's new house.

He had always either left Ann at the door or stepped in the kitchen through the back door and paid his respects to her mother. The antique furnishings, most of which came from the old Crutchfield home before Jerry and Janie moved in, were disturbingly out of place in the low-ceilinged room. Janie and other relatives had persuaded Amy to sell the huge plantation home she and Major Halbert had lived in and move into this small, efficient, Werner Park house. An invalid widow had no business in a two-story house, they argued, and she finally relented. But she insisted on bringing her plantation house furnishings. She said she wouldn't be comfortable around new things. Getting accustomed to a new house was enough. So the mechanically conditioned air blew in on the dark, gross furniture and the figures of Crutchfields and Halberts watched him from their giant gold frames. In the coolness and under the low ceilings they looked like people from another planet.

Ann hurried back into the room, bringing the loose-skirted, barelegged movement of a mid-twentieth-century woman. He loved her more than he ever had.

"Let's get out of here," he said, squeezing the firm, tanned, warm flesh of her arm.

"Well, by golly, let's do," she laughed, puzzled by the eager way he grasped her arm, and pleased by it too.

The rain had stopped. He was silent as they moved along the wet, winding streets of Werner Park to a through street near the high school. It was good to sit beside Ann and feel the glow of his love and know it was more than physical attraction alone. Much more. He wondered if the frustrations of romancing a Southern girl were altogether the fault of the girl. Doesn't a Southern boy share the blame? The foul-up last night, for instance, was his fault. His father had never tried to drive the Puritan fears into him as so many did, but his mother had. Sin was a monster to her and became a monster to him. It followed him into the Navy and afterward to New York, although up there he was able to consider the Monster more objectively. Sometime during his six years up there he lost the habit of thinking a brief prayer each night before he fell asleep. It was as if the wrathful Old Testament God actually did reside in the South. He remembered Brother Hardesty, the preacher at his mother's church, shouting—directly at him, it seemed—about "the Godless cities of the North." And, although God Himself remained below the Mason-Dixon line, the Monster perched on the bedpost when Phil went to bed with a woman, even up there. He sometimes avoided one of his Yankee girl friends for weeks after a night in bed with her under the eyes of the Monster. He wondered if Ann's laughter would chase the Monster from a bed they shared, if they shared one unmarried. Then he cursed his inability, after all these years, to cope with emotions his intellect told him were stupid and childish and the results of his mother's religious fanaticism, which grew more intense in the years after the night she found the telegram. But knowing his father pushed her down that cheerless, hopeless course somehow added to his own guilt.

"My, but you're quiet tonight," Ann said.

"I'm the quiet type."

He stopped to let two cars pass, then turned onto the graveled side road.

"Tell me more about the Allens," she said.

"John is one of those people who got disturbed during the depression and decided to spend his life trying to help people. He's from Atlanta. He became a Baptist preacher but, as he puts it, he discovered it was one hell of a job trying to be a regular preacher and a Christian at the same time. After a few years of that he started this missionary type work he does out here. First, this was an experiment in community farming. A place for refugees from the depression. Now there's no need for that, so Just-Ten Acres has become a sort of rural Bowery mission. You'd be surprised how many people in these hills—mostly Negroes—never entered a schoolroom. The Allens try to teach them how to take better care of themselves, how to farm better, and toss in a little practical religion on the side."

"Sounds like a grim life."

"I suppose so, but they seem to like it."

"Where does he get money to operate?"

"A couple of church groups contribute. And they sell a little corn and cotton and raise most of their own food."

"Do they have children?"

"A son—twenty-four or -five by now, I guess—a daughter who must be, let's see, about nine or ten, and I hear they had another daughter about four years ago. The son lives out in Arizona. He does similar work with the Indians. I think he's connected with the government some way."

"A fascinating family. Why don't you do a magazine article about them?"

"You sound like Mrs. Singletree. I'm going to do a feature about them for the *Dispatch.*"

"Who's Mrs. Singletree?"

He told her about the county school superintendent and his morning at the courthouse.

"I'm not sure I understand why you take such . . . abuse. But I'll try to remember from now on that we're newspaper people."

He stopped the car and kissed her.

"My," she said, a little breathless, "what did I do to deserve that? I want to write it down in my little black book."

"You said *we.* Not me, but *we.*"

"I guess I did, didn't I." She smiled and snuggled close to him.

"You sure did and I'm going to show you, make you understand, what a real newspaper can do."

"You don't have to show me anything about a newspaper, Phil. I don't love the newspaper."

He kissed her again until a car eased slowly by them on the narrow road. He waited until it was past and started the motor. As they rode deeper into the hills the car's hood rose and fell in front of them. Scrubby trees and their shadows and the erosion gullies, with their red clay insides exposed, spread on either side of them. Narrow, two-rutted roads trailed off from the main road every mile or two.

When they passed Shine Tatum's shack, with the yellow light filtering through the cracks in the walls, Phil saw a black Chrysler parked at the front gate.

"Wonder who's visiting Shine in a Chrysler Imperial," he said.

"Who is Shine?"

"The old Negro who lives in that shack back there."

"That is a fine car. What does he do, bootleg?"

"He runs a grocery store in town and farms. Never knew Shine to do anything wrong." The last was said thoughtfully.

"You sound *real* Southern." Ann laughed. "A Negro has a big car parked at his house, so you wonder if he's done anything wrong."

"I didn't mean it that way," he said. He told her about Shine's pickles and promised to take her to the store on Hooker Street someday soon.

Despite Phil's description of the Allens, Ann admitted later, she expected to see nervous-eyed, Bible-quoting fanatics. But, when they parked under the giant oak, the man who walked toward them from the porch of the farmhouse might have been a small-town banker dressed for a weekend in the country. He was of medium height and weight. His hair was gray at the temples and graying on top where it was clipped short. He wore horn-rimmed glasses and smoked a pipe.

"Well, well, Phil," he said, taking the pipe in his left hand and extending his right into the car through the open window. "I heard you were back. You rascal, what took you so long to get out our way?"

"John, this is Miss Davis, Ann. Anything special going on tonight? Thought we'd stop in for a chat."

"Heck, naw," Allen said. "Glad you came. Happy to meet you, Miss Ann. Come on in. Florence'll be tickled pink."

"Phil Arrow!" Florence cried, running down the porch steps. "We were just talking about you yesterday."

She was tall enough to kiss him without rising on her toes when he stepped out of the car to meet her. Your initial impression was that this was an ugly woman. Her nose was too large. Her cheeks were not fleshy enough, and she wore no make-up. But, Ann thought, she had never seen such beautifully clear eyes and skin.

Phil introduced Ann and they walked onto the porch, Phil with an arm around Florence, Ann and John following.

"Why don't we just sit out here," John said. "It's cooler." He went into the house to get two more chairs.

"I'll get us some iced tea in a minute," Florence said. "But I want to stay out here as long as Phil has to stand up with his arm around me."

"That's one good thing about living out here in the woods," John said, returning with the chairs. "We see so few people, except the farmers' kids and our own, anybody looks good to Florence." He winked at Ann.

He nudged the brown dog with his toe until it moved from the spot by the porch rail where he wanted to put Phil's chair. He put the other chair by his rocker.

"Here, Miss Davis, you sit by me. If they're going to spark all night we might as well strike up a friendship," he said.

"Are you an Ashton girl, Ann?" Florence asked when they were all seated.

"No, not exactly," Ann said, glancing at Phil. "I'm a New York girl at present. Kansas City is my home town. But my mother's people live in Ashton. She was a Crutchfield."

"Oh?" Florence said.

"Please, I say that only for identification," Ann said. "The Crutchfield name means nothing in Kansas City—or New York."

"She's an unusual Crutchfield," Phil said.

"That makes her an unusual person," John said. "You here to stay?"

"She thinks she's going back to New York this fall," Phil said quickly. "But we may talk her into hanging around for a while."

They sat and rocked in the bright moonlight that had followed the rain and drank iced tea and talked. Phil and John recalled hunting trips they had taken together until Florence interrupted one of her husband's stories to ask Phil if he still collected folk music records. He said he did and told her about the collection of Negro work songs he bought just before he left New York. It was an old record, he said, made by Alan Lomax at the Mississippi State Prison Farm in Parchman, but he hadn't heard of it until he moved to New York. And he added, "You know, Dad never cared anything for my other folk records. Didn't seem to anyhow. But this one is different. He's almost worn it out in just the short time I've been home."

"How is your dad?" John asked. "I haven't seen him in—oh, must be a month or two now. We used to have a cup of coffee and chew the fat every time I went into town."

"He's fine. Real fine. A little quieter than he used to be. But I guess it's a shock to realize you can't do the things you once could, especially to a man as active as Dad always was."

"Your father isn't all that old," Florence said.

"I know," Phil said, struggling for words that would end this part of the conversation. "But, well, you know what I mean. He seems to *think* he's getting old. I guess that's worse than getting old."

"I know what you mean. He'll get over it." Florence looked away from her husband's warning glare as she said it.

Phil looked at his watch. "We have to go," he said. "I've got to get up early and I was up kind of late last night." He looked at Ann and hoped he didn't blush.

Ann stood and the Allens stood.

"You come with Phil next time he comes," John said to Ann as they walked slowly toward the car. "And don't you wait so long to make it out here again, Phil."

"I won't," Phil said. "There're a couple of things I want to talk to you about." He was curious to know if John had heard anything about the rumor of the voting case, but he was reluctant to bring it up now because John might want to talk about it and he was ready to go, to be alone with Ann.

The moonlight was wonderfully bright and the night breeze cool and fresh as it filtered through the pines and oaks that surrounded the Allen house. For a moment, as they walked, the four were silent, listening to the crickets and other sounds of the night.

"It's a marvelous night," Ann said, closing her eyes and taking a deep breath of the cool air.

"These hills can be pretty at night," Florence said. "The night hides their ugly wounds."

After several goodbyes and promises to "do this again soon," Phil and Ann were driving down and out of the hills. As soon as they rounded the first bend in the road he stopped the car.

"Oh, dear me, sir, why are you stopping here?" Ann said, clutching her blouse front in mock fright.

"You, me proud beauty, are about to be kissed," Phil said and kissed her.

"When I kiss you the crickets sing louder than crickets ought to sing," he said.

"That's me, rubbing my toes together," she whispered. He kissed her again, then he began unbuttoning her blouse.

"The Allens are nice," she said, and her fingers gently massaged his neck and shoulders.

When he kissed her now he felt clumsy, heavily clumsy, and confined. He tried to move his body onto hers and bumped his knee against the emergency brake lever.

"Damn!"

"Hurt?" she mumbled lazily.

"Hit my damn knee."

"You're such a pretty man. I like to look at you."

"This is crazy. Let's go somewhere."

"All right."

———————————

Forty-five minutes later he turned off the motor under a blinking neon sign that stuck out awkwardly over the office door of a motel which seemed to have been dug back into the kudzu-covered hill beside the highway. He kissed her quickly, nervously, and went into the office. As he signed the register the desk clerk, a fat little man, licked his lips repeatedly as he talked and glanced past Phil trying to see what the girl in the car looked like. Phil wanted to smash his fist into the grinning face.

"How long you and the young lady going to be with us?" the clerk asked.

"Just tonight. My wife and I are driving through to Birmingham tomorrow. Long drive. We'll be leaving early so I better pay now. Save trouble in the morning." He hated whatever it was in him that made him lie to try to cover up what he and Ann were about to do. He hated himself for being unable to resist the compulsion to tell the lie. He hated the clerk for setting the whole process in motion in his mind.

———————

He closed the door to the room they were to share. He locked the door and looked around at the tiny, private world bordered by four green walls and containing—besides him and Ann—a bed, a chair, a TV set, a bureau, two lamps and "September Morn" hanging on the green wall over the bed.

"I've always wondered what a woman who went to a motel with a man felt like," Ann laughed, bouncing on the bed.

"Don't say that," he snapped; then quickly, "I'm sorry. It's that man out there. Greasy little bastard. . . . What we need is a drink. Don't know why I didn't think of it . . . I'll bet that clerk has some to sell. Probably charge a fortune but we do need a drink." He stepped toward the door.

"Phil."

"I'll be right back. Won't take a second."

"Phil."

"Yes?"

"Come here . . . come over here by me."

"Don't you want a drink?"

"No. I want you to come sit by me."

"Ann, I'm sorry . . . I shouldn't have—"

"Don't make this into something nervous and sneaky," she interrupted. "Look, Phil, if I was a girl you picked up in a bar you'd be pawing all over me. . . . Now, don't look so innocent. You're a man and I know you would. All I want are equal rights."

"Ann, for God's sake . . ."

"Okay, it wasn't a very ladylike way to put it. But you need shaking up. You think 'nice' girls can't have some things in common with the ones you don't consider 'nice?' Women were freed too Phil, not just Negro slaves. And we won't let you Southern gentlemen treat us like Dresden dolls you keep around to show off while the girls you keep on the back forty have all the fun. We won't. . . . That's another part of the Southern Way of Life that's gone."

He walked to her, sat on the floor and put his head in her lap.

She kissed him on the back of the neck.

"Come on up here with me," she said. "I can't reach you way down there."

10.

THEY WERE to arrive in half an hour and Janie was nervous. She was never ill at ease, of course, when she was hostess to a group of their regular friends, those in her own social class. (She hated to use the word "class" but could think of no other that was appropriate.) But tonight she must entertain rednecks and, even worse, their wives. That's what they were, rednecks. Or peckerwoods, as her father would have called them. They were crossroads merchants, plantation managers, and heaven knows what all. One was one of those self-ordained preachers. She could talk with them in their stores or at political rallies, she told Jerry, but having them as guests in her own home made her nervous.

"That why you asked Cousin Ann to come over and help you?" Jerry said.

"Frankly, yes. Ann seems to have a knack for putting people at ease—any kind of people."

"I wish you had asked me about it before you talked with Ann," Jerry said, unbuttoning his shirt. "She's been saying some damn shocking things at the Country Club lately. You should talk with her about it. People know she's your cousin, you know, and we can't be too careful with this campaign coming up so soon."

"Zip me," she said, backing up to him. "What about your bosom buddy, Phil? He's the one people are concerned about. They can overlook Ann as a Yankee who doesn't know any better."

"But she's your cousin. Anyhow, I've talked with Phil. We don't have to worry about him any more. He's learned his lesson."

"Are you sure?"

"Certainly I'm sure. He was out here last week. We had a long talk about it. Phil and I understand each other. He knows how I feel about things. He knows I'm not one of those rabble rousers and he knows that to get me in the governor's chair he has to keep quiet. But Ann doesn't have the interest of the state at heart. I'll tell Phil to talk with her. He knows if I don't get elected Mark Hadley will. And then lord knows what will happen to the state. Hadley would have the schools closed down in six months."

He walked toward the bathroom, naked now.

"What do I talk to these people about?" Janie said, a pout in her voice.

Jerry paused at the bathroom door. "Janie, I know you'd like to be first lady of this state. Right? Okay, then you may as well settle down and do some of the things you have to do to get there. You can't let your god-damned Crutchfield snobbishness stand in our way."

"I am not snobbish," she protested. "It's just that I'm nervous. That's the opposite of being snobbish. I'm afraid I'll do something wrong. For the first time in my life I don't know how to act at a party."

He saw that she actually felt inadequate and it amused him. "Look, honey," he said, "you may not know these people or how they act, but they damn sure know you and how you act. They've always known you and watched you and tried to imitate you—or imitate what they thought you were like. A Crutchfield is like a royal family to ordinary Ashton County folks. Sort of a tourist attraction. They know all about you and your background and they talk about it and every new item they learn like they discuss the goings on of a movie star. The best way to make a good impression is to put your most regal manner on and be the queen. They'll accept no less without criticism. So stop worrying."

He went into the bathroom. She was relieved. His words made sense. He certainly knew the people of this state. He should. He had lived in nearly every part of it when his father was teaching school. There were times when she wondered why she had married him. She hadn't been able to rid him of many of his common traits. It piqued her, for instance, for him to parade around in front of her naked as he had done just now. He was getting fat anyhow, and she couldn't persuade him to go on a diet. People trust a fat man, he would tell her and laugh his political rally laugh. But she had to admit he was going places. Suddenly she was lighthearted. Almost gay.

"Jerry darling," she said. "I'm going to have a drink. Do you want one?"

He stuck his lathered face into the bedroom.

"That's something else I forgot to tell you," he said. "We better not serve drinks tonight. Some of these hill people don't approve. I'll offer the men a snort in the library. But we better not take a chance on insulting the wives."

"Oh, great! Now you tell me I not only have to entertain these people but I have to do it sober."

He laughed. "Why don't you have a vodka martini? They can't smell that on your breath."

She wasn't gay any more. She went downstairs and while she was mixing a pitcher of vodka martinis Ann arrived.

"You better have a couple of these with me," Janie told her. "Jerry says we can't serve drinks tonight."

"I'll never know why you roped me in on this," Ann said. "Or why I let you."

"One Crutchfield never lets another Crutchfield down." Janie laughed.

"Crap."

"Ann, you shouldn't talk like that," Janie said, frowning over her martini glass. "You know you aren't in New York City. We were just discussing that."

"You were just discussing what?"

"You. You have to remember that Jerry is running for governor and what you say around people could lose votes for him."

"My God, Janie! You aren't serious."

"I am serious. It's bad enough that you've taken up with Phil Arrow."

"Did Jerry say that too?"

"No. I said it."

"Well, I should hope he didn't. Phil thinks Jerry is his best friend."

"He is. They grew up together. People know that and they know Phil well enough to know Jerry isn't responsible for what he says. Besides Jerry says Phil has promised to be careful about what he says and puts in that paper of his."

"Oh, is that what Jerry said? I'll ask Phil about that."

"Now, don't you go stirring up trouble."

"Look, if you're afraid I'll cause trouble, why don't I just check out of here now? I don't mean to sound childish. But you don't need me here tonight."

"Oh, calm down and have another drink with me. I'm not afraid of you embarrassing me in this house. You're a Crutchfield."

"Crap."

"My, what a charming expression," Jerry said, walking into the living room. "How's my favorite cousin?" He kissed Ann, then smacked his lips. "Tastes like a good martini. How about one for me before the folks arrive?"

"There's more in the pitcher," Janie said, nodding toward the tray on the coffee table between the small sofa and twin chairs in front of the fireplace.

Jerry poured a drink and shouted toward the kitchen door, "Precious, you better come out here and get this evil stuff out of sight before our guests start coming in."

"I'll put it away," Janie said, stepping to the coffee table to pour the last of the mix into her glass. "I'll split this with you, Ann."

"Never mind," Ann said. "I think you need it worse than I do."

Mr. and Mrs. J. Q. Perthman from Crutchfield Crossing were the first to arrive. They rang the doorbell ten minutes before the appointed time.

"I see we're the first," Mrs. Perthman said as she walked into the living room behind Precious. "We usually are. I told J.Q., if you say you're gonna be somewhere at a certain time, be there on time. Don't let them stand around waitin' for you half the night and then stand around later waitin' for you to leave. Be there on time and leave on time, I always say. Howd ya do, Miz Windham. I'm Bertha Perthman. Please call me Bertha."

"I'm so glad to see you, Bertha, Mr. Perthman," Janie said, squeezing Bertha's hand intimately and winking at her as if they shared a secret already. (Janie had learned that this always made older women like her.) "This is my cousin, Ann Davis. You may remember Mother's sister, Ruth. This is her daughter."

"Oh, yes," Bertha said. "Ruth was the one who married that Kansas City feller and went off up there to live, wasn't she."

"Yes, she was," Ann said. "Isn't it awful?"

"Ann's always joking," Janie said quickly, darting a frown at Ann. "Sit over here by me, Bertha. And please call me Janie."

"Oh, I will," Bertha assured her. "Fact I can hardly think of you as anything but little Janie Crutchfield. Us live at Crutchfield Crossing, you know, where your great-grandfather crossed the river when he first came here in 1827. We kind of feel kin to the Crutchfields."

What would Janie's mother think of that? Ann wondered as she listened from her corner. Janie and Bertha faced each other on the sofa and Jerry talked animatedly to Mr. Perthman over by the picture window. Janie's mother probably wouldn't resent the Perthmans' fancied familiarity she decided. In her latter years Aunt Penney became an almost fanatical reader of Faulkner. Ann remembered visiting her one summer—Aunt Penney's last summer—and hearing the pitiful, drunken old thing scream, "They're coming out of the walls! Tiny, crawling Snopes. Somebody call the Orkin man! Swish! Swish!" No, Aunt Penney would be as relaxed with Bertha Perthman and her silent, froglike husband as Janie was becoming. The Perthmans were not Snopes. The Perthmans stayed in their place. Snopes didn't. The Perthmans were storekeepers in Crutchfield Crossing and proud of it. Aunt Penney and Janie could relax with the Perthmans because they were principal allies against the aggressive "mongrel white trash." The Perthmans were allies because they lived by the rules of the System. They knew a Crutchfield was better than a Perthman and that there wasn't anything they could do about it. Didn't want to bother trying to do anything about it, in fact. "Putting something back for a rainy day" was enough to keep them occupied. Besides, cracking any part of the System might cause the whole thing to fall apart and the Perthmans were comfortable in the confines of the System. The only way a Perthman could become almost as good as a Crutchfield was to marry one. That's what Jerry had done. But Jerry was more Snopes than Perthman, Ann thought. Wonder what Aunt Penney would say about Jerry running for governor? Probably wouldn't surprise her at all. She'd shout something like "On to the White House!" and sulk back up to her room where she kept her favorite brandy and her Faulkner books. Ann saw Jerry and Mr. Perthman walk over and sit by their wives and she saw the look Bertha gave Jerry and knew he would never be a Crutchfield in Bertha's eyes. The children he gave Janie, yes. But not Jerry. This might be an interesting evening, after all.

The doorbell rang and when Bertha looked at Janie, Janie said, "Precious will get it," and Bertha said, "Of course," and shot a pleased look at her husband. Everybody in the state whose income was over seventy-five dollars a week had a Negro cook, but because this was Janie Crutchfield's house Bertha was going to make something impressive from everything she could. Anyhow, the colored help in most homes she visited wouldn't answer the doorbell if anyone else was nearer the door.

"You just can't get good, old-fashioned niggers any more," Bertha said to Janie, as they waited for the new arrivals. "Nowadays they want to come in at eight or nine and work no later than five. Why, my mamma had a girl who worked for her twenty-five years, raised all us kids, and she would come in at six, cook biscuits, and be there to do the supper dishes. Didn't live on the yard either. And love us! Lordy, she was just like one of the family. I remember when

Poppa died she came to the funeral and cried, just like one of us."

Precious came in ahead of Anse Hayes and walked on through to the kitchen. Anse was cashier at Hamp Auld's bank and the only town person invited tonight. His wife wasn't with him.

"Glad you could come," Jerry said, shaking his hand. "You know the Perthmans. This is Janie's cousin, Ann."

"Good to see you again, J.Q., Bertha," Anse said. "How you, Miss Ann? You're the one from Kansas City, aren't you?"

"I'm afraid so," Ann said, "although I live in New York now."

"Oh, New York?" Anse said. "That so?" He was short and stocky, with rounded shoulders. He wore round, steel-rimmed glasses and his front teeth protruded. He squinted through his thick lenses at Ann.

He looks like a mole, Ann thought.

"Where's the wife?" Jerry asked Anse.

"I was just about to take orders for tea and coffee," Janie said. "Which do you prefer?"

"I'll take coffee if you haven't got anything stronger." Anse laughed too loudly. "I'm just joking, Bertha. Oh, the wife has had a touch of the flu past few days. I told you that the other day, Jerry."

"Yes, you sure did," Jerry said. "Hope she's feeling better."

Janie went to the kitchen to tell Precious what everyone would drink and to see how she was getting on with Millie, the girl Janie hired to help Precious because the occasion was special. The doorbell rang again while she was out and Jerry answered it. He returned followed by a tall man and a short woman. The man was thickly muscular and his skin was leathery. The woman—about thirty-five, Ann guessed—was frumpy. Her hair was peroxide-burned and her flowery dress too tight around her hips.

"I believe everyone knows Mike and Rita Jean except Ann over there," Jerry said. "This is Janie's cousin, Ann Davis, folks. Ann, meet the Heaneys."

Ann saw the crinkles around the man's small, invasive eyes deepen and relax, as if a flash of sunlight had passed across his face.

He nodded to her. Rita Jean mumbled something Ann did not understand and tugged at her girdle, then jerked her hand away when she realized what she was doing.

Janie came back into the room and Jerry said, "Honey, you remember Mike and Rita Jean Heaney. They went to high school with us. It was Rita Jean Holifield then."

"Why, certainly," Janie said. Ann knew she did not.

"How are you, Mike, Rita? So good to see you again." They all sat down with their coffee and tea cups. Janie, Jerry and Bertha chattered on while the others listened, or pretended to listen, and sipped. Ann soon became conscious of Mike Heaney's stare and it was disturbing somehow until she shrugged it off and tried to strike up a conversation with Mr. Perthman, who sat nearest her. But he was stubbornly unresponsive as he surveyed the room and the people in it with his darting little rodent eyes, sucking on his snuff. He hadn't said a word that Ann had heard since he arrived. She watched him drink his coffee and wondered how he kept from swallowing his snuff.

Another couple—introduced as the Reverend and Mrs. Pat Grubbs—arrived. Then Jerry took the men into the library. Mrs. Grubbs and Bertha hovered near Janie, leaving Rita Jean Heaney sitting rigidly alone on the edge of her chair, so Ann moved over near her.

"I could use a little bourbon in this coffee," Ann said, taking a chance. "Couldn't you?"

"Boy! Could I!" Rita Jean said, her eyes lighting with interest for the first time since she entered the strange room. Then she retreated. "Not that I drink much, but I've had a terrible cold and it will loosen up your head, you know."

"That's what I mean," Ann smiled. "My head needs loosening."

"Oh, yeah, I see." Rita Jean smiled tentatively. "Mine too." And she giggled.

"What does your husband do?" Ann said.

"He's manager of a plantation," Rita Jean said. "The Blinken place out west of town. I bet you know the Blinkens."

"Oh, yes, I know Ches and his father. Ches plays a mean banjo."

"He does?" Rita Jean's eyes kindled again. "Say, I know who you are now. You're the one who goes with Phil Arrow, aren't you?"

"Well, yes. I have had several dates with Phil since I've been here this time."

"Yeah, I know. You seem nice. I'll give you a hint. Don't set near my husband. He goes nuts ever time you mention Phil Arrow, Junior."

"Oh? Why is that?"

"I don't know for sure. He won't talk about it much. He says it's because Phil Arrow, Junior, is a nigger lover."

Ann flinched visibly. "How interesting," she said.

The men came in from the library and before they were seated again Precious announced that dinner was ready and all went into the paneled dining room and sat, according to Janie's instructions, around the long, heavy table her grandmother had shipped to Ashton from Germany. Ann found herself sitting on the left of Mike Heaney.

"Brother Grubbs," Jerry said, "would you return thanks?"

Brother Grubbs (Ann found out later he was a Baptist preacher at a country church near his store in the hills near Crutchfield Crossing) asked the Lord to bless the food they were about to receive and thanked Him for all their "manifest blessings." Then he said "Amen" and raised his water glass and said, "Here's to the next governor of our great state." Everyone took a swallow of water and Ann thought, My God, Mr. Perthman hasn't gotten rid of his snuff yet! She noticed that Bertha glanced quickly at her husband then said, "Amen," as if she were saying something she knew he wouldn't approve. Then they began to eat.

Ann felt the presence of the immense man beside her as she heard the chatter of Bertha and Janie and Jerry, and now Anse, and through the clatter an occasional smack of the eating noises. He said nothing and appeared to concentrate on his food. She could not forget that here was a man who hated the man she loved. Finally, as if compelled, she said to him. "I understand you know Phil Arrow."

"Yeah, I know him," Mike Heaney said, without looking at her. And after a brief silence, he said, "I know you too."

"Oh?"

"Yeah. You probably don't remember me though."

He was looking at her now and she was looking at him.

"I'm sorry . . . I . . ."

"That's okay," he said. "I didn't expect you to."

It was then she saw something in his eyes that made her pity him. His eyes seemed to beg her to remember.

"I should remember." She smiled. "You wouldn't be an easy person to forget." It was the nicest remark she could think of at the moment. She hoped it soothed whatever put the hurt in his eyes.

"Thanks," he mumbled and turned his eyes back to his plate.

"Is everybody goin' to the Citizens Council meeting next week?" Rita Jean asked from the other end of the table. She sat at Jerry's right.

"Yes'm we, the wife and me, that is, intend to make it," Brother Grubbs said.

"So do Mike and me," Rita Jean said. "I just love to hear Mark Hadley speak."

"Rita Jean . . ." Mike began.

"Mr. Hadley is a wonderful speaker," Janie said quickly. "He's one of the few left of the old school. I'd enjoy him too."

Poor man, Ann thought, but couldn't help being amused, his wife blurts out and praises the host's political opponent and he's nervous enough as it is. But she was embarrassed for Rita Jean too. She was trying too hard.

"Oh, I'm sorry," Rita Jean said, her hand at her mouth as her husband's glare told her she had said too much, or something wrong.

"I'll be there," Jerry said, smiling at Rita Jean.

"Hadley was invited to speak before we knew you were going to run against him," Mike said roughly. "This is the big summer meeting, you know. We planned it months ago."

"Mike knows about things like that," Rita Jean said, "because he's an officer in the Citizens Council."

"Jerry told me," Janie said. "I think that's nice. What's your position, Mike?"

"He's sergeant at arms," Rita Jean said before Mike could answer.

"How nice," Janie said.

"That's more'n just being a bouncer like you usually think of it," Mike said, more to Ann than anyone else.

"Senator, I ain't seen you at any of the other Council meetings," Grubbs said to Jerry. He used the tone he used on members of his church who had missed service several Sundays.

"I'm not a member," Jerry said.

Ann saw all eyes turn toward Jerry. She was pleased. Maybe Phil was right about his friend.

"Oh?" said Grubbs. "You're not?"

"No," Jerry said, "I believe a public official shouldn't belong to any organization that must from time to time delve into politics. Any organization, I mean, but the Democratic party. I'm a Baptist, a Rotarian, a Mason, a past commander of the American Legion post here, and a Democrat. I figure that's all a feller needs to be to serve his country and his state."

I can never quite decide, Ann thought, whether Jerry is clever or absurdly naïve.

"With things going like they are in some places the Councils may be as necessary as some of the organizations you mentioned," Mike said, surprising Ann by putting so many words end to end. "You do believe in what the Citizens Council stands for, don't you, Senator?"

"I certainly believe in the Southern Way of Life and the rights of the individual, if that's what you mean," Jerry said smoothly.

"I'm glad to hear you say that," Mike said. "They's some who say you're too close a friend of Phil Arrow's to join the Council."

"Phil and I were friends long before the Council organized," Jerry said. "But our friendship has nothing to do with my politics."

"Why don't y'all ask Senator Windham to speak at the next Citizens Council meeting, Mike?" Rita Jean said, still warm from Jerry's smile and words that had saved her from embarrassment.

"I'm not on that committee," Mike said.

"I would like very much the opportunity to address the Ashton Citizens Council," Jerry said, smiling again at Rita Jean.

"Why, I think that'd be real nice," Bertha said. "J.Q. is on the board. Maybe he could bring it up at the next board meeting. Couldn't you, J.Q.?"

"Humph," Perthman said. At least that's what it sounded like to Ann.

"Good," Bertha said, very pleased. "That settles it. They usually do what J.Q. asks. It may embarrass you for me to say that, J.Q., but if you won't blow your own horn I have to. You know how it is." She directed the last to Janie, who winked in answer.

Rita Jean leaned over her roast beef to catch her husband's eyes and smile triumphantly at him. Janie saw Precious standing by the kitchen door then and said, "Oh, yes, Precious, I believe everyone is ready for dessert."

Millie appeared beside Precious and moved to the table with a tray of long-stemmed glasses filled with ice cream. Precious moved the cake from the buffet to the table in front of Jerry, who began slicing it and moving the slices around the table.

"I'm full as a pig," Rita Jean said, "but this looks so good I'm gonna eat it. Mike's always gettin' on me about gettin' fat. But when a girl's had four kids she don't have that girlish figure any more."

The Citizens Council wasn't mentioned during dessert nor during coffee, which they took in the living room. After coffee Janie played some Chopin on the grand piano, looking very beautiful and Southern, Ann thought, with the picture window behind her.

"I can tell J.Q.'s sleepy," Bertha said, after the third number. "And when he gets sleepy it's time for us to go. We never were ones to stay up late."

"Oh, must you?" Janie said, standing beside the piano.

"Oh, yes, child," Bertha said, standing too now. "I told you we were always the first to arrive and the first to leave."

Soon they were all gone and Janie, Ann and Jerry sat sipping from a new batch of vodka martinis.

"Well, darling," Janie said, "do you think we scored? Did the men promise to jump on the Windham bandwagon?"

"They didn't exactly promise," Jerry said, "but I feel pretty good about it. I expected no promises tonight. Perthman will do what Hamp Auld tells him; so will Anse. Grubbs will do what Perthman tells him."

"Why did you bother to have them over then?" Janie said. "Why don't we just concentrate on Hamp Auld. Gosh, I can talk to Elizabeth Auld."

"You don't handle Hamp Auld that way," Jerry said. "He plays winners only. If he sees that I impressed the Perthmans and the Grubbs, he might decide I'm a winner."

"Well, if you are a winner, why bother with Auld?" Janie said.

"I said he plays winners—those he believes can win with his help. And don't think he can't give it. He and his cronies control blocks of votes in every section of the state. But you have to be able to get a bunch of votes on your own. Nobody can control all the votes or even a majority. Auld and his bunch have been beaten a few times in the past, but the odds are heavy against you if you don't have their blessings."

"What about Mike Heaney?" Ann asked. "Where does he fit into this cozy little plan of yours?"

Jerry frowned. "I'm afraid I messed up by picking him. I wanted to show Auld's man, Anse, that I could handle the . . . well . . . more frantic element of the Council group. But there's something eating Mike where I'm concerned. I realized too late that . . . well, anyhow, I should have picked another representative of his group."

"Go on and say it," Janie said. "Ann won't mind. She's not that far gone on Phil. Mike Heaney hates Phil's guts for some reason and because you and Phil are friends he dislikes you."

———————

Mike sat with his friend, R. L. Squires, in the back booth at the Ninety-Six Inn, where they met and drank beer several nights a week. He told R.L. about his evening at the Windhams'.

"What the shit, Mike?" R.L. said, his freckled face flushed and his eyes watery because he had been waiting in that booth all evening for Mike. "You not gonna work for Windham, are you? Hell, he's Phil Arrow's buddy and you always said you wouldn't piss on Phil Arrow if'n he was burning 'side the road."

Mike took a quick swallow from the pint bottle that sat on the table between them. He chased the whisky with beer.

"I don't know," he said. "There might be something in it for me."

"I'll be damned," R.L. said, pushing his red hair away from his eyes. "I never thought I'd hear you say that."

"Not even when there's a fine piece of ass in the deal?" Mike grinned meaningfully over his glass.

"Whadda ya mean?"

"Just what I said."

"What fine piece you talkin' about?"

"The finest I ever saw . . . or you either."

"Well, dammit, tell me who it is. It ain't . . . naw, hell it ain't Janie Crutchfield. You're a cocksman, but not that good."

"Janie Crutchfield's a chunk of iceberg compared to the one I'm talking about."

"God-dammit now, tell me."

"You ever seen iceberg Janie's cousin, Ann?"

"You mean her? . . . I seen her out at the Country Club swimming last week when I was out there fixing the filter. I damned near popped my rocks just looking. Mike, ain't she and Phil Arrow thicker'n fleas on a nigger's dog?"

"Maybe so and maybe not."

"Yeah. Now I see what you up to. Now I see. Damn you, Mike, you're a slick one."

11.

GEORGE OSWALT FELT someone looking at him and he raised his eyes from the magazine. Facing him across the desk, shoulders hunched slightly and holding a brown felt hat with both hands at his chest, was a thin Negro man who might have been fifty and might have been seventy. Oswalt could never tell how old Negroes were. Chinese were like that too. This Negro wore new khaki pants and an old but freshly ironed khaki shirt. His shirt was buttoned at the collar but he wore no tie. His short, tightly curled hair was powder-gray. The black skin of his face and hands shone clean. He had been standing there for several minutes waiting for Oswalt to notice him.

"Whatta ya want, uncle?" the circuit clerk said.

"I want to register, sir," the Negro said, "to vote."

"Oh?" Oswalt pushed his glasses up on his nose so he could see this Negro better. "You sure?"

"Yes sir."

He's pronouncing his syllables deliberately, Oswalt thought, and that ain't like a nigger. He looked steadily at the expressionless black face. Then he said, "Why, sure, uncle. You just fill out this here paper and if it looks okay we'll register you right up." He handed a long sheet of paper across the desk and the Negro took it.

"Can you read and write?" Oswalt said, when he saw that the Negro seemed willing to take the test.

"Yes sir."

"What's your name, boy?"

"Theodore Ash Tatum," the Negro said, his face still expressionless. "And I'm sixty-four years old."

"I figgered you was old enough," Oswalt said. He spun the swivel chair and lifted the thick corduroy cover of a large book that lay on the counter behind him. Turning the long, heavy pages to the "T's" he followed his finger down the page until he came to the name. "Oh, yeah. You the Tatum nigger that runs that grocery on Hooker Street and has that buckshot farm out south of here. Right?"

"Yes sir."

"Call you Shine, don't they?"

"Yes sir."

"Well, Shine, now tell me what you think you wanta vote for. You know a nigger ain't voted in Ashton County long as I been circuit clerk, and that's a long time?"

"Yes sir."

"You still wanna vote?"

"Yes sir."

"Well, you just try and fill out that paper and we'll see if you qualify. Course you know it costs you two dollars poll tax ever year if you qualify."

"Yes sir."

"Well, then don't just stand there. Go on and fill out the paper," Oswalt said. He felt an unfamiliar excitement pass through him. This was the first nigger to ever try to register with him. He was almost happy. Now, why would he feel almost happy about something like that?

"Yes sir," Shine said, looking around for a place to sit and write.

"Got a pen?" Oswalt said, studying the Negro's face carefully.

"Yes sir."

"Then you can set right over there." He pointed to a chair near the door that opened to the corridor. He watched as Shine walked over and sat down in the classroom chair with the writing arm. He wanted to run out and tell Sheriff Copeland and the chancery clerk, across the hall, but he stayed in his chair. May as well let the old man take the test first. Then he could go across and tell it all to them. He saw Ches Blinken, Sr., walk along the corridor past the doorway and he started to call out to him, but decided against that too. He and the boys had talked about what they would do if a nigger came in and said he wanted to vote. They'd all agreed the best thing to do was keep calm and let him take the test. That's what the test was for. No use stirring up an unnecessary fuss.

After fifteen minutes Shine walked to Oswalt's desk and offered the sheet of paper to the circuit clerk.

"That was kinda quick, wasn't it?" Oswalt said, ignoring the paper Shine offered.

"It wasn't hard, sir."

"Zat so?" Oswalt took the paper then and glanced at what Shine had written on it. "Sorry. You fail."

"Sir?"

"You heard me. You fail. Flunk. It ain't right. You don't qualify. That plain enough?"

"What's wrong with my answers?"

"They wrong. That's what's wrong."

"How are they wrong?"

"Look, old man. I ain't got time to fiddle with you. You failed the test. Now get outta here."

"I have a right to know what I answered wrong." Shine took a deep breath, then he continued: "It is my right as a taxpayer and citizen of this country."

"You drunk, old man?"

"No sir. I don't drink."

"Then you better get outta here like I said before you get in bad trouble. You oughta know better'n that. If you was one of them zoot-suited niggers from Dee-troit or somewhere, I wouldn't be surprised. But you been around here a long time. You oughta know better."

A tall, light-brown Negro in a slick, tan suit walked into the office from the wide corridor. That's the first bald-headed nigger I ever saw, Oswalt thought. The appearance of the bald-headed Negro seemed to frighten Shine.

"Please, Mr. Oswalt, lemme register without no trouble," Shine pleaded. "I know I filled out the paper right."

"Damn it, Shine," Oswalt said, "I told you to get the hell outta here. I got another customer now, so git."

"I'm with Mr. Tatum," the bald-headed Negro said.

"You're what?"

"I'm with Mr. Tatum. I'm his attorney."

Mike Heaney was eating supper alone at the kitchen table when the telephone rang. Rita Jean answered it.

"It's for you, naturally," she shouted.

"Who is it?"

"Who's calling, please," Rita Jean asked into the phone, then shouted, "It's Rush Gamble at the hotel."

"What's he want?"

"Now, how do I know. Come talk to him and find out. I'm right in the middle of a program." She laid the phone on the table and went back into the living room where the television was.

Mike cursed and went into the hall and put the phone to his ear. "Yeah, Rush," he said.

"Look, Mike, we're having an emergency meeting of the Council directors tonight at the hotel here," Rush said. "Some crazy nigger is filing a voting suit against Oswalt and the county."

"Don't they know what to do about that?" Mike snorted. "What nigger is it?"

"That's the surprising part. It's old Shine Tatum. You know him, don't you? Runs that store on the Block."

"Yeah, I know Shine. Look, that ain't gonna be no big problem. I got some things I need to tend to."

"The meeting won't start till ten o'clock. Some of the others got things to tend to too before they can make it."

"Hell, there's something I was gonna do tonight. That's the trouble with this god-damned Citizens Council. They're scared to death of one nigger. You won't need me there."

"Don't get your bowels up," Rush said. "I'm just supposed to call certain ones. I've called you. If you can, come. If you don't think this is important enough, then forget it. Maybe we got the wrong man for sergeant at arms."

He hung up before Mike had a chance to answer. Mike cursed into the dead phone, then cradled it. Why tonight, of all nights? Nothing ever goes right for Mike Heaney. Well, god-dammit, he would go ahead with his plan. Handle that shithead, Rush Gamble, later. He was fouled up before—nine years ago. But not again. Not tonight. He took his jacket from the hall closet and put it on as he walked to the door.

"Rita Jean," he said, "I may be out late tonight. There's a special meeting of the Council board. Something important's come up."

"You didn't say anything about it before," Rita Jean said. "Can't I go with you?"

"No, dammit, you can't go with me. This is a special meeting. Some nigger is trying to sue the county for not lettin' him vote. Rush says it looks serious. Women ain't invited. It's just the board gonna be there."

"But you're just sergeant at arms. Why do you have to be there?"

"Cause, god-dammit, I'm on the board, cause I'm an officer just like the rest of them. Bein' sergeant at arms is being an officer too. It's more'n just a bouncer, you know, in an organization like that. If you had any god-damn sense you'd be proud of me for gettin' to be an officer in an organization like that. Not always naggin' cause I have to go to meetings. You know who the other officers are?"

"Yeah, I know." She slouched back into her chair and stared vacantly at the television. "The biggest men in town. I am proud of you, baby, you know that. I just wanted you to stay home with me tonight. There's good television on. You could get some beer and we could put the kids to bed early and . . . well, we ain't been alone together in a long time."

He stood at the door looking at her, sitting there, her fingers twisting the belt of her yellow, terry-cloth bathrobe. After dark and she hadn't put on her clothes yet. Always wiggling her round little ass at him before they married and rubbing up against him when they danced. She would never let him have it all the way then and he thought it was because she was a nice girl. A nice girl, wanting it as bad as he did but never giving it. Driving him crazy until he married her to get it all the way. But she stopped wiggling the day they got married, it seemed to him. She never made it even as good as it was before, when he imagined how it would be. At first it was "Oh, Mike, you're hurting me"; then it got to be so damned much trouble trying not to hurt her he just quit. You lose again, Mike. You're always losing. But not tonight.

"You don't need me to help you watch television," he said and turned and walked out the door.

He drove out the highway to Mannie's to buy a pint of vodka. Vodka doesn't leave an odor on your breath. He needed a drink or two but he didn't want her to think he was drunk. When he pulled open the screen door and stepped into Mannie's hut two men, leaning against the counter, drinking bourbon and Coke from paper cups, were listening to Mannie.

"Sure, I know old Shine," Mannie was saying. "Hi, Mike. . . . His place ain't far from here, between here and Just-Ten Acres. He always seemed like a good nigra to me. Never caused no trouble around here. Never known him to drink even. Just comes in here now and then for a carton of ginger ale or R.C.'s."

(Mannie didn't like to talk much about the race issue. He still remembered being pushed around and called a spick and a pepperbelly when he pulled bolls in West Texas before he came to the delta in the thirties. But the two men wouldn't be diverted from the voting test case. Everybody that came in that day talked about it, in fact. It wasn't that Mannie wanted to defend Negroes. He belonged to the Citizens Council. Paid his dues anyhow, just as he paid his dues to the Ashton Chamber of Commerce. He paid both as protection, not out of conviction. He just didn't like all this emphasis on racial differences. That's the reason he discouraged his cousins when they wanted to come out here from Texas and work for him. If too many Mexicans lived around Ashton, people would begin to notice that his skin was darker than theirs. Then instead of being unique he might be considered a threat. It was better to be unique.)

"What'll you have, Mike?" Mannie asked.

"Gimme a pint. . . . Hell, gimme a fifth of vodka," Mike said.

"Hi, Mike," one of the customers said. "You hear about that nigger trying to vote?"

"Yeah," Mike said. "I heard."

"Next thing you know they'll be wantin' us to cook for 'em," the man said.

"It's the by-God truth," his friend said, grimacing as he drank from the paper cup. He was Jim Perkins, who was a gasoline distributor. "It's time somebody did something besides sit around and talk."

"At's the God's truth," his friend said. "At's the by-God truth if I ever heard it. All anybody does is set around on their royal asses. There oughta be a couple of tar-and-featherin's and a few night rides like in the old days in Alabama. That's where I'm from, Alabama. I work outta Memphis now, but good old Bama'll always be home to me. By God, in Bama they don't just set around and talk."

He was district representative for the oil company that franchised Jim Perkins' distributorship.

"Like shit," Perkins said. "They ain't doing a goddam thing more'n we doing. We got a Citizens Council going."

"Citizens Council, shit!" the district man said. "That's just a god-damn country club far as I can see. Old ladies' sewing circle. Gimme the old KKK any day. They did things up brown. My daddy was one. He used to tell me about it. Take a nigger that got outta line and let him know in no uncertain terms that he better get straight and get straight quick."

"Yeah, well, the Council's got its eyes open," Perkins said.

"Don't you never think otherwise. When the time comes it'll do what needs to be done."

"That all you need today, Mike?" Mannie said as he handed Mike change.

"Yeah, I guess so," Mike said, turning to leave.

"Who's gonna do it?" the district man said. "One of those fat-ass bank vice-presidents you people are always electing to office in the Citizens Council?"

"We got more'n that in the Council," Perkins said. "When the time comes we got men. I'm a little too old, and crippled to boot, to do much, but, well, take a man like Mike here. He's an officer in our Council. Ain't you, Mike?"

"Yeah," Mike said over his shoulder as the black spring pulled the screen door shut behind him.

He got in his car and waited for the old pickup to chug by so he could back into the road and make the turn around to head back to the highway. Then he drove to the Dixie Drive-Inn at the intersection and ordered a glass of ice and a can of grapefruit juice. He sat in the car listening to the jukebox blare, drinking the yellow juice well laced with vodka, thinking about where he was going. Funny, how he had found out about it all. It was almost as if she had sent him a message. Rita Jean had hired the cook, Millie, for a day and the cook was saying all of a sudden, "Yes'm, Miss Ann going to stay over at the big house with the chillun while Mista Jerry and Miz Janie go to a big meetin' at the capital." The rest was easy to find out. She would be alone. At least she would until he got there. And there'd be no interruption this time.

He mixed another drink and called the Negro carhop and told him to bring a package of Dentyne gum. When he finished the drink he put three sticks of the gum in his mouth, mixed another drink and drove away carrying the glass between his legs on the seat. When he reached the lane that led to the Windham house he eased to a stop and looked both directions along the road, then turned left between the rows of pecan trees. He parked behind the high hedge, let the wad of gum fall from his mouth into his hand and pitched it into the hedge. Then he got out of the car and walked stiffly to the door. He pushed the button and drummed on his right thigh with his fingers as he waited. The door opened and Ann was there, her tall coolness framed by the doorway and the light from the hallway behind her. She wore knee-length shorts and a plain white boat-necked jumper. Mike felt sweat trickle from his armpits down his sides.

"Why, hello," she said. "For a moment I couldn't see you. I've been sitting in the dark watching television."

"I know how that is. . . . We watch television quite a bit at the house. . . . I bought a set, oh, bout a year ago I guess."

"I'm afraid you've missed Jerry. He went to the capital for some kind of legislative thing and Janie went along to do some shopping. I'm baby-sitting."

Mike cleared his throat. "Yes," he said, "I know. I wanted to talk to you."

"Yes?"

"I mean . . ."

"Oh, excuse me. Come in."

He followed her through the foyer and the living room into the playroom, watching her long, tanned legs. The flesh was smooth and round and firm, going up into the plaid material outlining her hips. His fists clenched at his sides.

"Here we are," she said. "Can I get you something? A tall, cool drink maybe. It's so muggy out tonight."

"Yeah . . . Yes . . . Thanks. . . . A tall cool drink. It sure is muggy out." He ran his tongue over his lips.

"Good," Ann said and turned toward the kitchen. "Precious, can you hear me?"

"Yes'm," a voice from the open doorway said.

"Would you bring us two tall glasses of lemonade? Be sure there's lots of ice."

"Yes'm."

"Now, please sit down, Mr. Heaney," Ann said, motioning to the big chair near the fireplace. She sat on a thick, brown corduroy cushion on the floor a few feet from him. "I'm at your service."

Mike cleared his throat. "Boy, it sure is muggy outside. That lemonade will taste good. My throat's dry."

"Yes. I don't know what we'd do without air conditioning."

"Me neither."

"You said you wanted to talk with me about something, Mr. Heaney."

"Well, yes, I did."

Precious came in with a tray that carried two tall, striped glasses of lemonade. She sat the tray on the coffee table near Ann and went back into the kitchen. Ann handed Mike one of the perspiring glasses and he drank from it thirstily.

"Aaah. Now that's good lemonade," he said.

Ann sipped her drink. "You were saying," she said.

"Yeah . . . well . . . I wondered first if you remembered seeing me before. I mean before the other night here?"

"You mentioned that we had met before."

"It was nine years ago. I just got back from Korea. I was a captain in the Army then. Got a battlefield commission in World War Two. You might have heard about it. Anyhow, I stayed in after that and got in on the Korea thing. I didn't set foot in Ashton from 'forty-three to 'fifty-two. I was a fat kid when I left and when I came back I was a captain. Went in a private."

"That's nice. You must have been a good soldier."

"They said I was." He drew lines in the frost on the glass with his finger. "I got a bunch of medals and they took me around to the Rotary and the Lions and Kiwanis clubs and the Blinkens asked me if I wanted to manage their place. My old man sharecropped for the Blinkens, so they knew I knew the place pretty good. Anyhow, it sounded pretty good to me so I got outta the Army. But what I was gonna tell was about that first week, no, it was in the second week, after I got back."

He paused, still staring at the glass.

"Would you like some more lemonade?" Ann asked.

"No, I don't believe so," he said, and when he reached down to put the glass on the coffee table Ann noticed that his fingernails were chewed ragged and his fingers were thick and rough and brown as cigars.

"What happened the second week after you returned home?" she asked, anxious for him to finish his story and go. She experienced again the pity she had felt briefly for Mike at the dinner party. But there was something else about him, something stronger than what she pitied.

"That was when I met you," he said. "You remember a dance you went to at the Country Club about then? I danced with you. There were several guys back from Korea then and they had a dance for all of us. Ches Blinken was one of them. Young Ches. You know he wasn't but a lieutenant and I was a captain. Course he wasn't in my company, but if he had been I'd been his boss."

Ann did remember the dance now. She should. It was the first "grown-up" dance she attended. She was visiting Ashton that summer. She was sixteen, or maybe seventeen. She had gone with Janie and Jerry and when Janie wasn't looking she sneaked sips of her cocktails. It hadn't taken many sips to get her tight. Oh, what a siren she thought she was that night! Entertaining the returned warriors. Flirting like mad. Getting the rush of her life. Floating three feet off the dance floor! It was the night Phil Arrow danced with her three times! He was so sad and serious. My, how she loved him! She had loved all the men there that night, but she had loved Phil most.

"Yes," she said. "I remember that dance. I remember it very well."

He leaned toward her, his tiny eyes bright. "I knew you would. That's why I wanted to tell you about it. I knew you'd remember it. You think so much about things when you're settin' around waitin' for something to happen in a war. And that night, at that dance, was everything I ever thought about. And you know why? Because you made it that. You made me feel like I was . . ." He reached out and touched her hand.

She withdrew her hand quickly and stood.

"What's the matter?" he said. "You act like I was poison or something. What's wrong with me? Tell me!"

"Nothing, Mr. Heaney," she said, knowing she should not have shown her fear. "You startled me, that's all."

"I startled you, did I? Well, I didn't *startle* you that night. You rubbed it all over me *that* night. You were ready to go outside with me *that* night. Said you were. Then Arrow—Lieutenant Philip Arrow, Junior—came along and you forgot about *Captain* Mike Heaney. Biggest night of my life, dammit, and he ruined it. Wasn't the first time, either."

Precious stepped quietly into the room, the hand she concealed under her apron clutched tightly around the wood handle of a long bread knife.

"Did you call me, Miss Ann?" she said.

Mike whirled, then strode rapidly out; through the living room and foyer and out the door. When he disappeared into the foyer Precious ran to Ann.

"You all right, Miss Ann?" she said, glancing at the door and back to Ann.

"Yes, thank you, Precious. He really didn't do anything. He just frightened me, that's all."

"I heard him."

"Precious, I want you to promise me that you won't mention this to anyone. There's no use causing a lot of trouble over something that didn't happen. You understand?"

"Yes'm. If you say so."

"I must have been tighter than I thought that night," Ann said, sinking into the sofa and laughing softly. "I'm glad I didn't decide to become a full-time siren."

Mike stood rigid on the porch and stared unblinkingly out across the long sloping lawn into the hot darkness. Then he stomped off the porch and kicked the tire of his car. His foot bounced away and the thump was barely audible.

"Damn her," he said through the tight bite of his teeth. "Goddam her! Damn the big-titted, snooty bitch!"

He pounded the hood with his fist and it rumbled. He got behind the wheel and the engine roared as he pedaled the accelerator. When the sedan lurched around the circular drive, stones scattered up and onto the porch.

Back on the blacktop road he reached under the seat and got the bottle of vodka and drank from it.

"Drink vodka, Mikey, so big-titted Ann Davis won't know you been drinking," he said aloud in the falsetto voice little boys use to imitate girls. He drank from the bottle again. "I'll bet those big tits aren't real. I bet if you poked them with a pin they'd sag like hound's ears."

It made him feel better to speak of her that way, so he thought of the vilest adjectives he knew and applied them to various parts of her body.

He drove to the Dixie Drive-Inn and bought a can of grapefruit juice and a glass of ice and telephoned R. L. Squires and told him to meet him at the Dixie and to bring some whisky with him. Damned if he would go home now and sit and listen to Rita Jean moan. He remembered the Citizens Council board meeting. He better go. An officer and board member should be there. He signaled for the carhop.

"You know Mr. R. L. Squires, don't you?"

"Yes, sir."

"When he comes tell him I'll be back in about an hour. Tell him to wait here for me."

The meeting was in the Hotel Ashton's small dining room, the one used by the Civitan Club for its weekly luncheons. The Rotary, Kiwanis and Lions used the large dining room. Anse Hayes was standing when Mike walked in. There were eight men seated in a cluster in the center of the room.

"Hi, Mike," Anse said, glancing at his watch. "You're not late. We were just starting."

"Sure," Mike said and pulled a chair from the wall to the fringe of the group and sat astride it, resting his folded arms on the back. "Go ahead. But I gotta go before too long."

"We're going to make it short and sweet tonight," Anse said. "Fact, we're going to dispense with reading the minutes. We simply want to talk about this thing awhile and decide what our first step should be."

"Want me to tell you what our first step as you call it should be?" Mike said, surprised to hear himself speak out at a board meeting. "We oughta go right out there to that black son of a bitch's shack and lay a little leather to his back. That's what our first step oughta be. Then there wouldn't havta be no second step."

"Now, Mike," Anse smiled. "You know we don't condone such things."

"You god-damned right I know it. That's what's wrong with the Citizens Council now." Mike saw the eyes of the other men—the town's richest and most influential citizens—watching him. Some of them nodded at his words. "You know what that bastard Carter over in Greenville called us. 'Uptown Ku-Kluxers,' he said. Well, he's just about right. Sissies would have been a better word. We don't never do a damned thing at these meetings but talk about what's the first step gonna be. We oughta get down off our high horses and get out the sheets and get things settled once and for all."

"There's a lot of truth in what he says," said Sheriff Copeland, who was sitting across the group from Mike. He patted the .45 pistol holstered at his side. "This is about the only thing some of them niggers is gonna understand."

Chester Blinken, Sr., stood. "Gentlemen, gentlemen," he said, shaking his bald freckled head to show his disapproval, holding his thick, short outstretched hands in front of him. "We organized to uphold the tradition of segregation of the races in a peaceful, lawful manner. I realize this is something we all feel very strongly about.

But this kind of talk will get us nowhere. Let's get on with the matter at hand."

"Colonel Blinken," Mike persisted. "What can we do about the matter at hand, as you call it, by discussing it?" The hard-nosed old bastard, he thought, he may be my boss but he don't own me.

"Mike," the Colonel said, leaning forward with both hands resting on his cane in the pose which meant he was going to give you some good advice, "the Southern traditions have been a vital part of my very being since I was conceived. My grandfather helped settle this great land. Helped dig it out of the underbrush with only his hands and a few slaves. There is Blinken blood on every battlefield from Appomattox to Vicksburg. A Blinken has never been afraid to fight for what he believes. But this is a different kind of war and these are different times. We must remember our Christian principles. We can and will maintain the Southern Way of Life without resorting to violence."

Mike wanted to say that what his grandfather did didn't pull a damn bit of water now. And it doesn't make you any god-damned better than me. Look what your fat-assed son did in Korea—nothing but run a PX—and look what I did. And my old man didn't help settle nothing, not even the god-damned grocery bill. You're not even a real colonel. Some governor just handed you a piece of paper saying you were because you donated to his campaign. But he didn't say any of these things.

"I don't like to argue with you, Colonel," he said, "but I believe you still have to fight for something you want. If we don't lay open some black backs and do it soon, the niggers gonna keep edging in on us and first thing I know one'll be settin' next to my little towheaded gal over in Sarah Weaver School. When that happens I'm taking my shotgun and going to school myself. I don't know how y'all feel about it, but I'm ready to fight and die in the streets to protect my little ole towheaded gal. How about you, Colonel, are you ready to fight in the streets for the Southern Way of Life? Or have you lost interest cause your kids are grown?"

Mike held his breath. But he saw that everyone was looking at the Colonel, not him.

"Well . . . now, Mike, now, I don't think it'll ever come to that in this great country of ours. We have laws and losing a legal battle or two doesn't mean we've lost a war. No, sirree. Not by a long shot, it doesn't. Why, Senator Wakefield was telling me just last week—"

"But if it did. If it came to that, would you?" Mike watched the others as they waited for Colonel Blinken's answer.

"Why, yes, of course. Certainly, my boy. All of us here would, I'm sure. Wouldn't we, fellows?" He glanced nervously around the room and as he looked at each of the eight men his look was answered by a quick nod.

Mike's eyes followed the Colonel's uneasy eyes as they skimmed the room. He saw each of the eight men nod. Men whose family names were posted on street signs and school fronts and arches at park entrances all over town. Names chiseled in concrete over store entrances and painted in gold on the windows of the offices along cotton row. They were the sons of sons. There was even a tiny community north of Ashton called Copeland Corners where Slim Copeland's people had settled. Not that the Copelands were much on a stick, but there were a lot of houses out there under old trees where Copelands lived under roofs put up by Copelands. And if a Copeland needed help he knew he could go there and get help. Yes, even Slim Copeland, and everybody knew a Copeland wasn't much on a stick.

"I'm sorry, Colonel," Mike muttered. "I guess I got a little excited. I wasn't questioning your . . . your . . ."

"Never mind, son," the Colonel said. "Don't apologize for your enthusiasm toward our sacred cause. Why, when I was your age—"

"That's right, Colonel," Anse interrupted. He wanted to get home early and he knew if the Colonel got wound up he would orate all night. "This is something we all feel very strongly about and must take action on immediately. So let's get on with the business at hand."

The Colonel nodded and sat down. Few had anything to say after that and Anse named a committee of three Ashton lawyers, from a long list of volunteers, to assist State Attorney General Anderson in defending Oswalt if the case actually got in the courts. All those present were asked "to give the matter much thought and prayer." It would be brought up again for more detailed discussion next week when the board met prior to the public meeting at the fairgrounds.

"There'll be Citizens Council officers from throughout the state at that meeting." Anse said. "We are not in this fight alone."

When Colonel Blinken said amen to close the prayer that adjourned the meeting the board members went immediately to Mike and shook his hand and patted him on the shoulder and mumbled that they "know how you feel, son." Even Hamp Auld, who rarely attended these meetings himself, paused on his way out to say, "There was a lot of good sense in what you said tonight, Heaney."

Mike stood by his chair until they all had walked past him and on into the lobby of the hotel. Then he walked slowly out behind them, not stopping to join the conversations that had begun in the lobby, and went to his car.

R.L. was waiting for him at the Dixie.

"Damn, Mike, you took long enough," R.L. said when he opened the door to get into Mike's car. He always left his car at the Dixie and they went in Mike's car. Mike liked to drive. "Where the shit you been all night?"

"To the Citizens Council meeting. I told you."

"Yeah, but I mean before that. I called your house and Rita Jean said you'd already gone. But the CC meeting didn't start till ten."

"You bastard. You didn't tell that to Rita Jean, did you?"

"Naw. Hell, you know better than that. But where'd you go?"

Mike pressed on the horn. "Where's that god-damned nigger? I need a drink."

"Where'd you go, Mike? You can tell me."

"Did you bring some whisky? I can't stand the taste of this Russian panther piss any longer. Who said it don't taste?" He tossed the half-empty vodka bottle onto the back seat.

R.L. pulled a pint bottle of Early Times from the right front pocket of his khaki pants. He was grinning. "Come on, tell me. If you didn't take me and Rita Jean didn't know where you was you was tomcattin'. Wasn't you, now?"

"I wouldn't say I was and I wouldn't say I wasn't," Mike said softly, looking past R.L., out the car window, across the broad new highway and the cotton field beyond it. They say that on a clear night you can see the levee, fifty miles away from here, because the Dixie was on a rise at the foot of the hills and the delta was so flat; but the moon was bright tonight when one of those clouds didn't cover it and he couldn't even see the Windham house. He drank from R.L.'s bottle and sucked on his cigarette. The young Negro carhop appeared beside the car then.

"Took you long enough," Mike said. "Bring us three Cokes and a bowl of ice. Bring some lemons too."

The carhop nodded and ran back to the building.

R.L. chased his drink from the bottle with a cigarette as Mike had done. "Come on now, tell me about it." Smoke followed his words from his mouth.

Mike blinked his eyes. That drink sure got to me quick, he thought, and it's been an hour or more since I drank the vodka. "A gentaman don't discuss such things," he said.

"Since when did you become a gentleman?" R.L. laughed. "You're sure funny, Mike. Real funny. Damn if you ain't."

Mike's big hand shot out and his thick fingers grabbed the material of R.L.'s shirt and lifted the surprised, slat-thin man across the seat until he was facing Mike's snarl. "I'm as much a gentleman as any of those fat-assed bastards," Mike said in R.L.'s face. "As any of 'em, you get that?"

"Sure, Mike," R.L. said, squirming loose carefully and easing back to his side of the seat. "I didn't mean nothing by that. I thought you were making a joke. Hell, you know what I think of those fat-assed bastards."

"Wanta have some fun?" Mike said.

"That's the god-damned idea, ain't it? You know me, Mike."

"Okay," Mike said, "just sit tight." He pushed the air vent around so the breeze the car made would hit his face. Then he turned the key and the motor caught and roared when his foot went down and the tires spun in the gravel, then caught and the sedan plunged toward the highway that led south.

———————————

The sedan skidded to a stop at the gate at the end of the path that led to the steps of the shack. Mike and R.L. stepped out into the dust cloud that flecked gold in the moonlight and caked when it settled on their sweating faces. Mike spat twice in rapid succession but the salty taste that squeezed out of his pores and ran down his hot face and into his mouth remained in his mouth. He wiped his face with his shirtsleeve and stood spraddle-legged beside the car and looked at the shack.

"That Tatum nigger lives here, Mike," R.L. said. "What're we gonna do?"

"We gonna scare some sense into his head, that's what," Mike said. "Gimme that bottle."

R.L. handed him the pint. Mike made gargling sounds as he sloshed the whisky around in his mouth. Then he swallowed it and sucked on his wet cigarette, rose to the balls of his feet and flexed his thigh muscles inside the khaki cloth of his pants and handed the bottle back to R.L.

"You think we oughta?" R.L. asked, looking over his shoulder at the main road that ran into the hills a hundred yards away.

"You mighty well right we oughta," Mike took the bottle from R.L.'s lips. "Somebody's gotta and nobody else's got the guts."

Mike stuffed the bottle in his hip pocket and raised his booted right foot and kicked the gate open. Then he strode resolutely along the foot-beaten path and clomped onto the bare boards of the porch floor.

"All right, you black son of a bitch, open up," he shouted at the unpainted door and kicked it.

No sound came from inside the shack and Mike kicked the door again. "We know you in there, Shine Tatum."

A thin, yellow light showed at the cracks bordering the door, flickered dark and showed again. The schuck-schuck of slippered feet moved toward the door from the inside.

"Now you showin' sense," Mike shouted. "We was just about to kick the god-damned door down." He turned his head and said over his shoulder, "And we could do it too, couldn't we, R.L.?"

R.L. stood statue-still a step inside the yard by the rail gate. A cloud moved across the moon, causing the darkness to press down upon him. Then the cloud moved past and the dark, silent hills sprang up behind the cabin again and the thin yellow light—brighter but thinner than the lamp light through the cabin cracks—splashed on the tin roof. The cabin door opened and he could see Shine's wrinkled black face clearly as the Negro held the lamp shoulder high to see who his midnight caller was.

"Let's get outta here, Mike," R.L. said, very low, then again, louder, "Let's get outta here."

If Mike heard he ignored it.

"What you want?" Shine asked, his face expressionless as he looked from the big man on the porch to the smaller, shadowy figure by the gate, then back to the big man on the porch.

"You know damned well what we want," the big man growled. "We gonna find out if you gonna keep on N-double-A-C-P'ing, you nigger son of a bitch, you." Shine had known they would come and he had known they would come at night. They always came at night. He had prayed it would not be someone like Mr. Mike. But somehow he had known too that it would be. What had the man in the yard said? It sounded like "Let's get outta here." Maybe he should try to reason with that one. He hoped the boy would sleep through it all. He could take the beating himself but the boy was only a baby really. Only a baby. He looked into the big man's eyes and the hand that held the lamp shook. You can always tell by the look in a white man's eyes if he is going to give you just a regular cussing out or if he wants to hurt you. This man must hurt him before he went to his bed tonight. Maybe if he fell to his knees and begged him not to hurt him he would be satisfied. But he knew he couldn't do that now. "Don't stand there with your eyes popping out," the big man said. "Say something. And it better be right."

"What do you want me to say, Mista Mike?"

"You know damn well what. You gonna stop this N-double-A-C-P'ing? Stop this crap about suing to vote. Don't ask me what. You know what."

"Mista Mike, I don't want to make folks mad at me, but I got to vote. It's my right."

Whack!

The lamp fell from Shine's hand when Mike's thick hand slammed against his cheek. The glass chimney smashed. The kerosene spilled out onto the dry boards of the porch floor and the flame from the wick spread oily and yellow and smoky over the spillage.

Mike struck out again and Shine's bony shoulder bounced against the door frame. He wished he would bleed. Maybe Mister Mike would be satisfied and go home if he would bleed for him.

"Come on, you bastard," Mike said as he grabbed Shine's loose nightshirt and jerked him off the porch. "Get in the car, R.L. We gonna show this nigger what we do to stinkin' black sonsabitches that think they as good as a white man."

He pushed and kicked the trembling but silent Shine along the path, through the gateway and into the back seat of the sedan. It was then that Shine, dazed by the blows, saw the flames growing on the porch.

"The boy! The boy!" he shouted. "The boy's in the cabin. He'll burn up."

"Let him burn," Mike said.

Joe Adcock, county coroner, squatted beside the body and chewed on a grass stem. The wind pushed most of the odor away from him but now and then it hit him full in the face and almost made him vomit. People always said, "Old Joe Adcock sure ain't afraid of a dead corpse." It helped him get re-elected every four years. So he squatted there beside this body as if the smell and the sight of it didn't bother him any more than it bothers a doctor to look at a gut he has just split wide open.

"I'd say it's been in the river, oh, bout two, three days," Joe Adcock said. "It's hard to tell though, the way the turtles got to it."

"Two, three days, huh?" Slim Copeland said. He stood a few paces away, focusing his eyes on a bush about ten feet the other side of the spot where the smell came from so the men behind him would think he was studying the condition of the body. "I think you bout right, Joe."

"I oughta be," Adcock said. "I been in this business a many a year now. You get so you can tell pretty quick when you've seen as many as I have alayin' on the river bank."

Jess Berkley eased up behind Sheriff Copeland. "I thought I'd bust a gut when I seen them legs sticking outta the water like that," he said, glancing quick at the body, then away from it. "I didn't touch it. Just left it right where it was. I knew better'n to touch it. Might mess up some evidence for you. Went straight to the store and called you. I know better'n to fool around with stuff at the scene of a crime before the sheriff gets there."

"You did the right thing," Copeland said, turning his back on Adcock and the body to talk to Berkley. "Course, we don't know yet if a crime is involved."

"Yeah, I know," Berkley said. "I couldn't see it was a nigger at first. I didn't know who it might be. Tried to think if I'd heard about anybody disappearing lately. You know, I had a cousin once who found a body in a river and he got a four-hunerd-dollar reward. Not that I'd want anything for just doing my duty and calling you. But if it'd been a white man there might'v been a reward of some kind, might'n they?"

"Lots of times there is," Copeland said. He took off his straw hat and fanned his face with it. "Sure is hot today. Summer's sure on us.

Let's get in the shade."

"Know what nigger it is?" Berkley asked, following Copeland from the clearing toward the cluster of trees where the cars were parked and where a dozen or so men leaned against the cars and looked across the clearing to the spot where Joe Adcock squatted beside the body.

"I think so," Copeland said.

"You find it, Jess?" one of the men said as they neared the trees.

"Yeah, I found it," Berkley nodded.

"Whur ja find it?"

"Upriver bout a quarter of a mile. You know where that dog-leg is?"

"Oh, yeah."

"You shoulda seen old Joe Adcock floatin' it side his boat down to this clearin'. He couldn't even get it out at the dog-leg. You know how crumbly the bank is there."

"I fished it a many a time. I know."

"One thing about old Joe, he knows how to handle a dead corpse."

"He ought to."

"Who is it?"

"Some nigger."

"Oh."

"Know which one?"

"Sheriff says he thinks so."

12.

"HEAR ABOUT OLD SHINE?" the tall man asked, feeling the stubble at the point of his sharp chin.

"Yeah," his stocky companion said, placing a carefully folded paper napkin in his saucer to soak up coffee the waitress spilled when she pushed the cup at him. "Too bad. Bring a lot of bad publicity to the town. I hate like the dickens to see it happen."

"Yeah," the tall man said through a yawn. "Me too."

"Rush, this coffee gets worse by the day."

"We got a new coffee urn last month. Look at it over there. Cost the owners a small fortune."

"Maybe that's it," the stocky man said, rubbing a napkin in quick strokes, back and forth, across his protruding teeth. "A new pot hardly ever makes good coffee. It's like gumbo, never clean the pot you make gumbo in. Ruins the flavor."

"You complained all the time before we got the new urn."

"Maybe it's the *way* you make it. You put eggshells in it?"

"I don't make it." Rush looked up at the clock on the wall above the large, shining coffee maker. Seeing Anse polish his teeth like that always bothered him. It didn't seem sanitary.

Colonel Blinken was red-faced, more red-faced than usual, when he came into the hotel coffeeshop. It was hot already (it wasn't nine o'clock yet, but the heat had come in with the daylight) and the short walk from his department store made him pant. "Whew!" he said as he sat on the counter stool to the left of Anse. "It's hot already.

This air conditioner sure feels good. Don't know what we did without them." He signaled the waitress with his right index finger, as if making a bid at a cattle auction. She brought the coffee, without cream or sugar. He had been drinking it black every morning since the doctor told him three months ago that he had to lose weight.

"It's getting summer all right," Rush said. "Course I ain't been out yet this morning. Night man went on a toot again and I had to be on the desk all night. Haven't even been to bed yet."

"You fellows hear about old Shine Tatum?" Colonel Blinken asked, frowning his concern.

"Yeah," Anse said. "We were just talking about it."

"I've known Shine twenty years or more, I guess," Colonel Blinken said, still frowning, "and I never knew him to do anything out of the way."

"Me neither," Anse said. "Why, our bank loaned him the money to buy that buckshot farm."

"Is that so?" Rush said, shaking his head.

"Oh, he'd already paid it all back."

"It's a terrible thing," the Colonel said. "The killing, I mean."

"Sure is," Anse agreed, nodding. "Could bring some mighty bad publicity to the town. Mighty bad."

"I guess it might at that," the Colonel admitted. He touched the steaming cup to his lips, but put it back on the saucer without drinking any of the coffee. He meant the old Negro's death was terrible, but, now that Anse mentioned it, this kind of thing *could* bring some mighty bad publicity to the town. Mighty bad.

"You know, I was in the courthouse not thirty minutes before Shine did it," Anse said. "Not thirty minutes before in he walked, big shitty, shotty, into Oswalt's office with that nigger lawyer from New York and tried to bluff his way into gettin' to register."

"I heard he was just as nice and polite as if he was asking Oswalt for his old shoes," Rush said.

"Sounds like it most probably was," Anse said. "That's the way with a nigger. Stand right there bowing and scraping like everything was normal and be stealing you blind out the back door and lying to your face about it."

"I know *exactly* what you mean," Rush said. "We had a maid here at the hotel we had to let go for stealing last week. Acted like a real, old-fashioned, country nigger gal—polite and hard working and all. We'd just raised her pay to fifteen a week when the hotel's head cook told me we was missing too much stuff out of the kitchen to be ignored as piddlin' stealing and last week we found out it was her—this maid—that was taking all that stuff. She didn't even deny it—except to say she didn't take all that was being taken. She claimed she had to take because she had four kids and her auntie was sick. And you know what she said? She said she took it because her kids needed a balanced diet. That's just what she said—'a balanced diet.' Now, niggers didn't talk like that before the war."

"Rush, I wish you wouldn't pay maids so much at the hotel," Anse said. "We get one at the house that's doing pretty good and first thing you know she's quit and working here. Or threatening to cause she says she's got a cousin working here making fifteen a week. Keep it up, I tell you, and everybody in town'll have to go up to fifteen."

Ches Junior walked up while Anse was scolding Rush for paying the hotel maids too much. He sat beside his father and it was easy to see that in twenty years he would be a freckle-for-freckle twin of the bald little man.

"You fellows heard about old Shine, I guess," Ches said.

"Yeah," Anse said. "We were just sitting here talking about it."

"I swear! I don't see how anybody could do a thing like that," Ches said. The waitress waited for him to order. Sometimes he ate breakfast there and sometimes, on a morning after a party, he drank milk instead of coffee.

"That's just what we were saying," Anse said. "Especially uh old nigger like Shine. You'd think he'd know better."

Ches looked up, surprised. "Shine?" he said. "Oh, you mean him trying to register. I meant I don't see how anybody in Ashton County could've killed him just for doing what he did. Hell, they could've scared him off without killing him."

"Nobody knows for sure yet what really happened," Anse said. "A lot of things could have happened. A lot of things. We don't know how scared he was of those New York niggers that talked him into doing what he did."

Ches pulled a newspaper from his pocket and unfolded it. "The *Commercial Appeal* says right here it looked like he was killed—the way his head was bashed in—before he was dumped in the river," he said, thumping the front page.

Anse and Rush and the Colonel bent forward to read the two-column headline in the center of the page.

"You gonna order now, Mister Ches?" the waitress asked. "Yeah, bring me a cup of coffee and two doughnuts."

"I'm surprised at the *Commercial Appeal,* putting something like that on the front page," Rush said. "His head could have been bashed by a floating log. That's not very reliable newspapering, I'd say."

"They must have a new man around here," Colonel Blinken said. He had read the *Commercial Appeal* every morning, after having coffee with the boys, for forty-five years and his daddy before him had read it every morning, after having coffee with the boys, for more years than that. *Commercial Appeal* in the morning, *Dispatch* in the evening. Why, they put the *Commercial Appeal* printing press on wheels during the War Between the States and moved it around out of the way of the Union troops and kept publishing a paper. You don't jump to conclusions about a paper like that. "That must be it," he added. "A new man wouldn't know Ashton County the way Horace does. If Horace had written it it'd have his name on it. They must have a new man."

"Yeah, you're right, Colonel," Anse said. "I saw Ken coupla weeks ago and he asked me how we liked the new man the *CA* had down here. I told him I didn't know, since I hadn't never seen the guy."

"I know the *Commercial Appeal,*" the Colonel said.

"I hope they haven't got another Yankee," Rush said. "Remember that DiMaggio fellow they had a year or so ago? The Italian that claimed he was Joe DiMaggio's cousin? He didn't understand *nothing* about this country. Boy! was I glad to see him leave."

"I'd hate to see them have a Yankee kid reporting for them too," Anse said. "Especially with a thing like this happening and young Phil back and all."

"I hadn't thought of that," Rush said. "I hate to see what he'll have in the *Dispatch* this afternoon."

"I don't see why you have to go jumping on Phil before he's even done anything," Ches said.

"We weren't jumping on him," Rush said. "But you know how he messes up a story involving niggers."

"I've never been chairman of a fund drive that I didn't get full cooperation from the *Dispatch,*" Ches said. "Full cooperation every time."

"Sure," Rush agreed. "But, like I say, get a nigger into something and the whole damn bunch over there goes crazy. Been that way ever since young Phil came back from the Navy. You remember the stink he raised about putting niggers' names on the memorial."

"Yeah, but what's so bad about that?" Ches looked at his father. "Dad himself here . . ."

"Son," the Colonel interrupted, "you ought to listen to what Mr. Gamble says. Think about it before you pop off, out of loyalty, and loyalty's a fine thing, mind you, but. . . . Well, just don't go around saying things you might be sorry for later."

"I know how young folks are, Colonel," Anse said. "They think us old heads get too excited about little things when it comes to this nigger issue. But we know there ain't no middle ground. Give 'em an inch and they'll take a mile, so to speak."

"Naw, don't worry about it none, Colonel," Rush said. "We know Ches thinks right. He's got a good solid states' rights, God-fearing background. But it's not every youngster around these days got the advantage of that kind of home life."

"I still don't see what makes everybody so down on Phil," Ches said sullenly. He never knew, exactly, how to react to the solid front he always faced when he disagreed with a member of his father's generation. "Do you know how Ashton got picked the cleanest city its size in the state? From a scrapbook full of *Dispatch* clippings, that's how. Why did we get the furniture factory? Mr. Arrow went up to Indiana, at his own expense, and talked to a newspaper friend of his who had gotten to be president of the company, that's how. How come we finally got the slums cleared up in the quarters across from the courthouse? The *Dispatch* ran pictures on the front page every day for two months of the filth those people lived in and showed everybody where their cooks were coming from before they put their hands in the biscuit dough, that's how come."

"Exactly the kind of thing we mean," Anse said. "He spent all that time and paper space taking up for those niggers in the quarters. Who had to put out the money to put toilets in all those shacks? The taxpaying white people of this town, that's who."

"You're mad because Hamp Auld had to put out some money," Ches said. "He owned most of those shacks."

"Now, son . . ." Colonel Blinken started.

"Don't think Mister Auld will ever forget about it either," Anse said angrily. "Just one more score he has to settle with the Arrows."

"I think that's a big part of it," Ches said. "I think Hamp Auld has it in for Mister Arrow and you fellows take everything Hamp Auld says as gospel."

"Son!" the Colonel said sharply. "You watch your tongue. You hear!"

"Yes, sir," Ches said, subdued by his father's tone.

"Don't worry about it, Colonel," Anse said. "He'll learn. We aren't worried about where a Blinken will stand when the time comes to be counted."

Herb Richards, who owned the service station across Main Street from the hotel, came in at his regular time.

"Hi, men," he said. He was a jittery man of average height, with a broad, owlish face on a thin, slat body. "Guess you heard about old Shine Tatum."

"Yeah," Rush said. "We been talking about it all morning."

"Guess everybody is this morning," Richards said, cracking his finger knuckles one by one. "Yeah, give me a cup of coffee."

"We were just sayin' how bad it is for the community," Anse said. "Look here in the *Commercial Appeal* already."

"I seen it," Richards said, cleaning the lens of his glasses with quick, jerky movements. "What you reckon they want to go puttin' stuff like that in the Memphis paper for?"

"It's nothing to what'll be in *Time* magazine this week, I'll bet," Rush said.

"Our own yellow sheet, the *Dispatch,* will be bad enough," Anse said, looking at Ches.

Ches appeared not to hear, concentrating on cutting the dough-nut with a fork, but a wave of pink passed over his father's bulbous face, moving up from his collar to the top of his freckled head.

"I don't know what an old nigger is thinking about to go get messed up in something like that," Richards said.

"Ain't it the truth," Rush said. "But you know they have no community spirit."

"I heard the nigger Tatum had been holding meetings out at his shack," Richards said. "Forty, fifty of 'em be there at a time; regular prayer meetings with everbody gettin' all voodooed up and raving about taking over the state. Regular Mau Mau meetings, I heard."

"You see, Ches," Anse said, placing a friendly hand on Ches's shoulder. "No telling what happened to Shine, mixed up with all that. He musta gone batty in his old age."

"Where'd you hear that, Herb?" Ches asked. "I hadn't heard anything like that."

"Preacher Grubbs from out at Crutchfield Crossings told me," Richards said. "Tell you something else. He said he heard it was all tied in with Just-Ten Acres and the Allens. You know Shine Tatum lived not far from Just-Ten."

"Be damned!" Rush said. "I never thought of that."

"Shows you don't know what goes on right here in Ashton County," Anse said. "Trouble is we're too gullible. Times has sure changed. Can't tell nowadays what's goin' on in a nigger's head."

"You see, son?" Colonel Blinken said. "You can't just jump up and defend people before you know what you're talking about. You always were impulsive." He smiled at Anse. "Guess we can't be too hard on a boy for being impulsive, can we, Anse? That's part of being young."

"Sure, Colonel," Anse said. "It's like I told you, don't worry about it. A boy with Ches's background is gonna stay hitched when the time comes."

"I wasn't talking about Shine Tatum or Just-Ten Acres," Ches said weakly. "I was talking about Phil Arrow and what the *Dispatch* has done for Ashton."

"I know, Ches," Anse said. "But the point is, the way times are you either on one side or the other. And I'm not too sure which side Phil Arrow's on."

Rush yawned and stretched his long arms over his head. "I don't know about you fellows but I got to get some sleep fore I fall on my face." He stood and stretched up from his toes.

"I got to get to the bank," Anse said and took a quick swallow from his coffee cup, gave his teeth a fast brush with his napkin and stood beside Rush.

Both men were reaching into their pockets when Colonel Blinken said, "It's on me this morning, men," and picked the green checks from beside their cups.

"I won't argue this morning, Colonel," Anse said. "I gotta rush. See you tomorrow."

"I'm too weak to argue," Rush said, following Anse into the lobby.

Richards swallowed the last of his coffee hurriedly.

"I gotta go too," he said, moving off the stool slowly.

"I got yours too," the colonel said, winking at him.

"Thanks, Colonel. See you, Ches."

The waitress picked up the three cups. "Want anything else?" she asked. "If not I'm going to get some breakfast before the nine-thirty coffee breaks start."

Ches was staring thoughtfully at the half doughnut he crumbled between his fingers.

The Colonel shook his head and when the waitress was gone he said, "Son, I don't want to fuss at you but you've got to watch your tongue. People around here are touchy about things now. It's not as if you were a kid. You're a grown man and people take what you say as coming from a grown man who knows what he's saying."

"What am I supposed to say when somebody says something I think is wrong? Dern it, I've known Phil all my life. Shouldn't I speak up for a friend?"

"Depends," the Colonel said carefully. "Heck, son, I know how you feel. I've always been close to Phil's daddy too. But you have to admit he's been acting strange lately. And you haven't been around Phil much to speak of in years. Don't forget he's lived up in New York City for, how long is it? Six years, or seven?"

"Six," Ches answered absent-mindedly, still crumbling the doughnut.

"Don't look so glum," the Colonel said and reached for his son's check. "I'll get this. You going out to the place today?"

"Guess I'd better," Ches said. "Mike's putting a crew of choppers in the field."

"See you later then."

"Dad?"

"Yes?"

"Dad, why can't anybody relax around here any more? How come all of a sudden you've got to be careful of who you take up for—friend or not? How do we know . . . I mean how *can* we know for sure who's who any more? Used to be all you had to know was somebody's name and you knew who he was."

"I don't know, son. . . . Something happened during the war, I think. It must have. Nothing's been the same since." The Colonel glanced about him and leaned closer to Ches's ear. "I'll tell you something for a fact, son. I haven't been comfortable here—right here in my own county—since that war . . . since Pearl Harbor. While the war was going on I had something to blame it on, of course. But since it stopped . . . I don't know. It just don't seem right somehow, not being comfortable where your roots are."

Ches looked at his father now. "I never heard you talk that way before, Dad," he said. "I thought it was just me that felt . . . I don't know . . . out of place or something."

"You *can't,*" the Colonel said quickly. "You can't feel out of place too. It's different with me. I'm old. I have reasons. . . . Driving past the factory on the way home every day is reason enough. Seeing that factory, that big brick factory, right where Granddaddy's house always was. . . . Cattle on prime cotton land. . . . Yeah, I have reasons to feel out of place, but not you, Ches. If you don't feel at home here, who does? Who can?"

Ches shrugged. "Anse and Rush seem to," he said.

"Yes, they do, don't they," the Colonel said thoughtfully.

"Aw, heck, Dad, forget it. I just got stirred up about Phil, what they were saying about him and all. I'm okay."

"Sure you are, son." The Colonel smiled now and pushed his right fist, which was wrapped around a dollar bill, gently against Ches's shoulder. "You and Mary Lee coming over tonight?"

"I guess so."

"Come on over. We'll have a couple while Momma's in the kitchen. Okay?"

"Okay."

The Colonel walked across the room to the cashier's cubicle.

"Hear about old Shine Tatum?" the cashier, a middle-aged brunette widow who was in the Colonel's Sunday school class, asked.

"Yes," the Colonel said. "We were just talking about it."

13.

"DON'T GET SO DAD-GUM EXCITED, Phil." Sheriff Copeland didn't take his eyes off the pistol he was polishing as he talked. "There wasn't nothing we could do until we found the body . . . or found something."

"But you didn't even tell my reporter Shine was missing," Phil said. He was trying to keep his anger—which was being stoked with a mixture of disgust and a strange, faraway feeling of hopelessness—under control, but Copeland's casualness was too much to watch and he snapped, "You may be stupid but nobody's as stupid as you're trying to act right now, Copeland."

"Take care what you say, Arrow," the sheriff said, squirming in his chair and glancing up at the two deputies standing by the door. "No reason to get more excited about one nigger leaving home than another. Nigger women run in here everday or so hollering that their men ran off. Usually he's up in Dee-troit or Chicargo, or maybe just as far as Stetsonville getting a little strange pussy. That right, boys?"

The deputies grinned and nodded.

"But this man had filed a civil rights complaint!" Phil said, the disgust and faraway hopelessness smothering his anger. "That makes it news."

"Well, now, I ain't in the news business," Copeland grinned. "That's your game. Mine's peace officering and I can't make up lawbreakers like you can news. That right, boys?"

The deputies laughed and nudged each other.

"Okay, forget it," Phil said. "But now that you've found the body you *can* take the boy's story seriously. Did he say who took the old man that night?"

"Naw," Copeland said, stepping over to the window air conditioning unit to adjust the vents so it wouldn't blow the papers on his desk. "He didn't see nobody. Even if he thought he did how could we believe him? He said it was about midnight."

Phil rubbed a palm over his hair and down slowly over his face, as a man rubs sleep from his eyes. "What *have* you found out, sheriff?" he asked. "You are investigating the case, I suppose."

"I had men looking around the riverbanks for clues," Copeland said, returning to his chair and lowering his bulk into it.

"What about the boy? Have you talked with him again?"

"What about?"

"Never mind. Where is the boy now?"

"How the hell should I know? It ain't my job to look after snotty-nosed nigger kids. That's for the welfare department."

Phil pivoted and brushed past the two deputies at the door. Outside in the heavy heat of midday he slowed his pace and rubbed the back of his neck. What a day to have a headache. He had only three, or maybe four, drinks last night but sometimes bourbon did him like this. This was a bigger story than the Emmett Till murder and he had nothing more than was in the *Commercial Appeal* this morning. Nothing, that is, except the remarkable fact that the sheriff seemed to know no more than a street-corner gossip did about the case.

"Hello, Phil."

Phil looked up and saw the Reverend Percy Stanford, the Episcopal rector, had walked up beside him as he stood pondering his next move.

"Hello, Mr. Stanford. How are you?"

"Hot," the rector said. He was a thin, little man of about fifty, with a sensitive, aristocratic face. He had come to St. Mark's Church from Richmond, Virginia, while Phil was in New York. Ann was Episcopalian ("My one Crutchfield heritage," she said), and Phil had gone to church with her and her mother the past two Sundays.

"Sure is." Phil smiled. He liked the little minister, liked the way he talked practical religion in his calm, literate sermons.

"Working on the Tatum killing, I suppose," Mr. Stanford said.

"Yes," Phil said. "But I'm not getting much."

"People are terribly upset about it," Mr. Stanford said. "I've had, oh, maybe ten phone calls today from people wanting to talk about it. I think a lot of people in this town feel guilty about it. Feel as if the town's attitude toward Negroes caused it to happen. They don't say that, of course. But I get that idea talking to them. That's why they call me about it, I think."

"I wish I could believe it," Phil said, his spirit rising at the suggestion. "Seems to me everyone wants to ignore it. Forget it happened."

"I'm sure it does," Mr. Stanford said, "talking to the people you have to deal with on the story. But don't forget that this town is not made up exclusively of Copelands. Don't forget people live in every one of those houses you passed on your way to work this morning. Decent people, honestly concerned with the moral atmosphere of the community their children will grow up in. Don't let the exaggerated cases you meet in your work cause you to forget the people in the ordinary little houses in the ordinary blocks all over this town."

"Thanks, Mr. Stanford," Phil said. "I needed that. Will you pardon me now if I run off? I've got a deadline."

"Sure, Phil," the rector said. "Come by and see me first opportunity you get. I'd like to talk more about this."

"I will," Phil said. Then he went back into the courthouse and telephoned Ranch. "Go ahead with Dunham's story," he told Ranch. "I don't have anything new. You might insert a graph saying that Copeland said this afternoon that he had no clues in the case."

"No editorial on it today then?" Ranch said.

"No, dammit, no editorial," Phil snapped and hung up. He lit a cigarette. He would think in here awhile. It was too hot outside. First thing he must do was find the boy, Cooter. Maybe he should write an editorial for the second edition. Ranch was disappointed that he didn't say he would. But what could he write? "Negroes should not be found in the river in Ashton County. It gives the community a bad name." That's actually all he knew, or felt, about the case now. The telephone calls Mr. Stanford had received. He would tell Ann about them. These were the people he had to keep in mind as he covered this story. These were the people who would come out of their decent, ordinary little houses in those decent, ordinary neighborhoods and demand justice when the *Dispatch* gave them the facts.

He walked into the long corridor and toward the double glass doors at the end of it. A Negro trustee in striped pants and a white T-shirt opened the door for him.

"Thanks," he mumbled and walked out and to his car.

He drove to Werner Park and when Ann was in the car with him he told her briefly all he knew about the case, wishing it was enough to erase the look of resignation from her face.

"I'm going to try to find the boy," he said. "Maybe I can get something from him that will be a lead. Copeland wouldn't recognize one if he heard it."

They went first to Shine's store on Hooker Street. A Negro man was sitting on the steps under the front door. When they got out of the car and walked to him he stood and nodded and held his beaten old hat in his hands at his chest as if he expected them to scold him. It was the one they called Crazy Tom, who worked for Shine when he worked at all.

"Hello, Tom," Phil said. "Have you seen Cooter today?"

"No suh," Tom said. "I ain' eben seed Mista Shine. I been comin' to wuk the las' three days now and Mista Shine ain't."

"Tom, Shine won't be here," Phil said. He hesitated, then decided someone had to tell him. "Shine's dead, Tom. Do you understand that? That's why I have to find Cooter. Do you have any idea where he might be?"

Tom's huge shoulders sagged. He sat down on the steps again and chewed his bottom lip. "Who I gonna wuk for now?" he said. His powerful body shuddered inside the faded blue overalls and the red shirt he always wore. (Ann had the uneasy feeling she was watching the enormous body of a warrior being moved by the mind of a child.)

"You don't know where Cooter might be, Tom?" Phil asked again.

"Mista Shine dint even tell me he was sick," Tom said. "Now hows come he dint? I coulda took him some chicken soup." Tears rolled down his shiny black cheeks and he turned away from them and ran around the corner of the store toward the alley.

"Oh, Phil . . ." Ann said, reaching to touch his arm.

"Don't worry about him," Phil said. "He'll be all right. He's learned to take care of himself no matter what comes along. He's like a stray dog. He's learned to survive on instinct."

He took her hand and they walked back to the car. "I suppose the logical place to start looking is the cabin," he said, sliding in under the steering wheel.

They drove to the Tatum cabin. The front porch was charred badly from a recent fire. Dunham's story had mentioned that. Shine's pickup truck was parked by the chicken house, about twenty yards east of the cabin. The door was not locked, so they went inside.

The main room of the two-room cabin was L-shaped. The walls and ceiling and exposed two-by-four rafters were freshly painted a dazzlingly clean white. The floor was battleship gray. Remembering how dark and cavelike most of these cabins were, Phil made another mental mark in Shine's favor. A crude table with a green oilcloth cover stood stiffly in the middle of the room, surrounded by five empty, cane-bottomed chairs. The kitchen equipment, crowded into the tiny inset made by the partition for the other room, was cold and unused on the shelves behind the black wood-burning stove. A large water pitcher, its porcelain glaze chipped, sat empty on the table. A gourd dipper hung on a nail by the stove and another pitcher, larger than the one on the table, sat in a small, zinc washtub on an unpainted table under the hanging gourd.

"This must be the boy's room," Ann said.

Phil looked into the tiny room: at the rumpled bed; the book on the floor by the bed; the silent clock on the varnished table by the bed; the magazine pictures of Jackie Robinson, Sugar Ray Robinson, and Sammy Davis, Jr., pasted on the faded wallpaper over the head of the bed; the two horseshoes nailed on the wall over the unpainted, Sears, Roebuck bureau.

"There's nothing here," Phil said. "Let's go."

"Shine slept over there, I guess," Ann said, pointing to the half-bed at the end of the rectangular main room opposite the kitchen corner. "He let the boy have the privacy of his own room."

"Yeah," Phil said.

On the way back to town he stopped at Mannie's and telephoned Ranch.

"Still nothing new," he said. "I'm looking for the boy now. Shine's nephew."

"Is the boy missing?" Ranch said. "Isn't that a story?"

"No," Phil said curtly. "It's not a story. I don't know whether he's 'missing' or not. He may have relatives he's staying with. Dammit, why don't they come in like ordinary people and trust you to help them? His own people are probably hiding him out somewhere."

"I don't really have to answer that one for you, do I?" Ranch asked quietly.

"No, I guess not."

"You going to write an editorial on it for tomorrow?"

"Not unless I find out more than I know now."

"Okay, you're the boss."

Phil stopped himself before he said, "And don't you forget it, damn you."

Back in the car he slumped into the cushion and stared at the dashboard until Ann asked, "Well, what next, Sherlock?"

"Damned if I know."

"I don't know much about these things, Phil," Ann said, lighting a cigarette, "but I just don't see how an old man can be dragged off and murdered without some clues being left. Hasn't the sheriff, or police, or whoever is supposed to do these things, found anything?"

"Not a god-damned thing."

"But they will . . . surely they will . . . won't they?"

"I don't know, Ann. It's not as if they were equipped to investigate a case like this. They even have to get the city police to take fingerprints when a grocery store is robbed out in the county. And those pistol-toting deputies know as much about police work as they learn watching television. I think they'd do something if they knew how."

"I should hope so."

"Look, darling, I'm beat. Do you really want to go to that Citizens Council meeting tonight? I've heard Mark Hadley and Governor Barrett rave and I can't see how you would be interested in anything either one of them has to say."

"Yes, I want to go. I've never been to a Ku Klux meeting. Should I wear my sheet?"

"Maybe it is a good idea for you to go. You're going to be surprised at how respectable it is. More like a big prayer meeting than a Ku Klux rally. Everybody dressed up fit to kill and . . ."

"Dressed fit to kill," Ann said. "That's a good one."

14.

THE CITIZENS COUNCIL'S open meeting was held at the stadium at the county fairgrounds. The grandstand was half filled when Phil and Ann arrived. That meant about six hundred perspiring people were there. The women, of course, looked cooler than the men, although most of the men wore suits made of the various new summer fabrics that had almost replaced the traditional cotton seersucker. A few men were dressed in khaki, but most of those who were stood in groups on either side of the narrow grandstand, smoking and chewing and watching the full-skirted women walk up the steep steps. A platform had been constructed on the race track in front of the grandstand and the special out-of-town guests and those who were scheduled to take part in the program sat on it, waving and shouting greetings to friends. Small, shouting children ran up and down the grandstand steps and played under it. Sousa marches blared from strategically placed loudspeakers, making conversation difficult.

"My God!" Ann said as she and Phil walked up the steep steps. "Are you sure this is the right place?"

"This is it." Phil couldn't help grinning at her bewilderment. "What did you expect, burning crosses and hoods?"

"I don't know. But I wasn't quite prepared for this. Why, it's more like a . . . a . . . well, a high school football game."

"How's this?" Phil pointed to a half-empty row above the bulk of the crowd. "Right on the fifty-yard line."

"Boy! When good old Ashton County organizes to hate niggers

it really does it up brown," Ann said, sitting on the rough planks and surveying the scene below her. "Where's the popcorn man?"

"You better keep quiet," Phil whispered.

"Why, are they looking for another victim? Look, there's Cousin Janie and Jerry. Hello, Cousin Janie! Oh, this is fun, Phil. Let's stay for the second lynching."

"Dammit, Ann, that's not funny."

"I know it."

"Ladies and gentlemen of Ashton County," the voice roared over the loudspeaker hanging behind them. It came from Anse Hayes, who stood before the microphone on the speakers' stand down on the track. Applause stopped him momentarily. Then he continued: "We are gathered here tonight to rededicate ourselves to the sacred goal of maintaining Southern traditions and the Southern Way of Life. We would not think of opening such a meeting without asking the Lord's guidance. I will now ask Brother Horace Stampley to give the invocation."

The Reverend Mr. Stampley, pastor of the Ashton Presbyterian Church, prayed cautiously. He asked that those present "search their hearts for the answer to the troubles that besiege our beloved Southland." He prayed briefly and tersely. Phil felt he did not approve of the meeting but, as many other Southern ministers, he probably was afraid that by refusing to attend and lead the prayer he would cut himself off from his congregation. The dilemmas facing a conscientious Southern newspaper editor were very similar animals.

The Reverend Mr. Stampley sat down and Anse stepped back to the microphone. He motioned to a thick-set, red-haired man in his early forties seated at the east end of the platform. The man stood and walked toward Anse and the microphone and there was a scattering of applause.

"Now, ladies and gentlemen," Anse said. "We have a most pleasant surprise for you. I don't have to introduce our state executive vice-president. You all know him as an outstanding journalist and tireless fighter for the rights of the individual in this age of the mixmonger. So here he is, Tom E. Simpson, better known as Whitey Simpson."

"Who is that?" Ann asked, and Phil explained that Simpson was one of three full-time employees of the state Citizens Council. He put out the monthly Council newspaper and wrote a four-times-a-week column for one of the capital papers and directed the Council's "education program" with the help of a former schoolteacher.

"Funny thing is," Phil whispered, "Whitey was once considered a radical. He's the youngest of six sons in a Hard Shell Baptist family. His dad is sort of a Hamp Auld type. Whitey was captain of the football team in college but after he graduated he couldn't seem to find his niche. He went to Europe for a few years and came back a changed man. Some say he belonged to a Fascist outfit over there. I don't know. Anyhow, he's been a little to the right of Louis the Four-teenth since he came back. When the Citizen's Council organized he was ready."

"As you all know," Simpson was saying into the microphone, "the weakest links in our plans for perpetual resistance to the mixmongers are, sadly enough, our very own children. They are so impressionable; tiny, helpless channels through which the mixmongers seek to infil-trate. With this in mind, your state Citizens Council has devised a plan to offset the plotters. After months of work I am happy to announce to-night the Council's statewide essay project for high school and junior high children. This is the natural follow-up for our highly successful elementary school storybook program so wonderfully handled thus far by Mrs. Bush. Students in our junior and senior high schools will be invited to write essays on assigned subjects such as state sovereignty and racial integrity. Cash prizes will be awarded the essays selected as best of those submitted each school semester. In conjunction with the project we are placing in the libraries of the schools sets of books es-pecially chosen as reference material for the contests. This material in-cludes Judge Tom Brady's *Black Monday* and other wonderful books. The students must, of course, obtain their material from this approved list of references. Well, folks, that's all I have to say, except that school administrators all over the state are co-operating wonderfully with us on this program. I just wanted to tell you about it tonight. Now I'll step down and let you hear the people you came here to hear tonight."

The applause was scattered. Phil hoped it was because those present were doubtful about the propriety of such an "educational" program. He feared, however, it was because Simpson was not a dramatic speaker and that many of those present had already heard about the program, which had been under way for several weeks since the beginning of summer school.

Anse stepped to the microphone and held his arms out, gesturing for silence. Then he said, "And now, ladies and gentlemen, the governor of our great state!"

The tall, gaunt man stood behind Anse, towering head and shoulders above him. His straight black hair was parted in the middle and shaved to the skin around his ears. He had the piercing eyes of an eagle and a large nose that jutted out of his bony face. His Adam's apple was enormous and bobbled like a fisherman's cork above the black bow tie as he talked. He wasn't as popular now, of course, as when he went into office almost three years before. But he was still a favorite at such meetings as this one and the applause was enthusiastic.

"Thank you. Thank you," Governor Barrett said. "It's always a pleasure to come up to Ashton County. I have so many friends up here and nowhere in the state is the true flavor of the old South so wonderfully preserved. It does my heart good to be here. But, ladies and gentlemen, I didn't come here to make a speech tonight. I came here to visit with you and to introduce the man you came to hear. As you know, during my term as governor of your state we have been able to fight back the relentless wave of mixmonger propaganda and keep peace while our sister states were torn with strife. We have been able to keep this peace because we have not wavered a moment. We have stood firm. My term as your governor ends a year and a half from now. And, according to the dictates of our state constitution, I cannot succeed myself in that office. It behooves the voters of this state, therefore, to select a man who will continue the unrelenting fight against the mixmonger hordes from the North. A man who will not waver. A man who will stand firm. Such a man, ladies and gentlemen, is your main speaker tonight. Such a man is Mark Hadley, an avowed champion of the Southern Way of Life. It is my proud and happy privilege to present him to you now. Ladies and gentlemen, Mark Hadley!"

It was an out-and-out endorsement of Hadley for governor and it surprised the people on the platform as much as it did those in the grandstand. Phil could see the startled expression on Anse's face as Hadley stepped forward and shook Barrett's hand and they smiled slyly at each other. It was a political bombshell dropped right in Jerry Windham's home town. And with Jerry seated in the grandstand, not even in a place of honor on the speakers' platform. As the applause built up slowly Phil watched Jerry loosen his collar and wipe perspiration from his forehead. It would be tough having to sit there now and listen to Hadley, but there was nothing else he could do. Walking out now would only make the situation more dramatic. And the more dramatic it was the more Hadley could capitalize off the talk about it that would spread quickly over the state. Well, Jerry may not be able to walk out, Phil decided, but he sure as hell could.

"Come on," he said to Ann. "Let's get out of here."

"I want to hear what Cousin Janie considers 'fine old-fashioned oratory,'" Ann said, but Phil stood and started down the aisle and she followed him.

As they picked their way out Hadley was saying: "I say we must get back to the fundamental truths. The world is degenerating to the alley cat morals of the days before the Flood. They are teaching our children that man is not a creature fashioned lovingly by the hand of God, the Father, in His own image. They are teaching our children that man is a mere accident of nature. A blob of chemicals that grew—evolved, if you please—like a tadpole changing to a frog. I stand here tonight, dear friends, and challenge any one of them highfalutin scientists to show me anywhere in the Bible where it says anything like that. Ohhhh! my friends, we must get back to the fundamental truths before it's too late. Look what they've done to Christmas—the birthday of our own dear Jesus Christ, who came to this troubled world to save us from sin. And look what they've done to Easter. Show me anywhere in the sacred Bible, dear friends, where it says anything about a big, fat Santy Claws and I'll hush up. Show me anywhere in the Bible, my friends, where it says anything about a egg-layin' bunny rabbit and I'll hush up. They can't show it to me. They cain't, because it ain't there, dear friends. It ain't there. And never mind that I say 'ain't' either. When I was comin' up on that Lee County farm we didn't have much time for school-ing. What we did have time for though was Bible readin'. And I say that if your governor—the present one or the next one—has to close the public schools to keep our race pure, then it won't be such a bad thing for all the sin they're teachin' inside those walls now. The tadpole religion. The Santy Claws Christmas and the bunny rabbit Easter. I say it wouldn't be so bad either for your governor, if necessary, to build a wall around this precious state to keep out those who would so corrupt our little children. Keep out the Walter Reuthers, the Northern press, the Commonists, the fellow travelers, the Moderates . . ."

The tall gate in the high, board fence which surrounded the race track (so people couldn't sit in their cars in the nearby fields and watch the stock-car races—the only kind of races held there now) closed behind them. They walked in silence the hundred yards or so up the gravel road to Phil's car. As they walked they could hear Hadley's voice and an occasional burst of applause, but it wasn't necessary out here to listen to his words.

"Are those the decent little people who live in those decent little neighborhoods you told me about?" Ann said, wishing immediately she hadn't said it.

"Yes, dammit," Phil said, opening the car door for her.

"If they come all the way out here in this heat to hear Hadley and Barrett and the rest of those nuts, how can you expect to reason with them?" she asked, then got into the car and closed her eyes as the door slammed loudly.

"What kind of crack was that?" Phil asked, when he had got in on his side.

"I'm trying to understand. You've been telling me how fine these people are. I want to know what they look like so I'll be able to recognize them if I'm going to live down here with you."

"Maybe it's a mistake for you to bother." His words surprised him, but he couldn't stop them. "Maybe you should live in New York where you never have to worry about who's decent and who isn't. Maybe you were meant to live in a sterile atmosphere like that—just not getting involved with anything your own little group doesn't approve of."

"Maybe you're right."

Both concentrated on the road as he drove her directly home. When he parked by the twin magnolia trees Ann looked at him across the space between them and sighed and opened the door and got out. He got out on his side of the car and walked behind her to the door.

"Well," she said, turning to face him when they reached the porch, "I guess I'll see you around."

"I guess so," he said, straining to keep from saying more, feeling juvenile but unable to do anything about it.

She went inside. He strode rapidly back to his car.

When he walked into the living room of his home his father was watching a Western movie on television.

"Hi Dad," Phil said, flopping into the chair at his father's right.

"Hi, son."

"What the hell are you watching?"

"A Western. I love 'em. Always have. This one has Bob Steele as the hero. You remember him."

"It's been a long time since I saw him."

"I saw him play a villain the other night. That's downright un-American. They ought not let the old cowboy heroes play villains, even if they do need the work. There oughta be a pension of some kind for them. Especially now. A kid sees Bob Steele as the hero in the afternoon on some rerun. Then that night he sees him as the villain on one of those modern adult Westerns. It's enough to shake him up psychologically. Heroes ought to be heroes and villains villains. It's the American way."

"I'm not so sure," Phil said. "But I'll agree it should be that way. Putting people in the correct category seems to be my main trouble right now."

The father studied the son's troubled face a moment, then reached out and turned off the television set.

"I thought you and Ann went to the Citizens Council meeting. Don't tell me it's over already." He looked at his watch. "Hadley never spoke less than two hours in his life."

"No," Phil said, rubbing the top of his head with a palm. "We left early. Dad, Barrett all but made a campaign speech for Hadley tonight. Right here in Jerry's home town. Hadley and his crowd knew Jerry wouldn't be up on the speakers' platform at a Council meeting. I don't know how they got Barrett to come out so early, but it sure puts the monkey on Jerry's back before he has time to get rolling. They're going to hang the 'moderate' label on him sure as shooting."

"Where's Ann?"

"I took her home."

"Oh? And it not nine o'clock. You two have a fight?"

"Dad, am I right about these people? I must be this time."

The father snuffed out his cigarette in the wide ashtray on the arm of his chair, stood and walked to the cabinet where the liquor was kept. "What do you mean?" he said. He took out a bottle of Scotch, placed it on the cabinet top and reached for a bottle of soda and two glasses.

"You know how I lashed out editorially before I went to New York. And you know what happened."

"What's that got to do with now?" Philip Arrow, Sr., asked the question quickly. He did not turn to face his son.

"Well, like you told me. I was losing my audience. People put up barriers against everything I wrote because I was trying to beat my ideas into them."

"Oh," Mr. Arrow relaxed and continued to mix the two drinks.

"Now I come back all set to go easy. To use the go-slow, logical approach. Be a part of the community. A voice among these people instead of a fire and brimstone preacher in a pulpit."

"And?" Mr. Arrow stepped over and handed a glass to his son and sat opposite him again.

"Thanks," Phil said. "And before I get started a harmless old Negro man is murdered and nobody seems to give a damn. The sheriff ignores it. Dammit, it looks now like the whole thing is going to be forgotten, as if a stray dog was hit by a truck on the highway instead of a human being killed and thrown in the river. I'm a newspaperman, Dad. Shouldn't I follow my conscience and put this whole mess in print as it really is? Or would that be making the same mistake I made six years ago? I think these people expect me to do that. I think they have the doors on their minds ready to shut as soon as I step out of line."

"You asking me for advice?" the father asked. "When I asked you to come back I promised I wouldn't give any more advice." He drank deeply from his glass.

"I thought I had everything all worked out then," Phil said. "It would have worked if this killing hadn't happened now. But this puts me on the spot—with Ranch, with Ann, with my conscience. I needed more time."

Mr. Arrow inhaled. "Why are you on the spot, son? Do you know something the sheriff doesn't know? Do you know Shine Tatum was murdered? If you don't know that, how can your conscience bother you?"

"Everybody in town knows that old man was murdered. I know it and you know it."

"I don't know it!" Mr. Arrow said, almost shouting. "I don't know it and you don't know it. Who are you, Jesus Christ? What right does a newspaperman have to accuse his neighbors? Pointing the finger. Forever pointing the finger. No wonder they hate him! No wonder they hate him no matter how much he tries to do for them! He's got no right to play God just because he happens to own a printing press!"

Phil saw the blood drain from his father's face and his eyes glaze over as if his system were shielding a physical pain that would have overwhelmed him if the shield had not been thrown up. He jumped to his father's side.

"What is it, Dad? Say, now, aren't we taking ourselves a little too seriously? Sit down a minute." He eased him back into the chair.

"Son, let's sit here and relax and get to know each other again," Mr. Arrow said. "We used to be close. It's been pretty damned lonely with you gone. Let's have a drink and relax. Make the night 'pass on way,' as the fellow says on that record you brought home."

"Okay, Dad," Phil said, but he knew the night would not "pass on away." If he had learned nothing else in New York he had learned that. He had to talk it out to someone. And he had to do it now. If he could only put some facts down and study them. Sure, he knew someone murdered Shine Tatum. Slim Copeland killed that Negro prisoner six years ago, too. But he had no facts then and he had none now. If he were a reporter on a New York paper he could write pages of emotional copy about the case with a clear conscience, because he knew a murder had been committed. But if he worked on a New York paper he would not have to face the people he accused. Before he could accuse his neighbors he must have facts. Ann should understand that. Ranch should understand it, too. But he couldn't ignore the killing, hard facts or not. If he had facts he could accuse a specific person. Without facts he would, if he did as Ann and Ranch would have him do, be accusing the entire population of Ashton.

He finished his drink. "I promised Jerry I'd drop by to see him after the Council meeting," he lied.

"Fix your old dad another drink before you leave. I think I'll just sit here awhile and listen to the record player." Phil mixed the drink and put it on the table beside his father's chair. He looked back at the man in the chair only once as he walked out the door.

When the son was gone the father sat thinking: I know a man who owns a little paper in south Mississippi. He has a son, younger than Phil but a grown man now. He taught his son to be a newspaperman too. Put him in the composing room when he was in junior high; in the advertising department when he was in high school; let him do a little reporting summers when he was in college. The boy studied business and marketing and advertising in college. Now he runs the paper and the father is an elder statesman type among the townspeople. Everyone is proud of the boy because he's made the paper an even greater business success. The boy was the state's "Outstanding Young Man" two years ago, in fact. He sure was. I'd forgotten that. And what did Philip Arrow do with his son? Pounded a so-called social consciousness into the boy and taught him all the god-damned clichés ever thought up by all the ivory tower journalism professors in the country. After his mother almost made a damned Baptist preacher out of him, it wasn't difficult. Truth is light, my son. Right makes might, my son. The good guys always win, my son. The boy soaked it all in through those big, trusting gray eyes of his. Then came the day. What a day! Sure he knew Copeland killed that poor old Negro drunk. God, would he ever forget that swollen head? But the Committee came that night and Philip Arrow, the senior, listened to them. These are tense times, the Committee said. A lot of publicity about a thing like this on the heels of the Supreme Court decision will ruin the town. You helped build this town, Philip Arrow. Do you want to see all your work and ours ruined overnight by a hotheaded kid, especially when the kid is your own son? Do you want that to mark him the rest of his life? No, you don't want that, Philip Arrow. But you don't understand. My son is a newspaperman. He's managing editor of this newspaper. He owns part of it. You don't understand what it means to a newspaperman to kill a story. What's more important to a newspaperman, Philip, killing a story or killing a town? Then Hamp Auld—silent in the background until then—put it another way. What's more important to a newspaperman, Arrow, killing a story or killing a newspaper? We'll kill your newspaper before we let that son of yours kill this town.

"Barrett really slipped me the shaft, didn't he?" Jerry said, handing Phil a drink. "I'll have to admit I wasn't ready for it. Goes to show, when you think you're big shit and take your eyes off the ground there's always somebody down there who's ready to throw dung up in your face."

"How many votes can Barrett swing to Hadley?" Phil asked.

"A hell of a lot," Jerry said, sitting in the big leather chair by the fenced fireplace. "Too many, with what he's built up over the years. Unless I can latch onto a chunk somewhere to offset it I'm in trouble."

"Got any plans?" Phil was reluctant now to mention his own troubles.

"I've been trying to think of someone I could get into the race to split the Citizens Council vote. But that would take more dough than I can get my hands on. I'd have to finance him, unless I could convince some joker he had a chance. And after Barrett's little surprise I'd have a fat chance doing it with anyone who wasn't an idiot."

"What about the Coast vote? The Council's not so strong down there, is it? Couldn't you offset Barrett with a big wet plank in your platform? Or, hell, promise them open gambling. It'd be better than letting Hadley win. They're gonna gamble down there anyhow."

"Well, well, Philip the All-American boy is getting practical. You said your eyes were opened in New York. I'm beginning to believe it."

"It's just that the most important thing now is to get you elected."

Jerry stirred the ice in his glass with a finger. "Don't go putting anything like that in the *Dispatch,*" he said cautiously. "It's better for people to think for a while that we're old schoolmates and nothing more. What I mean is, it wouldn't be good politics for the word to spread that you and I think alike on too many issues."

"Jerry, how long do we have to go on letting these people fool themselves? Contributing to the charade anyhow?" Phil said irritably. "Dad says I ought to ignore Shine Tatum's murder. You say you can't tell people we think alike. How long can politicians and news-papers keep this kind of thing up in this state?"

"What about Shine's death? What do you know about it? Has Copeland hit on anything new?"

"No."

"Then how can you do anything but ignore it? I talked to Cope-land this afternoon and he said he didn't have a single clue. Didn't even know, in fact, if the old guy fell in the river or was pushed."

"Jerry, you know and I know Shine was murdered. Hell, we've talked about this kind of crap too many times for you to sit there and tell me you don't know he was murdered!"

Jerry stepped to the window and stood looking out into the dark-ness that held the lights of Ashton, blinking in the distance. "Look at it this way, Phil," he said finally. "You can't say or do anything about Shine Tatum now. You raised too much hell about unimportant issues six years ago, so nobody will listen to you. If you had some-thing concrete in the case, you could. But you haven't. The day you start hollering 'murder' is the day everybody remembers you're a 'nigger lover.' Face it, Phil, you're an outsider in Ashton now. You can't do a damn thing until you prove to these people you are one of them again."

Phil rubbed his short hair, scratched his head, then rubbed his hand over his face. Then he said it. "I guess you're right. You and Dad. I wish I could make Ann and Ranch see it."

"Oho," Jerry said, smiling now. "Trouble with my luscious Yan-kee cousin, huh?"

"A little."

"Look, fellow, I wouldn't worry about that. If it's serious be-tween you, she's not going to let politics ruin it. She'll struggle. You just have to show her you know Ashton better than she does. As for Ranch, you don't have to worry about him. Hell, he works for you."

"I guess you're right."

"I know I am. Suppose you start raising hell, then find out Shine Tatum wasn't murdered. There is that chance, you know. Even a town is innocent until proven guilty. You talk about ideals. That's a pretty important presumption in this country. If any evidence turns up that says he was murdered, I'll be the first to tell you to open the gate. But if any evidence does turn up, how do you know the people of Ashton won't demand justice? You haven't given Ashton a chance."

"I knew I could see through this thing if I could find someone to talk sense with," Phil said. "I should have known you were the one."

Phil telephoned Ann from Jerry's and told her he was coming to get her. She said that she would be waiting. She was standing in the driveway when he drove up and ran to the car. He got out quickly and hugged her to him.

"Oh, Phil," she said. "I'm so glad you called. I called your house. I was trying to work up my nerve to call Jerry's. I'm such a smart aleck sometimes. I knew how upset you were about this killing and I needled you about it."

"I wasn't so sharp myself."

"I love you, Philip Arrow, Junior."

"I love you, Ann Crutchfield Davis."

"How did you know my middle name was Crutchfield?"

"I know the Crutchfields. Even if your mother did marry a Yankee, she was a Crutchfield."

She laughed. "Let's go somewhere. We can't stand out here in the driveway necking all night."

"Where'll we go?" he said, kissing her on the neck.

"I don't care."

"Let's drive out to Just-Ten Acres and have a quiet, sensible evening with the Allens."

"Quiet, sensible evening? Do you realize it's nearly eleven o'clock? This isn't New York, you know."

"Yes, that's one thing I do know," he said, half seriously, then continued lightly, "But the Allens have lived in New York. I need to unwind and they're the best unwinders I know. Unless you want to go to Stetsonville with me right now."

"That's exactly what I want to do," she said, snuggling against him. "But I have to keep up some kind of appearance for Mother's sake. She would never understand my leaving with you now. That is, she would understand but she wouldn't approve. Mother thinks a girl should be able to do anything a normal girl needs to do and still get home by one or two o'clock. If it takes you longer than that, there's something sinful about it."

"Let's go to the Allens then. At least we'll be moving."

They got in the car and he drove out the highway, turned and went past Mannie's store into the hill country—its gashed ugliness subdued by the darkness—past the dark cabin where Shine Tatum had lived. When he parked under the oak in front of the Allen farmhouse he decided they shouldn't stay because he saw no lights. Then he saw John walk to the edge of the porch and he cut off his headlights and stepped out of the car. John recognized the car and came toward them.

"Phil," John said, "am I glad to see you! I was afraid you didn't get my message."

"I'm afraid I didn't," Phil said, walking around to open the door for Ann, who already had it open and was getting out. "We decided to pop in on you folks in the middle of the night."

"Either way," John said, beside them under the oak now, "I'm glad you're here. We don't have a phone, you know, and I've driven that old heap of mine over these roads so many times it fagged out on me yesterday. Just when I needed it most."

"What is it, John?" Phil asked.

"I'm going to get a phone now for sure," John said. "Florence kept telling me the time would come when we'd need one. One of the kids get sick or something and we'd need somebody in a hurry. But I said, No, any time we need a doctor that old heap of mine will get us through those hills to old Doc Hogarth's quick enough."

"Stop kicking yourself and tell him," Florence said. She had walked out from the porch and stood now with an arm around Ann. "He's been talking like that all day. Works on that old car for half an hour then comes back in cussin' himself for not having a phone; then goes back out and tries to get the car running again. They're here now, John. Tell them."

"Come on up on the porch," John said. "Get us some coffee, Florence. I've drunk so much coffee I'm woozy-headed. Two more cups and I'd started walking to town. Florence, wake up the boy. I want Phil to hear him tell his story."

"What story, John?" Phil said, smiling at John's confusion.

"Come on up and sit first," John said, walking ahead of the rest. When Phil and Ann were seated and Florence had gone into the house, he said, "I went into town the other night to pick up some stuff—flour and meal, I think it was. Anyhow I got to talking to old Preacher Haines. You know the one who has that little church down by the river on the west end of town? He and my brother went to TCU together—my older brother. You never met him. Anyhow, it was late when I started back. Later than Florence likes me to be out in that old heap. But it was running all right then. Well, when I got past Mannie's a ways I saw this fire over to the left and realized it was about where Shine Tatum's shack was, so I stepped on the gas a little and headed for it. When I got near bout there this black Ford sedan jumped away from Shine's and whipped around the corner and past me like a bolt. By then I could see the fire was on Shine's porch and getting purty bad, so I whipped on in and by the time I got up to the porch the boy—Cooter—was out trying to put it out with a pitcher of water. Where's the boy, Florence? Oh, here he is."

As John talked, Florence had come out of the house with her arm around a sleepy Negro boy of about eleven.

"Cooter!" Phil said. "I've been looking everywhere for you."

"Hello, Mr. Arrow," Cooter said.

"Go on, John."

"There's not much else for me to tell," John said. "Me and Cooter put the fire out. It hadn't gotten very big. There was a shovel under the house and I shoveled some dirt on it and Cooter kept pouring on the water. But the main thing is, that was the night Shine was kidnaped. The men in the car that passed me had Shine in there with them. Cooter saw them."

"Who was it, Cooter? Who took Shine?" Phil had moved from his chair and was kneeling in front of the boy, a hand on each of his shoulders, restraining himself to keep from shaking him.

"It was Mister Mike and somebody else," Cooter said, his eyes round and bright and very much awake now. "I couldn't see who else. He stayed out in the yard. But it was Mister Mike Heaney up on the porch and hollering at Uncle Shine and slapping him and he's the one that dragged him off to the car."

"Mike. Mike Heaney!" Phil's hands dropped from the boy's shoulders and he knelt there staring at the design on the boy's pajamas.

"Yes, sir. Mister Mike Heaney," Cooter repeated. "The big white man from over at the Blinken place. He took Uncle Shine . . ." He stopped to swallow hard. Florence's grip on his shoulder tightened and her glance told Phil to hurry and get it over with.

"Cooter, are you sure it was Mike Heaney?" Phil said. "There's no possibility that you may be wrong. That it may have been someone who looks like him?"

"No, sir," Cooter said firmly. "I know Mister Mike. He comes in the store lots and gets Crazy Tom. Takes off and teases him like he does. I don't know anybody who looks like Mister Mike."

"Thanks, son," Phil said, touching the boy's cheek gently. Then he stood and faced John. "Why didn't you take this boy to the sheriff, John?" he said.

"I took him," John said. "Took him the next morning. I told Copeland what I saw and the boy told him what he saw. He said he would look into it. Next thing we heard a deputy came out here and got Cooter and took him in to the funeral home." He nodded to Florence and she took Cooter back into the house. "When the deputy brought Cooter back I asked him what had happened and Cooter said they showed him his uncle and that he was dead. They asked him if that was his uncle and he told them it was."

"My God!" Ann said.

"That lying son of a bitch," Phil said. "He told me he had absolutely nothing to go on. He said the boy saw nothing."

"Why would he protect Mike Heaney?" Ann asked.

"I don't know," Phil said. "Who can say what trips Slim Copeland's gears. Maybe he feels kin to a man who would kill a Negro."

Florence came back to the porch.

"I think he's all right," she said to John. "They learn to adjust very young."

"They have to," John said. Then he turned to Phil. "What are we going to do now?"

"There's only one thing to do," Phil said. "Blast this thing out into the open. I needed something concrete. Now I've got it."

"How many people will believe Cooter's story now?" John said. "If Copeland acts like he thinks it's a kid's imagination, that's enough for the others to build their usual rationalization process on."

"I think you're wrong, John," Phil said. "The rationalizations are made when no facts are presented. As long as Ashton has nothing more to go on than Copeland's word they're naturally going to make themselves believe no murder was committed. They can't do that if we give them facts."

"I hope you're right," John said. "But what about the Mack Parker lynching and the Emmett Till murder, to name two cases to the contrary?"

"This isn't Poplarville or Sumner, and the circumstances aren't the same," Phil said. "For one thing, a woman's not involved."

"I'm not arguing with you, Phil," John said. "I only wondered how you were going to get around Copeland's attitude. It's important. He's sheriff."

"As the politicians say," Phil smiled slightly, "I'll have to go straight to the people. To do that, by the way, I've got to get back to town and get to work."

Ann and Florence walked to the car behind Phil and John.

"You sit tight out here for a while," Phil said. "Guess I don't have to tell you to keep Cooter out of sight if anybody comes out this way." He opened the car door for Ann and she got in. He drove Ann home; then went to the *Dispatch*. The old elevator creaked and snapped as he rode it up to the third floor in the silent, empty building. He flipped the light switch by the elevator door and went to his desk, put paper in the typewriter, leaned back in the chair and lit a cigarette. Then he began typing:

Three days ago another Southern Negro was brutally, senselessly murdered. This time the animallike crime took place in Ashton County. This time it is Ashton County the nation and the world looks to for justice. This time the murder did not happen across the state, or in Alabama, or in Pearl River County. This time the people of Ashton County cannot sit and cluck their tongues and deplore it. This time it is our crime, committed by one of us. This time if justice is done we, the people of Ashton County, will have to do it.

A fine Negro man, who lived quietly among us for sixty-four years, was dragged from his cabin three nights ago by two white men, one of whom was seen and recognized. The person who saw this cowardly night rider has told his story to our sheriff. And his story is supported by the testimony of a second person, who arrived at the Tatum cabin in time to see the car in which Shine Tatum was whisked away. This is enough for any right-thinking law officer of average intelligence to build a case on. But our sheriff told the *Dispatch* he did not have enough evidence to even consider the possibility that Shine Tatum's death might be murder.

Deep within us we all know that this hard-working, quiet-living old man was murdered because he somehow pulled up from within himself the courage to demand that a basic right of his American citizenship be respected.

We have been hiding that knowledge behind the sheriff's statement that there was no evidence that a murder might have been committed. There is no longer anything there to hide behind.

He typed on furiously until five pages were filled. When he had finished he gathered the pages and read what he had written, making an occasional correction with one of the blunt copy pencils, then he clipped the pages together and laid them on the typewriter and leaned back in his chair, his hands interlocked behind his head. The AP and UPI machines in their cabinets across the room were loud in their silence. The white light from the single fluorescent fixture he had switched on threw thin shadows away from the desks and empty chairs. An unoccupied newsroom is like a graveyard at night, he thought. There's something phantasmal about it; invisible *things* seem poised behind every piece of furniture ready to jump into noisy action. The clutter on the desks—the copy paper, magazines, old newspapers (all newspapers are old once they have been read), the notebooks, the glossy, eight-by-ten photographs—all appear only temporarily still. The room looks as if it had been evacuated in the face of a fast-moving emergency. Newsrooms never look as if they were vacated in an orderly manner as empty business offices do. Newsrooms explode into action at the beginning of a workday and explode into coiled inaction at the end of it, like a movie run backwards. And a true newspaperman is never fully conscious except when he is in, or in contact with, a newsroom somewhere. He has to be plugged in like a coffee percolator.

Phil got up slowly and walked to Ranch's desk and dropped the editorial on it. Then he went to the elevator, switched off the light and rode down, with the squeaks and the silence filling the darkness about him.

Less than four hours later he was back in the brightly lighted newsroom. A shower and three cups of coffee assisted the few hours of sleep in making him feel he had another full day left in him. He walked to Ranch's desk and watched the big city editor read the last page of his editorial.

"Put that in ten-point type," he said when Ranch looked up at him. "Run it on page one in both editions today."

Ranch stood up, following his smile, and extended an ink-smeared right hand. "Welcome back, boss," he said.

Phil shook the hand perfunctorily. "Thanks, Ranch," he said.

"But I haven't been away. I have something *factual* now. That's all. I believe that's all the people of Ashton will need too."

"I hope you're right."

"I know I am. Trouble with you, Ranch, you been sittin' behind that desk taking crank phone calls so long you've gotten cynical."

15.

IT WAS 3:05 p.m. when the two panel trucks growled away from the *Dispatch* pressroom loaded with wired bundles of the second edition. The second edition is delivered to homes inside the Ashton city limits. The first edition is sold on the streets and put on buses and distributed to the smaller towns and crossroads communities in the five-county trade area around Ashton. The second edition bundles are dropped off, one by one, at appointed street corners in the various route districts. The route boys (the Little Merchants) meet the bundles and, when each paper is folded for throwing, they ride into the neighborhoods on their bicycles and motor scooters and cars (one *Dispatch* route boy rides a pony), sailing the tight folds across the lawns in the general direction of the front doors. This is done six afternoons a week in Ashton as it is in every Main Street town in America. If it isn't raining (and it wasn't in Ashton on this day) and if the neighborhood dogs are well trained, the folded papers usually remain where they fall until the breadwinner of each household arrives home from whatever work provides him (or her) with the paycheck that buys the bread and picks it up and takes it inside and unfolds it. It is then the work of the reporters and editorial writers and columnists and cartoonists comes alive.

Most people in Ashton look first at the front page, briefly, then turn to favorite inside pages. On this day, everyone read Phil's front-page editorial before turning elsewhere and some never read past the editorial.

In a rented cottage in northwest Ashton, near the cotton compress and the oil mill, a man in a sweat-stained khaki shirt sat before a humming fan and read it and cursed and called his wife and read it aloud to her. Halfway across town to the south, a schoolteacher, blue-tinted gray hair flowing down around her shoulders as she combed it from its tight bind, read it standing by the refrigerator. She walked to the front door and stood half an hour watching the small children play on the sidewalk. A Catholic priest read it and crossed himself and walked to the church next door and knelt before a figure of Christ. A Presbyterian minister read it and dropped the paper to his lap and closed his eyes and prayed. A retired Army colonel read it and laughed loudly. A Negro woman who taught American history at the Negro high school read it and cried softly. Philip Arrow, Sr., read half of it and dropped the paper to the floor at his feet; then he went to the cabinet and poured whisky in a glass and drank it.

"Phil is right," Ches Blinken, Jr., said to his wife after he read it. "We ought to show the world we don't condone things like this in Ashton County."

"Right about what?" Mary Lee said, looking up from the society page he handed her before he read the frontpage editorial.

So he read it to her. "My goodness," she said, "it sounds as if he knows who did it."

"Sure he does," Ches said. "Boy, I bet this'll make Slim Copeland turn blue. He told me only this morning he hadn't been able to dig up a single clue."

"What will your father say about this?" Mary Lee said, turning her attention back to the society page.

"Let's go over there tonight, honey. I'd like to talk with him about it," Ches said.

When R. L. Squires read it the paper dropped from his hands and he hurried into the kitchen and got a pint bottle from under the sink and poured a water glass half full and drank it in two long swallows. Then he rinsed the glass and chased the taste down with water.

"I'll be back in a little while," he shouted to his wife, who was in the laundry room ironing, and went out to his car and drove recklessly to Mike's house on the Blinken plantation east of town.

Rita Jean answered his knock and told him Mike was out in the northeast field counting weevils. He thanked her and drove out the dirt road until he saw Mike's pickup truck. Then he turned off the road and followed the dusty ruts that bordered the cotton field and parked behind the pickup. Mike stood, waist deep in green leaves, three rows in from the truck.

"You seen the paper?" R.L. asked, as he walked toward Mike.

"Yeah," Mike said. He was in town when the first edition of the *Dispatch* came out.

"Whatta you think we oughta do?" R.L. said.

"We ain't gonna do anything."

"But that son of a bitch sounds like he knows something. Talking about two witnesses and all that."

"So what?"

"Whatta ya mean, so what? Good God Amighty, Mike, if he knows . . . What happened, Mike? Tell me now what happened."

"What the shit you mean, what happened? You know good and damned well what happened."

The sun was balanced, blazing, on the flat horizon. There was no wind and sweat dripped down R.L.'s forehead and into his eyes. He blinked at the sting of it.

"But I can't remember. It's all fuzzy. Like I dreamed it."

"Stop blinking your god-damned eyes," Mike said, looking at R.L. for the first time. "It makes me nervous."

"Tell me, Mike . . . did I . . ."

"Did you what?" Mike looked down at the cotton stalk again and turned over one of the leaves and examined its underside.

"Did I hit him?" He couldn't ask Mike before. He knew Mike would think he was stupid. But he remembered so little of what happened that night from the time the car leaped away from Shine Tatum's gate. What he did remember came in quick, soundless pictures, or in sounds and odors without pictures. The dizzy race from the burning shack. Choking dust. Trees flipping past. Stopping and getting out somewhere. Riding again and stopping again and stepping out where the earth was sticky and the high umbrella of branches and leaves blocking out most of the light from the full moon. The metallic smell of the river. Him cursing and crying and Mike laughing. Ripping something hard and heavy from the damp earth. The bloody, wall-eyed face staring up at him.

"Stop blinking your god-damned eyes, I said," Mike said, walking toward the pickup.

"I wanta know, Mike. Did I hit him?"

"You damn sure did. You went nuts and started beating on him with that chunk of driftwood. I think he was still alive, too. I been thinking about it. I don't think I killed him when I hit him with my pistol in the barn. I think you killed him with that piece of god-damned driftwood."

"The barn?"

Mike leaned against the pickup. "Yeah, the barn. Don't you remember going to that old barn before we took him to the river? God, man, you *must* have been skunked!" He squatted in the shade of the truck and picked up a dry clod and crushed it with his fingers, then dusted his hands thoughtfully.

R.L. laughed. "I sure was. I sure was, all right. I wouldn't of done a thing like that sober. Would I?"

Mike spat. "No, you probably wouldn't, you yellow little bastard."

"I'm not yellow, Mike. I just wouldn't of gone batty like that. He was an old man."

"Listen, you stupid bastard." Mike pulled a handful of leaves from a stalk with an angry twist. "We killed a smart-aleck nigger that thought he could be a white man. We oughta get a medal. Hampton Auld himself told me, not two hours before we went out there, somebody oughta do something instead of just talk. They all wanted to. But it took Mike Heaney to get things rolling. Just like during the war."

"I don't want a medal, Mike," R.L. said, lighting a cigarette. "You got a drink on you, Mike?"

Mike stood, reached into the bed of the pickup, opened a gray toolbox and took out a pint bottle of Early Times. He handed the bottle to R.L.

"Thanks, Mike."

"Go easy," Mike said and grabbed the bottle from R.L.'s lips. "That's all I got out here." He drank and put the bottle back in the toolbox.

"Give me one more swallow," R.L. said. "You can't see weevils to count them now anyhow. It's getting too dark. Let's go in and get a bottle and figure out what we're gonna do."

"You just get your ass on back home and set tight till I call you," Mike said. "Go to work tomorrow like nothing happened. I'm gonna talk to a few folks."

"Okay," R.L. said, "but—"

"But nothing. Now, get home, dammit. Let me take care of this."

"Okay, Mike. Okay." R.L. stood a moment watching Mike stare at the ground. Then he walked to his car.

As R.L.'s car backed toward the dirt road, turned around and sped away ahead of the dust that glowed red in its tail lights, Mike got the bottle from the toolbox and drank again. He swallowed three times and he sweated. He put the bottle back in the box and squatted beside the truck. There was little natural light now. He reached and got another leaf and struck a match and put the flame to the weevil's cocoon. Then dropped the leaf and the match to the ground. I feel no more for that old nigger, he thought, than I do for that weevil. The weevils are bad this year. You just reach out and pick a leaf and there's one under it, digging in to make the cotton rot. Count how many weevils in a square yard of cotton stalks and the State College man tells you how many are in your field. You tell Old Man Blinken what the State College man said and he telephones you in a few days and says he's hired a man with an airplane to spray the poison. The guy with the plane has the fun and makes the money. A hundred dollars a day. Mike Heaney stays on the ground and counts weevils and the guy with the airplane zooms around, has the fun and collects the hundred dollars a day. Mike Heaney walks in the frozen mud and finds the Germans and the flyboys drop the bombs, then fly back to London and screw the Limey women. Mike Heaney loses again. . . . If he saw a man beating a good hunting dog he would stop him. If one of his hunting dogs died he would be sad. But he felt nothing for that old nigger. . . . You get close to a good dog. Live with him practically when you're in the woods. Get to know him. How can you know a nigger? . . . He laid a nigger girl once. Everybody does at least once. That's getting pretty close to one. Would he have felt anything if he had killed her? No. Laying her didn't make him know her. She was just a place to relieve himself, like taking a good crap. Same principle; something a man has to do and she was available. Leastways, she by-God got available damn quick when he told her to spraddle. . . . Why should he feel anything for an old nigger? A smart bastard trying to screw up things. Let one start voting and before you could say Battle of the Bulge the whole god-damned lot would want to. Then, sure as a boll weevil rots cotton, niggers'd be sitting down in the Capitol in the legislature, just like Governor Barrett said. No, the only thing he had to worry about was how much guts people had. They all wanted him to do it, from the governor on down to old freckle-faced Colonel Blinken. None of them wanted niggers all over the god-damned place, acting up. Leering at white women. . . . Leering at Ann Davis. . . . Trouble is, some women wouldn't *mind* at all if they thought they could get away with it. Never saw a buck nigger yet that wasn't hung like a mule. Women *know* that. Some would like it. Rita Jean'd probably *love* it if she could get away with it. Maybe that's why she didn't wiggle any more. Maybe he wasn't as big as she needed.

Like he told R.L., they oughta get a medal for what they did. A medal.

He broke clods in his hands and tossed the dirt against the side of the truck. Yeah, all he had to worry about was how much guts those people had—those people who wanted him to do what he had done.

He better go first to the one with the most guts, Hamp Auld.

He pulled the damp newspaper from his hip pocket and opened it and looked at the editorial again. That nigger-loving Phil Arrow! Acting like he was my friend in high school when we met in the woods hunting, then prance around those rich little bitches the next day, acting like he didn't even know me. At least the others didn't try to fool Mike Heaney. Didn't act friendly to him one day and like they didn't know him the next. The son of a bitch probably wouldn't even have danced with Ann Davis that night if he hadn't seen she was interested in Mike Heaney. Seems like every time Mike Heaney might win Phil Arrow steps in and Mike Heaney loses again. But not this time, buddy boy.

He stood and stretched the kinks from his tight legs. He would drive in and see Hamp Auld tonight. Now. He laughed. Hamp Auld had about as much use for the Arrows as Mike Heaney did.

The telephone in the hallway off Slim Copeland's living room jangled. The sheriff pushed his bulk from the chair with a sigh. He didn't want to answer it. It had been ringing all evening and every time he answered, it was somebody all stirred up about what Phil Arrow had put in his god-damned newspaper.

"Slim, this is Hampton Auld," the voice in his ear said this time.

"Am I glad to talk to you, Mr. Auld!" the sheriff said. "I been trying to call you. I been getting one phone call after another about that damned newspaper story. We got more nigger-lovin' sonsabitches in this town than I ever thought. You'd be surprised, Mr. Auld. They're wanting me to arrest somebody."

"That's what I called about," Auld's dry, clipped words said. "Mike Heaney's at my house. He wants to admit taking Shine Tatum from his shack that night. Him and R.L. Squires. Send a deputy out to Squires' house and get him. You come over here and get Mike."

Two hours later Slim Copeland telephoned the Memphis *Commercial Appeal*'s correspondent and told him he had taken Mike and R.L. "into custody in connection with the death of Shine Tatum, a male nigra."

Shortly after seven the next morning Phil walked off the elevator into the *Dispatch* newsroom and Ranch handed him a marked copy of the morning paper from Memphis.

Phil read it carefully and smiled. "That's the first time I haven't minded being scooped by the good, gray *Commercial Appeal,*" he said.

Ranch grinned happily. "Maybe you were right about these people, Phil," he said. "Dunham tells me Copeland got so many telephone calls last night he had to do something."

The telephone rang from the narrow table between the twin beds where Jerry and Janie slept. Janie pushed a hand out of the covers slowly. The air conditioner had been on all night and the room was chilled. When her hand found the phone she moved her tousled head out of the pillow and put the green receiver to her ear.

"Yes?" she said. "Yes. He's here. Jerry, it's for you."

"Who the hell?" Jerry asked, his eyes still closed.

"A man."

The curtains were pulled against the morning light so Jerry switched on the table lamp.

"What's he want?"

"How do I know?"

"Here, let me have it. Hello, this is Senator Windham."

"Senator Windham, I understand you'd like to be Governor Windham," the dry, mechanized voice said in Jerry's ear.

"Who is this?"

"This is Hampton Auld."

"Oh," Jerry said, sitting up straighter. "What can I do for you, Mr. Auld?"

"Let's just say we can do for each other. Are you awake now?"

"Yes."

"To put it briefly," Auld's voice said, "I been sitting back waiting. I don't trust a crackpot like Hadley, especially when he pulls a stunt like he and Barrett did the other night in my territory without consulting me. A man like that won't stay hitched. You listening?"

"Yes," Jerry said. "I'm listening. I make it a point to listen to any taxpaying, voting citizen in my district who wants to talk to me, Mr. Auld. That's why I've never lost an election."

16.

THAT NIGHT the Delegation called on Philip Arrow, Sr. Hamp Auld telephoned and said they were coming and Arrow thought of them as the Delegation with an upper case "D," because he knew the group that came would be essentially the same as the one that had come before, six years ago.

While he waited Arrow listened to the songs of the Parchman prisoners. A rich voice was telling again why prisoners sing when they work. ". . . if'n you sing, the day just pass on way." Another prisoner said, "I didn't do nothing this time, but the po-leece tole me I done done so much he wuz arres'n me in egvance, cause I's gonna do somethin'." The woodchoppers followed the song leader's chant and the broad axes chopped out a rhythm accompaniment. Arrow thought back to when his hair was not so white and Hamp Auld's skin was not so gray. It was a delicious memory because it was a time when the caution of old age had not bound him and he had struck out physically against a foe. It may have been the time when his present troubles began.

They were in the gymnasium at Teachers College and the annual meeting of the regional council was under way. There was an argument at the committee meeting. As usual, Hamp Auld—vice-president of the bank then—was on one side and he was on the other. He couldn't even remember now what the issue was. Yes, he did. He wanted to set better standards for the living quarters provided for the Negro field workers who were transported from one section to another during the peak work seasons. Most of them had to sleep in chicken-coop huts or on the ground. "Let's stop wasting our time on this crap," Auld had said. "The main problem is getting them where they're needed when they're needed. They can live anywhere. They're just like animals."

That's when Arrow had said it. Hell, he didn't know about Auld's family skeletons. "Aw, Hamp," he said, "you shouldn't talk like that. You probably have a good-looking black wench on your family tree somewhere like most everybody else in the county." Hamp Auld had hit him. Smack on the left cheekbone. It was a glancing blow and, although it hurt, he had reacted quickly. He floored Auld with a beautiful right cross. Sent him skidding across the slick gym floor! A couple of the committee members laughed. Maybe if they had not laughed . . . but they had and Auld never forgot. Arrow had friends too. Or thought he did. His side won about as many skirmishes over local issues as Auld's did.

Until 1954, that is. That's the year the sheep and the goats were separated, Auld said. The year the United States Supreme Court said segregated public schools were unconstitutional. The year Phil Junior's little crusades became "threats to the Southern Way of Life." The last time the Delegation came he knuckled under. And Auld himself wasn't even on the scene. This time Auld was coming in person. This time he must smell blood.

The doorbell chimed. Arrow turned off the phonograph and went to greet his guests.

"Come in, gentlemen," he said. He saw that each man carried a copy of today's *Dispatch.* "Come on in the living room and make yourself comfortable."

The Delegation—there were five this time—followed him into the living room. "Can I get you fellows a drink?" he said. "Or maybe some coffee?"

"No, thank you, Arrow," County Attorney Grady said. The others shook their heads.

"Well, sit down. Sit down," Arrow said. He sat in the big chair by the phonograph.

"Aw, sit down," Auld said.

Grady sat beside Auld on the sofa. Colonel Blinken sat in the small antique chair between the windows, where the curtains stirred before the night's first breezes. Anse, who was quiet for a change because his boss was present to speak for himself, remained standing behind the sofa. J. Q. Perthman from Crutchfield Crossing folded his arms and leaned against the wall under the arrangement of pen-and-ink sketches of plantation life done by the Ashton high school art teacher and presented to Arrow ten years ago by the school's Quill and Scroll Club for "The Ashton *Dispatch*'s continued meritorious service to the community it serves."

The Hampton Auld menagerie, Arrow thought. Perthman the puffed frog. Anse the rodent, wiping his front teeth. Colonel Chipmunk over there; poor old Colonel. Grady was a newcomer to the group. What was he? A weasel? His body kind of pyramided from his big ass to his pointed head, like a weasel's.

"You boys better let me get you a drink," Arrow said. "Give us something to do while we sit staring at each other."

"Hell-fire," Auld said. "You boys act like children. We came here to talk about this, Arrow." He held up his copy of the *Dispatch.*

"I see you have a copy of my newspaper there," Arrow said. "We make an error in the bank's annual ad?"

"No . . ." Auld began.

"Because if we did," Arrow continued, "you have a right to complain. I know you wouldn't try to tell us how to run any other part of the paper. Just as we wouldn't try to tell you how to run the bank." Have your fun now, Arrow, he thought, the test will come later.

"Apparently when the boys came to see you six years ago they didn't make themselves clearly understood," Auld said, ignoring Arrow's sarcasm.

"He knew what we meant," Anse said.

Why don't I tell them to get the hell out of my house? Arrow thought. Why don't I kick some asses?

"Did or not," Auld said, "it's come up again."

"What has come up again?" Arrow asked.

Auld reached into the leather briefcase and pulled out several magazines and newspapers. He tossed them on the floor at Arrow's feet.

"There," he said, "look them over. There's *Time* and *Life* and *Look* and some of those god-damned Yankee newspapers. Look at them. This piddling Shine Tatum thing is getting as big as the Emmett Till thing. Look at them. The good name of Ashton smeared. Lied about. Held up to the world for ridicule."

"What does that have to do with me?" Arrow said. *Why don't I kick some asses like a man?*

"Where do you think this all started?" Auld said. "You know damn well where. That son of yours. He had to go around hollering wolf for no good reason like he did before. Only this time the people had faith in you. Faith you would stop it. But you didn't. You let your community down, Arrow. You let your newspaper and your son be the cause of its shame."

"What about Heaney and Squires?" Arrow said. "Don't they come in for a share of the blame?"

"We have good reason to believe Mike and R.L. were the innocent victims of a diabolic plot," Grady said, looking at Perthman as he said it. "A plot instigated by Commonests, according to—"

"My God in heaven!" Arrow exclaimed.

"Don't act so surprised," Grady said. "We've known for years all this mixmongering was inspired by the Commonests. We didn't look close enough to home, that's all."

"What in the devil are you talking about, son?" Arrow said.

"You'll find out soon enough," Grady said. "Tomorrow night, in fact, if you come to the meeting—"

"Never mind that now," Auld said. "The point at hand is whether or not our distinguished editor and publisher has the courage to stand up and tell his son to stop this shameful campaign against his own community."

"What can I do? My son is a grown man."

"You either take charge of your newspaper or we'll be forced to take drastic steps," Auld said.

"What does that mean? That 'drastic steps' business?"

"We'll run your newspaper out of business," Grady said.

Auld frowned at him. "I wouldn't put it that way," he said. "We wouldn't run anybody out of business. But we would start another newspaper that would reflect the thinking of its people more accurately. And I don't think there's any doubt in any of our minds as to which paper the people and the advertisers would prefer."

Perthman shifted his weight from his left foot to his right one. Then he settled against the wall again and continued sucking on his snuff. The transparent white curtains floated out into the room on each side of the Colonel.

"Damned if those curtains don't look like wings." Arrow laughed. "Colonel, maybe that's a sign of something, huh?"

"What's the matter with you, Phil?" the Colonel said, pushing the curtains away with his elbows. "We came here in good faith. Why don't you say you'll do something about all this so we can all go home friends? This isn't pleasant for any of us."

"Isn't it?" Arrow asked, looking at Auld.

"Well, Mr. Arrow," Auld said. "We are waiting for an answer."

"What do you people want with a newspaper?" Arrow said. *Why do I stall? Why don't I kick five asses now?*

"We don't want to own a newspaper," Auld said. "But we want our community to have a newspaper that doesn't capitalize off sensationalism at the expense of the community."

"Capitalize!" Arrow said, raising his voice for the first time. "Do you know that in the past two days we have gotten four hundred sixty-four subscription cancellations and lost three advertisers? Do you call that capitalizing?"

"That proves there must be other motives behind what Phil is doing," Grady said.

"Yes, there are other motives," Arrow said helplessly, "but you would never understand them."

"See," Grady said to Perthman. "He admits it."

"Shut up," Auld said. "Those cancellations give you some hint of what would happen if we started a second paper here, Arrow. So let's stop wasting time."

"It isn't easy to turn your boy away," Arrow said. He turned to the Colonel. "You should know that, Colonel."

"*My* boy would never force *me* to turn him away," the Colonel said. "Philip, you don't really think Phil Junior would . . . would go against you—do you?"

"There is an alternative," Auld said.

"What is it?" Arrow said; too quickly, he knew.

"You're getting on up in years like the rest of us," Auld said. "Why not sell the paper? Go to Florida or the mountains and relax. Tell your son you can't stand the climate here any more. You haven't been looking too good lately. We'll give you a fair price for the *Dispatch.* He can't object to that."

Arrow looked slowly around the room, from the Colonel to Anse. "You have the papers in the capital parroting for you," he said. "Every paper in the state, in fact, but one or two. Why do you want the *Dispatch* too? At least my boy gives you something alive to fight in this intellectual desert."

"We didn't come here to talk in circles," Auld said. "We're prepared to make you a solid offer. Seventy-five thousand for the *Dispatch,* lock, stock and barrel."

"Shit, that wouldn't buy the linotype machines," Arrow said. *My protests are about as damned effective as the rusted reflexes of a punch-drunk fighter. I'm not going to kick any asses today.*

"That is our initial offer," Auld said. "To save time I'll admit we are prepared to go slightly higher."

Arrow stared at the carpet between his feet. "Give me a few days," he said. "I feel ill all of a sudden. Let me alone now, please. Let me alone. It would embarrass me to be sick in front of you."

"All right, Arrow," Auld said, standing. "Let's go, boys. I think Mr. Arrow will see it our way. I'm sure of it, in fact."

Colonel Blinken stepped toward Arrow's chair. "Is there anything we can do?" he said. "Call a doctor or anything? You turned pale as a ghost all of a sudden."

"No, thanks," Arrow said. "Just let me alone."

The Delegation walked into the hall and out onto the porch and the Colonel said, "I'm awfully worried about Phil. He hasn't been himself lately. Do you know he hasn't been to church in more than two years? That's a fact. I was telling my wife the other day—when a man loses contact with his church he loses something irreplaceable. I tell you, fellows, I'm worried about him. Things just haven't been right around here since the war—World War Two, you know. . . ."

17.

FLORENCE STEPPED OUT the back door and saw the dust. Then she saw the familiar gray car the dust seemed to be trying to eat. She stood on the tiny back porch and watched and frowned at the speed her husband was demanding from the old car. When she saw him skid to a reckless stop under the oak she put down the washtub of wet clothes and hurried around the house, wiping her hands on her apron.

"Something's wrong," she said aloud. "I knew he shouldn't have gone to town today with all this mess going on. That man's curiosity will get him yet."

He had not seen her on the back porch and had gone looking for her in the house. When she opened the front door he was walking toward her from the kitchen.

"What in the world is it, John?" she asked.

"I don't know for sure but the way Old Man Blinken looked when he told me makes me know it ain't something good—not for us anyhow," John said.

"What isn't good and what did Old Man Blinken tell you?" Florence said. "Sit down over here and calm down and tell me."

"Where's Cooter?"

"He's with the children at the pond. Eunice is with them, so don't worry."

John sat and fanned his face with a magazine. "It's so darn hot," he said. "I can't even think."

"Think or not. If you don't tell me something pretty soon I'm going to pop."

"All I know is that I was at the courthouse and I ran smack into Colonel Blinken and young Ches and Anse Hayes and Ross Grady," John said. "They were coming out of Copeland's office. When they saw me you'd have thought they'd seen a ghost. They practically pushed the Colonel at me. He mumbled something about a meeting tomorrow night. Said I should be there because it had to do with me. Said I may want to say something in my defense." He slapped the magazine down on the table. "I couldn't get him to tell me anything else," he said. "Now, what the devil do I want to say in my defense at a meeting at Bogue Nitta School?"

"That where the meeting's going to be?"

"Yes."

"What are you going to do, John?"

"I don't know. I called Phil. He said he would check around. He and Ann will be out here tonight."

"I don't think you ought to go, John."

Bogue Nitta School is seven miles south of Ashton. The people began to come into the auditorium exactly thirty minutes before the meeting was scheduled to start. They came through the wide triple doorway in pairs and threes and fours mostly. The sliding doors were pushed aside and remained so throughout the meeting because it was another hot night. The people did not talk more than was necessary after they entered the auditorium. They nodded to acquaintances already there, then sat in the little seats and concentrated on the people who sat up on the stage. They were told the meeting had something to do with Just-Ten Acres. That was enough to bring them out on a hot night. Rumors of "strange goings on" out there rose and fell like the tide in that section of the county. The favorite cropped up about four years back. It said that old Doc Hogarth, who visited the Allens occasionally and doctored the Allen children, was an abortionist and that to stimulate his business John and Florence Allen sponsored a teenage sex club. Requirement for membership in the club was loss of virginity.

Colonel Blinken and Ches walked onto the stage apron from behind the maroon curtain and moved along the line of chairs shaking hands with those who had got there ahead of them. The Colonel first, then Ches. (In the audience, a balding man of about fifty took his pipe out of his mouth and said to his neighbor, "Old Man Blinken and his boy ought to be in politics, they shake hands so good.")

"You haven't forgotten about the Sunday-school class Sunday, sheriff?" the Colonel asked Sheriff Copeland. The Colonel taught the adult class at the First Baptist Church.

"Yes, sirree," Copeland said. "I've got a couple of dandy questions to ask you about the lesson."

"Good," the Colonel said. "I believe in questions from the class. Stimulates interest. It's the democratic way. Like this meeting. Reminds me of the old-timey town hall meetings."

"That's exactly the idea," Anse Hayes said and turned to the man beside him. "That's what I've been telling Mr. Perthman here. When a matter of community-wide interest comes up the entire community should have a chance to speak out on it. That's grass-roots stuff. That right, Mr. Perthman?"

J. Q. Perthman nodded, sucking on his snuff-packed lower lip.

The Blinkens were at the end of the line of chairs when Ches whispered to his father, "I still don't see why I have to sit up here."

"Sit down, son, and be quiet," the Colonel said. "It wouldn't look right if you went down in the audience now."

At five minutes before eight John Allen arrived. He came in alone through the triple doorway and walked alone down the long center aisle to the foot of the stage.

"Should I sit down here or up there?" he asked, tugging on Colonel Blinken's pant cuff.

When John spoke the Colonel looked down and smiled and extended his hand. Then the smile faded and he withdrew his hand and turned to Anse. Anse said it was all right, he supposed, for Allen to sit up on the stage. But he could sit anywhere he pleased.

"It's all right for you to sit up here," the Colonel said to John. "But you may sit anywhere you please."

"I'll sit down here then," John said. "If I need to say anything 'in my defense' it won't be hard to jump up there where you are."

At five minutes after eight Anse asked Sheriff Copeland: "How many you think are out there?"

Copeland closed one eye and studied the crowd a moment. "I figure about three hundred, maybe three-fifty," he said.

"We may as well get started," Anse said to the Colonel. Then he turned to Perthman and said, "I always like to get a meeting started on time. Start on time and end on time, that's my motto."

Perthman nodded.

Anse turned back to the Colonel. "Go ahead," he said.

The Colonel walked to the microphone and pulled it near his mouth and said, "One, two. One, two." It came out, "One . . . un, un, un; two, ooh, ooh." Copeland got up and went to the right rear corner of the stage and turned some knobs on the control box. Then the Colonel's voice came through raspy, but clear.

"Ladies and gentlemen," the Colonel said, "before we begin I want to call on Brother Pat Grubbs from Crutchfield Crossing to ask the Lord to bless the purpose of this gathering. I believe I just saw Brother Grubbs enter the auditorium. Would you come on up here, Brother Grubbs, and pray through the microphone for all to hear?"

Grubbs had not expected this honor, but he was not made speechless by his surprise. In his profession, especially under the conditions in which Grubbs entered it, success largely depended on one's aptitude for expressing unpremeditated meditations. He was a self-ordained preacher—or, as he put it, ordained by God directly without going through a lot of college professors and other intermediates. This added to his prestige among members of his own flock in the vicinity of the tiny whitewashed church four miles southeast of Crutchfield Crossing. But, except during election years, he sensed that the people of Ashton "looked down on him." As he walked from his seat to the stage it was difficult for him to prevent a smile from replacing the serious, pulpit look on his angular face. He was pleased. A few weeks ago dinner at Senator Windham's house and now this. He decided to give them a real treat—one of his long, intense prayers. But when he stood before the microphone, his joy departed him and his prayer came out short and matter-of-fact. The moment before he closed his eyes he had seen the Reverend Percy Stanford walk into the auditorium with Phil Arrow, Jr. The Reverend Mr. Stanford's backwards collar always made Grubbs uncomfortable.

The entrance of Stanford and Phil Arrow also disturbed Colonel Blinken. It made him feel, for the first time, that perhaps he shouldn't be where he was. Ches had told him they ought to stay out of it. A lot of Episcopalians were fine people and he admired the dignity of the Episcopal ceremony. He knew the Reverend Mr. Stanford held moderate views on racial matters, although he was careful—the Colonel had been told—not to "come right out and say anything radical" from the pulpit of his church. Maybe his presence in the auditorium meant there were some good people in Ashton County who didn't approve of tonight's meeting. Important people. Maybe this was one time he should have listened to his son.

"Let's get on with the meeting," Anse whispered, nudging the Colonel with his toe.

"We're happy to see Brother Stanford here tonight," the Colonel said into the microphone. "Always happy to see our men of God take an interest in community affairs outside the church. I imagine Brother Stanford is like a lot of the rest of us here tonight. We know this is an important meeting but we know very little of what it is all about. I was asked to serve as master of ceremonies because it seemed desirable to have someone serve in this capacity who was not directly connected with the incident to be discussed here tonight. . . . Now I turn the meeting over to Mr. Anse Hayes, whom you all know I'm sure and who asked me to be master of ceremonies here tonight. Mr. Hayes."

Anse was puzzled by the Colonel's sudden nervousness. Usually the old goat talked too long. Maybe it was just as well; the crowd seemed to be getting restless. Heavy shoe soles scraped against the concrete floor and the coughing had started.

"Thank you, Colonel," Anse said. "I know you are all anxious to get into the business at hand. So without further delay I take great pleasure in presenting to you your esteemed county attorney, Ross Grady. Ross."

Grady nodded to Sheriff Copeland as he rose and stepped to the microphone. The sheriff had been waiting as expectantly as the crowd. He moved quickly to the table which held the baby-blue tape-recording machine and waited there for his cue.

"Folks," Grady said, "for many years the people of Ashton County have pondered the Just-Ten Acres puzzle. For years the good people of Ashton County have heard stories of the strange and mysterious goings on within the iron curtain around this so-called missionary settlement. But the good people of Ashton County are tolerant. The good people of Ashton County are patient. What you will hear in this auditorium tonight, ladies and gentlemen, will cause you to wonder if the good people of Ashton County have not been *too* tolerant and *too* patient."

He paused to sip water from one of the glasses on the table near the microphone.

"As you listen tonight," he continued, "we ask you to think back over the events of the past few weeks. Truly disturbing events in the history of our glorious county. Think first of an old nigger man appearing suddenly one day in the office of our circuit clerk and demanding that he be allowed to vote whether he could qualify or not. Think back to the fact—undisputed fact, mind you—that this same old nigger man, after living peacefully among us for over half a century, had met and broke bread with none other than a nigger lawyer from New York City. Met with him only a few days before he appeared in our circuit clerk's office. Think back too to the undisputed fact that the same nigger lived but a short distance from Just-Ten Acres and was known to be a personal friend of John Allen's. Now think back to the smears that have been wiped across the fair name of Ashton County in the past few days. Think of the headlines you have seen. Think of the front-page editorials you have read. Then think of who wrote those headlines and those editorials and think who only a week before all this came up wrote a glowing feature story in his newspaper extolling the virtues of John and Florence Allen and the work they were doing at Just-Ten Acres. Think of all this as you hear these nigger boys' voices on the tape telling about what they have seen and heard at Just-Ten Acres."

He signaled to Copeland with a nod. Copeland put the plastic wheels of the tape recorder in motion.

"This is your sheriff, A. O. 'Slim' Copeland," said the raspy voice coming from the machine and passing through the microphone Grady held near its speaker. "Standing here with me is our county attorney Ross Grady and Anse Hayes, er . . . assistant cashier at Mr. Auld's bank. *[There were whispers.]* Oh, yes, Anse is, as you all know, chairman of the county Democratic committee and vice-president of the Ashton County Citizens Council. *[More whispering]* Anse says he is not here as a representative of the Citizens Council. Okay, Anse. . . . What you are about to hear are the voices of the nigger boys who waved at a busload of white girls out on the Dobbsville road just three days ago. These little girls, Girl Scouts on their way to summer camp, were riding innocently by and these nigger boys waved and made undue remarks. These remarks were heard, luckily, by an alert citizen of our community, who desires that his name remain unknown. He heard one of them say—as the bus passed, mind you—that, and you ladies pardon me, that he'd sure like to roll in the hay with 'that little old blonde sticking her head out the bus window.' The other two, according to our informant, made similar remarks—some of them too vile to repeat here. Naturally, our informant informed us and the nigger boys were taken into custody."

Grady turned the machine off and raised the microphone to his mouth.

"Now you will hear the actual interview with the nigger boys," he said. "Some of the rest of this tape is difficult to understand. The machine is brand-new and some of us weren't too sure how to operate it then."

Copeland punched the button and started the plastic wheels turning again.

"You boys were acting a little smart out there, weren't you?" Grady's amplified voice asked.

"No, sir," three barely audible voices answered. Then a pause, and "Yes, sir . . ."

"Where you boys live?"

"At Forty Oaks."

"Forty Oaks community? Isn't that near Just-Ten Acres?"

"Yes, sir."

"You know Mr. John Allen?"

"Yes, sir."

"You ever go to any of those Sunday meetings of his?"

"Yes, sir."

"What did you hear about at those meetings?"

One of the boys—one with a soft hoarseness in his voice—gradually emerged as spokesman for the group.

"We heard about keeping clean and hy-gene and farming and God," the soft, hoarse voice said.

"Hy-gene?" Copeland's voice cut through the others. "What's that? It don't sound like something that ought to be taught niggers."

"Did Mr. Allen ever talk about the government?" Grady's voice continued.

There was a pause. Then the young Negro said, "Yes, sir, I remember once he said something about the government."

"What did he say? Go on. Don't be afraid to tell us."

"He said taxes is too high."

"Is that all you did on Sundays?" Grady asked quickly.

"No, sir. Sometimes we saw movies."

"Aaah. What were they about?"

"Hy-gene and farming and there was one my sister seen about having babies. Not how to, but how not to. She told me about it."

"One about what?"

"Hy-gene and farming."

"No. I mean the other. The babies."

"About how not to have babies. My sister seen it."

"Good God!" the sheriff's voice said. The crowd in the auditorium mumbled noisily a moment but the continuing talk from the machine brought the silence back quickly.

"Who was in the movies?"

"People. Doctors and nurses and people."

"White people?"

"Yes, sir."

"Colored people?"

"Yes, sir. My sister said there was."

"White people and colored people in the same movies. The ones about . . . how not to have babies?"

"Yes, sir. She said one had a chinee woman in it."

"Good God Almighty!" the sheriff's voice said.

Phil stood and waved a hand, asking for attention from the stage. Grady saw him and smiled and turned off the machine.

"Yes, Mr. Arrow?" he said.

"I think it's time someone asked what right you have to conduct a kangaroo court such as this," Phil said.

"Mr. Arrow," Grady said, "I'm sure you would like to defend your friends. But now is not the time. Wait until we have heard the entire interview."

The crowd was on its feet now. Shouting. Jeering. Waving cardboard fans it had been stirring the hot air with.

"Sit down, commie!"

"Go back to New York!"

"Let's hear the rest of it!"

Phil tried to shout over the crowd. "Those films came from the State Health Department," he said. "They're on venereal disease."

The Reverend Percy Stanford tugged at his coat and said, "It's no use, Phil. You're only making matters worse."

Phil sat down. The crowd became quiet immediately. Grady punched the button and the machine began to talk again.

"Is it true that the Allen children go swimming with colored children out at Just-Ten Acres?" Grady's question boomed over the speaker.

"I don't know." The answer came quietly. Muffled.

"You mean to stand there and tell me that if Deputy Sheriff Al Blackledge says he saw whites and niggers swimming together in that pond out at Just-Ten that he'd be lying?"

"No, sir."

"I seen a colored girl go in to get a baby out once," a shrill voice said.

"You did? When was that?"

"Bout three, four weeks ago."

"Tell us about it."

"The nigga gal was Eunice Gardner. She hangs around Just-Ten all the time. She told me she was their favorite baby-sitter. We was possum hunting over that way that day and went by to see if Miz Allen had any cookies, which she sometimes do. Just then we heard a holler and Eunice jumped in the pond and pulled the baby out. She said it ran over and jumped in before she had a chance to stop it."

(Near the center of the auditorium a man of about sixty, wearing steel-rimmed glasses, asked the younger man beside him, "What did it say? What did it say?" The younger man said, "Something about a nigger gal having the Allen's baby after she got raped . . . shhhh." Five rows back a fat woman in a polka-dot dress said to her husband, "Tell me what it said, Mac. I can't understand it." The husband said, without turning to face her so he would not have to take his gaze from the baby-blue machine on the stage, "Something about whites and niggers swimming together out there.")

"Did this nigger girl, Eunice, have on a bathing suit when all this happened? I mean, was she right in the pond with the Allen children?" Grady's voice asked.

"No, sir. She didn't have no bathing suit on. She just jumped right in without one."

(The man wearing the steel-rimmed glasses asked his neighbor, "What was that? Did I hear what I heard?" The neighbor, grinning, said, "You sure did." The older man slapped his knee. "God Almighty!" he said. "Niggers and whites swimming together without no clothes on. Right here in Ashton County!")

Finally, the machine stopped talking and began making a whirring noise. Sheriff Copeland punched the black button and the plastic wheels stopped. The white light you could see out in the auditorium cooled to red, then disappeared. The silence lasted until the tiny light disappeared.

"He oughta be strung up!" The shout came from the rear of the auditorium. It shattered the silence and three hundred voices rushed forth behind the single shout. "Please, ladies and gentlemen," Grady said, raising his right hand and shaking his head. "We must not let our emotions get the best of our judgment. We must continue this meeting in a democratic manner."

"Democratic, hell! Let's take care of him here and now," some voices demanded. Some of the people stood as they shouted. But none moved toward John, who sat motionless, his head bowed.

Grady continued to ask for silence and his amplified voice finally overpowered the others. "We have people living among us," he said, "who would overthrow our way of life. The only way to deal with them is in the good, old American tradition. We will ask for a show of hands on two questions. Sheriff Copeland, will you and Mr. Hayes count the votes, please?"

Anse whispered to Grady and the county attorney nodded and said into the microphone, "Yes, thank you, Anse. You are absolutely correct. John Allen, do you have anything to say in your own behalf?"

"Yeah, let him talk!"

The crowd wanted to see John Allen. It wanted to hear him say words. What does he look like? Does he have a foreign accent?

John stood up stiffly and turned to face the crowd. "What can I say?" he said. "I seem to be accused of something but I don't know exactly what."

"Get up on the stage!"

"We can't hear you!"

"Come up here and use the microphone," Grady said, bending down so John could hear him.

John walked to the end of the stage, climbed the steps and walked to the middle and took the microphone from Grady.

"I don't know what to say," he mumbled, "I was told of this meeting only yesterday. Now that I'm here I'm still puzzled. I heard some young Negro boys being questioned by some county officials. One said a baby-sitter pulled my child out of the pond. They said something about the movies we show on Sundays. What am I accused of?"

"How do you feel about segregation?"

"What?" John said, turning to Grady. "What did he say?"

Grady took the microphone and spoke into it. "The gentleman asked you, John Allen, how you feel about segregation. Is segregation right or wrong in your opinion?"

John inhaled and let the air out slowly. Then he asked, "Do I have to answer that here . . . now?"

"Mr. Allen wants to know if he has to answer that question here and now," Grady said into the microphone.

The harsh chorus rolled over them. "Yessssss!"

John struggled with the anger he felt inside him. He took the microphone from Grady and said into it. "I'll try to make this as concise as possible. I believe very sincerely that segregation is unchristian."

He pushed the microphone at Grady, "I think they've heard all they want to from me now," he said.

"Wait," Grady said. "We haven't voted yet."

"Voted?" John said. "Voted on what?"

"On whether or not you and your family should continue to live in this county."

"Grady, do you realize what you are doing?" John said. "No, of course, you don't. Go ahead and vote. You can mail me the results."

Then John walked off the stage down the short ramp. Phil was waiting there for him. They walked side by side up the center aisle and through the wide doorway.

When they were outside Phil said, "I don't know what to say to you, John."

"I don't know what to say to myself."

"Go on out to the farm. I'll see you out there later. Tomorrow. I've got to go in tonight and write the story of this meeting."

John nodded. They walked in opposite directions and in few

moments the sound of the motors of their cars blended with the cheers that came from inside the auditorium.

Phil drove to the *Dispatch*. He sat for thirty-five minutes trying to put what he had seen and heard on paper. Then the telephone on Ranch's desk rang. He got up and walked to the desk and lifted the receiver to his ear.

"Hello."

"Phil?" It was Mr. Stanford's voice.

"Yes."

"You should have stayed a little longer, Phil. You missed the big climax."

"You mean the voting? Hell, I know how that came out."

"No. The voting went as expected. Your friend Senator Windham came in."

"Jerry?"

"Yes. He'd been standing backstage apparently. Anyhow, he came out and asked to say a few words."

"Good old Jerry!" Phil said. "Why didn't I think of him. Those people will listen to Jerry."

"You don't understand, Phil," Mr. Stanford said. "Jerry announced tonight that he has volunteered to defend Mike Heaney and R. L. Squires in court."

18.

"HELLO."

Janie's soft voice broke through the protective crust which had formed around Phil's awareness. He had dialed the number hypnotically.

"Hello?"

"Janie, this is Phil. Is Jerry there?"

"No, Phil. He isn't. He should be here soon. Want me to tell him to call you?"

Did she know? If she did, did it mean anything to her? No, there were few here who would know what it meant. That it meant Phil and his editorials had been cut loose from the bank. He thought of the piece of driftwood he threw in the river the day he and Ann were on the sandbar—whirling wildly, then being drawn under by the inevitable.

"Yes, tell him I called. That I want to talk to him . . . no matter what time he gets in. If I'm not here I'll be at home. I'm at the paper now."

"All rightee," she said cheerfully. "When are you and Ann coming by to see us? I'm getting concerned about my pretty cousin. Are your intentions honorable, sir?"

"I'm sorry, Janie," he mumbled. "I can't talk now. Just tell Jerry."

He hung up and ran a palm over his hair and frowned at the half-filled page of type before him. He thought of Janie's blissful detachment and cursed her and thought how glad he was that he was not married to a Janie Crutchfield. He must marry Ann—right away, next

203

week. He could not lose her now. The paper in his typewriter waited. He tore it out of the machine and dropped it on the floor. He must see Ann now. Have her near him.

He typed some notes hurriedly and left them for Ranch to fashion into a news story tomorrow. His notes included Jerry's announcement. He telephoned Ann and told her what Jerry had done and that he would drive by for her. Then he went to Werner Park and they rode in silence to his house. They could not talk at her house with her mother and Aunt Amy hovering over them.

His father was sitting in the living room by the phonograph. The prison farm record was playing.

"Hello Ann. Hi, son," Arrow said. "How about you two stopping awhile and having a drink with an old man? I want to talk to you about something, Phil."

"I need to talk to you too, Dad," Phil said, knowing suddenly that he did.

"What about?"

"I can't sum it up," Phil said. "But somebody's all wrong. Me or everybody I've known all my life."

The father stared at his glass. "Why do you have to be like you are?" he said. "Why can't you be interested in putting out a good entertainment page?"

"What are you talking about?" Phil said.

"Before we let our hair down," Ann said, "and my woman's intuition says we are about to do just that, how about a drink?"

"I can use one," Phil said.

"You can sweeten mine up some," Arrow said, handing her his half-empty glass.

The chant of the prisoners' recorded voices came into the silence that followed Ann's departure for the liquor cabinet.

> It takes rocks and gravel, baby,
> to make a solid road, sugar.
> It takes a good-looking woman, baby,
> to make a good-looking whore....

Phil stepped across in front of his father and turned off the record player. "I can't take that now," he said.

"I should have turned it off," Arrow said. "Interesting record though. I've heard some of those work songs all my life and paid no attention to the words."

Ann brought their drinks. She sat on the sofa and Phil sat in the straight-backed chair opposite his father.

"All right," Phil said, "We have our drinks. Now, what did you mean by that entertainment page crack?"

"You went to the Bogue Nitta School meeting tonight?" Arrow asked.

"Yes," Phil said. "I was there."

"They put on a good show?"

"They sure did. The crowd loved it. Grady and Anse and Copeland are probably still taking bows."

Arrow drained his glass.

"How can these people swallow such crap, Dad?" Phil said.

"They are products of the System, son," Arrow said. "That's why I said you should use your energies putting out a good entertainment page or sports page. Forget the editorial page. We'll run garden columns and advice to the lovelorn. If you can't write editorials like a good, loyal Southerner you get kicked out of the game. That's the rule of the System."

"But I insist that I *am* a good, loyal Southerner," Phil said. "I was born here, grew up here. I love the South. Why can't I say what I think? Who made the rules for a System that allows only one side to speak out?"

"The rules just grew," Arrow said, showing interest now in his son's face. "They grew out of the dung of defeat. And it got so anyone who opposed them was thought to be from the enemy camp. So nobody bothered to break the rules for so many years that they became not simple considerations for a proud people's humiliation but sacred dogma. Then, when things began to happen that caused some to question the holy writ, it was too late."

"I haven't heard you talk like that in a long time, Dad," Phil said.

"No, I suppose you haven't."

"The trouble is I thought I could play by the rules and be honest with myself at the same time," Phil said. "Damn it, I still believe we could have done it if Jerry had stuck with me. But what can one man do alone?"

Pain fled across Arrow's face. His son saw it.

"I'm sorry, Dad. I didn't mean that the way it sounded. I had hopes Jerry could do something if he became governor without asking for Citizens Council help."

"What's Jerry done?"

"He volunteered tonight at Bogue Nitta to defend Mike and R.L."

"So now you are alone?"

"Hell, Dad, if Jerry can't trust these people any more than that, how can I?"

"Jerry *has* let you down," Arrow said slowly. "But before that I did. I let you down."

"Now, Dad . . ."

"No, let me finish. I taught you to be a newspaperman. Then I tried to make you forget everything I had taught you."

Ann held her breath and put her hands behind her back and crossed her fingers.

"I don't know what you mean," Phil said.

"I lied to you six years ago," Arrow said dully. "I was afraid and I lied to you. Afraid Hamp Auld would take the *Dispatch* away from me. I had fought all those years. I was tired. I could see the reaction of the Supreme Court's school segregation decision. It was a club in their hands. A weapon they hadn't had before. They told me if I didn't silence you they'd swing that club."

"Why didn't you tell me? We could have . . ."

"I know. But I was scared. Scared and ashamed to tell you I was scared. The easy way was to act like big daddy giving orders."

"All those years I was trying to believe the way I thought you believed . . ."

"Auld was here again last night, son. He wants me to stop you again."

"He does?"

Arrow stood up. "I'm not much good any more," he said. "I probably couldn't even write a decent news story any more. But I say, to hell with them. You're my editor. Whatever you say is okay with the publisher. I'll even cover the police beat if we have to cut the staff—for economic reasons."

Ann leaped to her feet and kissed the defiant old man. "Mr. Arrow," she said. "I love you."

"Well!" Arrow said, "maybe this integrity business has its own rewards."

"Dad, you mean it, don't you?" Phil said, standing too now.

"I never meant anything more in my life," Arrow said.

"I feel better already."

"Okay, partner," Phil said happily. "The trial starts in two weeks. We've got time to bust their little game wide open. If we keep pounding the truth into these people, it *will* penetrate. Jerry gave up too soon. We'll show him he did."

"Ann, mix us another drink," Arrow said. "This is a night for celebrating. The fighting Arrows are back in the newspaper business. Gonna die with our boots on and all that."

"We are not going to die," Phil said. "The grand jury's indictment of Mike and R.L. proves that."

"I hope you're right, son," Arrow said.

"I know I am," Phil said.

"Here are the drinks," Ann said.

19.

ON SUNDAY MORNING there were three of them. They walked out of the hotel lobby onto the wide, shaded porch about nine o'clock. They stood there stretching and talking awhile, then strolled leisurely across the street to the courthouse square. They were the only people on the square, of course, on Sunday morning, but that didn't seem to bother them. They examined the Confederate memorial statue, pointed at high corners of the courthouse building, then stood watching cars go by while the warm wind whirled leaves and paper about their feet. The heavy texture of the cloth of their suits alone would have marked them as strangers. But, added to that, they were uncommonly curious—even for tourists. They found out somehow that the men they saw driving by—slowly to get a good look at the strangers—gathered at The Grill or in the hotel coffeeshop every Sunday before church. They went first to the hotel coffeeshop, then to The Grill, and asked nearly everyone around questions most Ashtonians wouldn't even ask themselves.

People said what made them the maddest was the impudent way they asked the questions. Colonel Blinken said Yankees just naturally have an impudent way about them, especially Yankee newspapermen, which these three were. They arrived in Ashton Saturday on the afternoon plane from Memphis. Rush Gamble, the hotel manager, said they registered as representatives of the New York *Standard,* the New York *Daily Reflector* and the Chicago *Sun.* Rush said they must have stayed up drinking most of that first night because they came downstairs about three in the morning wanting something to eat and acting like it was his fault everything in town was closed. They finally found a taxi and went to Smitty's Motel Coffeeshop out on the highway. Smitty stayed open all night to catch the truck driver and tourist trade. He said they were pretty rowdy out there and asked him and the waitress, Alice, a bunch of questions about Shine Tatum. But, Smitty said, picking his teeth the way he always seems to be doing, they didn't learn a single thing in his place. ("No, sirree, bobtail bull.") He recognized their Yankee accents right away and could tell they weren't ordinary tourists. ("When you've seen as many tourists as old Smitty has you can tell. You can tell.") He told Alice to say no more than professional courtesy called for.

By noon Sunday everyone in town who took interest in local gossip—and that included a very large percentage of the population—knew they were in town, who they were and why they were there. The main topic of the discussions after church was how these visitors should be treated. Some said the town should go out of its way to be cooperative and friendly, what with the Chamber of Commerce spending all that money trying to get industries to move from the North to Ashton County. A few, of course, thought they should be run out of town, but nobody paid much attention to them. Finally, it was decided the town would be friendly and co-operative. ("You don't have to strain yourself—this is a free country and a man's got a right to be friendly to whoever he wants but if you run into one of them on the street just be polite.") Somehow—as it does in any small town—the word spread and by late afternoon everyone was tipping his hat or nodding at the visitors. Colonel Blinken and some of the lawyers from the Ash-Blinken Building invited them to the Yacht Club for drinks. ("Best not take them to the Country Club. The women and children will be running around out there in shorts and bathing suits, you know.") By the time they got to the Yacht Club to meet Colonel Blinken and the lawyers there were six of them. Two more from New York and one from Detroit. *("My Lordy, are they sending everybody down here?"—"No, sir, but it's a pretty big story up North."—"It is? Well, I declare!")*

On Monday, the day court convened, there were seventy-eight of them, counting television people with their noisy, clicking cameras and endless cables, and magazine writers. There was an artist from *Life* magazine. He sat on a folding stool throughout the trial and sketched frantically, but only one of his drawings came out in the magazine.

Monday and Tuesday, when only jury picking was going on, people got so interested in watching Yankee newspaper and television people they stopped talking about the trial. The *New York Times* reporter was invited to speak at the Rotary Club meeting on Monday. ("Well, hell, he's a Southern boy. Lives in Chattanooga.") He accepted the invitation and many Rotarians were relieved when he did not mention the race question. He talked about the "great economic potential of the South." Called it "a frontier, with tremendous untapped resources."

There were, of course, reporters there from Southern papers— New Orleans, Memphis, Baton Rouge, Jackson, Birmingham and Little Rock. One could pick them out because they were more properly dressed for the climate, in tropical weight suits or sport shirts without coats. But they fraternized so uninhibitedly with the others that local people were inclined to lump them all in the same category—a somewhat alien class, not to be wholly trusted because they carried with them the ominous power to place what they saw and heard and interpreted from it before the eyes of thousands of newspaper readers. Ashtonians read little, if any, of what the out-of-town reporters wrote in their hotel rooms each night. Some tried to get the special Western Union men, sent in for the occasion from Memphis, to tell what they punched out on the machines. But these telegraphers were a clannish group too and stubbornly uninterested in talking shop after hours. Finally, the town became convinced that what was being written was bad for Ashton County, the state, and the South in general. So, after a few days, the hat tipping and the friendly nods stopped and wherever the reporters went they were met by noncommittal stares, and their questions more and more were answered by grunts and shrugs. Some members of the Rotary Club decided, after discussing it awhile one night, that the *New York Times* man, Chattanooga resident or not, had indirectly insulted the South in his speech about "untapped resources."

Throughout the tedious process of selecting the jury the reporters wandered in and out of the hot, smoky courtroom, peering at the crowd with their curious, probing eyes; sitting sometimes in the audience and sometimes at the tables Circuit Judge Conrad K. Hansberry had ordered placed for them on the crowded raised area behind the rail where the drama was to be enacted. The tables snugly surrounded the jury box and the long polished table where the attorneys would sit and there was one on each side of the judge's desk. (It is an old courthouse and there is no regular "bench" from which the judge can preside above the confusion on the courtroom floor.) The photographers, with their chrome-trimmed black boxes of assorted sizes and shapes and brown bags hanging from their shoulders, squatted on the floor as near as possible to Judge Hansberry's desk. The judge allowed them to bring their cameras inside the courtroom, but warned them sternly that pictures could be taken only during recesses. One shutter snap during the trial proper, he said, would get them all evicted.

Even on Monday the courtroom was filled. The aisles were jammed until Judge Hansberry rapped on the scarred desk with his gavel and announced that no one would be allowed to stand in the aisles because of fire ordinances and ordered the deputies to keep them clear. And even on Monday some spectators who had been to Sumner to watch the Emmett Till murder trial brought lunches and iced tea in thermos jugs. On Tuesday Pete Handley, the courthouse custodian, had his four sons selling cold Cokes and candy in the courtroom and in the corridors. By Tuesday, too, the ladies of the Magnolia Garden Club had set up a temporary booth on the square in front of the courthouse and were selling sandwiches and hot dogs. That afternoon the Jaycees put up a similar booth at the other end of the square to raise money for their Christmas street lighting project.

The I. C. Railroad track runs by the east side of the courthouse. Joe Chu, a descendant of a Chinese couple who came to the region back in the thirties when some plantation owners brought in coolie labor, has a small grocery store facing the street that runs parallel with the tracks across from the square. The newspaper reporters started going over to Chu's for lunch because he sold beer and the store was handy and the food was inexpensive. Two or three would pool their money and buy a loaf of bread, a stick of bologna and a jar of pickles and make sandwiches right there in the store. Joe Chu and his wife were very happy during the trial. They did more business that week than they ordinarily did in a month. The television announcers and cameramen didn't patronize Chu. They preferred the air-conditioned comfort of the hotel coffeeshop.

On Tuesday at 11:33 a.m. the final juryman—number thirteen, in case one of the regular jurymen became ill during the trial—was agreed upon by the defense and the prosecution. Judge Hansberry recessed for lunch until two.

At ten minutes before two, the first whip of excitement snapped in the crowded courtroom. Three Negro newspapermen walked in and asked Sheriff Copeland for permission to sit behind the rail at a press table. Sheriff Copeland looked at them thoughtfully. Then he said, "You mean you boys are newspapermen?"

"Yes," said the tallest, who wore a gray, Italian-silk suit. "Here is my press card."

The other two—one short and constructed stockily and with very black skin, the other a little taller, with light-yellow skin—dug into their pockets for wallets and produced similar cards.

(Sheriff Copeland hardly looked at the cards. He tried to decide what to do. Under ordinary circumstances this would have posed no problem for him, but Judge Hansberry had warned him repeatedly that "if any trouble pops up out there, Slim, I'm going to hold you responsible. The eyes of the world are on Ashton now and we're not going to let anything happen that will make us look foolish.")

"Just a minute," Copeland said and hurried to the small room behind the judge's desk. Judge Hansberry was rising to his feet to enter the courtroom and end the recess when Copeland closed the door and leaned against it breathing heavy as if he had sprinted fifty yards. "Judge," Copeland said, "there's three niggers out there that say they are newspaper reporters. One's from Pittsburgh, one's from New York City, and the other one's from Chicago. They want to sit at the reporters' tables. What am I going to do with them?"

"Don't get in a sweat, Slim," Judge Hansberry drawled. He turned and looked out the window and said to the court reporter who traveled the circuit with him, "I knew I should have retired last year. I would have been fishing somewhere right now if I had. Let me think a minute."

———————

In the courtroom a man leaning against the rear wall cracked his knuckles and it could be heard all the way to the jury box. The two ceiling fans hanging over the area behind the rail moved so slowly that flies rode around on the black blades. A small piece of dried, brown plaster, brittle with age, fell from the ceiling onto the shoulder of the tallest Negro reporter. He brushed it away nonchalantly, whispered something to the stocky one, and all three laughed and looked up at the ceiling.

"Smart-aleck sonsabitches," a man's voice from the audience said.

Two deputies—ruddy faces set in forbidding frowns—came out of the judge's office carrying a table between them. "Make way!" the one in front ordered the photographers, and they took the table to the aisle on the west side and placed it near the middle windows, outside the rail. They went back to the judge's room and came out again immediately. This time the one in front carried a chair and the one behind carried two chairs. They motioned with their heads to the three Negro reporters. The Negroes looked at each other and shrugged and walked over to the table and sat in the chairs the deputies pushed at them.

Judge Hansberry entered the courtroom moments later and the bailiff chanted, "Everybody rise! The circuit court of Ashton County is now in session." Everyone stood and Judge Hansberry sat and rubbed the back of his neck with the handle of his gavel, then tapped on the desk with the gavel and everyone sat down. Judge Hansberry nodded at District Attorney Robert Lee Featherstone, who stood and nodded at the judge, indicating he was ready to begin.

District Attorney Featherstone wiped his damp forehead with an already soiled white handkerchief. Stuffed the handkerchief back into his right hip pocket. Pushed his chair back against the long, polished table and edged his way around, behind Ross Grady, to a spot at the immediate right of the judge's desk, between the judge and the jury. He looked first at the confident coolness of his opponent, Jerry Windham; glanced quickly at the silent, waiting crowd, then down at his yellow note pad—where he found only the doodling he had done as he waited for the judge to end the recess. He sighed at the pad and faced the Jury.

"Gentlemen," he said, nodding to the thirteen somber faces, "you have been selected by the defense and the state to sit in judgment on two of your fellow Ashton Countians who are charged by the state with the crime of taking a human life. This is indeed a serious responsibility."

He paused and looked at the water pitcher, surrounded by glistening glasses, on the table he had just walked away from.

"You have been chosen, as I said," he continued, "to sit in judgment of fellow Ashton Countians and, as you have been chosen for that duty, it is my duty to present the state's case against them to the best of my ability. It is not my duty to sit in judgment. It is my duty to present the evidence gathered in this case and to present it in an unbiased manner."

He looked now at the tables where the newspaper reporters sat, busily taking notes.

"It is also my duty as a sworn public officer," he said, still watching the reporters, "to emphasize to you that, under the eyes of the law, it is just as much a crime to kill a nigger as it is to kill a white man. Each of you was asked several times, during the jury selection period, if you would be influenced in any way by the fact that the deceased was a . . . a colored man. You each said it would not."

He emphasized "not" and turned away from the reporters to direct the remainder of his opening address to the jurymen.

"I am bound by the oath of my office to present the evidence in this case to you," he said. "Then, gentlemen of the jury, it will be your duty to decide whether or not the evidence which has been presented is enough to convict these two defendants. When I have presented the evidence, with the able assistance of the honorable county attorney, Ross Grady of Ashton, my duty will have been done. My conscience will be clear. I will then be able to wash my hands of the case. Knowing that I have, to the best of my ability, fulfilled the requirements of my oath, I will be able to go home that night and get a good night's sleep. It is your duty, gentlemen, to reach a decision, when you have heard the evidence, that will allow you to do the same thing—go home and get a good night's sleep. Thank you, gentlemen. That's all I have to say to you at this time."

Featherstone wiped his wet forehead again and walked back to his chair. Grady put a hand on his shoulder as he sat down and said, "Nice going, Bob. Very appropriate, I say."

Judge Hansberry nodded to Jerry. "Senator Windham, are you ready?"

"Yes, your Honor," Jerry said. He glanced at his notes on the yellow legal pad on the table, pushed his chair back with the backs of his legs as he stood, and spoke from that spot. He faced the jury. The crowd was to his left, because his chair was at the end of the table, and the judge to his right. Mike and R.L., in that order, sat silent at his left with their backs to the crowd, as they had throughout the hours the jury was being picked. Mike kept a chew of tobacco in his mouth because Jerry had told him it might be wiser if he didn't smoke behind the rail, although the judge allowed smoking in the audience. Periodically, Mike glanced swiftly around him and lifted a pint cardboard container to within a few inches of his mouth and spit in it.

"Your Honor," Jerry said. "It is so hot in the courtroom I would like to request permission for myself, and anyone else who wishes, to be allowed to remove my coat. Being a country boy I kind of work better in shirtsleeves."

A murmur of appreciation moved around the room. Several jury-men smiled and nudged each other.

"Request granted, Senator Windham." Judge Hansberry smiled. "I would take my coat off too, but I've got a hole in my shirt. You gentle-men representing the state may do likewise if you wish."

As he and Featherstone and Grady removed their coats and hung them on the backs of their chairs, Jerry turned so he could see Phil's grim face among the faces at one of the newspaper tables. Then he put his attention on the jury.

"I consider it a privilege," he said, "to be able to stand here before you gentlemen of the jury today and defend my former schoolmate and his buddy. I consider it a privilege because this is not an ordi-nary trial. The state has charged that Mike Heaney and R. L. Squires did willfully and knowingly and with malice aforethought kill and murder one Theodore Shine Tatum. But I know that their only crime was being a bit overzealous in their love for their state and its sacred traditions. The state has charged that Mike and R.L. went to Shine Tatum's shack in the hills of Ashton County—near the place they call Just-Ten Acres—and dragged the nigra into their car and took him somewhere—somewhere, mind you—somewhere on the river and, after killing him somehow—somehow, mind you—dumped his body into the river."

He turned now to face the press table where Phil sat.

"Now, I want the gentlemen of the press to hear this," Jerry said. "Especially those from the Northern press. If this charge can be prov-en—and in the great tradition of freedom of the individual on which this great nation of ours was founded, it must be proven; the defendant does not have to disprove anything—then I will be the first to say that Mike Heaney and R. L. Squires should be found guilty and given the maximum sentence."

He moved his eyes from left to right, gazing briefly into the eyes of each juryman.

"That maximum penalty," he said slowly, "is, as you know, death in the gas chamber."

He poured some water from the pitcher into a glass and drank one swallow from it.

"But," he continued, "if the state fails to prove this charge—and remember the charge is murder, not kidnapping, not trespassing, not anything else which might be mentioned in the course of this trial, but murder—if the state fails to prove this charge, then it is your duty to set these defendants free. And this charge must be proven, according to the majestic laws of our land, beyond a *shadow* of a doubt. A shadow of a doubt."

Jerry took a deep breath, then continued: "And let me tell you, gentlemen, just one of the many things the state must prove before these two Ashton County boys can be legally convicted. The state must first prove that a murder was committed. Let us not forget that for one minute. Just because a grand jury issued an indictment does not mean that a murder has been committed. A grand jury may issue an indictment for many reasons. A grand jury can issue an indictment on the slimmest of circumstantial evidence because an indictment is not in any way a conviction. It is only an admission that *perhaps* a crime has been committed and *perhaps* there is enough indication that this person or that one was involved. But when the case gets in court, gentlemen, it is a different story. Then the crime and the involvement of those charged must be proved beyond a *shadow* of a doubt. So, the first thing the state must prove is that Shine Tatum was murdered. And believe me, gentlemen, there are those among us today who believe sincerely that Theodore Shine Tatum is walking the streets of Chicago or Dee-troit this very minute—very much alive—and laughing with his N-double-A-C-P friends at the headlines that are putting a smear across the good name of Ashton County."

"Why doesn't Featherstone object?" the whisper cut through the silence. It came from Phil.

Featherstone looked questioningly at Grady, then stood and said, "I object, your Honor."

"On what grounds, Mr. Featherstone?" Judge Hansberry asked.

"Well . . . on the grounds that he's not supposed to talk about things like that now," Featherstone said, wiping his face with the soiled handkerchief. "Things that haven't even come up yet and have nothing whatsoever to do with this case."

"Objection sustained," the judge said.

"Yes, sir," Jerry said.

Featherstone sat down. Grady frowned at him.

"That's about all I have to say now, gentlemen," Jerry said to the jury. "I put my trust in you gentlemen to follow the dictates of your conscience and do what is best for your community and your state."

"Are you gentlemen ready to proceed?" Judge Hansberry said as Jerry sat down.

"Give us five minutes," Grady said.

Judge Hansberry nodded. "There'll be a five-minute recess. But in order to avoid delay, I will ask everyone to remain seated. You may talk but do not leave the courtroom unless you intend to stay gone."

The tall windows lining each side of the courtroom (six on each side) were opened as wide as they would open, inviting any breeze which might stir outside to come in and move the smoke. But there were no breezes with strength enough to do that. The smoke was stirred only by fifty or so small, round, cardboard fans and as many folded newspapers and magazines fluttering in front of faces in the audience. The windows were ten feet high. There were no curtains or shades and broad and bright shafts of sunlight angled down through them. The smoke drifted up through the shafts of light and hung, gray and wispy, against the ceiling. In the narrow balcony, above the stir and murmur on the main floor, Negroes sat hunched forward, peering through the smoke. Sweat ran shiny down their black and brown and yellow and uniformly expressionless faces.

Phil looked up at the balcony. "That's the second jury up there," he said to Alex Rushmore, the New York reporter who sat beside him at the press table. "Waiting to see if the white people of Ashton County will call it murder when a white man has killed a Negro."

"All right, bailiff," Judge Hansberry said, tapping on his desk with the gavel. "Call the first witness."

"Call Sheriff Copeland," Featherstone said.

Copeland stepped out of the crowd behind the judge's desk and stood by the witness chair.

"Do you solemnly swear to tell the truth, the whole truth, and nothing but the truth?" the bailiff said, squinting and holding the Bible under Copeland's heavy left hand.

"I sure do," Copeland said.

"State your name, please?" Featherstone said when Copeland had squeezed his bulk into the witness chair.

"My name is A. O. Copeland."

"Are you the duly elected sheriff of Ashton County?"

"I am."

"And that's the county we in right now?"

"It is."

"Sheriff Copeland, as you know, this is the trial of Mike Heaney and R. L. Squires, charged jointly with willfully and knowingly and with malice aforethought killing and murdering one Theodore Shine Tatum. Would you tell the jury, in your own words, what you know about this case? Just start back when it first came to your attention and tell the jury what you know."

Copeland shifted his weight and faced the jury. "Well, sir," he said, "it was about midnight the night of June seventeenth, or early the morning of the eighteenth, whichever way you look at it, when I got this phone call. It was John Allen, the one that calls himself a missionary and lives at Just-Ten Acres. He, Allen, said he was calling from old Doc Hogarth's. He said he had been driving by Shine Tatum's shack and there was a fire—"

"I object," Jerry said. "He can't tell what was said to him in a conversation. That's hearsay. Let Allen testify for himself."

"Sustained," Judge Hansberry said, his eyes closed as he leaned back in his chair and listened.

"Just tell what you did after you talked with Allen on the phone," Featherstone said.

"Well, after I talked to Allen I went back to bed," Copeland said.

"And then what happened?"

"I went to sleep."

Featherstone frowned at the titter that came from the crowd behind him. "I mean what happened next in regard to the case?" he said.

"Well, next some people told me—"

"I object," Jerry said.

"Yes," Featherstone said. "Sheriff, you can't tell what people told you. Just tell what you actually did next in connection with this case."

"Let's see," the sheriff said. "If I can't tell what people said about it, I guess the next thing I did was go out to the river and look at a body."

"And why did you go to the river?"

"Cause Jess Berkley telephoned and said . . ." Copeland looked at Jerry. "Well, anyhow, after I talked to Jess on the phone I went to the river—down where that dog-leg bend is—and saw this nigger's body sticking up out of the water."

"Then what did you do?"

"I called Joe Adcock, the coroner. He floated the body down to the next low place and put it out on the bank."

"And whose body was it?"

"I object," Jerry said from his chair. "There has been no testimony yet that would indicate Sheriff Copeland could have identified the body."

"Sustained."

"That's what I'm trying to do, judge," Featherstone said, some irritation showing in his voice. "I'm trying to show how he identified the body. Very well, sheriff, what did you do then?"

"We took the body in to the nigger funeral home," Copeland said. "Leastways, it was took in. Then I sent a deputy out to Just-Ten Acres, where Shine Tatum's nephew was staying with the Allens. He brought the boy in to look at the body."

"And what did the boy say?"

"I object," Jerry said. "Let the boy testify for himself. Neither of the defendants was present when he looked at the body."

"Sustained."

Featherstone stepped within reach of the water pitcher and poured half a glassful and drank it. "Sheriff Copeland, did you examine the body?"

"Yeah, I looked at it."

"Did you determine the cause of death?"

"I figured he drowned."

"Didn't you tell me you found signs of violence?"

"His head was bashed in, if that's what you mean," Copeland said. "But that could have been done by something floating past it."

"But it also could have been done before the body was thrown into the river, could it not?"

"I guess so."

Jerry stood this time. "I object," he said. "We do not care what the sheriff guesses. Only what he knows for a fact is pertinent."

Featherstone wiped his forehead. "Did you call a coroner's jury together?"

"Joe Adcock did," Copeland said. "That's his job."

"And what did the coroner's jury say?"

"I object," Jerry said. "Let the coroner, if he is called to testify, make his own report."

"Dad burn it, Slim," Featherstone said. "You arrested Mike and R.L., didn't you? Why did you do that?"

"Actually, they kind of turned themselves in," Copeland said. "They said they heard some talk about the body we took out of the river being Shine Tatum's and they wanted to get it all cleared up. They said they went out to the Tatum nigger's shack one night and took him off and talked to him about filing that voting suit, then let him go. They said with all the talk that was being stirred up by the Ashton *Dispatch* they didn't want anybody to think they were afraid to face the truth."

"Never mind all that, sheriff," Featherstone said. "Did you or did you not arrest Mike Heaney and R. L. Squires on the charge of murder in connection with the death of Theodore Shine Tatum?"

"Yeah, but like I said—"

"Never mind," Featherstone interrupted. "Just answer the question, yes or no."

"Yes."

Featherstone looked at Judge Hansberry. "That's all for this witness right now, judge. I might want to call him back though."

Judge Hansberry tapped on his desk, then laid the gavel down and pulled his watch from the tiny pocket at the waist of the dark-blue, wash-and-wear pants. "Gentlemen," he said, "if you have no objections I am going to recess this case until nine o'clock tomorrow morning. It looks as if it might go on for several days and the court has some other, minor cases to dispose of. We can do that this afternoon and it will clear the docket for this session."

"No objection," Jerry said.

"That's all right with me, judge," Featherstone said.

"Very well, gentlemen," the judge said, and the crowd began to rise noisily to its feet. "Let's have order, please," the judge said, rapping sternly on his desk. "Everyone will remain seated until the jury has filed out. Deputies, see that no one leaves until the jury is clear. Now, gentlemen, you will have to spend the night here. Quarters have been provided for you. You will remain together at all times and refrain from discussing this case with anyone. If you have messages—to your wives or business associates—just tell the bailiff. He is there to serve you. Let me caution you again against talking about this case with anyone even among yourselves—until all the testimony has been given. That's all for today, gentlemen. You will follow the bailiff. See you in the morning."

The five farmers, two storekeepers, one minister, one truck driver, one retired railroad brakeman, one insurance salesman, and the pharmacist who was the alternate juryman, stood and followed the bailiff. Single file they marched, their eyes straight ahead, through the rail gate and up the middle aisle as the white spectators watched from both sides and the Negroes watched from overhead.

When the door closed behind the last juryman in the line, Judge Hansberry tapped on his desk and said, "This trial will continue tomorrow morning. As soon as the courtroom is cleared I would like to see the district attorney and those others who have business in the court other than that in connection with this trial."

He rapped sharply on his desk and the crowd began to move toward the exits.

20.

MOST OF THE NEWSPAPER REPORTERS had managed to get rooms on the fourth floor of the Hotel Ashton. (The hotel is the only building in Ashton more than three stories tall. It is eight stories. A split in its brick outside wall runs across the front, which faces Main Street. The split is filled with cement and looks like a jagged scar. The scar has been there since four months after the hotel was put up in 1949 and doesn't seem to be getting any wider, but City Engineer Rube Hawkins says someday one side of the building will sink away from the other side and "it'll be hell to pay." Then, Hawkins says almost every time he drives past the hotel, the city council will be damned sorry it gave permission for the extra floors over his objections.) The three reporters who arrived the Saturday night before the trial began were given fourth-floor rooms and when the others started arriving Rush Gamble decided to put them all up there together. ("No use putting them around with the other guests," Rush told Anse. "They'd just keep everybody awake.") The Tuesday night after Copeland's testimony had got the trial proper under way, Phil went up to Alex Rushmore's room. Doors to most rooms on the floor were wide open, he saw as he stepped off the self-service elevator into the narrow, dimly lighted hall. He heard Billie Holliday's haunting voice singing of her troubles with a man. He discovered the music came from Alex's room. The door of 404 was open. Alex sat before a portable typewriter that stood on top of its black case in a chair pushed against the wall at Phil's left. Joe Rivers of the New

York *Daily Reflector* faced the two windows. Rivers' typewriter clattered steadily. Alex's was silent.

"God!" Alex said to his typewriter as Phil entered the room, "everything I write reads like a poor man's Faulkner. What's your lead?"

Rivers picked a sheet of copy paper from the bed beside him. "The bravest man in Ashton County today is eleven-year-old Cooter Dunbar," he read. "How's that?'

"Horse shit!" Alex snorted. "Oh, hello, Phil. Joe, this is the bravest son of a bitch in Ashton County today. Meet Phil Arrow. Have you seen the stuff he's been writing in the Ashton paper? Hell, it's rougher than ours and these people are reading it. How do you get away with it, Phil?"

"I'm not sure I will." Phil smiled, and sat on one of the twin beds.

"Glad to meet you, Arrow," Rivers said. "Met your man Harden yesterday. He gave me most of the background stuff I had in my story last night. Appreciate it."

"Have a drink, Phil," Alex said, nodding toward the bottle on the bed table. "I'll finish this soon." He bent to the record player on the floor beside his chair and put on another record. In a moment the hoarse, penetrating voice of Bessie Smith shouted, "Twenty-five cents! I wouldn't pay twenty-five cents to go in nowhere. . . ." Then she began singing about a rent-raising party in a Harlem tenement house.

"I don't see how you concentrate with that hollering going on," Rivers said. "Glad I got most of my story done before you came in."

"Kiss my ass," Alex said and began typing.

"What are you trying to do, win the Pulitzer Prize?" Rivers taunted.

Page Crowder, manager of the Ashton Western Union office, came in then. "Are you finished yet, Mr. Rushmore?" he asked. "It's getting a little late."

"Here's my stuff," Rivers said, handing six sheets of paper to Crowder. "Come on, Alex, chop it off. Let's get down to the serious drinking. This man has to get home to the wife and kiddies."

Crowder took the copy from Rivers and smiled gratefully. "I would like to get home," he said apologetically. "The home office said to pull all stops to give you fellows service though, so I'm not complaining, mind you. But I would like to get home. All you fellows coming in and sending stuff out sure has been something. The home office sent four special operators down from Memphis to help out, but those fellows work just eight hours. Union, you know. I'm manager of the office here, so I don't come under the union."

"Hear the man?" Rivers said. "What're you doing, trying to make it rhyme?"

"If you'd keep your goddam mouth shut a minute I could finish," Alex said. He was typing rapidly now.

"I don't make as much noise as that damn record player of yours," Rivers said. But he poured a drink and sat sipping it until Alex finished, which was about ten minutes later.

Alex scanned the last page he had written and put it with four others and handed them to Crowder. "Sorry I kept you up," he said.

"That's okay," Crowder said, taking the copy and hurrying out of the room. "The home office said to pull all stops to give you fellows service, so I'm not complaining. Good night."

Alex walked to the table by the bed Phil sat on and poured whisky from the bottle and dropped a single ice cube into the glass. "Here's to the South—the deep South," he said, holding the glass up, "the land of the four-dollar hotel room. That's what these people are fighting for. The four-dollar hotel room. I say it's worth a fight."

Phil raised his glass, then drank from it. These men may be writing a lot of hasty impressions, he thought, but put it all together and it is a lot nearer the truth than what is being written for the papers in Jackson and Memphis and New Orleans. The stories in the Jackson papers will come through the editing and rewriting to make the trial a contest between the NAACP and the state. The stories in the Memphis and New Orleans papers will come out so cautiously worded that an innocent reader will never suspect the emotions of the community will play a more vital role in the outcome than the testimony.

Doug Johnson, the state's Associated Press correspondent, came in followed by Rafe Saunders of the *Capital City Record* and a young reporter Phil had not met.

"Hello, Johnson," Rivers said. "How's the United Press?"

"Rocking along, I suppose," Johnson smiled. "Last UPI man I saw was a little weary from trying to keep up with my rugged pace, but I suppose he'll survive. How are you city slickers making out? Need anything from *your* Associated Press?"

"Yeah, you just keep sending your colorless dispatches," Rivers grinned. "You see, we're not really here to cover the trial so our papers will need your crap. We're really here to organize a Mau Mau movement."

"I wouldn't doubt it," Saunders said. Red crept up the back of his thick neck and over the bald skin of his head.

"Don't doubt it a minute." Alex grinned. "Like to join? The dues are small and you only have to kill one white plantation owner a month."

"Bull shit," Saunders said.

"How do you Southerners make shit a two syllable word?" Rivers asked.

Roy Bannister from Chicago walked in then and said, "Say, I just heard about a place not far from here that's an all-Negro town. Why don't some of us rent a car and go over there?"

"Hell, me and Alex went up there last night," Rivers said. "Nobody would talk to us."

"That bastard kept telling everybody, 'We're on your side,'" Alex said. "No wonder they wouldn't talk to us."

"They've learned not to trust many white people," Phil said.

"I bet they trust you," Saunders said.

"I hope they do," Phil said, trying to hide his irritation.

"Rafe, we better get on to bed," Johnson said. "Tomorrow's going to be a long day in court."

Phil knew Johnson felt that, as the AP's representative in the state, it was his responsibility to avoid a clash between two paying AP members. He felt sorry for Johnson, having to write to please papers in this area and those in other parts of the country at the same time.

"Guess you're right," Saunders said, looking at the grinning faces around him. "I'm in the wrong crowd anyhow."

"See you guys tomorrow," Johnson said. He walked out and Saunders followed.

"What's with that guy?" Rivers said. "Sheeesh!"

"He's a hatchet man for the Southern Way of Life," Phil said.

"Doesn't he ever take time off?" Rivers asked.

"Not often, if ever," Phil said. "There are some of the best reporters in the country down here. Guys whose insides are itching until they're almost psycho because they're forced to soft-pedal race stories, but there are the Rafe Saunderses too. He's no reporter. He just draws wages and writes what he thinks his bosses want him to write. Can't blame him too much, though; he's not intelligent enough to have any original ideas."

The telephone rang. Alex answered it. "Hello . . . Yes, he's here," he said. "Phil, it's for you."

It was Phil's father. "There's someone here who wants to talk to you," he said. "Tonight. I think you better come right on home."

Phil looked at his watch. "Okay," he said. "Who is it?"

"Rather not say on the phone, especially with this call going through the hotel switchboard," his father said; then added with a laugh, "You there, Rush?"

"Okay." Phil grinned. "I'll be right out."

He said his goodbyes and was soon parked in the driveway of his home. A black Chrysler Imperial was parked at the curb. He walked into the living room and his father and a tall Negro man in a tan suit stood to greet him.

"Phil, this is Duval Stoneham. Mr. Stoneham is the attorney who came down to represent Shine in the voting complaint. He's got an interesting story to tell you."

21.

THE FIRST WITNESS Featherstone and Grady put on the stand the next morning was Jess Berkley, who had found the body in the river.

After he was sworn in and his identity established for the record, Featherstone said to him, "Tell the jury, in your own words, what happened to you on June twentieth that has bearing on the case being tried here today."

Berkley nodded to Featherstone and said, "Yes, sir, Mr. District Attorney." Then he turned to the jury and said, "Well, that was the day I was floating the river from Loose Nigger bridge. Hadn't been too good a day. There was a little too much wind and it was hard to judge the corners or stay still in the boat long enough to really concentrate. Fore I knew it I was at the dog-leg. That's when I seen it. The body. The legs were sticking up out of the water. Well, sir, I nearbout had a conniption. But I knew enough about detective work to know not to bother the body. So I started the motor up and went to shore. Had to go down about a quarter of a mile to the clearing because the banks are so high and crumbly at the dog-leg. You ever floated that river you know that."

"You went to the first place you could come out of the river and then what did you do?" Featherstone said.

"Well, I went and called the sheriff," Berkley said.

"And what did you tell the sheriff?"

"I told him I'd seen a dead nigger in the river."

"Did you tell him anything else?"

"I told him where I'd seen it."

"Anything else?"

"That's all I knew."

Featherstone looked down at his legal pad, then up at the judge. "That's all," he said.

Jerry stood. "Mr. Berkley," he said, "did you know whose body it was when you saw it in the river that day?"

"No, sir. I just knew it was a white man or a nigger."

"Oh? So you actually could not tell whether it was a white man or a nigra? When you first saw it, I mean."

"No, not at first, anyhow. I seen later, though, it was a nigger."

"By later you mean after it was put out on the bank, don't you?"

"Yeah, I guess so."

"I see," Jerry said. "No more questions."

The state's next witness was Joe Adcock, the county coroner. He walked briskly out of the witness room to the witness chair, nodding and smiling at his friends.

"Put your left hand on this Bible," the bailiff said, squinting up at him.

"Shoot, if I didn't know to do that I'd be pretty dumb as many times as I've been in court," Adcock said.

"You swear to tell the truth, the whole truth, and nothing but the truth, so help you God?"

"I do."

Featherstone stood by his chair this time, as Jerry did when he questioned a witness. "State your name, please," he said.

"Joe Adcock."

"Are you the duly elected coroner of Ashton County?"

"Have been for twelve years now."

"On or about June twentieth did you have occasion in the pursuit of your duties as coroner to investigate the death of a body found in the Big Tom River?"

"I sure did."

"Would you tell the jury about it, please?"

"I was at the drugstore across from the funeral home eating a banana split when a deputy—Dogan, I think—came in and said I was needed. He informed me that what was alleged to be the body of a nigger male had been purported to be found in the river south of town. I went out and got in the old ambulance—the one we use for such occasions, not the new one we use in the big funerals. Then I proceeded to drive to the spot on the riverbank where Dogan said the sheriff was waiting at for my arrival."

"And did you empanel a jury to investigate the cause of death?"

"Yes. Like always, I called together a jury and we pronounced him dead."

"Did you or did you not tell me before this trial got under way that there was considerable discussion among the members of that coroner's jury about whether the cause of death had been drowning or a blow on the head?"

"Well, yes—"

"I object," Jerry said quickly. "The official report of the coroner's jury can speak for itself. Any discussion that might or might not have gone on during the jury's investigation is hearsay of the worst sort. The point is that a final decision was made."

"Sustained," Judge Hansberry said.

"But, judge," Featherstone said, "there was no other investigation made. No autopsy, no nothing. If there was any doubt—"

"I object," Jerry said. "If the honorable district attorney is going to testify, I insist that the jury be removed from the courtroom while he does."

"Well, Mr. Featherstone," the judge said, "do you wish to argue the point? If so, I will ask the jury to step out for a moment."

Grady tugged on Featherstone's coat. When the district attorney bent down, Grady whispered, "Bob, let's get on with it. Windham's right. You can't gain anything by arguing when he's right. Let's get on with the trial."

Featherstone rubbed the handkerchief across his sweating face. "I suppose you're right," he said, and stuffed the damp wad into his hip pocket. "But damn Windham. He's trying to make a fool of me. I don't like it."

"You're imagining things," Grady said. "He's just the aggressive type."

"Maybe so," Featherstone said tiredly. "Maybe so."

"What do you say, Mr. Featherstone?" Judge Hansberry said.

"Call the next witness." Featherstone sighed. "Call Bedford Jackson."

Bedford Jackson made his way across the crowded space between the witness-room door and the witness chair. He stood stiffly by the chair, his right hand raised and his left hand on the Bible held by the bailiff.

"Do you swear to tell the truth, the whole truth, and nothing but the truth, so help you God?"

"I do."

"Your name is Bedford Jackson?" Featherstone said curtly.

"Yes, sir."

"What is your business?"

"I am an undertaker. I own Jackson Funeral Home."

"Did Coroner Adcock bring a body to your place on the afternoon of June twentieth?"

"Yes, sir, he did."

"And was that body allegedly the body of Theodore Shine Tatum, a male nigger?"

"Yes, sir. It was his body."

"How do you know it was the body of Shine Tatum?"

"I had known Shine Tatum more than twenty years. We belonged to the same church and were close personal friends. I would have recognized him if he had been in that water two more days."

"That's all," Featherstone said.

Jerry leaned over the polished table toward the witness, propping on his hands. "You say you and Shine Tatum belonged to the same church," he said. "Didn't you also belong to the same N-double-A-C-P chapter?"

"I object," Featherstone said.

"I am only trying to establish their relationship," Jerry said. "And, as I will bring out later, it could have a great deal to do with this entire unfortunate case."

"Very well," Judge Hansberry said. "But if you do not connect it with the case I will have this part of your cross-examination stricken from the record."

"Thank you, your Honor," Jerry said. "Now, Bedford, answer the question. Were you and Shine Tatum active in the N-double-A-C-P? As a matter of fact, aren't you still an active member of that organization?"

"Yes, sir," Jackson mumbled, looking at his hands.

"Speak up so the jury can hear you."

Jerry's words were clipped and commanding. Jackson's head snapped up. "Yes," he said, directly at the jury. "I am a member of the NAACP. And Mr. Tatum was a member." The thirteen jurymen shifted in their chairs.

"That's all," Jerry said and sat down.

"Who's the next witness, Bob?" the judge said.

"The boy," Featherstone said. "Call Cooter Dunbar."

The bailiff, without moving out of his chair, reached back and pushed open the door of the witness room. "Cooter Dunbar," he shouted.

Cooter, dressed by Florence Allen in his best Sunday clothes, stepped timidly into the courtroom and walked to the witness chair after the bailiff pointed to it. He sat with his hands folded in his lap. As he had waited to be called, John Allen had largely succeeded in removing his fear with a quiet, friendly voice and a firm hand on his shoulder. But when Cooter stepped through the doorway he was nervous and frightened again. He had never seen so many people crowded into such a small place before. And all of them were white people. They squatted on the floor and he had to step across their legs to get to the chair pointed out by the bailiff. When he stood by the chair he looked across the tops of the heads of the men with the leather bags hanging from their shoulders and saw the face of Mike Heaney. Heaney leaned forward on his elbows and stared at him with his tiny eyes.

The bailiff's voice startled Cooter.

"Sir?" Cooter said. He had not heard what the wrinkle-faced white man had said.

"I said put your left hand on this here Bible and raise your right hand," the bailiff said.

Cooter remembered his instructions.

"Do you swear to tell the truth, the whole truth, and nothing but the truth, so help you God?"

"Yes, sir."

"The answer is 'I do,'" the old bailiff grumbled.

"I do," Cooter said.

"Now, Cooter, don't be nervous," Featherstone said from his chair behind the long table. "Tell those gentlemen over there what your name is."

"Cooter Dunbar."

"Where do you live, Cooter?"

"Out on my Uncle Shine's place."

"Is that south of Ashton, just into the hills?"

"Yes, sir."

"Were you out there at your Uncle Shine's on the night of June seventeenth?"

"Yes, sir."

"Now—tell these gentlemen what you heard and saw out there that night."

"I was in the bed asleep and I woke up to some noise. Somebody was banging on the door and hollering to open up. Then I saw the light through my door cracks and I knew Uncle Shine was up and answering it. When Uncle Shine went out on the porch I went to the front window and watched and listened."

"Go on," Featherstone said. "What did you see and hear then?"

Cooter breathed deeply, then said, "The white man at the door called Uncle Shine a lot of names. Everything happened so fast after that it's hard to tell it all. But the man hit Uncle Shine. I saw that. Hit him in the face and his lamp fell on the porch. That's what started it burning. Then the white man pulled Uncle Shine off the porch and out through the gate and into the car." Sobs were beginning to break into Cooter's voice.

"Then what happened?" Featherstone said and bit his bottom lip.

"I ran out on the porch," Cooter said. "I hollered for them to bring Uncle Shine back. Then I saw that the fire was getting big and I ran in the house and got a pitcher of water and when I came back out Mr. Allen was there."

"That was the last time you saw your Uncle Shine until you identified his body in the funeral home?" Featherstone said.

"Yes, sir," Cooter said, smearing tears across his face with the back of his hand.

"All right, Cooter," Featherstone said, closing his eyes and tilting his chin up, "now tell these gentlemen if you see the man who came to the door that night and dragged your uncle off."

Cooter looked left, then quickly back at Featherstone. "Yes, sir," he said.

"All right, Cooter," Featherstone said, his eyes still closed. "If you see that man in this courtroom today point him out for these gentlemen. Just stand up right there and point him out."

Cooter stood slowly and raised his right hand and pointed a finger at Mike Heaney.

Mike concentrated on peeling a callus in the palm of his left hand. His face displayed a contemptuous half-smile.

The silence of the courtroom was tangible, tightly coiled.

"Are you pointing at Mr. Mike Heaney?" Featherstone asked.

"Yes, sir," Cooter said.

The silence disintegrated into whispers and the scuffling of feet.

Four rows from the rail in the center section Ann turned to Philip Arrow, Sr. "Mike admitted taking Shine," she said. "The sheriff testified to that. Why is everyone acting so surprised?" Arrow leaned over to whisper an answer when a man's voice behind them said, "I never thought that nigger kid would stand up there and do it." Arrow smiled and shrugged. Ann chewed her bottom lip angrily.

Judge Hansberry hit his desk with the gavel. "Order," he said. "Order! The court will tolerate no more such outbursts. Go ahead, Mr. Featherstone."

"You can sit back down, Cooter," Featherstone said.

"Now, you say that is the man who banged on the door of your uncle's cabin that night. Hit your uncle. Cursed him. Dragged him off in the car while his cabin was burning?"

"Yes sir."

"Did you hear him say anything about wanting to talk to him?"

"No sir."

"Did you get the idea from the way he handled your uncle that he was driving off somewhere merely to 'talk things over'?"

"I object," Jerry said. "What he thinks is not pertinent."

"Sustained," the judge said.

"Very well," Featherstone said. "Now, Cooter, you are certain that is the man you saw that night?"

"Yes sir."

"That's all, your Honor."

Jerry stepped through the squatting photographers to stand beside the witness chair.

"Cooter," he said, "you said you stayed there at the cabin and fought the fire."

"Yes, sir."

"And you said that when you went back in the house for water and came back outside John Allen was already there, didn't you?"

"Yes, sir."

"So John Allen just suddenly popped up on your porch? Did he say how he happened to be so close by?"

"He said he was driving home from town."

"Oh, he was just driving home from town? At midnight. Kind of late for a preacher, isn't it? All right, Cooter, where have you been living since your uncle went away?"

"At Just-Ten."

"Where at Just-Ten, Cooter? Whose house, I mean?"

"At Mr. Allen's house."

"I see. And where do you sleep?"

"In the little room in the back of the house."

"And where do you eat, Cooter?" Cooter looked at his shoes.

"I asked you a question, Cooter," Jerry said. "Where do you eat out there? Do you eat in your little back room?"

"No sir."

"Then where do you eat? Do you eat at the same table with the Allens? At the same table with the Allen children?"

"Yes, sir."

"That's all, your Honor."

"Don't surprise me none," a woman on her right said into Ann's ear. She was about fifty, plump and soft. She fanned the hot air with a recipe pamphlet from the State College Home Economics Department. "Don't surprise me at all. I've heard about the kind of things that go on out there at Just-Ten."

Judge Hansberry rapped on his desk. "If you ladies and gentlemen out there don't keep quieter, I'm going to clear the courtroom," he said. "One more such outburst and we'll finish this trial behind closed doors. Who's your next witness, Mr. District Attorney?"

"Call John Allen," Featherstone said, pushing up from his chair tiredly.

"John Allen," the bailiff said, and John came out and stood by the witness chair until he was sworn in. Then he sat down and folded his hands in his lap and faced Featherstone.

"Your name John Allen?" Featherstone said.

"It is."

"You operate a farm southwest of town commonly known as Just-Ten Acres."

"Yes, sir."

"Now, Mr. Allen, will you tell the jury what you know about the happenings at Shine Tatum's cabin on the night of June seventeenth?"

"I had been into town to buy some things and overstayed talking with a friend of mine. It was about midnight when I started home. Just as I got into the hills I saw this fire over where I knew Shine's cabin was. I hurried up a bit and as I got to the turnoff this car, a black sedan, sped away from Shine's gate. I didn't see who was in it. I went right to the cabin because of the fire. The boy, Cooter, told me later, after we put the fire out, that somebody had come and—"

"Object," Jerry said. "Let him tell only what he saw himself."

"Sustained," Judge Hansberry said. He was leaning back in his chair with his hands behind his head, elbows out.

"No more questions," Featherstone said.

"Mr. Allen," Jerry said from his chair, "just what do you do out at that so-called farm of yours?"

"I object," Featherstone said.

"I believe the witness's occupation is generally considered pertinent," Jerry said. "In this instance, in fact, it could have a great deal to do with the case. His occupation and preoccupation, that is." He smiled at the jury.

"Go ahead, Senator," Judge Hansberry said.

Grady leaned over and whispered to Featherstone, "Take it easy, Bob."

"Thank you, sir," Jerry said to the judge. "Now, Mr. Allen, will you answer my question?"

John spoke to the jury. "We try to teach some of the people in that area—or anyone who asks for it, for that matter—how to take better care of themselves. How to farm better and how to be better citizens. That's about the only way I can describe it. Some folks have called us missionaries. I suppose, in a way, we are."

"You mean you think this state needs missionaries?" Jerry said.

"There are people here—anywhere, for that matter—who need some help," John said.

"Most missionaries are ministers of the gospel," Jerry said. "Are you an ordained minister, Mr. Allen?"

"Yes."

"And have you ever had a pulpit?"

"Yes."

"Where?"

"I was pastor of a church in Selma, Alabama, and later in Greenwood, Mississippi."

"As I understand it," Jerry said, "you were pastor of a pretty good-sized church in Greenwood. Why did you leave that to live as you do out in these hills, away from all contact with regular community life?"

"I felt I could do more important work out there."

"I see," Jerry said. "And just what organization sent you out there? Where do you get funds to operate? Surely not from your . . . your new congregation."

"No single organization," John said. "Several groups contribute. We've even gotten contributions from people in Ashton. Not lately, I'll admit. Anyhow, our books are open for inspection at any time, Mr. Windham."

"I see. But you didn't bring your books in with you today, did you?"

"No. Of course not."

"I see. All right, one more thing, Mr. Allen. Didn't the people of your own community ask you to move your operations elsewhere? Didn't the people of your own community call a meeting at Bogue Nitta School just two weeks ago and ask you to take your family and leave?"

"I object," Featherstone said. "This man is not on trial."

"When a man stands up here and tells a story that supposedly backs up the tale of a key witness, I say his character is very important," Jerry said.

"Objection overruled," Judge Hansberry said.

"All right, Mr. Allen," Jerry said. "Isn't it true that your neighbors met and voted to ask you to leave the community for the general good of the community?"

"There was a kangaroo court out at Bogue Nitta," John said. "There was no meeting of my neighbors."

"That's all," Jerry said to the judge. "No more questions."

"Who's your next witness, Bob?" Judge Hansberry said. Featherstone looked at his yellow pad. "Judge, could we have about five minutes?"

"Sure, Bob. Court recessed for ten minutes."

Newspaper reporters sprinted to the telephones and special Western Union booths downstairs. Photographers and television cameramen went into action. The bailiff was asked to bring Cooter out and, directed by the photographers, the boy pointed, as he had done on the witness stand. More pictures were made of Mike and R.L. The sons of the courthouse custodian moved up and down the aisles selling peanuts and cold drinks.

Featherstone had asked for the recess because John Allen was the last witness on his list.

"Dammit, Grady," he said. "Surely there's more to be done than this. Didn't you and Copeland make any kind of investigation?"

"Don't blame me if you don't have a case," Grady said, turning his back on two photographers who were aiming their Speedgraphics at him and Featherstone. "I'm just your assistant in these cases."

"But you know how we've always worked," Featherstone said, ignoring the flashing of the Strobe units. "I've got five counties to cover. I have to depend on you county attorneys."

"I know you're overworked, Bob," Grady said. "You're overworked, so just relax. They're not going to convict these boys anyhow. So ride it out. There's nothing to convict them on. You've lost cases before and you'll lose them again."

"I know some of you young guys don't think I'm much of a lawyer," Featherstone said. "But dammit it don't seem right. All this don't. You know as well as I do that Mike and R.L. killed that old nigger. They killed him and we ought to show people that this state doesn't condone that kind of thing. I'm as much for segregation as anybody. But we can't go around killing people."

"You talk like you've been reading Arrow's paper."

"By God, I have—some. I don't care what he believes about some things. He's right about this. It's wrong, Ross. Just look around you. All these television people and newspaper reporters. The whole damn country is looking at us. They tell me there's even one here from London, England. The whole world is looking, Ross. The whole world."

Featherstone puffed on his cigarette and studied the jurymen, who were drinking Cokes brought by the bailiff and watching the curious antics of the photographers.

"Maybe if I put it to them the way I feel it they'll understand we can't let this go by," he said thoughtfully.

"Bob, I think it's time me and you had a little talk with a mutual friend of ours," Grady said.

"What mutual friend is that?"

"Hamp Auld. He wants us to have lunch with him one day this week," Grady said. "I think this is a good day."

"What does Hamp Auld want to see me for?"

"He just wants to see you, Bob, that's all. He told me the other day he hadn't seen you in months. I'll call him and tell him we can make it to lunch with him. You don't have anything else planned, do you?"

"No . . . I guess not."

"Good. I'll run out and call him now." Grady pushed his way through the crowd and went into Judge Hansberry's room. He returned a few minutes later and said to Featherstone, who stood exactly where he had left him, "It's all set."

22.

PHIL PUSHED TOWARD the door, trying to move faster than the ponderous pace of the crowd. The wide, scattered pattern of mass converged to a four- or five-abreast file as it moved into the doorway, which Phil finally reached and was popped out into the corridor like a squeezed watermelon seed. As he half stumbled out he bumped into Jerry.

"Sorry," Phil said, as he would to a stranger.

Jerry glanced about quickly and saw that the people, no longer a mass, were concentrating only on getting out to eat lunch as soon as possible so they could get back in time to get seats. "Hi, Phil," he said tentatively. "I've been hoping I'd get a chance to talk with you a minute."

"We don't have anything to say to each other." Phil started to walk away.

"No, wait. . . . Don't be that way. I'll explain all this if you'll give me a chance. Come out to the house some night and I'll explain it all. . . . You said yourself the most important thing is to get elected."

"There are a couple of more important things. But I guess I took too much for granted . . . thinking you understood that," Phil said, stopping, hoping Jerry would say something to erase his disappointment in his best friend but knowing that no explanation short of blackmail or threats on Janie and the children would erase it and knowing too that such a dramatic explanation was out of the question.

"But I've got to get in before I can do any of the things we talked about, Phil. I've got to get *in.*"

Phil studied Jerry's face a moment, then he said, "I'm sorry for you, Jerry. This business is beginning to eat at you, isn't it?"

Jerry's face changed instantly from a look of pleading to one of anger. "Don't waste your sympathy on me, pal," he snapped. "You're the one who needs it, not me!" He turned abruptly and strode away.

Phil watched him until the door closed behind him. Some of the disappointment was blurred now. At least, he thought, he can't do what he's doing with a clear conscience. Knowing that Jerry's conscience was nagging him also made Phil feel better about his own situation. He preferred the uncertainty of his future to the certainty of Jerry's. He looked at his watch. He wanted to tell Ann about the new development. It had been too late to call her last night after Duval Stoneham left.

He turned toward the exit opposite the one Jerry had taken and saw Ches Blinken standing a few feet away, leaning against a drinking fountain, watching him. He obviously had been watching while Phil and Jerry talked. Maybe listening; he was near enough to have heard at least part of what was said.

When Phil turned he seemed to surprise Ches out of deep thought, or concentration on what he had heard. Ches's face flushed pink.

"Hello, Ches," Phil said. "Hot enough for you?"

"Uh . . . yeah, Phil. Sure is." Ches patted the gleaming aluminum surface of the drinking fountain foolishly. "Can't seem to get enough water."

"Try turning around and bending over," Phil said, and walked past Ches and out the door.

Outside he stopped and wiped his face with his handkerchief. Admit it, he heard himself thinking, admit the sweat on your face is as much the cold sweat of fear as hot sweat squeezed out by the humidity. And it was the worst kind of fear—the fear of failure. Seeing Ches and knowing he had heard the brief conversation with Jerry put the fear in him. No, it had been in him since the day he walked into the *Dispatch* newsroom after returning from New York. Seeing Ches only made the fear flip over in his stomach like a sleeping Copperhead poked with a stick. Ches represented failure, just as he had once represented security. The Blinkens owned the largest department store in Ashton. This meant they were the biggest advertisers in town.

I must be getting old, Phil thought. I never worried about offending advertisers before, not even the Blinkens. He walked slowly toward his car.

"Especially not the Blinkens," he said through his teeth, and slapped the top of his car. The metal had absorbed the sun's heat all morning and it burned his hand.

He cursed and climbed into the oven-hot interior of the Ford, started the motor and drove away from the curb.

When he parked in his driveway Alex was emerging from a taxi and he remembered that he had invited the New York reporter to lunch. He had misgivings about it now because Alex's presence would complicate his telling Ann about the new witness Stoneham had found. But he decided Alex could be trusted to withhold the story until it unfolded in the courtroom.

"Hi, Alex," he said. "I'm afraid we'll have to do on sandwiches today. But Ann builds a pretty tasty sandwich."

"Anything will be better than those dry bologna and cheese things I've been eating at Joe Chu's." Alex grinned. "Let's go in and see what she's got." Phil opened the door and they walked into the coolness of the air-conditioned room.

23.

WHEN JUDGE HANSBERRY was behind his desk again and order was restored, Featherstone stood and said, "Judge, a new development has come to my attention and I would like a little time to look into it before we proceed."

"Is this necessary, Bob?" Judge Hansberry asked.

"I believe it is," Featherstone said. "At least I want time to find out."

"Why didn't you take care of it during the noon recess?"

"It was brought to my attention only a few minutes ago," Featherstone said.

"Very well," Judge Hansberry said.

"I object," Jerry said.

"I said, very well," Judge Hansberry said. "Court is recessed for twenty minutes."

Grady stood beside Featherstone. "I still say you ought to tell Phil Arrow to take a flying leap," he said.

"I can't do that," Featherstone said. "If he has something, it will come out later anyhow. And if he could go around saying I refused to listen, it would be worse than it is now."

"Didn't anything Mr. Auld said sink into your thick skull?" Grady said.

"I have the boy in the chancery clerk's office," Phil said, leaning across the rail behind them.

"Good. Fine," Featherstone said, wiping his face with his handkerchief. "Let's see what you've got, Arrow, and it better be good."

Phil led the way out of the courtroom, down the dimly lighted, narrow stairs and into an office near the foot of the stairs on the first floor. Ranch and a tall, narrow-shouldered Negro youth with frightened eyes waited there for them.

"You know Ranch, don't you, Mr. Featherstone?" Phil said.

"How do you do, Ranch," Featherstone said. "Boy, that air conditioner feels good." He pulled the damp cloth of his shirt from his stomach and stood in front of the humming window unit.

"Hello, Mr. Featherstone," Ranch said, grinning happily at Phil.

"What does the boy have for us?" Featherstone said, turning his back to the window unit.

"This is Sonny Broadhead, Mr. Featherstone," Phil said, nodding toward the youth. "He lives with his folks on a farm east of Ashton near the county line. To make it brief, since we don't have much time, I'll tell you what he told us. Then you can take it from there."

Nineteen minutes after Judge Hansberry rapped for the recess Featherstone re-entered the courtroom and escorted Sonny Broadhead up the center aisle as if he were a prisoner. As they walked they pulled a blanket of silence behind them. Featherstone, gripping the youth's elbow, guided him to the bailiff.

"Put him in the witness room until I clear this with the judge," he told the bailiff. Then he went to his chair.

"These god-damn reporters have been driving me crazy," Grady said. "I didn't tell them anything though. Not that I knew what to tell. What did you decide to do? Who is that nigger kid?"

"He's a witness," Featherstone said.

"Mr. Auld won't like this."

"He don't have to like it," Featherstone said. His voice was almost a whine. "He's not district attorney. I am. The boy's got something to tell. What do you want me to do . . . kill him?"

"Let's have order," Judge Hansberry said. "Now, Bob, what's on your mind?"

Featherstone turned and faced the judge. "Damn Hamp Auld,"

he mumbled. "Damn Mike Heaney. Damn Phil Arrow. Damn them all."

"What did you say?" Judge Hansberry said.

"I would like permission to put another state's witness on the stand, your Honor," Featherstone said.

"I object," Jerry said. "The state has rested its case."

"What I ask is not so irregular," Featherstone said, his voice suddenly lifeless. "It's done all the time."

"Your Honor," Jerry said, "I know nothing of this witness. I have not been informed either of his identity or of the gist of his story."

"When he tells his story," Featherstone said, "the court and Senator Windham will know as much as I do. If you'd like, judge, we can discuss this in your chamber. Then you can decide if it is important enough."

"I don't suppose that's necessary," Judge Hansberry drawled. "If you think it's important, Bob, then I'm willing to go along. So be it."

Jerry turned to the jury and shrugged his shoulders. Then he sat down.

"Bring the Broadhead boy in," Featherstone said to the bailiff.

Sonny Broadhead edged out of the witness room cautiously, glancing from side to side nervously, and, following the bailiff's directions, went to the witness chair.

"Do you swear to tell the truth, the whole truth, and nothing but the truth," the bailiff said swiftly, "so help you God?"

"Beg your pardon?" Sonny said.

"For heaven's sake, bailiff," Judge Hansberry said, "talk slower so the boy can understand you. The nigger's never been in court before. You can see that."

The bailiff frowned and repeated the oath.

"Oh, yes, sir," Sonny Broadhead said, nodding his head vigorously. "I always tells the truth. You can ask anybody. I been sanctified."

"Just answer the question yes or no," the bailiff said. "I mean answer the question, 'I do.'"

"I do."

Featherstone stood by his chair. "Now, Sonny, tell those gentle-men over there exactly what you saw and heard that night at the old barn on the Sanders place."

From the corner of an eye Featherstone saw R. L. Squires reach and grab Mike's shoulder. Mike slapped the hand away without tak-ing his eyes off the boy on the witness stand. Featherstone looked quickly at the jury. It was watching Sonny Broadhead. All thirteen men were watching Sonny Broadhead.

"Go ahead, Sonny," Featherstone said.

"Yes, sir," Sonny said, his thin, angular face reflecting his ea-gerness to please. "Well, one night not long ago I was coming home by myself when I heard this noise in the old barn out on the Sanders place. First, my thought was to run. It was way late and, you know, spooky. But then I saw this car was parked in front of the barn and the lights was shining in the barn. I knowed that old barn hadn't been used for nothing in years, so I was curious. You know, curious. I went over there to see what was the trouble."

"You said 'trouble,' Sonny," Featherstone said. "What made you think there might be trouble?"

"Well, I thought there might be trouble because I heard this hol-lering and screaming like somebody was being whupped."

"Go on," Featherstone said.

"Well, he was. Was being whupped, I mean," Sonny said. "That nigga was getting the whupping of his life. It was two white men doing it. Two white men standing over him taking turns kicking him and hitting on him, it looked like."

The youth was captured again by the horror and fascination of what he had seen. The horror and fascination that had made him tell the story over and over to anyone who would listen. Tell it as if he were hypnotized by it. He had seen white men beat black men before, but he had never seen the beating continue after the blood showed.

"I watched like I couldn't take my eyes off what I seen," he said, breathing more heavily. "Like I was voodooed or something. Then the big man said, 'Wait a minute,' and he bent down and looked at the old nigga real close and said, 'You had enough?' And the old man say something I couldn't understand and the big man kick him and tell him to get up on his feet, but the old man was limp out then. That's when the little white man said, 'I think you killed him.' And he started crying like a baby. Then the big white man picked up the old man and throwed him in the trunk of the car and they backed out and drove off."

"And where were you all this time?" Featherstone said.

"I was at the side of the barn, the west side, looking through a crack I knowed about being there. I peeked through it one other time . . ." Sonny's momentum almost made him tell about the other time. The thought of what he saw the man and girl do that time made him forget for a moment the fright the other story made him feel.

"Now, tell us, Sonny," Featherstone said slowly, "you recognize any of the men you saw in the barn?"

"Yes, sir," Sonny said. "I recognized both the white men. One was Mr. Mike Heaney and the other was Mr. Squires. I used to pick cotton for Mr. Heaney and Mr. Squires used to come out to the field and stand with him all the time."

"Did you recognize the nigra man?"

"No, sir. Most likely I couldn't have if I'd knowed him like a brother, his face was so bloody."

Featherstone dropped the yellow legal pad to the table. His face was pale and the deep wrinkles under his eyes were shadowed. "That's all, your Honor. No more questions."

Judge Hansberry studied the youth's thin face. Finally he turned to Jerry. "Any questions, Senator?" he asked.

"Yes, sir," Jerry said. He walked to the witness chair and folded his arms across his chest and looked down at Sonny. "What did you say your name was, boy?" he said curtly.

"I didn't say, Mr. Windham," Sonny said. "Nobody ask me that."

Laughter cracked across the long room. Some of the jurymen laughed. Then, as abruptly as it came, the laughter stopped. "Order!"

Judge Hansberry said. "Order!" But he said it to a room that was already silent except for the cadence of an asthmatic wheeze somewhere in the audience. "It does appear there has been somewhat of a rush to get you on the stand and off again," Jerry said. "We're going to slow things down a bit. Tell me what your name is."

"Sonny Man Broadhead."

"Where do you live, Sonny Man?"

"Out on the bogue, near Loose Nigga Bridge. Where the old one was and where they're putting a new one down."

"Is that also near Just-Ten Acres?"

"Yes, sir. Just this side of it."

"I see. You live very near Just-Ten Acres."

"Yes, sir."

"Tell me, Sonny Man, what were you doing wandering around out there as late as you say it was?"

"I'd been to the Crossroads."

"Do you often walk around that late at night?"

"When I been to the Crossroads I do."

"Where is the Crossroads?"

"That's where we go."

"Where you what?"

"Where we go. Where we hang around at night. All of us who live around the bogue do."

"I see. It's where you hang around at night. Do you have anything to drink when you hang around there at night?"

"Sometime."

"On this particular night—the one you just told about—did you have anything to drink that night?"

"Well, er-ah. Yes sir. We—least I—had maybe two, er-ah, beers."

"So you say you had two beers. You sure you didn't have three?"

"Maybe I did have three."

"Four?"

"No, sir."

"Remember, boy, you swore to tell the truth. You swore to God you would tell the truth. You don't tell the truth now and you get in a lot of trouble. See that sheriff behind you with that pistol?"

Sonny jerked his head around and looked down at the holstered gun on the deputy's hip.

"Maybe I had four," he said. "I can't remember exactly. I stayed around there a long time, but I wasn't drinking fast. Not chug-a-lugging, I mean."

"I see," Jerry said to the jury, then turned back to Sonny. "You said you knew Mike Heaney because you picked cotton for him and you knew R. L. Squires because he came out to the field to visit with Mike. Is that the only time you ever saw them?"

"Yes, sir."

"It's been almost a year since the last cotton was picked."

"Yes, sir."

"Then it's been a year at least since you saw Mr. Heaney and Mr. Squires. Is that right?"

"Yes, sir."

"You actually wouldn't know either of them if you saw them right now, would you, Sonny? You see them in this room? You don't, do you? Come on now, quick! Don't wait for a signal. You don't see them in here, do you?"

"No sir."

"No more questions," Jerry said, and walked back to his chair.

Judge Hansberry looked across the heads of the kneeling photographers at Featherstone.

Grady whispered in Featherstone's ear. "You put the boy on the stand, Bob," he said. "Let well enough alone. Drop it now. You put him on the stand. That's all you can be expected to do."

"Well, Bob?" Judge Hansberry asked.

"No more questions," Featherstone said.

24.

JERRY'S STOMACH BURNED. He had eaten half a box of Gelusils and it still burned. When this trial was over, he decided, he was going to the Baptist Hospital in Jackson and check in and tell them to examine him from head to foot. Too long now he had told himself the fire in his stomach was caused by a simple acid condition. It was an ulcer. He was sure of it. God, if he could get this trial behind him. Behind him and forgotten. It was necessary that he do what he was doing. No use letting remorse drag on him now. It was necessary and he had to carry through with it. He made the routine motion that the judge dismiss the case from lack of evidence and the judge overruled it.

"Does that mean he thinks we're guilty?" Mike asked Jerry.

"No," Jerry said. "It doesn't mean a damn thing. Just relax. It's routine."

"Senator," Judge Hansberry said, "who's your first witness?"

"Call Duval P. Stoneham," Jerry said.

Stoneham strode out of the witness room and stood stiffly by the witness chair as the bailiff swore him in. He looks like one of those Watusi chiefs, Jerry thought, as he stood and appeared to study his note pad until the bailiff finished. Then he said, "State your name."

"Duval P. Stoneham," the witness said.

"Where do you live, Stoneham?"

"New York City."

"You live in Harlem up there?"

"No, I live on Riverside Drive."

"You people can live anywhere you want to up there, can't you?"

"No, I'm afraid not."

"What do you do for a living, Stoneham?"

"I'm an attorney."

"Isn't your present client Theodore Tatum, better known as Shine?"

"He was. I was advising him on some matters."

"Oh, you were advising him on some matters. Just what matters might that be?"

"I don't believe I have to answer that question. It has nothing directly to do with this trial."

"Are you trying to do the district attorney's job for him?"

"No."

"You tried to, didn't you? You tried to volunteer to help prosecute these boys, didn't you?"

"I offered my services. Yes."

"Well, now, if the honorable district attorney had accepted your offer, Stoneham, just who would have paid your fee? Your client, Shine Tatum, is supposed to be dead. He couldn't pay it, could he?"

"I wasn't thinking of a fee when I offered to help."

"Stoneham, you are a member of the N-double-A-C-P, aren't you?"

"Yes, I am."

"Isn't it a fact that the N-double-A-C-P sent you down here to help Shine Tatum in his attempt to break the laws of this state?"

"Mr. Tatum felt he should be allowed to vote in the county where he paid his taxes. I came down here to advise him about that."

"That's a long trip, Stoneham," Jerry said. "Even for a New York lawyer. Who paid for it? Surely not old Shine Tatum."

Stoneham looked past Jerry at Featherstone. The district attorney sat limp in his chair, examining his fingernails.

"I see you'd rather not answer," Jerry said. "Very well, no more questions, your Honor."

"No questions," Grady said.

Judge Hansberry sat forward in his chair and squinted through his glasses at Featherstone, who still did not look up from his hands. "Very well," the judge said. "Who's your next witness, Senator?"

"Call Mr. Anse Hayes," Jerry said.

The bailiff leaned back and opened the witness-room door. "Mr. Hayes," he said. Anse walked out, smiling at the jury, and made his way to the witness chair, followed by the bailiff, who swore him in and returned to his chair by the door.

"Your name is Anse Hayes?" Jerry asked.

"Yes, sir."

"How long have you lived in Ashton, Mr. Hayes?"

"All my life."

It was easy from then on. Jerry's stomach eased a bit. These were his witnesses. People who answered his mechanical questions mechanically. As Anse Hayes told of the Bogue Nitta meeting, Jerry let his mind drift ahead to the campaign he would soon be submerged in. When Dr. Marvin Holbrook was testifying that, in his professional opinion, the body he saw at Jackson Funeral Home was the body of a much younger man than Shine Tatum had been, Jerry allowed himself to think of the inauguration. He would have two thousand colonels. That's something he should have thought of before. Promise every redneck who would bring in a few votes a colonelship. These honorary appointments were usually reserved for the men who made the heaviest campaign contributions. Why not have a few colonelettes? That was an angle. Promise the appointments to women and they would bring in twice as many votes as the men. . . . Why did Phil have to be so god-damned stubborn? Sitting there with his big-shot newspaper friends, looking righteous. Why doesn't he move back to New York? It's where he belongs. I'll do more for this state by making a couple of compromises than he will with all his high-blown idealism. If he moved back to New York, we could still be friends. . . . The last of nine character witnesses—none of whom had been cross-examined by the prosecution—was saying, "Yes, sir, I've known Mike Heaney all my life just about. I never knew him to be a man of violence." (His war record alone is enough to indicate he is a man who enjoys violence, Phil thought. Why the hell doesn't Featherstone cross-examine them? He was doing fine, then suddenly he quit.)

"Thank you, gentlemen," Jerry said to the final character witness. "The defense rests, your Honor."

Judge Hansberry looked at Featherstone. "Any further questions, Mr. District Attorney?" he asked.

"No questions," Grady said. Featherstone seemed not to hear.

Judge Hansberry's eyes remained fixed on the district attorney a moment. Finally he said, "Very well," and looked at his watch, lying on the desk in the coils of a silver chain. "There'll be a fifteen-minute recess. After that each side will have thirty minutes to sum up its case to the jury." He tapped on his desk with the gavel and the noise and movement erupted.

"You didn't put on much," Mike grumbled as Jerry sat beside him and began studying his notes. "Why didn't you let me get up there and say something? I woulda told them a god-damn thing or two."

"That's *exactly* the reason I didn't put you on the stand," Jerry said, not looking up from his notes.

"Don't sit there talking to me like I'm a dope or something," Mike said roughly. "I wouldn't have picked you for my lawyer anyhow if Mr. Auld hadn't talked me into it. You and your god-damned big house and—"

"Mike," Jerry said angrily. "Keep your damn mouth shut so I can get this jury speech organized in my mind. I'm trying to save your stupid neck and talk is about all we have to do it with. Personally, I don't give a god-damn if you wind up in the gas chamber, but I don't want to lose this case."

Mike slumped back in his chair and stared toward an empty chair behind the judge's desk.

"Where's your wife and kids?" Jerry asked. "You were supposed to have them here."

"They'll be here," Mike said. "They damn sure better be here." He looked over his shoulder. "Here they come."

Rita Jean was walking toward them in the center aisle. She held a hand of each of the two Heaney children. She wore a black dress and white cotton gloves. The children's faces were shiny from the scrubbing she had given them. She nodded solemnly to acquaintances who spoke to her. Jerry stood and told her to let the children sit with Mike. He lifted the girl over the rail and Mike lifted the boy over. The boy wore khaki pants, a white, short-sleeved sport shirt, and black, ankle-high motorcycle boots with brass rings dangling on each side of each boot. He was dressed exactly as his father was dressed.

"How do I look, Senator Windham?" Rita Jean whispered.

"You look fine." Jerry smiled. "Just fine. Now you sit right there. Hoak has been holding this seat for you. Thanks, Hoak."

The short, fat man in the seat directly behind Mike stood and nodded to Rita Jean. "Hello, Miz Heaney. That's all right, Senator," he said. "Any time I can do anything for you, you just call on old Hoak." He reached across the rail and patted Mike's shoulder. "Good luck, Mike, we're with you all the way."

"Thanks, Hoak," Mike said.

R.L., who had been silent since Sonny Broadhead testified, turned and smiled weakly at Hoak. "Yeah, thanks, Hoak," he said. Then he said to Jerry, "I don't know why my wife wouldn't come down here with the kids, Senator. She just wouldn't. She said it wouldn't be good for them. I don't know what's got into her."

"That's all right, R.L.," Jerry said. "Don't worry about it."

"How's the fighter?" Mike said to his son. The boy was six and a half.

"Fine, Daddy," he said.

Mike put the boy on one knee and the girl on the other. "I want to sit with Mamma," the girl said. She was five. She began to cry.

"Let her sit with Rita Jean," Jerry said. He stood and lifted her back across the rail.

"Old Mikey wouldn't cry," Mike said, shoving his son's chin

with a heavy fist. "Let the sissy girls sit back there. Senator, you know what this boy did. He went to the dentist, see, and when the dentist stuck his finger in his mouth he bit the hell out of it. When his mother said, 'What did you do that for?' he said, 'Well, I told him he better not hurt me.' How about that? He's just six, you know. Tough as nails."

"I told him he better not hurt me." The boy giggled.

"See, what'd I tell you." Mike patted the boy on the back.

"Yes, I see," Jerry said.

"Maybe we could send a deputy out to my house and bring the kids down here anyhow," R.L. said. "A deputy could make her let them come, couldn't he?"

"That's not necessary," Jerry said. "Just relax and forget it. I've got to look over these notes. We don't have much time."

R.L. leaned over and took the boy's chubby hand. "Hi there, Mikey," he said. "You remember your old buddy, R.L., don't you? How would you like to sit on my knee after a while?"

"Better be careful, R.L." Mike laughed. "He'll bite you. Hell, no, he don't want to sit in no laps!"

R.L. rubbed a hand over his face. "I just thought . . ."

"If you two don't get quiet," Jerry said, "I'm not going to know what the hell I'm saying to that jury."

"Yeah, we better get quiet and let Senator Windham get ready, huh?" R.L. said; then added, "I don't think they'll find us guilty. Do you, Mike?"

"Shut up and suck your thumb," Mike said. "Hey, Mikey, smile for the camera."

The photographers, most of whom had taken the recess to go after Cokes, had discovered Mike's family and were busily photographing them. Television reporters were talking to Rita Jean. She listened carefully, then nodded and leaned over the rail toward Jerry.

"Mr. Windham, these gentlemen are television people from New York," she said. "This one right behind me in the blue suit is from the Dave Garroway Show. They want me to go outside with them and be interviewed on television. Imagine! It's all right, isn't it?"

They'll make a fool of her, Jerry thought, but she'll never know it, so she'll enjoy it. "Tell them you can go as soon as the jury goes out," he said. "That will be in about an hour."

"I'm going to be on the Dave Garroway show," Rita Jean told Mike.

"Great," he said, and turned away from her.

Rita Jean stuck out her tongue at her husband. She did it quickly and moved away quickly, as if she expected Mike to strike her. When she turned to the television reporters she was smiling. "My attorney says it will be all right after the jury goes out," she said. "That should be in about an hour."

A photographer from the New York Reflector *was taking a picture of Mike and his son when Rita Jean stuck out her tongue. Her face, tongue extended, appeared three columns wide on the front page of the* Reflector *the following day. The caption said that Mrs. Heaney was sticking her tongue out at the* Reflector *photographer.*

Judge Hansberry's entrance chased the spectators back into their seats and the photographers sheathed their equipment and squatted on the floor around the judge's desk again. Jerry looked over his shoulder at Rita Jean, hoping she was looking properly sad.

"Mr. Featherstone," the judge said, "are you ready?"

"Yes, your Honor," Featherstone said. He stood up slowly and wiped the sweat from his face.

"Very well," Judge Hansberry said, placing his watch on the desk and winding the chain around it. "The bailiff will tell you when your time is up."

Featherstone spoke deliberately. As he talked he stared over the heads of the jurymen.

"Gentlemen," he said, "at the outset of this trial I told you that it was my sworn duty as your district attorney to present to you whatever evidence was available in this case. This I have done to the best of my ability. I have presented to you all the evidence available. I did this because I sincerely believe that it is the duty of the state to be adequately represented in a case such as this one, a case which is under the scrutiny of the entire nation, the entire world, in fact. . . ."

His voice trailed off and he poured a full glass of water and drank it all before he continued.

"Many red herrings have been dragged across the path since this trial began," he said. "I beg you. As a fellow Southerner, I beg you. Please do *not* be distracted by these red herrings. It was my unpleasant duty to present what evidence was available. It is your duty to consider that evidence and that evidence alone in reaching your decision. In my own humble way, men, I did my job. I did my job and I can go home tonight and sleep. It will soon be in your hands. In your hands. I pray the decision you make will allow you to go to your beds and sleep the sleep of the undisturbed. That's all I have to say."

Featherstone sat down. Grady looked at him, disgust twisted his face into a near-snarl. "What did that red-herring crap mean, huh?" he said.

"You know very well what it meant," Featherstone said. "You were at Bogue Nitta School that night. Why didn't you sit over next to Windham during this trial, Grady? You were on their side."

"You're a stupid old man." Grady, grinned. "You're through."

"I know," Featherstone said. Then he looked up and added, "Unless this jury finds your friends guilty."

Jerry walked to the witness chair to give his final speech to the jury. He faced the panel, with his back to Judge Hansberry.

"Gentlemen," he said, "there is little that I need say. You have heard the testimony and in that testimony there has emerged a definite pattern. A pattern which shows clearly how this tragic burden came to be dumped onto this peaceful community. These are indeed trying times for the people of the South. There are those who would go to any extremes to destroy the very foundations of our Way of Life. And for what? Well, that is for you gentlemen to decide. What does this well-known situation have to do with this case? I don't think I need tell you gentlemen. You are intelligent enough to know.

But just for the record let me review what has passed before our eyes here this week."

He glanced at the crowd and saw that most of them leaned forward as if straining to hear, so he spoke louder. "First, an old nigra man is visited by a nigra lawyer from New York City. Then that old nigra—Shine Tatum—goes down to the courthouse right here in Ashton and says he all of a sudden wants to register to vote. He's lived among us all these years, mind you, and never before bothered to try to vote. But after that visit from that New York nigra—and whatever went on before that—he decides he wants to vote. Next, we hear that Sheriff Copeland is told that a body has been found in the river. A badly mangled body that is difficult, at best, to recognize as either that of a white man or a nigra. You remember the testimony of Jess Berkley. Then out of nowhere John Allen comes down with a little nigra boy in tow, saying that body is the body of Shine Tatum. Let's see who John Allen is. John Allen, gentlemen, is the man who only a few days ago faced his neighbors at Bogue Nitta School and declared that segregation was unchristian. Unchristian. He is the man his neighbors asked to leave the county because they considered him a dangerous influence. I don't have to tell you how you should take any story John Allen told on this stand. Told with a straight face, after swearing to God that he would tell the truth. Then, to support John Allen's tale, they send in a real ringer. A real ringer, gentlemen. You remember him. Sonny Man Broadhead. Another raggedy-tailed nigra kid, mind you. They built their case against these two fine, upstanding members of the community with the stories of two raggedy-tailed nigra kids and John Allen. And they expect you to send these two men to the gas chamber on that."

He paused to drink a glass of water. Over the rim of the glass as he drank he saw the look of disbelief on Phil Arrow's face. He looked away and continued:

"What about the cock-and-bull story told by Sonny Man Broadhead? What about it? Special witness Broadhead told of seeing two men which he said were Mike Heaney and R. L. Squires beating an old nigra in a mysterious barn somewhere in the hills after midnight. How many beers had Sonny Man had that night? He wasn't certain. He counted up to four, but admitted it may have been more. I say, gentlemen of the jury, that even if Sonny Man Broadhead thought he was telling the truth—which is a matter of conjecture—a nineteen-year-old nigra kid with five or six beers under his belt, walking along a dark road in the hills after midnight is liable to see and hear anything. . . . But then I asked special witness Broadhead if he saw Mike Heaney in this courtroom. You remember me asking that. And he said no he didn't. He didn't recognize Mike Heaney although Mike Heaney sat, big as life, not ten feet from him. And they expect you to believe that this nigra kid, staggering drunk and in the dark, recognized Mike Heaney as he peeked through a crack in a ghostly barn in the hills. Ridiculous!"

Jerry had planned to bring Phil's name and the *Dispatch* into his speech at this point. He meant to point out that it was Phil who brought Sonny Man Broadhead to Featherstone; that it was Phil writing in the *Dispatch,* who had, more than anything else, brought the mobs of Yankee newsmen to Ashton; that Phil, with a "questionable record on the race issue," had only recently returned to Ashton after living six years in New York City. He had intended to say these things when he stood up. But now he watched the faces of the jurymen. I have them, he thought, they are with me. Why go on? Old Man Auld would grumble because he didn't "nail the Arrows to the cross," but why go further than is necessary to win the trial?

"Ridiculous, I repeat," he said. "Yes, utterly ridiculous! But that's the story, gentlemen. That's the story they would have you believe. It is all the more ridiculous because they think they can come down here and tell such a story and that you, a representative panel of Ashton Countians, will believe it. Will be stupid enough to believe it. Well, that's where their propaganda has backfired. Backfired like an old Model A Ford. And, gents, if you remember the old Model A like I do, you remember that when they backfired you better watch out or you'd get the dickens burned out of you. Yes, sir, they preached the lie of the ignorant, backward South so much they came to believe it themselves and when you come back into this courtroom with a verdict of 'not guilty' you will let the world know that the South is not ignorant and easily fooled as the world has been told by the Northern press and the jelly-spined liberals. And when these so-called gentlemen of the press go back into their hotel rooms tonight to write their stories for their New York papers they will stop and wonder if what they have been writing up to now is true. That is what your 'not guilty' verdict will do, gentlemen of the jury—make the world stop and think about the South and what has been said about it up to now. With that in mind, I agree completely with the Honorable Robert Lee Featherstone's words: 'I pray that the decision you make will allow you to go to your beds and sleep the sleep of the undisturbed.' That's all, gentlemen."

Jerry filled his big chest with air. Then exhaled slowly, giving the effect of a long sigh. "That's all, gentlemen," he repeated at the end of the sigh. "It is now in your hands." He bowed his head, raised it and smiled, turned and walked back to his chair at the end of the table.

"Hey, that was pretty good. Huh, Mike?" R.L. said.

"Yeah," Mike admitted, watching Jerry as he walked toward them. "I may vote for you for governor yet, Senator."

"Keep your god-damn vote," Jerry said, with more feeling than he intended. "I did my job for my reasons. You're lucky I had those reasons, that's all. I don't need your damn vote."

"Like hell you don't," Mike said in a hoarse whisper as Jerry sat down beside him. "I know what your reasons were. My vote. My vote and the votes of all the people that think what I done was—" He was interrupted by the look of surprise on Jerry's face.

"Then you really did—" Jerry began, hating Mike for making it impossible for him to pretend any longer.

"I meant what I'm accused of . . . Aw, blow it out your ass." Mike turned away from Jerry's stare.

"You shouldn't talk like that to Senator Windham," R.L. said, a worried frown wrinkling his flushed, freckled face. "Anyhow, you ought not cuss in front of your son."

Mike put a hand on Mikey's knee, possessively. "I'll raise my kid," he said, "You raise yours. Why didn't your kids ever come down here, by the way? Ashamed of you or something?"

"Naw, it's not that, Mike. My wife just didn't think they ought to see me here and hear all the things. . . . She took them to her folks' house."

Judge Hansberry tapped on his desk. "All right, gentlemen," he said. "If you have your instructions ready I'll look them over."

Jerry shuffled through the papers in front of him and selected three white sheets. Each had three short paragraphs typewritten on it. He stepped near enough to the judge to hand the papers to him. Grady had walked around the table to deliver the prosecution's instructions.

"You did a good job," Grady said to Jerry. "A real good job. You realize, Senator, that I had to sit over here because I'm county attorney. Otherwise . . ."

"Yeah," Jerry said, "I know." He found himself looking directly at Phil.

"If you gentlemen have any discussion about the instructions, we can go into my office," the judge was saying.

Grady scanned the three pages Jerry had given the judge. "These are satisfactory with us," he said.

"Senator?" Judge Hansberry offered the other set of papers to Jerry.

Jerry looked away from Phil's eyes and motioned for the judge to keep the papers. "No, that's okay," he mumbled.

When Jerry and Grady were seated again, Judge Hansberry told the jury: "Gentlemen, you have been a patient and attentive jury. I compliment you. Your real job is now beginning. The bailiff will escort you to your room and give you these instructions from the court telling you how the law applies in this case and the specific verdicts you may return with. You may take as long as you believe necessary to arrive at a fair and impartial decision, gentlemen. When you have reached that decision, send the bailiff to me."

He rapped on his desk and said to the crowd: "The jury will be allowed to file out before anyone else moves. Please continue to be as cooperative as you have been." He turned to the bailiff. "Mr. Bailiff, you will lead the jury to its room now, please."

The bailiff marched to the judge's desk and took the instruction sheets from him. He nodded to the jury. The thirteen men stood in concert.

"Pardon my oversight, gentlemen," Judge Hansberry said. "I forgot about Mr. Amboy. Mr. Amboy, you are the thirteenth juryman. The 'just in case' man, so to speak. However, since your colleagues, fortunately, seem to be in excellent health, your job is finished. You are dismissed, sir. You can get your check in the chancery clerk's office."

Mr. Amboy, a pharmacist at Walgreen's downtown, appeared puzzled. He leaned and whispered to the bailiff and the bailiff whispered to him. Then Mr. Amboy smiled a self-conscious smile and waved a vague salute to the others in the jury box and stepped aside to let them march past his chair, which was on the outside end. He followed them out of the railed-in section and up the center aisle. When they walked out the door he leaned against the back wall. The judge rapped for the recess and a sizable group assembled around Mr. Amboy immediately asking him how he would have voted if he had remained on the jury.

Most reporters hurried out of the courtroom to telephone or telegraph their newspapers that the jury was out. The photographers resumed their relentless picture taking. The television reporter from the Dave Garroway Show, followed closely by representatives of CBS and ABC networks, escorted Rita Jean out of the room.

Phil did not leave the press table while the jury was out.

He watched the movement at Jerry's end of the long table near the rail; watched Jerry accept the premature congratulations and the wishes of "good luck, Senator" from those able to elbow near enough to shake his hand or catch his attention across the tops of the heads of the crowd around him. Mike stood beside Jerry, his back toward Phil. The well-wishers went from one to the other. R.L. remained seated, nodding anxiously when someone remembered to call to him. At the other end of the table Grady was in animated conversation with several people, calling out to others as they passed him leaving Jerry and Mike. Featherstone sat slumped in his chair, his face ashen, seeming not to hear nor see the crowd that moved about him and ignored him as he did it.

Phil looked up and watched the black, dusty blades of the ceiling fan circle slowly over Featherstone's head. Then he looked past Jerry at the Negro press table. The Negro reporters sat silent, another island of stillness in the random motion of the crowd. He looked at the door that had taken the jurymen and tried to imagine what they were saying and thinking now in that tiny, hot room across the corridor. What did all they had heard this week add up to in their minds?

Suddenly he felt a limpness, of mind and body. What those men heard this week—as they heard it and now as they thought about it and discussed it—must pass through layers of fear and distrust, which had stagnated a hundred years, before it reached their normal reasoning processes, if it ever did.

"Well, what do you think?" Alex asked, returning to the press table from a telephone.

"I don't know, Alex," Phil said softly. "I'm damned if I do."

Exactly twenty-nine minutes (according to the Associated Press) after the main door of the courtroom closed behind the last juryman in the line, a deputy sheriff opened the door and the bailiff came in and looking neither right nor left limped up the center aisle through the rail gate and the maze of tables and chairs and milling people to the door of the judge's office. He knocked three times on the door with an open palm and when the door opened he said, "They're ready, your Honor."

The news spread quickly, but no more quickly than the silence.

The news moved from the main door with the bailiff as he limped down the center aisle. People who saw him knew why he had returned and they told people who didn't see him. The silence spread in the opposite direction, originating behind the rail in the group that surrounded Mike and Jerry. Suddenly none of them are certain, Phil thought, watching the smiles invert and the group disintegrate into embarrassed individuals. Some of them, those who happened to walk away in that direction, took notice of Featherstone for the first time since the recess began. Some of those who noticed him paused to speak to him or pat him on the back or on a shoulder. Featherstone did not acknowledge the salutations.

Six minutes after the bailiff knocked on the door of the office the twelve jurymen stood in a semicircle facing Judge Hansberry.

"Have you gentlemen reached a verdict?" Judge Hansberry asked.

"We have, your Honor," said the foreman, who stood at the end of the line on the judge's right. The foreman was Pete Roundtree, a planter with three thousand acres north of Ashton.

"Read it, please," Judge Hansberry said, "then hand it to me."

In the silence between the judge's words and those spoken by Pete Roundtree Phil counted seven clicks made by the circling ceiling fan.

Pete Roundtree cleared his throat and held the sheet of white paper shoulder high and read, "We find the defendants not guilty."

25.

WHEN PHIL PARKED in his driveway the half-darkness of dusk was moving in rapidly from the east, bringing with it a fresh wind that had not been there for more than a month.

"Going to rain," Mr. Arrow, Sr., said from the back seat.

"Yeah," Phil said. "Breeze feels good." Neither he nor Ann nor his father moved to get out of the car. They watched Bill Satterfield, who lived next door, walk into his front yard and look up into the swaying green branches of the trees he had planted when he bought the house thirty years before.

"Last time it rained—when was it, two weeks ago?—anyhow, it was hotter than no rain," Mr. Arrow said, not interested in what he said. "No breeze at all."

"It rained the night we visited Florence and John," Ann said. "Not the last time. The time before that."

"Yeah, it was hot that night until we got into the hills." Phil nodded.

"Have you seen John?" Ann asked, more interested in an answer now. "They aren't going to pay any attention to that meeting thing are they?"

"I don't know." Phil studied the steering wheel. "John said he might go to Arizona and work with his son. He and Florence have gotten real fond of Cooter. John said they'd probably go to Arizona now, if for no other reason than to get Cooter away from here."

"It would be wonderful for him," Ann said. "Now, I hope they *do* go."

"They probably will," Phil said.

Bill Satterfield wandered back into his house and, as if this were a signal, Harlan Monroe, the neighbor on the other side of the Arrows, walked into his yard and began mowing the grass. The silence, except for the clatter of Harlan's hand mower, was exaggerated, as it sometimes is before a rain, especially at dusk before a rain.

"It's *so* peaceful here." Ann yawned. "As if all that . . . back there never really happened."

"It happened all right," Phil said, frowning.

Ann began massaging the tense muscles of his neck and shoulders.

"Got a cigarette?" he asked.

She pulled a red package from her purse, took a cigarette from it, lit it and handed it to him. He inhaled, squirmed deeper into the cushion and let the smoke drift from his mouth.

"Why don't you go on down to the paper now and get your story written, then come back and we'll all get philosophically drunk?" Mr. Arrow said. "Get it over with and take tomorrow off."

"Ranch is doing the final chapter of this old Southern melodrama," Phil said. "Nothing to say anyway, but 'pore old Shine. He gone whur de good darkies go.'" He slapped the steering wheel.

"Take it easy, son."

"Take it easy?" Phil sat up and faced his father. "You're damn right I'll take it easy. . . . What else can I do? It doesn't matter what you write. If the dear readers disagree they're ready to boycott you; run you out of town. If you tell them *only* what they want to hear, you're great . . . for a while . . . then they complain how dull the paper is. Face it, Dad, this town's not big enough for an honest newspaper." He tossed the cigarette out the window and slumped into the cushion again. Then he added, "This state's not big enough for an honest newspaper."

"You sound like me, son. . . . Me, that is, before you convinced me I was wrong. And I *was* wrong. So are you." Mr. Arrow leaned forward and put a hand on Phil's shoulder.

Phil sat up again. "Prove it, Dad. Prove it to me. Show me one . . . just one . . . of those decent people from one of those decent little houses who read what I've been writing these past two weeks and read it with an open mind. Show me one and I'll admit I'm wrong and stay here and face anything."

"Phil! You're not thinking of leaving, are you, not now?" Ann asked.

Phil laughed. He leaned across the steering wheel and laughed loud and his body shook.

"What's so funny?" Ann asked.

"Nothing," Phil said, leaning back against the seat. "But I thought you didn't like Ashton. I was going to show you how fine and good these people are. . . . I was going to show *you.*" He laughed again.

Ann laughed too now. "Is that why you've been stalling?" she asked teasingly. "And I thought it was because your intentions were not honorable, sir. I thought one dreary day you would send me a note saying, 'It's been fun, but goodbye.' Phil Arrow, you're a nut. You don't have to sell me a town. It's not the town I want to live with."

Both stopped laughing. Phil reached over and put a hand on her knee.

Mr. Arrow cleared his throat self-consciously. "You two don't mind if I go in the house and mix myself a drink, do you? . . . No, I didn't think so. I'll have the ice out when you decide to come inside." He opened the door and got out of the car.

Phil and Ann came into the living room ten minutes later. His father raised his glass and nodded solemnly.

"Old Man Monroe couldn't cut his grass for sneaking looks at us." Phil smiled. "We came inside to let him finish before the rain." He turned to Ann. "I'll take Scotch and a little water."

"At your service, master," Ann said, and went to the liquor cabinet.

When she brought his drink Ann saw that Phil had fallen back into his gloom. Mr. Arrow sat in his favorite chair, the leather one beside the phonograph, some of the old defeat showing again in the deep lines of his face and the slump of his shoulders.

"The fighting Arrows!" she said, and wished immediately she had not, so she added, "Here, darling, take your medicine. It'll make you feel better."

Phil looked up at her sharply. His eyes studied her face as he took the glass from her hand. He sipped the drink, then said calmly, "Are we that disgusting?"

"No, Phil. I'm sorry."

"Don't apologize. We are," Phil said. "We sure are. Disgusting as hell. The fighting Arrows—with our tails between our legs. It's my fault, talking the way I did out in the car."

"What do you think we ought to do, Philip?" Mr. Arrow asked, an edge of anticipation on his voice.

"Just keep going, Dad. Just keep at it." Phil stood up. "I'm going to call Ranch and tell him to raise holy hell in that story. Let Mike sue us if he dares. And he won't. He's not likely to want to go into court again over this thing."

"Let's drink to the fighting Arrows," Ann said, and the pride showing in her eyes as she lifted her glass and looked at him excited Phil; frightened him a little too, because the moment he saw it he challenged himself to keep the look there. Knew he must keep it there.

The doorbell rang.

"Who the hell could that be?" Phil said. "I'll see," Ann said. "You two relax."

The two men watched her walk into the hall. Seconds later they heard her say, "Well, this is a surprise. Come on in." When she walked back into the room she was followed by Ches, Jr.

Ches took three steps into the living room and stood there, holding a gray straw hat with both hands belt high in front of him.

"Hello, Ches," Mr. Arrow said cordially. "We're taking our medicine. Have a dose?"

"Thanks," Ches said. "I can use it."

"Bourbon or Scotch?" Ann asked.

"Bourbon . . . on the rocks."

Ann went into the dining room. Ches remained where he was, rotating the hat with nervous fingers. He looks like a small boy called before the school principal, Phil thought, and remembered Ches had acted the same skittish way in the courthouse corridor—as if he thought he had done something wrong or he had bad news to tell.

"Sit down, Ches," Mr. Arrow said, nodding toward the sofa. "You look like a man with something on his mind."

"Matter of fact, I have," Ches said, as if he wondered how Arrow knew. Phil smiled at Ches's naïve surprise; but an anxiety began to gnaw. He wondered what Ches came to say that made him so nervous.

Ann brought Ches the drink and sat beside him on the sofa. Ches downed a swallow then leaned toward Phil, resting his elbows on his knees, gripping the glass with both hands.

"Phil," he said, "I've come to tell you that no matter what Hamp Auld and that bunch does, we're going to keep on advertising in the *Dispatch.*" He drank from the glass again and his face reddened. "It may be silly, coming over here like this to tell you we're going to keep on doing something we've been doing for twenty-five years, especially when we haven't even talked to you about not doing it . . . but . . . well, I thought you might like to know. Things being the way they are and all."

"Thanks, Ches," Phil said, pushing the words out over a lump in his throat and feeling his body relax. "Thanks. It's sure not silly to us to know you feel that way at this point."

"Have you and your dad talked about this?" Arrow asked.

Ches faced him. "Yes, sir. He . . . he would have come with me, but . . . well, frankly, he's the one who said it was silly to walk in on an old friend and announce you were going to keep on doing what you'd always done."

"I can see his point," Mr. Arrow said. "Yours too. I appreciate both of them."

"What you've been writing makes darn good sense, Phil," Ches said, as if he had planned to make a speech and was determined to get it all said. "It's like you said—*a man* was *murdered.* Nobody threatened to burn our homes and steal our silver. I don't understand how it got all twisted around so. Something's gone haywire in this town lately. Dad says it's because of the war. I don't know. I guess I realized how bad it had gotten the night of the meeting at Bogue Nitta School. I . . . I saw them make my dad act like a coward. First time I ever pitied him. That's not a nice feeling. . . . Anyway, that's why I came."

The silence was broken by the doorbell. Ann went to answer it and was followed into the living room this time by Colonel Blinken.

Before anyone else could speak, the Colonel said, "I decided if Ches was determined to come over here I better come too. You might think I didn't stand behind him."

Arrow walked over and shook the Colonel's stubby hand. "Glad you did," he said, and they looked at each other until both were embarrassed. Then Arrow said, "Now . . . let's not talk about it any more tonight. Sit down, Colonel, and have a drink. How's your cotton look?"

Relief spread across the Colonel's face. "Looks good," he said, and sat in the chair opposite Arrow's in front of the fireplace. "By the way . . . we're getting a new manager for the plantation. Ches's going to run things out there until we find a good man."

Ann collected glasses and went for refills and a drink for the Colonel.

"One thing more before we change the subject," Colonel Blinken said firmly to Arrow. "Don't expect me to go along with your boy here on any and every thing he comes out with. I won't. But, like my son says, if everybody who disagreed with newspaper editors tried to run them out of town we wouldn't have any newspapers. What I'm trying to say is, I'm going to keep on working with the Citizens Council. It's our only hope down here, I'm convinced. Now don't frown, Philip, the Council's not what you think. My daddy fought the Klan and I would too. The Council's different. It's made up of responsible community leaders. People who have a stake in—"

The rock crashed through the window, bounced across the carpet and stopped at Ches's feet. The three men sat motionless for a moment before Phil ran to the front door. The others followed closely. When Phil threw the door open yellow light from the burning cross in the yard danced on the porch and on the dark forms of the shrubs and the trees. In the street four men scrambled into a 1955 Studebaker. Each wore a white pillowcase over his head. The yellow light flickered on their backs and on the car. Doors slammed shut and the car sped away.

Ann came out, still carrying the tray with four full glasses on it.

"My God!" she whispered, staring at the flaming cross. Phil examined the startled disbelief fixed on Colonel Blinken's face and wondered if the Colonel recognized the car too. It belonged to Anse Hayes. In a town the size of Ashton you see the same people so often you get so you can recognize them as far away as you can see them—walking or riding.